CHARLIE HUSTON

Catchpenny

Charlie Huston's previous novels include *The Mystic Arts of Erasing All Signs of Death, Sleepless, The Shotgun Rule,* the Henry Thompson trilogy, and the Joe Pitt casebooks. He lives with his family in Los Angeles.

Catchpenny

CHARLIE HUSTON

Catchpenny

— A NOVEL —

Vintage Books
New York

A VINTAGE BOOKS ORIGINAL 2024

Grateful acknowledgment is made to the following for permission
to reprint previously published material:
Hal Leonard LLC: Lyric excerpts from "Troy," words and music
by Sinéad O'Connor, copyright © 1987 Hipgnosis SFH I Ltd. and
"Never Get Old" words and music by Sinéad O'Connor,
copyright © 1987 Hipgnosis SFH I Ltd.
All Rights administered worldwide by Kobalt Songs Music Publishing.
All rights reserved. Reprinted by permission of Hal Leonard LLC.
Richard Sterling Streeter: Lyric excerpt from "Feel Like Dyin,"
by Richard Sterling Streeter copyright © 1997 by Richard Sterling Streeter.
Reprinted by permission of Richard Sterling Streeter

Library of Congress Cataloging-in-Publication Data
Names: Huston, Charlie, author.
Title: Catchpenny : a novel / Charlie Huston.
Description: New York : Vintage Books, 2024.
Identifiers: LCCN 2023020424 | ISBN 9780593685082 (Vintage Books
Trade Paperback) | ISBN 9780593685099 (ebook)
Subjects: LCGFT: Novels. | Paranormal fiction.
Classification: LCC PS3608.U855 C378 2024 | DDC 813/.6—dc23/eng/20230926
LC record available at https://lccn.loc.gov/2023020424

Book design by Nick Alguire

vintagebooks.com

Printed in the United States of America

9 7 5 3 1 2 4 6 8

For Virginia, the love story.
For Clementine, the magic.

—c

I don't do anything in order to cause trouble.
It just so happens that what I do naturally
causes trouble.

—Sinéad O'Connor

Catchpenny

PROLOGUE

CIRCE'S MOM STARTED THE RITUAL after she heard the detectives talking at the end of the third day.

"Time's up on this kid," one of them said to his partner. Missing teenagers were never found after three days. Not ones who disappeared like Circe had. Without a trace.

That overheard comment sent Circe's mom to her daughter's bedroom, desperate to do something hopeful, anything that would signal to the universe that she *knew* her daughter would be coming home. She started the ritual with hope, and without understanding what she was doing. She only knew what she wanted. She wanted nothing to change. She told herself that when Circe came home, everything should be exactly how she had left it. So she took pictures of Circe's bedroom, documenting where everything was, careful not to step on the shag rug in the middle of the floor because she didn't want to mar any of Circe's footprints. She felt better in the room, but it was only after she stepped into the hall that she realized it was the smell that had soothed her. The heavy scent of Circe.

It wouldn't last long if she wasn't careful. She checked to make sure the window was shut, but leaving the room, she felt a stir of air on her bare feet through the crack at the bottom of the door. A possible escape route for molecules that had once clung to Circe's skin and hair. Using a roll of black duct tape, she fashioned a baffle that she could adhere to the bottom of the door to seal the crack. Then she remembered the central-air vent in the floor. She was about to go back inside the room when she became aware of her own scent. Her soap and shampoo, the fabric softener on her T-shirt. These might interfere with the purity of Circe.

She stripped and took a shower, scrubbed herself raw with a washcloth. On a shelf in the bathroom cupboard was an unopened package of underwear, and in the hamper a sports bra that smelled faintly of her own sweat and nothing more. She put these on and went back into Circe's room and taped over the floor vent. For good measure she ran tape around the edges of the window. Then she left the room and started a load of laundry, washing several pairs of shorts and T-shirts and some underwear and a few bras in plain water. She ran them through two cycles and then left them to air-dry in Circe's bathroom in the hope that any odors they absorbed there would match the smells of her daughter's bedroom.

The ritual had begun. The once-daily visits to the shrine of her daughter. The stripping naked, the careful washing, the clothing of herself in specially prepared vestments. The prayerful entry into the temple. Prayerful because she never stopped hoping, believing, that the next time she opened the door she would find Circe in her bed, having snuck back in as silently as she had snuck out the night she disappeared.

Did Circe's mom really not know what she was doing? Considering her family history, it would be hard to believe she had no inkling. But she claimed ignorance to the end. All she wanted, she would say, was to preserve that link to her daughter, a fading scent that proved Circe had been there. Proved she had lived.

Whatever Circe's mom's intentions, her actions had consequences.

Six days and nights passed, and the smell of her daughter

began to fade. She stood outside the door one evening, asking, praying, begging. She was afraid to ask for too much, scared to beg to be awakened from a nightmare and find everything as it had been before. That felt like a jinx. Her requests had become smaller and smaller until there was just the one thing she was willing to ask for. She'd only ask that her daughter's scent would linger a little longer. Deep in her pillow, in the kangaroo pocket of her favorite hoodie, in an unwashed bandana. Circe's scent had faded from so many things. Even Dizzy, the stuffed bat that Circe had kept on her bed since childhood, had become so void of scent that her mom had let herself remove it from the room so she could carry it around. She had it with her that evening as she prayed.

Let the sage and dirt and citrus smell of her daughter hide in just a few places. Let there be something she could bury her nose in and bring the feeling of Circe into her. She asked for that, silently. What mattered wasn't who or what she implored, what mattered was the power of her wanting. What mattered was the meticulousness of the ritual she'd created. What mattered was the stuffed bat she clutched in her hand, pressed into the hollow of her throat as she prayed before opening the door. That unique object of her daughter's affection, that fuzzy *curiosity*, that was what mattered most of all.

When Circe's mom opened the door and saw that someone was in the bed, she knew it wasn't her daughter. She was spared that twist of cruelty. It wasn't Circe; it wasn't anyone she had seen before. It wasn't anything she had ever suspected might exist.

It was a darkness in the darkness, very still in the moment she opened the door, then suddenly aquiver, as if it had been startled. But it wasn't a shadow. It was a cloud. It rippled as she stepped into the room. Her fist clenched. Something was in her daughter's room. Something was on her daughter's bed. For the first time in a week she was filled with emotions more powerful than despair. She was filled with fear and rage. She wanted to crush the cloud, the stuffed bat's crumpled wings sticking from either end of her balled fist.

The cloud had a shape when she first opened the door, a shape that was dissipating now. A large animal, somehow poorly made. It reminded her of knotted rags. She rushed across the room, and the cloud ripped itself to tatters, became a fluttering of scraps. They were all over the room, fleeing from her as if her anger and fear drove them. Up the walls to the ceiling, into the high corners, down the walls to the floor, away from her. She screamed and flailed her arms, jumped on the bed to try to get at them, jumped down, chasing. In waves, they poofed out of existence. Just like that. Gone, gone, gone. She stopped screaming, stopped trying to punish the cloud for being in her daughter's room. She stopped moving. The remaining cloud specks calmed, gathered, drew toward her. She didn't move, only breathed. The little mass, no bigger than a penny, all that remained of the cloud, floated in on the tide of her breath, and slipped up her nose.

It was Circe, an odor deep and pungent and present, the strongest trace of her that her mom had smelled since the night the girl went away. Longer than that. Because this wasn't teenage Circe, this was toddler Circe. Doughy spit-up, powder, her downy hair, a little poo. It hit her and she couldn't stand up. She fell to her knees, bringing the poor mangled bat to her face to wipe her tears. And that's when she remembered that the bat, Dizzy, had not always been Circe's favorite. Before Dizzy there had been Sparkie, a malformed rag pony they had made together. Circe had loved Sparkie, keeping the toy in her grubby hands until it was coated in dirt and baby food and drool and snot. Then she saw Dizzy on a drugstore shelf, discounted the week after Halloween, and she'd had to have it. She began to sleep with Dizzy under her chin instead of Sparkie. Taking advantage of the opportunity, Circe's mom had carried Sparkie to the washing machine. She'd been about to add the rag pony to a load of towels when she caught the scent of the thing, the thick, lush rankness of it. It smelled like her daughter's tiny childhood. She'd dropped Sparkie in a Ziploc bag and then dropped that inside a second Ziploc and then dropped the whole thing in a plastic bin where she kept little mementos. If Circe asked for Sparkie, she would give it a wash and turn it over. If not, she'd see if she could preserve that lovely, disgusting odor. Circe never asked about Sparkie, and her mom forgot. Until that moment on the floor of her missing daughter's room with that fantastically rank, fantastically undeniable Circe smell in her nose.

There had been several homes during the years after she got Circe away from her father. This one had been theirs for a long time now, and the meticulousness that had inadvertently created the ritual of entering Circe's room was not a new quality. Organization was necessary to their lives. There was a lot to keep straight in the story she told people about herself and Circe. Remembering Sparkie, Circe's mom knew just where to look.

She left Circe's room, went down the hall to the trapdoor in the ceiling, grabbed the toggle at the end of a short piece of rope, pulled, and the spring-loaded step stair unfolded. She climbed, Dizzy still in her hand. Her fingers touched cobwebs, were coated in them, and then found a pull chain. A quick tug and a bare bulb popped on. It was a small, drywalled attic with twenty or so stackable plastic crates, all labeled. She found CIRCE'S KID STUFF under two other crates, tucked Dizzy under her arm while she shifted them, and then unsnapped the lid. Right on top, sealed in those double bags, Sparkie. Dizzy was still under her arm; she let the little bat fall to the floor as she reached into the crate. She unsealed the first bag, took out the inner one, and held it in front of her face, pausing for a moment, then peeled it open and stuck her nose inside. Nothing. It smelled of nothing. Less than nothing. A vacuum. She had a feeling that if she kept the bag open it might suck all other smells out of the air and remove them to some other place. She suddenly felt ill. She almost threw up in the bag. She started to reach into it, to remove Sparkie, but no, she didn't want to touch that thing. It was wrong. Something was wrong with it. It was dead. No, not dead—it was sick.

An inkling then, a feeling of wrongness. Transgression. And denial. Had she done something she shouldn't have? Something she'd promised herself she'd never do? Had she crossed the barrier between? No. Impossible. Something had happened, yes, but it wasn't her doing. She wasn't like that. She snatched Dizzy from the floor, backed away from the crate and down the steps and pushed the trapdoor back up into place, wishing it had a lock.

Her prayer had been answered. The hidden scent of her daughter, lingering for years in Sparkie's knotted body, had been transferred to her daughter's room where she could find it. She didn't know how. She told herself she didn't know how. This wasn't her. She couldn't have made that happen.

But she knew something about inexplicable happenings. Her own father and his secret life. Circe's father. The hole in the ground. Demon deep in the Chasm. Stories to scare children. The truth hiding under the lies. Everything she had run from.

It was awful to think it might be back in her life. Her tidy, organized, brightly lit life. She was terrified to think what it might mean. But she knew now with no doubt that Circe was still alive. Somewhere, her daughter was alive.

She'd need help to find her.

Instead of help, she got me.

ONE

I WAS LYING IN BED, daydreaming about things I'd like to steal.

Big-ticket items that would solve all my problems at once. Things like the Declaration of Independence. The stones from the pockets of Virginia Woolf's suicide coat. The Narcotics Bureau badge President Nixon gave Elvis. Harriet Tubman's revolver.

There was a time I could have gone after legendary curiosities like those, a time when someone else would have put up the capital for the job, all the mirrors and mojo I needed. My expert services were an expense serious collectors were willing to pay for. Those days were past. I wasn't the go-to sly in Los Angeles anymore, hadn't been for a long time. I'd made a couple of wrong bends, blown a job here and there, and that high-end business had gone away. The last fourteen years had been one long skid. Now it was a constant hustle to make ends meet. Freelancing, stealing when opportunity presented itself, selling off low-grade curiosities to pay the bills. No one to blame. Unless blaming myself counts.

What I needed just then was something notional. I'd have liked to steal a set of baby teeth. Complete and old, passed down as a family heirloom. *Here, child, these were your great-grandmother's baby teeth, and now they are yours.* That kind of thing takes on significance because no one knows what to do with it. Who's gonna be the jerk to finally throw those teeth out? No one. After a couple generations a family is stuck with that kind of stuff and it becomes a *curiosity*. I could make good profit off an intimate little curiosity like that. But I didn't know where to find a set of old baby teeth. Shoes that someone had worn on the Selma to Montgomery march would also have been good. Or an Inuit scrimshaw that had passed hand to hand through gambling debts and pawnshops. It was the lucky charm of a guy who hit nine straight points shooting craps in Reno, walked out of a casino with more money in his pocket than he'd ever had in his life, and got run over by a car that blew through a red light. That would be good.

The strings of events and random occurrences that turn any average object into a curiosity. The accumulated emotion soaked into otherwise banal objects. I could dream up that stuff at will, but what I needed was a real score. To find it, I'd have to get out of bed and leave my apartment. Two things I didn't want to do. Bed was the place for me. It had been like that on and off for many years. The general trend was me marooned on my bed for longer and longer periods of time. Why get up? Everything was pointless, and so was I.

I should really just kill myself, a voice in my head sometimes suggested.

That's what I was most afraid of, the I-should-kill-myself voice in my head. It sounded just like me. Well, it was me. Not that I was bipolar, or suffered from schizophrenia or paranoia. My diagnosis was persistent depressive disorder. With the emphasis on *persistent.* I'd been wrestling in the mud of depression since I was a kid. Back then I'd mostly had weeks' or months' long cycles of depression punctuating an otherwise average youth. Average for a kid who'd been abandoned by his parents as an infant. Still, even carrying that emotional baggage, I could go as long as a year or two without being dragged into a depressive cycle. That had changed when I was about twenty; the cycles got longer and longer until they lasted years. Until depression became my new normal.

Right then I was in a record-setting hole. My depressions had always ended, but I could never believe one would end when I was inside of it. I needed someone to give me a reason to get up. Maybe someone I owed money to would come over and beat me up and tell me to pay them. That had happened once, and it definitely got me motivated and up on my feet. But I didn't want to get beaten up.

I could call Shingles, maybe. She worked at a suicide prevention hotline and was the single happiest and most optimistic person I had ever met. Maybe you had to be happy and optimistic to handle listening to suicidal people all day. But I don't know—her persistent happy optimism made me mad sometimes. Like, give it a rest already. I didn't think I had the energy for Shingles's ebullience just then.

I turned my head and looked at my phone, which was as much as I'd moved in more than an hour. I had a landline. Cellphones are too perilous. All that black shiny glass. You have to look at yourself reflected in it every time you want to make a call or find out what kind of body wash your favorite celebrity uses, and then you have to ask yourself, *Is that really me looking back at me or is someone else inside there looking at me?* The whole internet is like a giant mirror. A swampy reflecting pool for the world. Viscous and unclean, mottled, distorting.

I have a thing about mirrors. I know too much about them. Mirrors are my profession, reflections and likenesses. For a good thief, a true *sly,* that's where the art of it is. In mirrors. And I am a true sly. At my best, I was the kind of sly who made things disappear from thin air, but when I'm in a depressive cycle, I'm total crap. Clumsy, slow, easily rattled, full of doubt, second guesses, and uncertainty. I was daydreaming about stuff

I'd like to be stealing, but if I'd tried to pluck candy from a baby just then, the baby would have caught me, turned me over to a cop, and collected a reward.

So maybe Shingles would cheer me up, I was thinking as I stared at the phone. But what if Shingles didn't cheer me up? Then I'd feel worse. More sleep—that was the way to go. When you sleep, you don't have to do anything. The world goes along without you. How nice.

I closed my eyes. The phone rang.

My phone, it doesn't have voice mail. It will ring until whoever is calling runs out of patience. I started counting rings. When it passed five, I knew it wasn't a spam call. When it hit ten, I knew it wasn't Shingles or any of my other associates. When it hit twenty, I knew it wasn't anyone I owed money to. I got curious. Who the hell was it? After five more rings I figured the caller's persistence was worthy of some effort on my part, so I picked up.

"Yeah?" I said.

"What's wrong with you?"

A voice from the past. I stopped breathing.

How often had I hoped to hear this voice? How often had I hoped never to hear it again?

"Nothing's wrong with me."

"Why'd you take so long to answer?"

"I'm answering now."

"Are you in bed?"

"Um."

"How long have you been in bed, Sid?"

I'm Sid. I'd been in bed more or less continuously for more than a week.

"What do you want, Francois?"

His name was Francois. Over a year since the last time we'd talked. Fourteen years since we'd worked the big jobs together. Since we'd been brothers to each other. Not that I dwelled on any of it. Not much. Not more than constantly. What did he want now?

"Are you depressed, Sid? Are you off meds and thinking about killing yourself?"

I'd been off meds for years.

"I'm good. Just resting up. I have a gig later," I lied.

"A gig for who? I need something today."

"Just a gig. It's flexible. I can maybe move it. What's your thing?"

Francois was quiet. There were traffic noises in the background, the murmur of radio voices. There's always traffic in the background when Francois calls, always radio. He drives a cab.

"You there, Francois?"

"I'm thinking. I'm thinking that you're full of crap. I'm thinking you're up your own ass, feeling sorry for yourself. I'm thinking you'll screw up anything you try to do. I'm thinking I should hang up and call another sly."

Well, none of that made me feel better about myself.

"I've been down, but I'm on the upswing now," I lied some more. "I'm so slick, I could steal a snail's shell and it wouldn't know I just turned it into a slug."

"What the fuck does that mean?"

"I don't know. I thought it would sound cool."

"Don't use that line on anyone else, Sid."

"What do you need, Francois? What's the gig?"

Would he call another sly? I didn't think so. It wasn't self-confidence that was telling me so, it was the simple fact that he was calling me at all. Either no one else was available or he wanted me specifically. But he didn't want to want me. He was trying to figure his options.

"Come on, Francois, you got no one else. What's the gig?"

"Pretty hungry for it, aren't you, Sid?"

"I owe rent to Minerva."

He sucked air through his teeth, an audible wince.

"I don't want trouble with Minerva. He send any manikins after you?"

"It's not that bad. I just need to pay him."

"That what your gig is about?"

"What gig?"

Oh, shit, I blew that one.

"I mean. Yeah. That's what it's about."

"You're a terrible liar, Sid."

He hung up.

I didn't bother hanging up my own phone. I didn't even let go of the handset. I just lay there and waited for the line to start that terrible bleating that tells you that you're off the hook. And I was, totally off the hook. No one was going to be depending on me. I could go to sleep now. But before that happened, there was a knock at the door. Loud, insistent, constant.

I got out of bed, went to the door, and let Francois in.

"How long were you out there, Francois?"

"Long enough to make up my mind. Let's go."

"Where're we going?"

"Sunland. To see a lady. Put on some clean clothes."

The only thing I had that was clean was my favorite T-shirt. I put it on and we left.

Sunland is a desert foothills community of light industry and horse ranches within driving distance of Downtown L.A.'s towers. Northbound traffic was free-flowing, so we got away from my scabby bungalow court in Pico-Union without problems, but the southbound stuff heading for downtown was snarled for miles. An epic jam that didn't have any apparent cause beyond the sheer density of traffic. I stared out the window at the people in their cars while Francois gave me a bad time about what I was wearing.

"You didn't have anything else you could put on?"

We were in his cab. One of those green and white minivans. The names of four or five different taxi companies had been scraped off the doors and painted over. The current name was FRENCHIE'S CAB CO. Francois was the entire company. He wasn't French—his mom had just liked the name. The guy had a lot of style. Crisp white guayabera shirts, seersucker shorts, orange espadrilles, and a rattan walking stick that was pure affectation. His close-cropped hair was receding, but still dark, showing just a few speckles of gray in his neatly trimmed goatee and pencil mustache. He wore thin gold hoops in his right earlobe, one thick gold hoop in his left earlobe. A dapper pirate with mahogany skin.

"You look like a punk," he said to me.

He wasn't wrong, but he didn't mean punk in the sense of a young jackass. He meant the other kind of punk. The cool kind, I'd say. My black straight-leg jeans had both knees blown out. My black Levi's trucker jacket was frayed at the collar and cuffs, the left breast pocket studded with a bunch of those nickel-size band badges you find in smoke shops. My belt was cracked black leather riveted with chrome spikes. My sunglasses were aggressively rectangular, too big for my skinny face, and had a matte-black finish that prevented the lenses from carrying reflections. I don't wear jewelry, don't have tattoos, but I do have some interesting scars, a thick tangle of them in the middle of my chest. I won't admit to how many decades I'm pushing because I'm vain, but I look like I'm still comfortably inside my thirties, because I am heartless. Being heartless helps to keep one well preserved. My hair is thick, blue-black. At the time, I was letting it run wild. I wasn't in the state of mind to care. My vanity would come back along with the rest of my interest in life when my depression cycled out. My vanity always came back. Like a toxic bad habit. The clean T I'd put on was a Sinéad O'Connor *The Lion and the Cobra* shirt. The real deal from way back, with the European release photo of her screaming her face off. Tissue-thin, soft as silk. I'd had it a long time. It was my touchstone, an intimate curiosity entwined with my life story. The kind of thing everyone in the racket keeps on them to focus the course of their personal mojo. Standing five foot three and built like a fourteen-year-old, I do not intimidate, but if anyone touched that shirt they better kill me. Because before it was my favorite shirt it was Abigail's favorite shirt.

Abigail.

I'm not ready to get into that now.

I looked out the window as we swooped through the interchange from the Glendale Freeway to the Foothill. Southbound traffic was still packed.

"They doing construction somewhere?" I asked.

Francois glanced at the opposite lanes.

"It's that protest. Downtown. People are coming in from all over."

A protest was news to me. Then again, the fact that it was daytime was news to me.

"What are they protesting?"

"I don't know. It's one of those things organized on social media. Not my wavelength. Kids protesting everything, I think."

Protesting everything. Well, they had a point.

"So what am I stealing?"

"Nothing."

"Nothing?"

He looked over at me, slouched nearly sideways in the passenger seat, bonelessly sprawled because it took too much willpower to sit up straight.

"If I sent you to steal something right now, Sid, you'd get two steps into the Vestibule, lie down on the floor, and take a nap."

I lifted my head.

"I'm perking up. The prospect of work is perking me up."

He turned his eyes back to the road.

"I'll pay you to listen to a story. That's all. Listen and give me your opinion. The rest of it is too important. I can't use a fuckup."

I didn't bother to argue with his assessment. It was accurate enough.

We got off at Little Tujunga Canyon Road and Francois drove us up Kagel Canyon past a couple of ranches, a worm farm, turnouts for hiking trails. Finally, he took us onto a private dirt road through the chaparral, scrawled northwest, winding up a ravine between two ridges. There had been no gate at the bottom, just a mailbox, but the sides of the road were planted with steel poles, each one topped with motion-activated lights and cameras. Someone was security-minded.

The road ended where the two ridges butted against a lower slope of the mountain. There was a chicken coop and a goat pen, a stable, a small corral, a water tank, propane. At the back of the property was a ranch house. A 1930s combination of adobe and shingle construction, it had been freshened up sometime in the 1980s or '90s. Typical of Southern California ranches, the property was heavily planted with palms, citrus trees, and eucalyptus. It wasn't far short of idyllic.

Francois parked the rattling minivan. He took a packet of Drum tobacco from the storage compartment in the armrest and started to roll a smoke, blending the shreds of tobacco with some flakes of hashish.

"Now what?" I asked.

"Go knock on the door. Listen. Ask whatever questions you need to ask, come back here, and tell me what you think. I want clean eyes and ears on this thing. No biases." He lit up, took a drag. "Show me how perked up you are."

"Screw you," I said. But I got out of the car and walked to the house, following a path of flagstones. I'd wanted a proper job to get me up and moving; instead I was running an errand.

I knocked on the door. It had been painted red to invite good fortune, but what they had was me on their doorstep. I knocked again. There was a plastic plate set in the doorframe, slick black with a fish-eye lens in the middle. I turned my face from it, avoiding my own reflection. I looked around. There were more poles standing all over the perimeter of the property, more cameras. Whoever lived here either had something worth stealing or a strong case of home-invasion paranoia. I started to knock again, but the door was yanked open before my knuckles could hit the wood.

"Who are you?" the woman asked.

I pointed at Francois, still seated in his cab.

"I'm with him," I said.

She hadn't looked overly friendly when she first answered the door, but she positively glared at Francois. He saw her look and did this weird half shrug, half head-shake thing. An embarrassed apology of some kind.

"Him," she said, like she wished he'd die while she watched.

"So you two know each other," I said.

She looked at me again.

"What are you supposed to do?"

"Listen to you, ask questions if I have any."

Her eyes flicked to Francois.

"Typical."

Something hit her, and she pointed at my shirt.

"You always wear that?"

I looked down at my chest: Sinéad O'Connor, the tiniest bird, hair shaved, screaming defiance, fists crossed over her heart.

"Yeah, pretty much."

She squinted, suspicious about something.

"You didn't put it on special today?"

"I wanted to wear a clean shirt. This was clean."

She jutted her chin. She didn't like something. I didn't know what.

"Okay. Let's say I accept you're telling the truth. Can you help me?"

She didn't say it like she wanted me to help her to steal something. She meant could I help her with her trouble. Something was keeping her up all night. Something was making her grind her teeth. Not much past thirty, she was wearing cargo shorts and a plain white T-shirt, a lanyard with several keys dangling from her neck. Her skin was light cocoa, a scatter of freckles on her nose, short, kinky, coppery hair in a boyish cut. Hollowed eyes, thinned cheeks, ragged nails. Whatever her trouble was, she was being consumed by it.

No one had said anything about a gig that involved someone who needed help. I was trying to figure out if I could help myself, not other people. This woman was facing a tragedy. I didn't need to be anywhere close to tragedy. Then again, tragedy is where you often find the most interesting curiosities. The eternal dilemma of the sly. Strong emotion fosters curiosities, but its presence is a hazard.

Could I help her?

I didn't know what to tell her, so I took the path of least resistance. I told the truth.

"No. I probably can't help."

She nodded.

"At least you're not a liar."

"Well," I said. "Don't get carried away."

She pointed at Francois. "He stays outside."

I turned, raised my voice.

"You stay outside, Francois. No one wants you."

He flipped me off.

I turned back to my host.

"He'll wait."

"You know him well?"

"I've known him a long time."

"That's not the same thing."

"That's right."

She gave me one more long look, then swung the door open and stood aside.

"You can come in. I'm Circe's mom."

"Circe's mom," I said, stepping inside. "So that would make you Perse."

"No," she said, "but you're not the first nerd to make that joke." She closed the door, snapped the locks, one two three, a practiced rhythm.

There was a gun cabinet in the entryway, two shotguns. A small-bore birding gun, the kind of thing ranchers keep for crows and gophers, and a twelve-gauge pump with a collapsible stock, the kind of thing people keep to blow big chunks off of other people. There was a bandolier hanging on a peg next to the twelve-gauge; all its loops were filled and I was betting the gun was loaded. I was also betting that the key to the cabinet was on the lanyard she wore around her neck. She could pick it from the bunch by touch, open that cabinet, and be armed in seconds. I had a sudden feeling that she might have been holding that shotgun moments before she opened the front door.

"I'm Iva," she said.

"Sid."

She didn't stick out her hand so I didn't stick out mine. I followed her through the living room. The curtains were drawn, no lights on. There were blankets and a pillow on a well-worn green sectional, a water bottle and a few books and a toothbrush on a glass-topped coffee table with chipped corners. She'd been bedding down out here in front of the TV. Sleepless, bingeing seasons of cooking shows or something equally harmless. I couldn't see anything that was obviously worth stealing.

Of course anything can be a curiosity. Anything can be loaded up with emotional significance because of its proximity to volatile circumstances or because it is itself a focus for fervor. Anything can be imbued with that special combination of feels known as *mojo*. I didn't invent the nomenclature, by the way; I just use the terms of art that my venerable calling has inherited.

A square of old carpet could be soaked with mojo. If, for example, it was the place where a beloved dog slept every night. A dog that once saved a baby's life by barking the parents awake when the infant had fallen asleep on its tummy and was suffocating. The child, growing up, having been told the story, would cuddle next to the dog, thinking that they would never have had a life if not for Fido. Then, after the dog died and the kid left home and the owners decided they could finally remodel, they discovered that they couldn't get rid of that piece of carpet. They cut it out and saved it, rolled it and carefully stored it in a cedar chest with the rest of the family heirlooms. Grandma's box of baby teeth and all that. When their child cleaned out the house after Dad died and Mom was moving to a senior living complex, they found the roll of carpet. Confused for a moment, they unrolled it and fell apart, burying their face in the carpet, drenching it in tears of love and sorrow and pent-up emotions. Those experiences, that specific history, could soak the nasty piece of carpet in a load of sweet, sweet mojo. Anything, absolutely anything, can carry mojo.

And mojo is power. A path to getting things you want. A means of doing the impossible.

But it's tricky using mojo. There are rules to how it works. There are rules and also there are no rules. Because at brass tacks we're talking about magic. Although I try not to employ that overly loaded word. Rules and no rules. Mostly it doesn't make a lot of sense to me, so I keep it simple and just steal magic stuff for other people to use. Iva's place was feeling like a dud. Nothing worth stealing so far.

She took me to the kitchen. Windows behind the sink faced out to the garden. It had been spring-planted and maintained until recently. Now it was dry, going to seed. There were dishes in the sink. The coffee maker was on and there were several open bags of coffee nearby. Corkboard covered one wall. Snapshots and kid art. I got a glimpse of a mother-daughter photo and looked away. I didn't want to see Iva and her daughter, Circe, smiling and happy. I knew something bad had happened. Keep it simple and in the present. Minimize entanglements. I had my own problems.

Iva sat down, but her posture remained rigid. Like she was ready to leap up at the least noise. The sound of her daughter's key scraping in the lock. She had something in her hand, a plush toy. I realized she'd been holding it the whole time, like she didn't know it was there. Occasionally she brought it to her nose and then pulled it away, taking a sniff and then frowning. She saw me noticing and crammed the toy into the side pocket of her shorts.

"So are you a detective or what?" she asked.

What to say?

"I'm a thief."

"He brought me a thief. Why?"

Good question. By then I had an idea of what Francois wanted from me.

"Sometimes I can find things that have been stolen."

"You think my daughter was stolen?"

"I don't know anything yet."

"That's two of us."

It was no good, me being there. She didn't want me, she wanted someone who could help her. And I didn't want to be there anyway. Where did I want to be? With Abigail. I wanted to be with Abigail. I felt that very deeply for a moment. It wasn't a new feeling. Wanting to be with Abigail was something I felt almost constantly, but only occasionally became aware of. Abigail was dead. There was only one way for me to be with her, and I wasn't ready. Not yet.

I watched Iva staring out her window at her dying garden.

"I gather something happened with your daughter. She's missing?"

"Missing. *Missing*. Ha!" She didn't laugh, she said the word *Ha!* "Circe is not missing. She is. *Gone*. Don't ask me. Don't ask me what I mean by *gone*. Don't ask me how *gone* is different from missing. *They don't file gone-children reports*. That's a joke one of the cops made to my face. *Missing* is like she's somewhere not where you left her. My sunglasses are missing. My keys are missing. My wallet, my left sock, my sanity can all be missing. My daughter is *gone*."

That seemed to wear her out. She was lost in the gone-ness of Circe. Needed a nudge to get going again.

"How'd that happen?" I nudged.

"I. Don't. Know." Her hand wandered to her cargo pocket and pulled out the stuffed toy. It was a bat. An old thing, beloved. I started to reach inside my jacket, going for my compass. I wanted to draw a bead on it, see if it would get a quiver from the needle. The toy of a gone child, comforting the hysterical parent. It could be mojo-loaded. But my hand stopped on its own. The toy bat was mortified. Not *mortified* as in humiliated, but as in dead, bled of its essence. Whatever mojo it once held was drained off. Strange things were happening here. Maybe there was something worth stealing after all.

I sat up a little.

"She's gone," I said. "Okay. Tell me. She was here and then?"

Iva waved the bat toward the bedrooms at the back of the house.

"She snuck out. Normal teen stuff. A week ago. She snuck out to go hang with her friends. They were doing this thing that night. Circe, she homeschools. She has a community. Clubs. When you're a homeschool family, you have lots of extracurricular stuff. But she had an essay she had to finish. I told her she couldn't go to meet her friends till that was done. She snuck out to meet them. And then she was gone."

"She didn't come home?"

"Gone, I told you, she was gone. I don't have words. She was there, they said, her friends. She was there, and then she was. Gone. Not there."

I leaned forward a little.

"She," I said, balling my hands and then flashing them open. *Poof!* "She disappeared?"

Iva rubbed the bat all over her face, exhaled.

"Gone."

It was starting to feel like there was an angle here for Francois. I didn't like the idea that he wanted me to ferret something out, something I didn't even know what it was, and then he was going to use some other sly to steal whatever there was to steal. I wanted to know what I was being used for.

"How did you say you know Francois?" I asked.

She blinked, confused by the jump I'd taken.

"Um. From before. He helped us. Me and Circe. You know." She tugged at the toy bat's wings. "Look, do we have to say it? I know that there are things. I don't know how to say it without it sounding crazy. But Francois used to talk about it. I wouldn't have called him if something hadn't happened here. Something besides Circe being gone. Because the cops, they could be right. She might be missing in some totally normal way. I wanted her to be somewhere I could understand. But too much has happened now. Nothing is normal. So can we just agree for a second, for this conversation, can we agree that it doesn't sound crazy for me to say that I know magic is real? You know all this. I'm not crazy. I'm not. It's real. I've seen it be real."

Magic is real. There it was. Out in the open.

"Sure," I said. "Okay, I know what you mean."

"Of course you do. You're Francois's guy. You've done this before."

"Sure."

"You're one of the mojo people."

Mojo. The word came out of her mouth like poison. That revulsion, that desire people have to not believe something when they've experienced the inexplicable—that's not denial, it's common sense. Whatever Iva had seen or gone through in her life, wherever she'd rubbed against mojo, her mind had decided to selectively edit the narrative. She had a powerful need to be living in a world governed by rationality. She didn't want to return to whatever had happened in her past. Even with her daughter disappeared, she was fighting to go no farther than the fringe of remembering some mojo madness that she'd barely escaped.

Still, I had to ease her a little farther if I was going to learn anything valuable.

"When Circe disappeared last week, you didn't go to Francois right away. Something more happened to make you go to him."

"Yes."

"Tell me."

She spread the bat across her open palm, stroked it gently with the fingers of her other hand.

"I can try."

So she told me the story about smelling Circe in her room. She didn't know it, but she was telling me a story about casting a spell. I could see she'd created a ritual, and she'd charged it and thrust it past an intangible membrane that separates real and unreal with the love crammed inside a worn, plushy bat named Dizzy. *Madness* is just another word for magic.

But she was leaving something out. Could have been that Circe was a junkie or that Iva had an abusive boyfriend. Could have been any kind of thing that she didn't want to reveal because it would be a bad look and she wanted to pretend none of it mattered anyway. I'm a thief, not a detective. I barely knew what the heck I was there for. But she was hiding things. Fine.

I couldn't judge her. After all, I was hoping I might find something worth stealing while I poked around her house. We're all
only human.

Iva was chewing the end of Dizzy's wing. She pointed at my
eyes.

"Do you ever take those off?"

She meant my sunglasses. I took them off.

She leaned toward me, staring into my eyes. It was uncomfortable.

"You haven't even looked at her," she said. Shot her eyes to
the wall behind me, then back into my eyes. She wasn't going to
look away. She wasn't going to blink. She wasn't going to give me
an out until I looked.

Whatever. Nothing I saw was going to make me feel the least
bit conflicted or obligated or like I had to suddenly start caring
about anyone but myself. Why not look? No reason at all. So,
fine, I turned around and looked at the wall.

Mistake.

A life up there. Photographs. The whole life of a girl. Toddler
to teen. But there weren't going to be any new pictures. Because
she was gone. No more story of Circe and Iva unless someone
found her.

I turned back to Iva, put on my sunglasses.

"Show me her room," I said.

TWO

CIRCE HAD A SINÉAD O'CONNOR *The Lion and the Cobra* poster on her bedroom door. European cover art.

Iva looked at the poster, looked at my T-shirt, and waited.

I nodded.

"Yeah, okay, I see why you asked about my shirt."

"She loves that album."

I was still looking at the poster. I was glad I'd put my sunglasses back on. I was trying not to cry and I didn't want Iva to know. That would have been embarrassing.

"I love it, too," I said.

"It mean something, you and Circe loving the same album? You wearing that shirt today?"

I shook my head.

"It means we both love Sinéad O'Connor. Just one of those coincidences."

I knew it might be more than that. The closer you get to mojo stuff, the more coincidences tend to abound. It's not a rule, just a possible indicator. Don't make it a thing.

Why I felt like crying was because it touched me, the idea that *The Lion and the Cobra* meant as much to this kid as it did to me. Nearly forty years after its release, this girl was crushing on Abigail's favorite album, putting up the poster that matched my dead wife's shirt. I felt a twinkle of recognition, like not only did I now know something about Circe, but that she might understand something about me. One nerdy brat to another. I wondered if she'd done what I did when Sinéad died. Had she lit a candle and listened to that first album while sprawled on the floor, hoping that death might be a mercy? I bet she did. For a moment, I was sure that she'd mourned exactly the same way I had. For a moment, I felt not alone.

Then it was gone, the feeling of connection, and I was sure that what the coincidence meant was that Circe was dead. The idea that the universe would hand me a feeling as good as that and not have attached a price tag to it was beyond my ability to conceive. I was going to pay for having suddenly felt connected to Circe. I had no doubt in my mind that that feeling meant something horrible must have happened.

"Are you okay?" Iva asked.

I'd been standing frozen, staring at the poster, and one or more tears might have leaked out from under my sunglasses.

"I'm fine."

"You sound like you're trying not to cry."

"No. All good."

"At first I thought you were trying not to sneeze. But then it was more like choking back sobs."

"Can we go in?" I asked, eager for a change of topic before I really did start sobbing.

She stepped in front of me. She was still carrying Dizzy around.

"I need you to do something first. If you give me a bad time or act like it's stupid, I don't know what I'll do."

She opened a linen cupboard in the hallway. On the top shelf was a stack of Tyvek coveralls. She took two of them down and handed me one.

"It would be better if we showered first, but I'll settle for this."

I tugged at my pants leg.

"Do I have to undress?"

She held up a restraining hand.

"Just put this on. I can't really smell her in there anymore. I just don't want to change anything. Humor me."

We put on the coveralls. There were latex gloves, booties for me to slip over my shoes, and hair bags. All of it was pink.

"Can I say something?" I asked. She didn't say no, so I said it. "I feel like we're about to enter a Hello Kitty crime scene."

She didn't laugh, but she didn't get mad at me, either.

"Okay," she said, "me first."

She rushed in, like she needed to clear the threshold before something could hold her back, and then she stopped, turned slowly to me, and waved me forward.

I went in, and froze.

The ends of Iva's mouth tipped up, tipped down. She didn't know what to feel as she watched me get hit by something and become dumbstruck.

"You feel it, too," she said. A statement.

She was right. I felt it. Like stepping into deep, flowing waters, a powerful tug just a few degrees below body temperature. The current pulled at my innards. If I stepped farther into the stream, it would grow in power. Out in the middle, out in the deepest part, it might sweep me away. I took another step toward Iva, and it was gone.

"When did that start?" I gasped.

"Last night," she said.

I nodded.

Mojo was coursing powerfully through the room. Now I knew for certain there was something worth stealing. Something very special. I looked around. Circe's style of interior decor was *More is more*. The walls were covered with layers of posters, postcards, handbills, snapshots, drawings, little plastic toys, dolls, doll clothes, two dog collars, stolen street signs, deflated helium birthday balloons, candy packages, game boards, plastic flowers, and I don't know what else. There was a lot of it, stuff on stuff on stuff. Text was woven into the layers: pipe cleaners bent so they spelled out lines of poetry were cut off by a cereal box; letters from magazines, clipped ransom-note-style, listed book titles; typewriter pages were covered in single phrases à la *The Shining*. There were a lot of *H*'s and double *R*'s, part of a word or phrase that repeated around the room, but were cut to pieces by other junk. Squares of brightly colored patterned fabric hung in billows from the ceiling, along with long dangles of silk ribbon. It felt like the spoors of an entire childhood had been released in the room and grown into a perversely beautiful fungus of pop culture.

"It started with pictures from magazines," Iva said. "Then some snaps of friends. You know. And then." She moved her hands in expanding arcs, describing something that grew and grew. "She just keeps going with it. Then she'll rip down a section and throw a bunch away and start over. Always revising, remaking."

Iva lifted her face to the ceiling, into a thicket of frayed ribbon ends, letting them caress her cheeks and chin.

"What is she into?" I asked.

"She's a teenager. It's something different all the time. She's obsessed for a month and then done. Gardening, sewing, shooting guns, a couple of TV shows, playing the keyboard, space, silversmithing, cross-country running. Homeschool kids get into all kinds of oddball stuff. She's into her friends. They message all day, hang out."

"What's she most into right now?"

"She has a band, I think. It's not like she tells me details. But mostly she's into theater and online gaming."

Theater. *Crap.*

"What kind of theater? Musicals?" I was hoping for musicals. Musicals are mostly harmless.

"No. It's more performance art meets classical? It's a school thing. Circe and some of her friends wanted to make their own class combining their art history and culture studies requirements. They can do that."

"What did they combine?"

"Theater, medievalism, and comparative religion."

That was an unusual and striking combination of seemingly random elements. *Bad mojo*, it screamed at me. I tried to be casual.

"This was their idea?"

"I think so."

"Iva. This was their idea or someone gave it to them?"

She heard the sharpness in my voice as I failed to be casual.

"What is it? What's wrong?"

"Who gave them the idea to combine those specific classes?"

"They wanted to combine classes with theater. Make them more fun. And the teacher, the mentor who does theater, he made some suggestions."

"Who is this guy, the mentor?"

"A drama teacher. He's accredited by a bunch of homeschool organizations. Vetted. His fingerprints are on file, background checked. They have to do all of that."

"Sure, sure. Of course. I'm just asking."

"Why?"

"She was with friends the night she went gone. She snuck out because there was a club thing she wanted to go to. What was it?"

She started kneading Dizzy, squeezing the bat over and over like a tension ball.

"Theater club."

"Where?"

"At the barn. The mentor guy has a small orchard with an old barn that he converted to a kind of theater. They do *The Music Man*. They do *Annie*. I've been there. It's cute."

"The kids were going to rehearse that night?"

"Yes. But the police talked to him when they talked to her friends. All of that has been checked out."

"What's the play?"

"I told you, they wrote their own play. Why are you asking about the stupid play?"

I was looking at the walls while I asked her these questions. Something jumped out from the patternless pattern.

"On the wall there, under the black scarf, that's a mirror, right?"

Iva looked at the large oval I was pointing at, hanging on the wall over Circe's bed. It was draped with a black cashmere scarf, an ornate frame decorated with gold spray paint peeked from the bottom.

"Yeah, it's a mirror. What are you looking for? What is happening? Where is my daughter?"

I unzipped my pink coverall and took out my compass.

"I want to check something."

"What is that? What are you doing?"

What it was, was a compass, small, about the size of a quarter, old, made of cheap brass. Straight from a box of Cracker Jack back when Cracker Jack toys were worth having. It was part of my kit, the pieces of this or that I kept tucked in my pockets to make my job easier. Most anyone in the mojo racket carries a compass, especially slys. Some have elaborate, collapsible numbers that tuck into aged leather sheaths. Some have commando models with titanium covers. Some wear them as jewelry, the reverse side of an antique brooch. Only thing the compasses have in common is that none of them has a needle. Or not a needle that can be seen. It's there, but just hovering outside awareness, somewhere in a crease of the universe. If you want to see it, you need to be practiced in the art of forgetting the world around you. You need to have a gift for remembering that none of it is really there. Reality, it's just what we agree we all want it to be.

Why bother with it at all?

I was in Circe's room, a little guy affecting Ramones' punk style, frequently a drag to be around. Iva was behind me. Circe had a turntable, hipster teen that she was. *The Lion and the Cobra* was on the spindle, I could see the sleeve, a vintage copy, not a repress, standing on top of the turntable lid, leaning against the wall, partially covering a series of drawings stapled there. The drawings leapt out, sketches of a stage, set designs, costumes. Iva moved behind me. It was all so real, all so tangible and vivid and undeniably the real world.

I made it all go away.

It wasn't there anyway, and for a twinkling I was able to let myself remember that fact. It takes practice to be able to do it. Lots of practice. Or lots of natural talent. I let myself remember the world wasn't there and poofed it out of existence.

Poof!

Suddenly my compass had a needle. It started as a glimmer, a pinprick of shine. If there is a curiosity at hand, it will stretch and brighten and take on substance and point the way, showing you where the mojo is hiding. How brightly it shines and how definitively it points the way depends on the strength and proximity of the curiosity. I knew from the tug of current I'd felt when I came into the room that something powerful was there. I was guessing the compass was going to point at either the Sinéad O'Connor album or the covered mirror. Instead, the needle blazed, snapped into length, and swung this way, that way, spinning, buzzing as it whirled, and became a searing disc of light.

"What is that? What is that light?" I heard Iva from far away elsewhere.

A voice began to speak in Gaelic, reciting a psalm from the Bible. And then Sinéad O'Connor began to sing.

Young woman with a drink in her hand,
She likes to listen to rock and roll

The turntable had clicked on and the tonearm lifted and dropped. "Never Get Old" was playing at full volume.

She moves with the music
'Cause it never gets old

The light from the compass became blinding. I squinted against it. Something was there, a scrawl of shadow in the light. Standing in front of the turntable. Someone was there.

"Circe!" I heard Iva scream.

She shoved me and I fell into a wall as she lurched past me, arms spread. The shadow wavered when she reached it, bled away into the light. Iva stumbled and her shoulder rammed the turntable, knocking it off its shelf. The needle scraped along the grooves and hung up on the spindle, rasping the paper label.

There was a world. I was back in the world. The compass light was gone, needle gone, a new crack splitting its face. Iva came at me, swung a fist, and caught me on the side of the neck.

"What are you doing? Make her come back! Make Circe come back!"

I ducked and ran out of the room with her at my heels.

"Where are you going? Help me!"

She was hysterical. Who wouldn't be? She was having experiences that shouldn't be real, but they were. The scent ghost, and now this. Her daughter was gone, but there had been the shadow of her daughter in the room with us. It had something to do with magic. She felt like she was going insane. She chased me into the hallway, stopped, listed into the wall, and slid down it, hands over her face, Dizzy's frazzled wing poking from between her fingers.

I closed Circe's bedroom door.

"Iva."

She moved her hands from her face.

"Was that her?" she asked me.

I put my back to the wall across from her.

"No."

"What was it?"

What was it? A great big pile of *I've never seen anything like that before* is what it was. There was so much mojo pumping in that room, it was cutting courses directly from Iva's heart. All of her need to see Circe was painting a ghost in the air. I did my best to explain. Which I hate. Explaining anything magic is begging to sound silly, be misunderstood, and make people mad at you.

"Things like this don't happen on their own, Iva. The scent ghost you saw before. That shadow. Those things come from us. The urgency of you wanting Circe to be here."

She cut me off.

"Don't blame this on me. It's not my fault."

"I mean, it may be accidental, but you are doing it."

She shot up straight, like something had pulled her up the wall. She took a step and got in my face. Rancher woman. I had little doubt she could beat me up.

"I can't do shit like that," she hissed at me. "I don't do magic. That's *you people*."

I tried to edge away.

"Emotion," I said, "powerful emotions like you're feeling, they can make things happen. Not on their own. You wanted something so much. You made a ritual out of going in her room. You cast a spell."

"Are you telling me that I made my daughter disappear?"

"No. But the scent ghost and that shadow of Circe, yes."

"Get out now!" She pointed at the front door. "Now!"

I walked fast to the door, Iva right behind me. She popped the locks and yanked the door open.

"Out!"

I walked out. Francois was sitting behind the wheel of his cab.

Iva gave me a shove to hurry me on my way.

"Get this asshole out of here!"

I walked to the cab and climbed in.

Francois started the engine.

"I knew you'd fuck it up," he said.

Who was I to argue.

THREE

I HAVEN'T ALWAYS BEEN A THIEF.

I didn't always know about mojo. There was a time when the only thing I knew anything about was music. I was a singer. My gift was in my voice. No need for false modesty. You might have heard of me. About the same time Nirvana was exploding, and Pearl Jam and Radiohead and all those angsty white rock bands, I was on the verge. If things had rolled my way I would have been the edgy singer-songwriter who broke through.

My voice got me things, did things for me, made people want to help me. My voice opened doors and cleared ways. It took me right where I wanted to go. It took me to one of the biggest managers in the music scene.

Munroe.

She heard me sing at her party. By the firepit at her place in Laurel Canyon. Terraces climbing up a hillside, her house at the top. Getting an invitation to the party wasn't that hard, but getting called up to the house was another thing. Abigail got us to the party.

I met this guy at the juice bar, Sid. He was into me, invited me to a party. Guess where we're going tonight?

I didn't need to guess. It's what we'd known would happen when we got to L.A. It was why we came to L.A. At eighteen I left the Baltimore group home I'd grown up in and headed west to be a star. That was an electric time for me, when it seemed like depression was in the past. I sang a wandering path from gig to gig, making enough money along the way for the next bus ticket. My voice led me to Abigail, pulled her to me in a West Texas honky-tonk. She joined me on the road, and somewhere between Santa Fe and Las Vegas she got her hands on a five-year-old copy of *Rolling Stone* that featured a spread on Munroe and her party. *That's it, baby*, Abigail said, putting the magazine in my lap. *That's where you need to be.* I sang us to L.A. so we could get invited to Munroe's party so I could sing and be discovered by Munroe. That was my career plan.

And it totally worked.

The night we went to the party, it was just like in my dreams. Bunch of crazy L.A. types around the bonfire. Sun just gone down, pink sunset tingeing the hilltops across the canyon, a chill coming into the air. The fire starting to roar. Girls in bikinis, guys in trunks, legs and torsos, all that beautiful skin getting goose-pimpled. Beach blankets going over laps, ponchos slipping over heads. Bottles of whiskey and wine, crack of beer cans opening. Pool chlorine, lilac, and weed. Even if you'd never been to Munroe's party, you knew it was time for the guitars and harmonicas to come out. It was 1993, but hootenannies never went out of style for Munroe. This was her open mic, her star search for new talent. I wasn't the only one looking to be discovered that night.

Some girl got it started, covering Pat Benatar, "Hit Me with Your Best Shot," doing it in this breathy, agonized, downbeat growl. It was good, and she knew it was good; that's why she dove in first. It was intimidating. You could see other singers rethinking about going next. But I wasn't even waiting for her to finish.

I started to sing, strumming the melody on my guitar. Under her. Supporting. Then letting it fly a little. She looked at me as I came over the top of her voice in the chorus. People stopped chatting. A couple of musicians looked my way, probably expecting to see another girl singing. My voice was throaty but high. The bullies at the group home had teased me for having a girl's voice when I sang. People that night at the party heard me, then saw I was a dude. I started to hit my strings harder, staying with the singer's tempo, but upping the energy. She kept her growl, I went higher yet. Now she was backing me up. Focus swung. Eyes on me. I went into my falsetto, a sweet, gravelly thread. The girl knew her big moment was being stolen. The thief was already in me back then. It just wasn't my profession. The girl was stuck singing backup to me. I'd snagged her spotlight and I wasn't going to let it go.

I gave them classic singalong hits. Bowie, "Heroes"; Prince, "Let's Go Crazy." And hits of the moment. "Are You Gonna Go My Way," "That's the Way Love Goes." When they were warmed up and ready for anything, I glanced at Abigail and she nodded back to me. It was time. I started to sing a cappella. My own song now.

"Feel Like Dyin."

The fire's crackle and the bustle of the party, the breeze in the trees; as my voice went up, unleashed, all sounds faded. Couples making out in corners lifted their faces. Guys sharing a hookah dropped the hose and came to see. Late arrivals climbing the stairs stopped talking and tiptoed to the top.

> When I get close enough to you
> To feel you breathing
> I can smell the smell of you
> And my heart stops beating
> Take me down, take me down, take me down, my love.
> I feel like dyin whenever you're around
> I feel like dyin whenever you're around.

Up above, on the balcony of the house, a figure hovered, swathed in linen that fluttered in the night air, tiki-torchlight glinting off chunks of amber at her throat and wrists. Munroe. Listening to me and my magic voice.

I set down my guitar after that, ignoring the crowd's pleas for more. A few minutes later a guy in a white jacket asked me and Abigail if we'd care to come up to the house. A few days after that, I signed with Munroe. A few months after that, I was wrapping recording sessions on the EP that Munroe was going to use to score my label deal. A few hours after that, Abigail was dead. Murdered. I'd seen her killer. A killer with my face.

Somehow, impossibly, I was her killer. I had to catch myself. I had to kill myself. Nothing was impossible once I knew that mojo existed. So I made a deal. I sold my magic voice, and I had my heart cut out.

These things, they change a person.

I haven't always been a thief. I haven't always been like this. You would have heard of me. But now there I was, dressed head to toe in pink, rattling down a dirt road in a minivan with a cabbie who was tearing me a new butthole.

"What did you do?"

Francois was driving angry.

I braced a hand on the dash.

"I listened and asked questions. Like you told me."

We overshot a corner and Francois hit the brakes, bringing us to a skidding stop just before we plowed into one of the steel poles that lined the road.

A moment of silence as dust settled around us. Then Francois folded his arms over his chest and eyed me.

"So what do you think?" he asked.

"I think she's afraid of something and you don't want to tell me what it is."

"She's afraid her daughter's dead."

"Not that. This setup here."

I pointed at the security lights and camera mounted on the pole we'd almost hit.

"The lights and cameras. Guns. House at the back of a ravine so no one can come up behind her. What's all that about?"

"Just give me your opinion."

"About what? How am I supposed to help if you don't tell me anything?"

"Was it a grab? Did someone take the kid?"

I unzipped my pink coverall and started to wrestle out of it.

"Was it another sly? That's what you want to know?"

"Yes."

"I don't have enough information to say."

"Useless."

"You know the kid was into theater?"

He jerked his head at me.

"Since when?"

"Recently. So that's an angle."

He shook his head.

"No, I don't think that's it."

"Why? I know you helped Iva with something before. Give me the background. If I can get a picture of the whole thing, then I can tell you if the kid was slyed away. If I can get a bead on technique, I can give you a name. Maybe even sly her back. That's what you really want, yeah? Get the kid back?"

He gave me nothing, just restarted the van and drove us down the ravine.

This guy and his secrets and his silences. What hadn't we been through together in the past? He comes looking for me, but he doesn't want to tell me anything. It wasn't the first time we'd been through something like this. The last time was four-teen years ago, which was also when our friendship bottomed out and became a business relationship. Now he was treating me exactly like he had back then, acting like I'd done something wrong, but not telling me what it was.

"The heck is this about, Francois? Did you come around just to relive old times? Ask for my help and then close me out?"

No answer. We drove in silence. Francois in angry silence, me in gradually gloomier silence. I'd felt like I was perking up for a minute there. Interest got under my skin and made me forget how dumb and pointless everything was. The way my compass reacted in Circe's bedroom. That shadow. I'd never seen that before. Like there was so much mojo, the compass didn't know where to point. So much mojo it could be directed by Iva's desire to see Circe and then pull some kind of shadow of her into the room. There was no single curiosity in that room. Not one or two or even three. It was something else. Something I'd never even heard of.

The room was the curiosity.

Whatever Circe had done, assembling the pieces of the collage that was her room, whatever it meant to her, it added up to way more than the sum of its parts. It was imbued with mojo way beyond what I was used to seeing. That kind of feeling usually takes a lifetime to accrue, more than one lifetime. Maybe the kid was some kind of super mojo battery or something? If you could get your hands on that mojo, you could get a lot done. If you coursed that mojo just right, you could cut a trail ahead of you that would put your life back on track.

I was down deep, looking for anything to drag me to the surface. Circe was maybe a rope. I'd been pulled along for a moment, but now she was slipping loose. I felt like if I could just keep after her, I might get somewhere. It was a sudden rush of positivity that I had not felt in years, but it was fading, fading.

It was a long drive home. Southbound traffic was getting worse as we approached downtown. Police and traffic copters were circling. I saw a couple cars with hand-painted banners anchored to the doors, the kind sports fans make when they go to root at a big game.

SCREAM BEFORE IT'S TOO LATE, read one.

SHE RISES—WE FALL—SHE RISES, read another.

I saw several variations on a design with a scribbled black circle. Words that seemed like English at first glance, but then appeared to be in a kind of code. Like elaborate graffiti tags I couldn't quite unbend into messages I could read.

"Fucking protest," Francois said, veering onto the shoulder to take us past a row of cars and down the Washington Boulevard off-ramp.

He was frustrated enough with the traffic to forget that I was getting the silent treatment.

"Entitled kids unhappy with the world."

"I think it's an ageist cliché to call young people entitled," I said.

"Fuck what you think," he said, jerking us to a stop outside my bungalow court. Dead lawn, drooping brown palms, overflowing dumpster, rattling AC units in the windows.

"Get out," he said.

I got out. That rope I wanted to latch on to, it was almost out of reach. I took a last grab.

"The theater angle, Francois. I think there's something there."

"Stay out of it. I don't want you around screwing things up."

He leaned over and grabbed the door, pulled it closed, and sped away from the curb.

I was alone again. Me and my problems. My many debts. I really needed to steal something soon. It would be a hell of a thing, if you could steal that room. Francois didn't seem to know about all that mojo. Iva had no clue what it meant. It was possible that I was the only person in the world who knew there was a curious room flooded with mojo up in Sunland. How would a sly go about it, stealing a room? It was a place as much as it was a thing. Would it lose its mojo if you moved it? Maybe I didn't have to steal it. Maybe I could sell the information.

It was bad thinking. I'm not pretending otherwise. I was indulging in bad thinking because I was a thief, not a hero. I didn't help people, I stole from them.

Ah well, time to go in and see how my bed was holding up without me. I unlocked my door and went inside my bungalow and two of Hillary Minerva's manikins grabbed me and slammed my face into the closet door and started going through my pockets.

Home sweet home.

FOUR

"MAKE SURE he doesn't have any mirrors on him," someone told the two manikins.

Hands emptied my pockets, taking out my compass, keys, a few dollar bills, lock picks, bicycle chain, pocketknife, wallet, glass cutter, and three linty Tic Tacs.

"Just this junk," one of the searchers said, handing off my stuff.

"All right, let him go," said the someone else in the room.

I turned around. The manikins were both new faces, but I knew their types. Nostalgia manikins. Pop-culture cliché archetypes of a past era. One was wearing a 1984 Los Angeles Raiders Super Bowl jersey, Gargoyle sunglasses, snug black track shorts, a white fanny pack, and a museum-grade pair of Air Jordan 1 sneakers. The other was sporting oversize lawyer glasses, a Tommy Hilfiger sweatshirt, pleated jeans, and Top-Siders. Typical Hillary Minerva manikins. His 1980s obsession extended well beyond his specialization in curiosities from that decade. Even his muscle had to have the look.

"You got any money, Sidney?" asked the other person in the room.

This one I knew. Real people. Not a manikin. Lloyd Fonvielle, Minerva's less-than-enthusiastic dogsbody. Thin-lipped and narrow-hipped, Lloyd always let his long, lank hair hang in a greasy fall over half his face. The other half exuded a petulant boredom that only abated when it expressed a flash of sadistic glee. He wasn't yet thirty-five, but looked hard-ridden, verging on burnout. He'd been a hotshot sly, his talent discovered when he was barely sixteen. He caught fire about the time I bottomed out fourteen years ago. At his height he tried for a big score, looking to retire rich. He went after a Kennedy curiosity. Jack Ruby's gun is what I heard. Kennedy stuff is sly catnip. Mojo as pure as it gets. Generations' worth of obsessive grieving and second-guessing about what-might-have-beens.

Now, if the gun Jack Ruby used to assassinate Lee Harvey Oswald had been in the hands of the private collector in Florida who bought it at auction in the 1990s, the job would have been a snap for Lloyd, but *that* gun was a painstakingly crafted replica. Most of the big Kennedy assassination relics that are in the hands of millionaire collectors or the Smithsonian or the vaults of the Secret Service, those are replicas. The originals, the actual curiosities, those were slyed away long ago to be hoarded by heavy players in the mojo racket, players who one simply does not screw with.

It was an expensive job. Lloyd needed a load of mojo just to set it up. He put his heart in pawn with Minerva to raise the capital. Then he went into the mirrors for Ruby's gun, and got tripped up, lost the thread. Strayed. How long? A couple of seconds. It doesn't take long. He popped out in Nebraska somewhere, dazed and dumbstruck. When he remembered who he was, and scraped up the cash to get back home, he was broken and indentured to Minerva for the foreseeable future. He hated Minerva, loathed working for the banker, but he was stuck as long as the man had his heart. Minerva knew Lloyd wished him ill, but he didn't care. Minerva was the type who liked having people under his thumb. Why else would he be a banker?

"Money, Sidney, do you have any?"

"No," I said. "I'm tapped."

"You owe Minerva back rent."

"I know."

He had my stuff, looking for anything valuable, but it was all crap.

He flipped my compass like a coin.

"You wayfind with this thing?"

"Yep."

He dropped it on the floor.

"What a piece of shit."

He rifled through my wallet, dropping scraps of paper, my driver's license, Ralphs club card, and found the single photograph I carry.

"Oh, hey, is this her? Is this your wife that you killed?"

I grabbed for the photo, and he held it over his head to keep it away from me.

"I'm just looking, man. Here. Take it if it's so important."

He offered me the photo, waited for me to reach for it, and then snatched it away and giggled.

I grew up in a group home. Skinny boy with girly locks and a heavenly voice. I know a thing or two about being bullied. Sometimes you have to take it. Payback can wait.

I put my arms at my sides.

"Minerva sent you to mess with me, Lloyd. I'm messed with."

He shrugged and offered me Abigail's photograph again, saw I wasn't going to take the bait, and flipped it to the floor.

"She's not as hot as I thought she'd be."

I bent to pick up my stuff.

"Tell Minerva I said message received. I'll have his rent in two days."

I had no idea when I'd have Minerva's rent or how I was going to get it.

Lloyd smiled. He had one of those smiles that barely reached his incisors and exposed the entire height and depth of his gums. An eel's grin.

"We're not messengers, we're couriers."

He snapped fingers at the manikins and they grabbed me and pulled me toward the door.

"Minerva wants to see you in person."

They had a black late-1980s four-door Bronco Centurion around the corner.

"Nice ride, guys," I said when I saw it. "I was afraid we were all gonna have to cram into a DeLorean or a Porsche 944 or something. I appreciate the elbow room."

I did get plenty of elbow room, but I also had a sack on my head and was shoved into the back and told to lie on the floor.

"Lloyd, hey, Lloyd, you know I know where Minerva's office is, right? He's in Hollywood on Hammond in that strip mall with the great Thai place." No answer. "I can give you directions, Lloyd. Lloyd, Lloyd, Lloyd. Names with two L's are an odd thing. You ever looked into that? Why two L's, Lloyd? And also, Lloyd *Fonvielle*. That's not your real last name, is it? Did you make that up? Oh, wait, is your whole name fake? *Ow!*"

Lloyd had leaned over and punched me in the ribs.

"Shut up. I don't want to hear your voice, and I'm not taking that bag off your head. No one's letting you get a look at a rearview mirror."

Rearview mirrors? That's what he was worried about?

"Rearviews, Lloyd? That's your concern? What am I gonna do, turn myself into a snake and slither through? You give me too much credit, man. Could you do that? When you were hot shit, I mean. Could you do that crazy snake thing and sly tiny mirrors straight up? You must have been a real stud before you burned out and ended up being Minerva's gofer."

"Turn up the damn radio," I heard Lloyd say.

"Doesn't work. All we got are Mr. Minerva's cassettes." That was one of the manikins.

"Fine. Just drown this asshole out."

That was the last thing I heard him say because I was soon being blasted by Bon Jovi. I don't think they picked "Wanted Dead or Alive" on purpose, but it really tickled me. Being so tickled made me think about Circe and my earlier grim thought that she was probably already dead. Now I didn't see why that had to be true. I was sure she was fine. And also, I thought I would really be able to help with finding her and getting her and Iva out of whatever jam they were in. Not just that, I bet I could make enough cash and mojo helping Circe that I could clear all my debts and have enough left over to finally zero in on Abigail's killer. I could feel it—I was right around the corner from being able to catch and kill myself.

This was a great day!

Coming out of a depressive cycle and returning to baseline normalness can feel like having bags of wet sand lifted from your back. The sense of relief, the ease, the clarity. The world is no longer your enemy. You are no longer your enemy. It's better than getting high; it's like being rescued. But it's a process. You only gradually become aware that you feel different, and you never know right away if it's the real thing. Usually, it's weeks before you can be certain that a cycle has ended. And then it's time to start the countdown to when the good feeling will be taken away again.

But I wasn't easing out of my depression, I was exploding out of it in a transformation that felt like taking a sip of Jekyll and Hyde soda pop. Bam. Those tingles of positivity I'd felt when I left Circe's home had been the leading edge of something I'd never felt before. A single-stage release from depression. Undeniable and unprecedented. It felt unnatural. I was certain that it was unnatural. And I was pretty sure that I knew how such a thing had happened.

Circe's bedroom.

Mojo is never neutral. It is flavored, characterized by the emotions that it springs from and the purpose to which it is coursed. Something about the course in Circe's room had drawn me straight out of my years-long depressive cycle with no transition. I knew I was right about that. I had my head bagged in the rear of a stuffy SUV with blown springs, and I had rarely felt better in my life. I was buzzing and rushing. I was confidence personified. Just in time to visit my banker.

FIVE

HILLARY MINERVA got into mojo because of eBay.

Well established as a partner at an exclusive merchant banking firm, he'd entered the twenty-first century and a wide sea of middle-age doldrums at the same time, and found both lacking. The events of the early aughts—9/11, Middle East wars, the internet, climate doom, hanging chads—were so very lame. It all made him feel old. He missed his glory years. He missed the 1980s. They were vibrant and cool. An actor for president, *Just Say No to Drugs,* Hulk Hogan, the Go-Go's, Central American CIA drug deals, *Star Wars* weapons, the Los Angeles Olympics, the fall of the Berlin Wall, the AIDS quilt, the Rob Lowe sex tape, keytars. All of that belonged to the eighties.

He decided to embrace his passion for the idealized past, cashing out from his banking job and putting everything into an upscale 1980s memorabilia shop. It was while he was accumulating stock that he began noticing odd bidding patterns on eBay, how an apparently mediocre collectible could suddenly generate a bidding war. At first he thought he had some gaps in his knowledge of desirable kitsch. But it wasn't the relative collectibility of Swatch watches or mint in-box *Star Wars* action figures that he needed to bone up on. Gradually he came to understand that there was a secret underlying value to his new business. He'd thought he was discovering people who shared his eighties jam, but they had another jam entirely. He stumbled into what was then the new world of online mojo bargain hunters. You couldn't know for sure if anything you bought online was a proper curiosity, but the low prices often made it worth taking a shot. Once Minerva realized what he'd uncovered, he got very excited.

It's a rumor, but people say that when Minerva found out about mojo, he wanted to use it to literally return to the eighties. He wanted to live his own version of *Back to the Future*. Whatever he really wanted out of mojo, he didn't get it. For one thing, mojo does not allow for time travel. No amount of mojo is going to bend that rule. The other thing was that Minerva had no facility for using mojo himself. He tried to learn, but had no *feel*. He was a cold fish. He'd discovered that magic was real, but that his dreams were beyond him. So he settled back into banking, a business where he had experience, and his lack of emotion was an asset rather than a hindrance.

But the man never gave up on the eighties. If he couldn't retreat to the past, he was determined to bring as much of it to himself as he could.

Minerva was sporting red vinyl pants and a pink T-shirt covered in pastel geometric shapes and random squiggles of primary color. His thinning hair, dyed pitch-black, was all business in front and all party in back. For a guy in his sixties, he did a good job of making the look work for him. He was perched on the edge of his glass-topped desk when Lloyd walked me in.

"Sidney Catchpenny, as I live and breathe. You're the last person I expected to see skipping into my office today," he said.

I gave him twin thumbs-up.

"Hillary, you're beautiful. I know you want to talk about how much money and mojo I owe you and how I'm going to pay it back, but that limits the scope of what I can offer you. Future opportunities, that's where we need to focus."

Lloyd slapped me. Big swing, palm into the front of my face, out of nowhere. It sent me to my knees.

"Shut the fuck up."

Minerva gave a pained expression, ran a hand through his hair.

"You should have a little patience with the man, Lloyd. He's been through a lot. He's going to go through worse very soon."

"The worse for him, the better for me, Hillary."

Minerva turned his head, a slow swivel to Lloyd.

"What was that you just called me?"

Lloyd looked lost for a moment.

"What?" He pointed at me. "This asshole called you Hillary."

Minerva nodded.

"This asshole and I have history. This asshole was a rare talent. You're a cocky wannabe who didn't know how to play the game and ended up with his life in hock to me."

Lloyd looked at the floor, fists balled, jaw tight.

"Fine, I'm sorry."

Minerva stepped closer to him.

"Try again."

"I'm sorry, Mr. Minerva."

"Go away, Lloyd. Go think about the nine years you have left indentured to me. Stew on that."

Lloyd headed for the door.

Minerva snapped his fingers.

"What do you say before you go, Lloyd?"

"Yes, Mr. Minerva. I'll do like you suggest me to, Mr. Minerva."

"Good."

The door slammed. Minerva frowned at me.

"Don't get blood on the carpet, Sid."

I tipped my head back and put my cupped palm under my nose as I stood up.

"Right, yeah, sorry."

Minerva plucked several tissues from a box on his desk and shoved them in my face.

"You got plans today, Sid?"

I wiped my upper lip and chin.

"Evolving plans. I need to see where it's going. Could take a few days. But the payoff, it's going to be huge. You're in for a cut. Mojo. Ample remuneration. *Remuneration.* Word trips me out. I don't know why."

Minerva pointed at a chrome-and-black-leather tube chair.

"Sit, Sidney, and chill."

I sat as he returned to his perch on his desk.

"You seem a little high-strung, Sid. Back on your meds?"

"Who needs meds? I'm naturally ebullient."

He took a few seconds to scrutinize me a little closer.

"Maybe you're on something not over the counter?"

I shook my head.

"Whistle-clean. Squeaky." I made little squeak noises like a cartoon mouse.

His eyebrows drew into each other like they wanted to consult.

"This is weird. I'm unused to seeing you when you're not covered in self-loathing."

I patted my own chest.

"Me! New and improved!"

He gave the tail of his mullet a little tug, clearly not sure what to make of my bright-eyed bushiness. I didn't blame him. No one had seen me like that in a long time. I didn't recognize myself. I felt newer and shinier every second. Why was it I hated myself so much? I was a pretty great guy!

Minerva must have decided he felt the same.

"I'm glad you're in such a good mood, Sid. I want you to go to a party."

Ooh, I liked parties. No, I hated parties. But I liked everything right then. Still, a party wasn't what I had in mind.

"Thanks, no, got things to do."

"You speak of opportunities," he said. "That's what this is. You go do this thing for me, and I give you a little more time to pay me."

"Yeah, but like I said, I have a whole very profitable thing I'm working on. Remuneration, remember?"

"Look, Sid, you are going to go to a party for me. *The* party. Munroe's party. Got it?"

At the sound of Munroe's name, I became considerably less ebullient.

"Munroe doesn't like me."

"No one *likes* you, Sid. They use you."

I got up, shaking my head.

"I won't go back to the party."

The only thing in Minerva's office that jarred the 1980s vibe was a double-door J. Baum safe from the early 1900s towering behind his clear Lucite chair. He slid off the desk and circled to the safe and began spinning the twin dials.

"Never say never, Sid. I, for instance, never tell my clients that I will never sell off their deposits. That would be dumb. I house them, keep them secure. In return, I am paid fat stacks of cash. It is a highly remunerative business model. But only if depositors pay. If they fail to pay, I have to seek said remuneration elsewhere. Through the selling of said assets. Now, let's see what we have in here."

He swung the door open, revealing shelves lined with large canning jars, each jar filled with a viscous ocher fluid. Floating within each jar was a beating human heart. Minerva took out one of the jars and set it on his desk. A hand-lettered paper tag hung from its metal clasp on a loop of butcher's twine: CATCH-

PENNY, SIDNEY JAMES—HARVESTED SPRING 1994. He rested his palm on the top of the jar, as the heart inside began to pump harder and faster.

I could feel it, hear it. I never stopped hearing it, not entirely, no matter how far I might wander. If I ever stopped hearing it, I would be lost, somewhere, forever. I needed someone like Minerva to look after my heart, but that didn't mean I liked it. I hated it.

He watched the rapid beat of my heart, gave a whistle.

"Nervous, Sid? Feels like you're nervous about something. Or scared?"

I could feel my heart hammering in the empty shell of my chest, but where my fear lived I couldn't say. Was it broadcast to me from my heart or did I signal the fear to the disembodied organ? I knew I wouldn't survive if it was ever destroyed, but would it go on without me? When I died, would it still beat with fear? Would it still ache at the thought of Abigail?

"Put it back in the safe, Hillary."

Minerva didn't move, his point apparently not made to his entire satisfaction.

"Tell you what: I'll give it to you. No strings. You keep it for yourself. Not like you have any enemies who'd want to get their hands on it."

A sly's heart is a potent curiosity. Aside from what it means to a sly, it has intrinsic value. That's why I needed a banker like Minerva in the first place.

He picked up the jar and held it out.

"Take it."

"I'll go to the party. Just put it away."

Minerva circled his desk to the safe.

"Thanks, Sid. I appreciate that."

He set the jar back in its spot and closed the door and gave the twin combination dials a few twists to scramble the tumblers.

I felt my heart calm, the beat becoming steadier and softer, the sound of it fading, the doors of the safe buffering its insistence, leaving only a murmur in my chest.

Minerva patted the safe.

"Better?"

"Why do you want me at the party?"

"Go to the party and get this for me. Easy and done."

He picked a photo up from his desk and sailed it to me. I took a look. Black and white, old, and faded. It looked like a small piece of wood that had been carved into a knife. I looked again.

"Is this a bone?"

"It is. Go get it for me."

"You need a dog."

Minerva laughed, segueing into a bark.

"Ruff-ruff! Ruffruffruff!"

"You don't have to be mean about everything, Hillary."

"You don't have to make everything a total pain in the ass. I have an errand that needs running. Go run it."

It was all wrong. Minerva wanted me to go to Munroe's and fetch a bone? Knowing how Munroe and I felt about each other, it was asking for trouble.

I looked at Minerva.

"Why are you trying to make trouble with Munroe?"

He folded his arms.

"I want the bone, not trouble."

"So send Lloyd. You send me to Munroe to pick up some curiosity she's selling you, that's a provocation."

"I do not want to make trouble with Munroe. That would be dumb. She could hurt me, and I don't like being hurt. But you're right. The bone is not all I want. Munroe has something going on. She's bringing in manikins, more than usual. I'd like to know what she's up to without being obvious about it. So I made an offer on that bone. It's an excuse to send someone to the party.

Very casual. Lloyd would push too hard. You know the party. If Munroe is cooking some big move, you'll see signs."

"Munroe will know something's up."

"You're just fetching the bone, coming back here, and telling me about the party. And don't be so sure she doesn't want to see you. She always has a soft spot for a former protégé."

That was all very crooked and bendy. Also, was it weird how both he and Francois wanted me to go places and look around and report to them? I didn't like it. I wanted to keep things simple. Find out more about Circe and her room. I wasn't going to the party, but I had to match Minerva's bendy crookedness with my own. Make him think I'd run his errand.

"Okay, I'll need some money. I'm gonna have to get a taxi or something."

"Lloyd will take you."

I headed for the door.

"Great. Send him to my place around nine or ten."

"He'll take you now."

"It's daylight. Party is still in barbecue mode. Munroe will be in her aerie."

"You show up, ask for the rib, she'll see you no matter the time of day."

He put a hand on my shoulder.

"Do this, Sid. And make a good job of it."

"Hillary, I'm gonna do so good, you're gonna cancel my debt."

He pulled the door open.

"One never knows. But if you screw it up, I'm going to have Lloyd peel your face off."

I took a step out from under the hand on my shoulder.

"That's unnecessarily grim."

He chucked under my chin with his index finger.

"Such a pretty face has got to be worth something to someone."

Lloyd and the two manikins were waiting outside the office in the storefront. Locked glass cases filled with eighties-era jewelry and watches, every piece choice. Walls hung with limited-edition Nagel and Hockney prints, anime movie posters, and autographed mug shots of John Hinckley and Mark Chapman.

Minerva nodded.

"Take him to Laurel Canyon, Lloyd. No bag and no beatings. He's on the team."

Lloyd shoved his hands into the hip pockets of his jeans.

"Whatever you say, Mr. Minerva."

Minerva waved.

"Ciao, Sid. Don't screw it up."

He closed the office door.

Lloyd and the manikins led me out to the Bronco. Dak, the one in the Raiders jersey, was climbing into the driver's seat. Lloyd was standing at the front passenger door. Neil, the manikin with the *L.A. Law* look, was holding the rear passenger door open for me. If I got in that truck I wasn't getting out until we arrived at Munroe's. Minerva was threatening me with face peeling. I knew from experience that Munroe could make that feel like a mercy.

"In," Lloyd said. "No bag and no beatings leaves plenty of leeway for pushing and shoving."

Keep it simple, I thought. Whatever my move here, I needed to keep it simple. No flare, just avoid getting into the truck. I tucked my hands into my jacket pockets and started to dance a soft-shoe.

"Uh-oh," I said. "Looks like I'm having an attack of dance fever."

Lloyd's features got more pinched than usual.

"In the truck, asshole."

I ignored him, just kept dancing.

"Can't get in right this moment. These fevers gotta run their course."

Neil turned to Lloyd.

"Is he crazy?"

I did a spin, pulled my bicycle-chain-wrapped fist from my pocket, and slammed it into Neil's face as I came around. I felt his jaw crack, heard the sharp, grinding tink as his face fractured, saw the shiny glint that showed deep in the spiderweb of fractures that shot across his chin and cheek and down his neck. A couple teeth spilled from his mouth and fell to the ground as I pushed him into Lloyd and sprinted toward Sunset.

Yes, it's true that I am a slight-framed guy who got picked on at the group home. It is also true that I learned to survive that bullying by being equal parts patient, a fast runner, and a very dirty fighter. I didn't like hitting Neil. Aside from hurting your hand, it is an unpleasant sensation to hit a manikin as hard as you can. The tinfoil feel of their skin, the glassy splintering of their bones. It causes an instinctive recoil, the unnaturalness of the sensations. People spend a lot of time digging into mirrors looking for just the right reflections they can use as free labor, but you never know what you'll end up with. Some will break in a stiff breeze while others can be dropped from a skyscraper and barely be chipped. Some you punch as hard as you can, thinking you'll shatter its head, and all you manage to do is give it a bad crack. My hand was throbbing from the punch; I shook it out and let the bicycle chain fall to the sidewalk. It wasn't a curiosity, just something to hit people with.

I ran into traffic on Sunset. Brakes squealed, horns honked. I ran straight across to the opposite sidewalk and into the near–pitch darkness of the Rainbow Bar & Grill, clipping my knee on a chair and limping toward the back of the restaurant. The AC was blasting frigid and I could see the outlines of tourists in the red vinyl booths as my eyes adjusted. "Ace of Spades" was blasting on the sound system. A server in ripped fishnets, a black leather miniskirt, and a cropped pink Sex Pistols T-shirt stepped in front of me.

"You want a table?"

I pointed toward the deeper gloom at the back of the place.

"Bathroom," I said.

"It's for customers."

We reached the men's room door. I pulled it open.

"I'll have a lemonade."

She put a hand on my arm.

"Strawberry or regular?"

"Regular."

"Normal or fizzy?"

"Normal. No. Fizzy sounds good."

Sunlight flashed at the front of the restaurant as the door was yanked open and two aggressive silhouettes ran in. Lloyd wouldn't be able to see me yet, his eyes would still be adjusting, but he'd have a good idea why I'd come in here.

"I'm gonna poop my pants," I said, pulling free from the server.

"Gross," she said, as I yanked the bathroom door closed and locked it.

"Don't think about not paying for that lemonade," she yelled through the door.

I didn't say anything. I was checking out the mirrors over the twin sinks. I've spent a lot of time scouting Los Angeles, taking note whenever I find a mirror that's in a good location. Any mirror will do in a pinch, but some mirrors have a dash of their own mojo. That makes things a little easier.

Places like the Rainbow Bar & Grill have cultural resonance. A mecca of the heavy-metal heyday on the Sunset Strip, that dive has seen a lot. Fame and desire and desperate yearning are dripping from the dining room walls, and the bathrooms have played host to unknown numbers of fights, sex frolics, ODs, and crying jags. Mirrors are powerful because they hold our gazes. Intimate moments when we look into ourselves. We're raw in the mirror's face. We imprint them with shadows of ourselves, negative images burned into the glass. Emotional residue collects and seeps into the tain. And if you know the ways and means, you can use that mojo to reach right into those mirrors and do amazing things. You can *sly*.

The mirrors in the Rainbow men's room should have plenty of mojo. I slipped my compass from its bag, blanked my mind, forgot the world and all its mundane realities, and watched as the needle flickered, gave a slight pulse, waggled between the mirrors, and faded.

Crap.

Both mirrors had been slyed recently. It would be years before they were juiced back up.

"Sid! Open up. I know you're in there." Lloyd, banging on the door.

Emergency procedures.

The mirror is a surface that presents the illusion that it contains a depth, an illusion that hides the fact that the mirror is a door. A gateway. A window. Something that allows passage into something else. Except nothing is there. How to go through that nothing?

I'll tell you how I did it.

I peeked down at the cluster of small band badges pinned to the left breast pocket of my Levi's jacket. Mostly these were straight from the dollar box on the counter at a Melrose Avenue head shop, but I always wore at least one that was uniquely collectible. A curiosity. These rarities were part of a larger collection that had been put together by a notorious 1970s rock-'n'-roll groupie named Pegleg Wanda. In the cocaine glory years of rock, a one-legged teen hottie had been a perverse attraction that few rock stars could deny. According to legend, every time Wanda scored, she kept tally in two ways. She put another notch on her peg leg, and she added a band badge to her collection. Recognizing the mojo potential of that collection, Munroe had bought it from Wanda when the former groupie's notoriety was at its height after the publication of her memoir. When I started slying for Munroe, she'd passed the collection to me—tools for my new trade. I'd kept them when I left Munroe's employ, using them in sundry pinches over the years until only a few remained. I was judicious about putting their still-potent mojo to use, but I wasn't going to get stingy with myself when there was a severe beating waiting just outside the bathroom door.

Slam!

Something rammed hard against the door. Dak's shoulder, I assumed.

I pulled a Peter Frampton badge off my jacket, one of Wanda's trophies. I let myself forget about that. I forgot there was a universe with rules and laws that govern its operations. And while I forgot reality, I placed the hand holding the Frampton badge flat against one of the mirrors. The next part was hard. I exerted something deep inside myself, a collection of arcane muscles that have atrophied in the rest of the species, but I have trained to strength. A humming began to emanate from the button, with a second hum, a harmonic resonance, coming from the mirror itself.

"I hear what you're doing in there!" Lloyd. Very pissed.

Slamslamslam! The door couldn't take much more abuse.

A vibration rippled from the badge in my hand into the mirror, making the men's room waver in reflection as the door gave out and Dak stumbled through, with Lloyd behind him. And then the rippling center of the mirror where my hand was pressed became liquid, my arm plunged deep, and I threw myself forward.

Cold ran up my arm as it disappeared into the mirror, and then the room was tilting, as if the wall with the mirror mounted on it became the floor. My own face, twisted in reflection, came at me, and then I and my reflection washed into each other and I was covered in the cold and dragged down and felt the mirror snap back into place behind me, like ice closing over someone who had fallen into a frozen lake.

Description fails after that. Inside the mirror there is no inside. There is nothing. I simply popped out of a different mirror elsewhere in Los Angeles. I was able to find my way out of nothingness because I have an anchor here. My heart. Tucked safely in Minerva's safe. I went into the mirror in the Rainbow Bar & Grill's men's room, entered an absence of existence, and wayfound myself out another mirror. As for exactly where I emerged, well, I had a plan, remember? I had a specific reason to run away from Minerva's errand and Lloyd's anger.

Circe.

That teenage gone girl and the mojo in her bedroom were my golden ticket out of all my troubles. Not only did that room have tremendous value, but it also seemed like its specific flavor of mojo could flip me out of depression. If I could soak some of that into a talisman that I could carry around, my sad days might be at a permanent end.

Better than that, Circe and Iva really needed help. So I had a chance to do something awesome for people I didn't even know. But I was going to need some more information. Francois wasn't going to tell me anything, and Iva might shoot me if I knocked on her door. I needed some clues. *Clues.* I liked the sound of that. Looking for clues. Figuring things out. Helping the innocent and the beleaguered. Yeah.

Which explains my destination and why I was squirming my way through the mirror on Circe's bedroom wall, making a supreme effort to be utterly silent as I tumbled out onto her bed, hoping I wouldn't alert Iva and risk her blasting a hole in my stomach with her shotgun.

The mirror was a large oval in a thrift-store baroque gilt frame. I was grateful for the generous dimensions. I spilled out onto Circe's bed on my stomach and lay there for a moment, feeling more than a little impressed with myself. It had been a long time since I'd pulled a move that tricky.

"Yes," I whispered to myself. "I rule."

I rolled onto my back, and found myself looking at myself. For a moment this made perfect sense. I had, after all, just come out of a mirror.

"Hey, big guy," I said, still pumped about how awesomely I had escaped Lloyd and slyed my way to Circe's bedroom.

My reflection did not simultaneously mouth the words I spoke. There were other disturbing qualities to this reflection. Its hair, while fantastic, was worn in a greaser ducktail, piled high and swept back. Yes, it was clothed almost entirely in black, as I was, but it was wearing a suit with a snug, mod cut and a mohair sheen. Its shirt was softest gray and its skinny tie had alternating horizontal lines of pink and black. Its shoes were red. Long, pointy-toed oxfords, elaborately perforated in swirls and curlicues. It wore no socks, my reflection. I hated its style. This reflection did not wear a Sinéad O'Connor T-shirt.

It was standing, my reflection, quite close to where I was sprawled on Circe's bed. It had something in its hand. A compass. Black alloy, its cover decorated with a white enameled skull. The cover was closed. My reflection was about to take a mojo bearing on the room.

I smiled at me.

I mean that my reflection smiled at me. I myself was expressionless. My grin of exultation had been slapped off. My face could not express what I was feeling. I couldn't understand what I was feeling.

I made a move, lurched up, thinking I'd grab it, but it was faster than me, much faster. It leapt like a diver, sprang with its arms extended, describing a graceful arc over the bed, over me, cutting seamlessly into the big oval mirror, a sea otter slipping into its element, barely rippling the glass as it passed through the surface.

What? How? It can't do that, is what I thought as it went through the mirror, and my head went inside out. I got to my knees and gripped the edges of the mirror. I would follow it, find it. I had to. I recognized it. I knew it. How could I not? The last time I had seen it was when it murdered Abigail thirty years before.

SIX

I PREPARED TO LUNGE through the mirror.

Mojo swirled in Circe's room. This would be easy. I would dive into the mirror and track that thing to the end of nothing and finally have it in my hands and batter it into fragments. For that instant, I was singing. Some hungry part of me that lived for revenge opened its mouth, and out came a perfect and harmonious tone. So beautiful. I lurched at the mirror, and stopped myself, and the song died inside me.

I couldn't chase myself, no matter how much I wanted to. It wasn't a matter of priorities, it was a matter of possibilities. Nothing and no one can be tracked inside the mirrors. You go in there and find a way out. There is nothing else to be found. It had been here, in reach, and I'd missed my opportunity to break it. A bigger question: how had it dived into the mirror at all? Manikins can't sly, they can't use mojo to do anything. I must have missed a detail. Had a hand been thrust out of the mirror? Had some hidden sly pulled that thing inside? However it had been done, it was gone now. But it had been here, as real as I remembered it. Here.

Why here? Why would it be in Circe's room? Me and it here together. That couldn't be coincidence. So. The way to find out where it might have run to was to find out how and why it had come here. Thirty years I'd been trying to find myself, looking for revenge; it couldn't be random chance that brought us together here and now.

I was feeling more and more a deep connectedness between everything that was happening. Whether that connectedness was authentic or a symptom of my newly hyperactive brain was a worthwhile question I didn't bother to ponder. Let everyone else concern themselves with rational explanations—I knew better. There was some very hinky action going on, and I didn't believe for a second that it wasn't tied up together somehow. Probably. Maybe. Anyway, I'd need to investigate further.

I moved to where my reflection had been standing and felt the tug of the mojo current still flowing in the room. I took a step back. The fact that this course had flipped me out of depression suggested it was directed toward change of some kind. But there was no reason to think the change had to be benevolent. If I waded back into it, it might return me to a depressive cycle. I stayed clear of it and focused on the physical surroundings.

My reflection was here for a purpose. Looking for something, maybe? Start with that. I turned myself around, rotating slowly, letting my eyes skip along the feverish collage of Circe's walls. I wanted to find her friends and track down the theater mentor. How to do that? I rotated, letting my pixilated thoughts fuzz around my head. My head and Circe's room had a lot in common just then. Everything was everywhere and none of it seemed to make any sense.

Hapax legomenon.

Wait. What? "Hapax legomenon"? I stopped rotating. Why did I think about hapax legomenon? That's not the kind of thing I usually think about. Where did it come from, all of a sudden? I tried to shake my head clear, and started rotating again, reversing direction, slowly, slowly, eyes open. Where was it? There! The words jumped at me from a piece of paper on the wall near Circe's turntable.

HAPAX LEGOMENON.

What was a Greek term that means something like "said

only once," and refers to the single use of a word in a written work, doing in a teenager's bedroom? I mean, even if you're a researcher for the *Oxford English Dictionary*, you're not going to see that term put to use every day. The words HAPAX LEGOME-NON were at the top of a flyer, its bottom hidden under a strip of black-and-white photos of a man in a suit and tie shooting pool. I picked at the tape holding the photos to the wall, carefully peeled them back, and peeked at the flyer behind them.

Hapax Legomenon

A mystery play in three acts:
Hope Eclipsed by Black Despair
Death and the Danse Macabre
The Harrowing Call and Demon's Rise

The Old Barn Theater—Advance Ticket Sales
at Plow House Coffee Co. Physical and in Person.

The whole thing was a combination of hand-lettering and 1990s computer clip art. The borders were as densely layered with symbols and icons and faces snipped from magazines as were the walls of Circe's room. It was one of those times I kind of wished I had a phone. I'd have liked to take a photo so I could study the design, see if there were clues lodged in it; I didn't want to take it with me and risk marring the pattern of the room and the mojo flowing in it. I had to be happy with the fact that not having a phone meant that my memory did not suffer from the typical twenty-first-century atrophy. I could easily remember the address of Plow House Coffee. That would have to do. I smoothed the strip of billiards photos back over the flyer.

Circe's turntable, with *The Lion and the Cobra* album jacket atop it, had been returned to its perch on the dresser. Iva must have straightened up. I was tempted to take the album off the spindle, slip it into its sleeve, and take it with me. I still had no idea why Circe's mojo was so potent, but her favorite record was bound to be worth quite a bit. My fingers tingled with temptation as I touched the jacket, but I settled for leaning it away from the wall so I could get a look at the drawings behind it.

I'd caught a glimpse of them when I'd been in the room with Iva. Pencil, pen, and watercolor. They looked theatrical. A few were sketches of stage sets peopled by stick figures made of squiggly black lines, each of them given a rich dash of red at their neck, as if they wore scarlet scarves. There was a banner planted downstage, a long pennant stretched to its full length, the end forked. The design on the banner was a black circle made of crisscrossing hashmarks. A spiky circlet that evoked a crown of thorns, bisected horizontally by a streak of red that matched the scarves on the figures. The only other piece of scenery was upstage, a backdrop covering the rear wall. Another circle, much larger, encompassed the backdrop, but was painted in many colors. It looked like a crude map of a massive city laid out in a ring with nothing at its center. Another rendering featured a view from above the stage. This one showed little but the floor of the stage itself, and another circle, solid black, appearing to be a massive hole, big enough to fill the emptiness at the center of the ring city on the backdrop.

One of the sketches was different from the others. Not a stage rendering. On this one, the circle motif from the stage design was repeated, but it served as the outline of a wide-open mouth in a screaming face. Emerging from the mouth were a series of concentric black rings, each larger than the last. Representing a silent scream? Text had been penciled in and erased. There were several tries at a caption, but apparently none of them had pleased. I could pick out the impressions of a few words. SCREAM. RAGE. ABYSS.

I turned in place again. What had my reflection been looking for? What did it want? I stopped rotating. If it wanted to kill me, it had just passed on a good shot. I'd been defenseless on my back. But it waited until I saw it, and then it smiled and ran. Ran from me or ran to pursue someone else?

Circe?

I had to find my reflection. Find that thing and batter it with a hammer until it shattered into a bazillion tiny shards. And I had to figure out how to get at the mojo in Circe's room. I was still a thief, after all. Once I knew she was safe from my reflection, I could focus on robbing her. I was going to need all the mojo I had to get that job done. I didn't have much, and it was all back at my apartment. Would Lloyd think I was stupid enough to go back home after I got away from him? It didn't really matter. I needed that mojo. I'd have to take a chance.

I lived life on the line that bordered stupid and clever. It's called being sly.

I climbed up on Circe's bed and faced myself in the mirror. This would be easy; mojo was everywhere in the room. Making sure not to direct too much into the mirror was the challenge. I didn't want to get caught in a tide that washed me across the country. I did my thing, opened my mind, forgot existence, imagined where I was going, and slid myself into the surface of the glass. Strong, clean, aching, and angry. That was the feel of the mojo in Circe's room as it washed me through the mirror and I fell out of another mirror, one that was bolted to the wall inside my bedroom closet, transitioning from freezing, endless blankness into stifling, humid darkness, and banging my head against the clothes bar as I stood up.

My hand found the pull cord and I yanked on the light. I kept my spare kit in the closet. Back of the shelf, behind several milk crates full of jumbled old cassettes. I bought them by the handful at swap meets and culled them for loose mojo. Mixtapes were a good medium for deep emotion. People used to put a lot of feeling into creating their own mixtapes. They had to match songs from different artists and genres, transitioning from song to song while building to a climax and trying to fill the length of the tape perfectly so that it didn't end with minutes of hissing silence. All of that effort directed at a purpose. The perfect accompaniment for a Midwest road trip, consolation for a friend who has lost a loved one, booty shakers for a dance party. Of course most of them had been made by someone hoping to get laid, but that didn't make the effort any less sincere. If you were patient, you could skim a nice bit of mojo off junk like that.

Streaming playlists had absolutely gutted the market.

I pulled down one of the crates, clattered the cassettes onto the floor, flipped the crate, climbed up, and let my hands find the cigar box hidden at the back of the shelf. Inside was my last hundred and fifty bucks, my remaining three Pegleg Wanda groupie badges, and a car safety hammer. One of those little hammers with pointy steel nubs at the head; you're supposed to keep it in your glove box to break windows so you can get out of your car if you ever drive into a lake. I pocketed the money, pinned on all three badges, and slipped the car safety hammer inside my jacket. In a cardboard box on the floor I found a small notepad and a novelty pen with a topless hula dancer who dropped her skirt to reveal a mermaid's tail when you turned her upside down. Now I could scribble my thoughts, get organized, plan the next step of my quest to find Circe and shatter my reflection and steal a boatload of mojo. But first, I really needed to pee.

So I opened the door and stepped into my bedroom and a pair of California Highway Patrol cops grabbed me and slammed me against the wall and started going through my pockets.

"Lover doesn't carry mirrors," said a voice, "but take those band buttons off him. He might do something sly with those trinkets."

Weeks I'd been lolling on my bed, desperate for something to happen to give me evidence that the world was still spinning and I had some place in it. In all that time, nothing had happened more interesting than a fly landing on my hand and me playing a game with myself to see how long I could stay perfectly still so it wouldn't fly away. I got pretty good at that game. And then, wham! Today comes along and I get roped by

Francois out of the blue and manhandled multiple times in my own place.

My new set of manhandlers were also manikins. They emptied my pockets and took my badges, and spun me around. Both were in black leather jackets and jack boots, khaki uniforms, with nightsticks, .38 police specials on their Sam Browne belts, snug gold and blue helmets, and mirrored Ray-Bans. A couple of preening neo-Fascist skull breakers, circa 1977. His and hers. He had a YMCA mustache, she had a sleek ponytail peeking out at the back of her helmet.

"Don't move," Mustache told me.

"What now?" Ponytail asked a woman sitting at the end of my bed.

The woman was leaning back on her elbows, long legs crossed at the knees, squinting at me with mismatched eyes, green and blue, her grin disconcertingly snaggletoothed in an otherwise ethereally beautiful face.

Perilous Sue.

She gave the mattress a poke with her index finger.

"As lumpy as ever, Catchpenny. And your sheets need washing. Ah, well, not my concern any longer. Not for some time, eh, lover?"

She pushed herself up from the bed.

"Munroe wants to see you."

I thought about fighting, trying to take a dive back through the mirror in the closet, but Sue was a different creature from Lloyd. Lloyd was a dangerous creep. Perilous Sue was a monster. Pretty much literally a monster. I didn't want her mad at me.

"Want to hear something funny, Sue?" I said.

She gave her long frock coat a brush.

"Tell me. I could use a laugh."

"I was just coming to see Munroe."

SEVEN

IN THEORY, if you can do one thing with mojo, you can do anything with mojo.

Not anything, but any of the areas of specialization. The schools. That's in theory; in actual practice, anything you do with mojo is so damned hard to master, no one has the time to study in more than one school. Everything you do with mojo is dangerous and prone to boomerang on you. Lose focus at the wrong moment and the mojo you want to use to curse your father and speed his death so you can inherit his fortune may wrap around and hit you back, perhaps manifesting as a subtly irritating rash in your crotch that distracts you while you're driving him to his dialysis appointment. You take a hand off the wheel to scratch yourself and you veer into the next lane, getting plastered by an eighteen-wheeler that sends you into a telephone pole, killing both you and your old man, so that your sister, who you loathe, ends up with the whole estate. That's an example drawn from life. And as mojo-related cautionary tales go, it's pretty soft stuff. It could be much worse. Existentially worse. People get lost. Inside themselves, inside the mirrors, inside curiosities. There is so much space inside of everything, you can get lost anywhere and never come back. The risks of generalization are fantastically high, so everyone ends up specializing in just one school. Everyone except for Munroe.

Munroe was a school unto herself. The school of being frighteningly adept at the arts and sciences of mojo. She was a vehemancer by disposition, able to draw raw emotion from the atmosphere as people were generating it. That alone was scary. It's a volatile practice, prone to mishaps. Handling raw mojo is like messing with sweaty sticks of dynamite. One slip, and boom! You're gone, literally blown up, swollen and popped. To be an effective vehemancer is a lifetime's work. But Munroe was also skilled at auspicing, coursing mojo to a specific purpose. And she was an outstanding limner, a drawer of manikins. But she could not sly. She never went into the mirrors herself. Never dipped a pinkie or a toe. She needed hired help for that errand.

Whatever else she did or was, Munroe was also a heck of a hostess and threw an amazing party. One way or another, sooner or later, everyone came to Munroe's party. Her door was open and the party was raging. Had been for more than fifty years. The festivities never ceased, rambling up and down the jumbled tiers and decks of the great white house that clung to the side of Laurel Canyon. It was a haunted place for me. Specters of my past were everywhere to be found, many of them covered in blood. Then again, the place was haunted for everyone who came there. The ghosts were part of the attraction.

The first time Abigail and I went to the party, the night I attracted Munroe's attention with my voice, we came panting up the flights of zigzagged stairs from the street and saw the ghosts of Jimi Hendrix, Janis Joplin, and Jim Morrison playing nude Marco Polo in the pool with a gaggle of less-recognizable guests. We knew to expect that sight. Everybody knew to expect to see a few dead-celebrity impersonators upon arrival. In the pool or working the grill or bartending, all of them unsettlingly identical to the dead stars they emulated.

Where does she find them? Abigail had asked me.

I'd taken a moment there at the gate, ostensibly to catch my breath, but more to gather my poise after seeing the trio of dead rock stars frolicking in the pool.

Central casting, same as the movies, I told her.

Dead celebrities were only one of the party's exotic attractions, but they garnered particular attention from both the press and new arrivals. The party had been haunted through the years by JFK, RFK, JFK Jr., Marilyn (of course), and James Dean (also of course). Natalie Wood, John Lennon, and Sid Vicious had had their day. Munroe would always have a smattering of well-known cadavers from the last twenty or thirty years mixing in, but her real interest was in the freshly dead.

That first night at the party, in 1993, Abigail and I saw Audrey Hepburn, Andre the Giant, and Rudolf Nureyev, all recently deceased at the time. Over the next months, as we became regulars, and as the early nineties took their toll on the rolls of fame, we met the ghosts of Mick Ronson, Thurgood Marshall, and Brandon Lee. Few things I've seen in my life have stuck with me like the sight of a crowd of spectators cheering the arm-wrestling ghosts of Richard Nixon and Charles Bukowski. And I've rarely been as moved as I was the night Kurt Cobain's ghost sang a cover of "American Pie" less than two months after his suicide. No one could imagine where Munroe found them. They were so flawless in appearance and manner that they came to be called ghosts. The rawness of her gesture, displaying these fantastic mimics just after someone had died, was especially thrilling. People loved the tastelessness of it.

If they only knew the truth.

Coming through the gate, with Sue leading the way and the cops before and behind me, I caught sight of David Bowie and Prince mingling and making themselves available for a succession of selfies. Those two had been dead for several years. More recently demised, Charlie Daniels, Charlie Watts, and

Charlie Pride had a jam going on fiddle, bongos, and guitar. There'd be an even more recent reaper's crop hanging about somewhere.

The pool lights hadn't come on yet, the midsummer sun still hanging above the canyon. Two blondes wearing sunglasses designed by someone with a fondness for neon ski goggles were bobbing in the pool on inflatable lounge chairs. The deck was littered with the detritus of a party. Wet towels draped the rails around the pool deck, and the white canvas walls of the cabanas expanded and contracted in the which-way breeze as if they were pumping oxygen for a quintet of shirtless beach bums puffing on a towering, five-hose hookah.

As we climbed to the next tier, the firepit, I could hear voices raised in chorus. The hootenanny had begun. Coming into view, I saw Munroe's current cadaverous main attraction. Tina Turner in her prime was covering Taylor Swift's "Anti-Hero." As we climbed the next flight of stairs, I heard a sting of electric guitar join in and the crowd went berserk. I looked down as Eddie Van Halen stepped into view and they swung into Olivia Rodrigo's "deja vu." It was actually pretty cool.

Doubtless Munroe had written their set list. She always sought to give the audience exactly what they wanted, wrapped inside what they didn't know they could ever have. She left nothing to chance when her artists went to work, living, dead, or otherwise. The duo was surrounded by a halo of glowing screens, dozens of guests streaming the show from their phones.

I looked up at the house, jutting out from the canyon wall, cantilevered, looming. No sign of Munroe on the balcony. She didn't need to check on Tina and Eddie. She knew when she had a hit on her hands.

If Minerva gravitated to the 1980s out of loving nostalgia for his own youth, Munroe cultivated her particular vision of Laurel Canyon Hollywood demimonde mythology with far more calculation. She'd settled in Los Angeles for a reason. She knew the power of fantasy, particularly the methodically manufactured kind that is designed to creep into people's hearts and minds and breed wants and desires. Munroe aspired to romantic timelessness, fever dreams of what it might have been like once upon a time here in La-La Land. She built a bastion in the canyon for the cool, sexy, lost, and bad L.A. that everyone wished they could have been around for.

The dead celebrity ghosts weren't the only manikins Munroe used to set her scene. The party was studded with L.A. and Hollywood clichés that enhanced her desired atmosphere. Perfectly tanned Century City agents, West Hollywood leather lads, Venice Beach burnouts, Chinatown mah-jongg hustlers, a USC Trojan in his football jersey, Sunset Strip rockers, Valley girls, and more. A *Playboy* bunny playing backgammon with a guy who exuded the creepy, vacant-eyed charm of a Scientologist, sun-baked cowboy stuntmen, fad-dieting Malibu Colony matrons with bones jutting behind age-spotted skin, Boyle Heights lowriders in white tank tops and Panama hats, Dogtown skater boys, aging silicon queens with orange-skinned sugar daddies, Muscle Beach bodybuilders in pastel Speedos, and a clutch of pale-faced screenwriters squinting against the sun as they gathered around a bottle of free whiskey and bitched about residuals.

"Hey, man."

A Melrose punk shuffled to a stop in front of me: leather jeans, cracked Doc Martens, the crest of his mohawk stretching him to seven feet. He took a photocopied band flyer from a thick stack and shoved it into my hand.

"Move it along." Ponytail cop frowned at him, placing a threatening hand on her baton.

The mohawked kid shrugged and slouched away, passing flyers to the other guests. He was a cliché type, but he was real people. One of those lower castes that make a demimonde a demimonde. I followed my escort up the next flight of stairs.

Manikins, whether they were dead celebrities or just local color, were not the bulk of the party. Mostly the party was a mass of real people that added to itself, diminished and then replenished, but never dried up. In the predawn morning hours, the party might reduce to bodies passed out on couches, couples hidden under king-size beach towels on air mattresses, and exhausted caterers filling garbage bags with half-eaten hors d'oeuvres and empty bottles. But as the day went by, it would repopulate.

The last and smallest of the many tiers of Munroe's patio was an intimate deck just below the house. A lush thickness of carpets and rugs had been layered over the tiled floor with dozens of cushions tossed about for what Munroe called *the lounging*. The lounging was being accomplished that late afternoon by a couple dozen pretty young things and a few manikins. The phones were out and active. Digital mirrors, cameras faced around for selfies, a silent chatter of social media commenting on the audible chatter of the party itself.

I eyed the litter of humanity and pseudo humanity lolling about, chatting, drinking, eating, smoking, sniffing, and flicking eternally at the screens of their phones. The surface of the deck had become topographical over the years, the carpets and rugs lumping up, spreading, ripping, rolling their corners. If I took out my knife and cut into them, I could have found an accounting of the years. I wondered how far I'd have to slice to find one that Abigail and I had lounged on.

"Are you stalling, Catchpenny?" Sue asked me.

I'd gotten lost in thought, looking down as more people were streaming up from the knotted streets of the canyon. It was clearly going to be a big night. Munroe must have something special planned. And Minerva had been right when he said she was bringing in more manikins than usual. The higher we'd climbed, the more I saw. Not just the usual party candy. There was a lot of muscle. Bodybuilders and stunt cowboys, the motorcycle cops bracing me. I could see plainclothes detectives, a couple of boxers, some South Central gangsters. Munroe didn't usually keep that much of the hard stuff around. Manikins tended to be either deeply vain creatures with outsize confidence in themselves or insecure and full of self-loathing, products of the mirrors they were limned from. Neither was entirely stable.

"I'm not stalling," I told Sue. "Just taking it in."

Local-color manikins helped maintain the base of the party, the famous manikins added spice, while real people were the soup. But the party wasn't there to nurture them; they were there to feed the party. The party was a churn of energy. Mojo feeding itself, and thus feeding Munroe.

No one came to the party without leaving a taste of themselves in Munroe's mouth. The more they came, the more she nibbled. Keep coming, keep giving in to the growing addiction of feeling that you were a part of something bigger than yourself, something cool and special, and the more of yourself would be consumed. You could spot the longtime partiers in an instant. Mortified, stripped of all mojo except the bit that kept them motivated enough to have another drink, take another puff, laugh like they were having the best time of their lives, but their lives were as good as over.

Ascending finally to the house itself, Sue parted a white curtain, standing aside, giving me her gnarled grin, and we went through into sudden quiet. The CHP manikins would stay outside. Munroe didn't like manikins in her house. A rival had once sent a trio of hitmen drawn from the stainless-steel mirrors in the high-security wing at San Quentin. Sue had gone at them with a poker from the fireplace, expecting to smash them hither and yon and leave the sweeping up to the housekeepers. Instead, the iron poker had clanged off the first one's skull and sent a numbing shiver down her arm. Way the story is told, that night is as close as Sue's ever come to taking the worse end in a fight. As it was, she came out in one piece because Munroe stepped in. She has ancillary courses devoted to her safety and protection running every which way inside the house, and she tapped one that ran from the hooded gas fire in the middle of the main room. It focused mild heat into a hairline of combustion, a razored wand of arc-welder intensity that she slashed through the stainless manikin killers, carving off chunks of them, which she still kept scattered around the lawn behind the house like the half-melted remains of a garden sculpture. Then she tracked down whoever had sent them for her and indulged the mean side of her nature.

It all ended well enough, but Munroe had learned a lesson. No real person was insane enough to attack her directly, but a freshly limned manikin can be made to do any foolish thing. Now the house was coursed with violent streams of mojo that would splinter or melt any reflection that moved against her.

The bottom floor of the house was open-plan, a sprawl of empty space. No furniture, no decoration. White, clean, and quiet—just the hiss and flutter of burning gas from the circular hearth at the center of the room, yellow flames in a pile of blue glass pebbles. A space to serve as a buffer between the party and Munroe. Invitation only. A spiral of stairs corkscrewed up through the ceiling in a far corner, the final ascent to the lady of the house.

"You know the way, lover," Sue said, tipping her perfectly chiseled chin toward the stairs.

I climbed.

A legendary maven of the music business with an unrivaled ability to discover talent, Munroe had enjoyed a run of success that was unparalleled, but, unlike so many other super managers and mega agents, she never grabbed at the offered brass ring of her own label. Munroe stayed with talent, close to the music, intimately involved with her artists and their fans. In the studios and the clubs and the arenas. Where the mojo got made.

People in the mojo racket said that Munroe had gotten her start as a vehemancer at Woodstock. Rumors abounded about how she skimmed mojo from the zeitgeist event of an era-defining generation. Not true. She told me herself how it really went down. She got the idea to use rock concerts to gather mojo when she was at the Monterey Pop Festival, two years before Woodstock. She wasn't the only one who saw the potential, and she knew more than one mojo fiend would be packing into a VW bus to make the trek to Woodstock. She didn't want the competition. Instead, she started cooking up something from scratch. A free concert in the Bay Area, away from San Francisco, somewhere more isolated, where she could have her own security and make sure no other vehemancers crashed the party to skim her mojo.

It was the first big investment of her nascent mojo and influence. She burned everything she had in order to see that the Rolling Stones and Grateful Dead free concert in Golden Gate Park would be moved to the Altamont Speedway near Livermore. To heighten the emotion surrounding the show, she arranged for the Hells Angels to work security.

Well, that all went to pieces, Munroe would gleefully admit.

Not that she regretted the beatings, the mortal stabbing of Meredith Hunter, the two hit-and-run deaths, and the LSD case drowned in an irrigation canal. Those things didn't diminish the emotion generated at the concert or its later reputation; they just changed the nature of the mojo she reaped from the event.

It was rough stuff, bracingly raw, she'd told me.

Realizing that mojo could be drawn off a live concert wasn't original to Munroe. Creating a party that was a kind of perpetual-motion mojo machine was her stroke of brilliance. No matter how much of the party's mojo Munroe recycled to keep it going, there was always more than enough to surfeit herself. Although truly, Munroe was never sated. As much mojo as she coursed for her own good fortune and security, she banked more away. There was never enough for her.

Appetite was her salient quality. Munroe, ever hungry for more.

I went up the stairs and emerged into the lounge. Decorated in shades of gold, silver, black, and white, this was Munroe's reception area. Beyond an open archway was her office, and beyond that her bedroom. And somewhere beyond that, a chamber filled with one of the most potent collections of curiosities in the world. There was only one mirror in the entire house, a huge one mounted on the ceiling over her California king–size bed. It was a dare, that mirror, a tease to any sly who thought they could steal from her. A dare no one had ever taken.

"Sidneeeeeey!"

Munroe came swooping at me as I topped the stairs, her arms spread, her rogue's grin in place, face turned for me to kiss as she gathered me to her, mashing first one cheek and then the other against my lips, and then grabbing me by the back of my head and turning it this way and that as she returned the kisses. The golf ball chunks of amber on her necklace dug into my chest while the assorted pieces of turquoise, ivory, jade, and onyx on her wrists dug into my back. For all her size and voluptuous heft, Munroe's embrace felt sharp-edged.

She took me by the shoulders, holding me at arm's length, her nails and her many rings digging into me.

"Look. At. You. Look at you. You came. I'm soooo glad you came. I told Sue. I said, *He'll come. Just wait, he won't miss a party.* And here he is. Here. He. Is."

She gave a squeeze of her long-fingered hands with each of those last three words. I had smears of her rust-red lipstick on my cheeks and my clothes were saturated with the citrusy eau de cologne that had been formulated just for her during her long-ago modeling career, before she'd aged out and turned to music as another pathway to relevance. I felt marked. Like I'd been rubbed by a cat. It sure seems like affection, but it's pure territoriality. *This is mine.*

I cocked a smile.

"How could I stay away after you sent a personal invitation? You look amazing. As always."

"Sidney, you are a liar."

"Don't. No. You look fantastic."

It was true—she looked amazing. Munroe was happy to let herself age naturally, but mojo ensured that her aging was graceful and striking. She'd had her hair cropped close on the sides, the top kept long, parted sharply, pomaded and combed, and she had allowed it to go entirely gray. It was the haircut of a 1950s stockbroker and it suited her. I've seen magazine spreads and paparazzi snapshots from her prime. Several hung on the walls of her lounge. Covers of *Vogue, Elle,* and *Vanity Fair,* along with candid snaps. Munroe laughing as Grace Jones inhales a line of coke out of the hollow between her breasts, Munroe with a hushing index finger to her lips and a naughty wink as she slips into a nightclub men's room with Warren Beatty in tow, Munroe scampering nude, backlit by the setting sun on Pismo Beach. For as long as her modeling career lasted, Munroe had been never less than provocative in both style and lifestyle.

She grabbed a fistful of my hair and gave it a tug. "That hair. I'd kill for your hair." She noticed the picture of Sinéad O'Connor on my T-shirt.

"That old witch, huh?"

I plucked at the bottom of the shirt, straightening it a bit.

"What can I say, I'm a fan."

Munroe blinked slowly.

"Ugh, Sidney. I mean, *ugh.*"

"So she wouldn't sign with you, does that make her untalented?"

She flexed her fingers, gave them a wiggle, and her smile flattened.

"I cannot wait. I. Can. Not. Wait. Until I get my hands on one of her mirrors so I can limn up her manikin to play the party."

She settled herself on a high-backed gold divan.

"I'll have her singing Phil Collins for weeks."

I thought about that for a moment.

"She'd demolish 'In the Air Tonight.'"

Munroe laughed.

"She would. You're right. She would."

I didn't think there was much real danger of Munroe finding a mirror with a strong enough reflection of Sinéad for her to be able to limn a manikin. There was little doubt that O'Connor had been some kind of adept herself. And no one in the racket would ever spend enough time in front of a single mirror to leave a usable impression.

Munroe's hand wandered as of its own will to a massive phone perched next to her on the divan. Fingers danced over the screen, her eyes moving back and forth between it and me.

"These people," she said about something on her phone. "What did you think of Tina and Eddie?"

I clapped a few times.

"Bravo."

She flicked and tapped her screen, barely looking up.

"It's low-hanging fruit, I know. But these people. You have no idea what it takes to keep them focused these days." She flipped her phone over, hiding the screen from herself. "It used to be they'd come here and never want to go. All their attention was on the party. But these things."

She waved a dismissive hand over her phone.

"Appalling. Unless people have something they can take a picture of or do a selfie with, they don't pay attention at all. They just dick around with their socials. It's not what it used to be, Sidney, the party does not perform as it once did. Do you know the next great frontier for curiosities, my little thief? These things."

She flipped her phone, screen-side up.

"People care more about their phones than anything else

they own. There will come a day, not long off, when the only curiosities worth stealing will be phones. Old-timers like me need to find new sources of mojo. I've always said the party can't last forever. Mark me now. The. Party. Can. Not. Last. For. Ever." She gave her phone a last look. "Ah, Tina and Eddie are trending. What kills me is that I can't get my hands on any of the mojo these leeches are generating with their posts. I can skim their enthusiasm for the show as they watch it, but the mojo that comes off the reactions to their posts? It all leaves the party and goes away. It literally dumps into the fucking internet. The waste is dreadful. How is a girl like me to survive?"

Munroe was not alone in this lament over modernity. As smartphones had proliferated, massive amounts of mojo that used to get attached to curiosities or people or events or any of the several foci where a savvy operator could get at the stuff was now bound up in the World Wide Web. And when mojo got sucked into the internet, that's where it stayed. Internet mojo was out of reach. Period.

"You seem to be getting by okay," I said. "The party is as lively as ever, despite all the new dead people."

Her smile was back.

"Oh, Sidney. You make me laugh. It is so good to see you. What are you drinking?"

"I'll have whatever you're having."

"I'm having a bloody bull. Sue, a bloody bull for Sidney, plenty of lime, and I'll have a freshener, please."

Sue moved behind a small wet bar in the corner and began mixing drinks.

Munroe picked up her phone again and flicked the screen, reading.

"What do you think, Sidney, are people right?"

"About what?"

"Is the end of the world nigh?"

Not the conversational bid that I had been anticipating. My

brain spun on that for a moment. The end of the world? No idea
what that was about.

"Why do you ask?"

"It's in the air. People are worried about it."

"Should they be?"

She laughed.

"Any reasonable person should be worried about the end
of the world. Nuclear weapons abound, climate disasters rage,
political unrest, pandemics, all that stuff."

Where was this going? No clue.

"We live in complicated times, I guess."

"So no thoughts on the impending end of the world?"

I shrugged.

"If it goes, it goes."

"Mmm, well," she said. "Happier thoughts. Here's your drink."

Sue appeared beside me so silently that I flinched.

"Bloody bull, lover," she said in a voice that belonged on
radio. "Extra lime."

I took the sweaty highball glass from her hand.

"Thanks."

She nodded and returned behind the bar.

"Suicide cults!" said Munroe, as if she'd been pondering my
favorite movie title and had just come up with her best guess.
"What do you think about suicide cults, Sidney?"

"Suicide cults?"

"As a phenomenon, I mean. What do you think about them?
Sign of the times?"

"I do not think about suicide cults ever."

"Cults committing mass suicides. You don't think about
that?"

"Nope."

"You just dwell upon your own suicide."

She was suddenly hitting very close to home. Why, I didn't
know.

"I don't have a suicide to dwell upon, Munroe. Here I am, sans suicide."

"Oh, Sid, you're a terrible liar."

Well, that stung.

"I'm a good liar."

"Let's test that proposition."

Uh-oh.

"Where did you go with Francois today, Sidney?"

Where did I go with Francois? Why did she know what I'd been doing?

I glanced at a window, tipped my head that direction.

"Lot of new manikins around the place," I observed, taking a stab at changing the topic.

"I asked you a question, Sidney," she said, deflecting my lame attempt.

"I heard you."

She was right about me and lying; I'm not very good at it. *You have a face like a book,* Abigail told me when we met in Odessa, Texas. *A children's book with nothing but pictures,* she teased. She'd been waitressing in a honky-tonk where I was playing. I'd noticed her, anyone would have, and I was trying to pick her up. Anyone would have. It wasn't my ungentlemanly intentions that she could decipher so easily—I hadn't tried to conceal those—it was how completely smitten I was by her. *We've just met and I've got you twisted 'round my little finger, don't I?* she said. I laughed and told her no such thing was true. And that's when she said the bit about my face being a picture book.

Lucky for you that I can't resist an open book, she said.

I love your voice, she said later that night in bed at the motel where she was living. *And your hair,* she said. A couple of days later we left Odessa on the bus together. Three weeks later we were married in Vegas by a guy dressed like Elvis. A year later she was gone. Me and my open-book face and my voice and my hair had charmed her to death.

I was caught in that reverie and wondering what lie I could tell that Munroe might believe when Perilous Sue butted in.

"Lover told me something funny when I picked him up. Told me he was on his way to see you."

Munroe flashed a look of theatrical surprise, raised eyebrows and all that.

"Were you, Sidney?"

"Sure," I said. "Minerva asked me to drop by."

"Yes?"

"He asked me to come by and grab that bone he bought off you."

I was on firm footing here truth-wise. I might not have known anything about what was going on, but Minerva had absolutely wanted me to go to Munroe's and get a bone.

Munroe blinked, laughed.

"Grab the bone?" she managed to get out between gasps of laughter.

"That's what Hillary said."

She wiped her eyes.

"I've missed you so much. No one makes me laugh like you do. Grab the bone." She took a deep breath, regaining composure, and pointed at my glass.

"You haven't touched your drink."

Of course I hadn't touched it. I'm a terrible liar, not a dummy.

"Yeah, I'm not drinking this."

"Not enough lime?"

"No, it's drugged."

Munroe shrugged. *Well, of course it is.*

"Sue," she said, "help Sidney to imbibe."

Sue was suddenly clamping a hand on the back of my neck, squeezing in a way that had me opening my mouth wide to groan in pain. With her free hand she steered the cocktail to my mouth, tipped the glass, and bloody bull streamed down my open gullet and over my chin and cheeks. I coughed and choked, bloody bull exploding from my nostrils in a fine spray.

"Get him a towel." Munroe, always thoughtful.

Sue let go of my neck and shoved a towel into my hand. I covered my face, hawked, and spat, but plenty of the doped cocktail had gone down my throat. Whatever it was, I was going to be feeling the effects soon enough.

Munroe patted the divan next to her.

"Come sit."

I didn't move.

"Sue, would you mind escorting Sidney over here?"

I surrendered my pride and walked over and sat on the divan before Sue could force me to. But I sat as far from Munroe as I possibly could. So there.

"Now, Sidney, you had to know something like this would happen if you came here. You haven't been to the party for years and years. If you show up, I'm bound to be curious."

I folded my arms, kept my mouth shut.

Sue stepped over, and I waited to be hit, but all she did was offer Munroe the junk her manikins had taken from my pockets, including the photo of the bone Minerva had given me.

"He had this on him."

Munroe picked up the photograph, flashed it at me.

"Do you know what's irritating about patriarchal annexation, Sidney? How obvious it is. It's like, the most natural thing in the world is birth, you know. So if there's an original human being, if god is going to make a first single human, why is she going to add a step for herself by making a guy when she can just make a woman? A pregnant woman. There's a whole story about it. Lilith, the original mother-wife. But that won't do for the church fathers, will it? Nope, first human needs to be a man, no matter how illogical that may be. Anyway, this bone here, it is a rib. Adam's rib. Pure bullshit, of course. The man never existed. But this bone has been venerated for over nine hundred years in the belief it is Adam's rib. People have fought and died for it. More than one crusade was waged expressly to take possession of it. It is steeped in all the obsession and blood and faith that religion can muster. Satanists got their hands on it at one point and carved it into a knife so they could pollute it by using it to sacrifice virgins and all that nonsense. It is a superior curiosity, unique, powerful, and it was excruciatingly difficult to obtain."

"Wow," I said.

"And yet, Minerva asked you to come over and casually request I give it to you."

"He gave me the impression he bought it from you."

"He doesn't have the price. Not half of it."

"Huh."

"You're a bright boy, Sidney. If Hillary had no arrangement to acquire the rib from me, why did he send you to pester me?"

Crap. Crap. Crap. I'd been right about what Minerva wanted from me.

"He wanted to cause trouble."

"Yes. Why?"

"I don't know. He said you're up to something. All these new manikins. He thinks you have a scheme or something. He wanted me to come over and peek around, see what I could see."

Suddenly, it got dark.

"Don't close your eyes, I have more questions."

Don't close my eyes? Oh, right. I opened them.

Munroe stroked my hair. Who could blame her?

"Francois came to me, Sidney. He wanted to contract a sly. But he wouldn't tell me what he wanted to steal, so I told him no. And then he went to you."

"Francois came to you before me?"

"Yes. What did he want you to steal for him?"

Sometimes I don't have to lie. A bad liar, drugged to my eyeballs, spilling my story to anyone who wants to ask, I can sometimes just tell the simple truth and it works out okay.

"Nothing."

Munroe tangled a finger in a lock of my hair and gave it a pull.

"You're a thief. What else would he want you for?"

"I don't know. To check it out."

"He wanted you to case something?"

"Mmm, yeah, sort of like that. So tired."

She gave my hair a hard yank.

"Not yet. Case what?"

"Case. Case? I'm not a detective. I just steal stuff. I'd like to steal that rib you got."

She looked at Sue.

"Tell me again what you saw at his place."

I looked at Sue, too. I was interested in this. And it was nice to have someone else answering questions for a change.

Sue put her hands on her hips, drawing back the wings of her frock coat. She wore a holster under her right arm. Oiled leather, it held a knife, its handle longer by an inch than its broad, single-edged blade. I remembered the feel of that blade going through my skin. Not good.

"I staked out lover's place. You were right. After you told Francois he'd have no help from you, he fetched up at Catchpenny's abode. I followed them to Sunland. Up a private road they went. Came back some ticks later. Followed them back to his place. Lover went in and came out with Minerva's skinny creep and a couple fragile-looking manikins. I followed to Minerva's junk shop. Lover came back out with the creep and the retro dolls. He caused a ruckus and ran. They all went into the Rainbow. Creep came out with his muscle, lover did not. I called you. You said go to lover's place, wait for him there. You said he'd run home soon enough. You were right."

I looked up at Munroe's face.

"I hate that I'm so predictable to you."

She gave my hair another tug, pulling hard this time.

"End of the world, Sidney. Suicide cults. What do you have to say?"

"Grim. Grim stuff."

She tangled both hands in my hair, yanking, shaking my head back and forth.

"Someone is working big mojo, Sidney. I want to know who it is and where the mojo is coming from. Say yes if you understand."

I understood, but I couldn't say anything because my tongue was made of lead.

Munroe dropped my head and rose, waving Sue over.

"I have to change for the show."

Hands in pockets, Sue jutted an elbow at me.

"Bring him along?"

Munroe shook her head.

"He doesn't know anything. He's best left here, where he can't get into trouble."

"So Minerva's not the other big player?"

"He's desperate and impotent, sending Sidney to stir me up because he doesn't know what's happening. Someone is making a big play, but it's not Hillary Minerva."

"Might be we should hold off on plans until I suss out whose fuckery we're dealing with."

Munroe cocked her head like she was listening to something.

"Too late to stop now. Hear that? Open the doors."

Sue opened the French doors that led to Munroe's private balcony. Music wafted in.

Munroe looked at me. My head was hanging off the side of the divan, so she was upside down.

"Hear it, Sidney? Bring back memories?"

I heard it. Someone singing. A voice rising from the terraces below. Sounded like Munroe had a new star on her hands. A star who was singing with my voice.

Then the floor disappeared and everything went black.

EIGHT

MY VOICE SANG AND SPUN around me as I fell down the dope hole Sue had dropped me in.

Munroe had finally found someone to give my voice to. Well, it was hers to give. I'd sold it to her fair and square. Sold my golden tonsils for a load of mojo, and traded that to Sue for a dire service indeed. Oh, no. Nope. Stop. Don't think about that. Spiraling in drugged darkness, I did not want to be thinking about Sue and her knife and . . . Too late.

I was thinking about the past and all the many terrible choices I'd made, and I fell right into the middle of them. Landed on my back with a flat smack, the Earth rolling beneath me. Not the Earth, a bed. King-size. California king. Munroe's waterbed. As wide as it was long. It had been stripped to its bladder. The surface should have been blue, cool, and rubbery. It wasn't. Instead it was pinkish, warm, and smooth. Except for the seams. Seams? There were stitched seams where several pieces of something had been sewn together to make the bladder. Odd. And those little brown nubs, what were those? Looked like . . . nipples? Aw heck. It was skin. I was on a waterbed made out of somebody's skin. More than one somebody. And that was not water inside. Blood. Human-skin waterbed filled with blood. This was not good. What had I done? What deal had I made?

Munroe was standing beside the bed. My ankles and wrists were bound. Perilous Sue was there. She reached inside her coat and slid her odd knife from its sheath. Munroe marked the spot, drawing an *X* in the middle of my chest with her rust-red lipstick. Sue gave her knife a twirl. I saw myself in the mirror above the bed, splayed nude, confused, wanting my heart to be gone so it would stop hurting so much. Was it too late to change my mind?

Yes, it was.

Sue's knife went into me, cutting. A gifted sly, she knew this rare corner of the art. How to sever the wellspring of emotion and bind the wound with a course of mojo that would leave me alive. Oh, but it hurt. Her knife cut deeper, pierced me through and into the bed. The bladder burst. I could see myself in the mirror on the ceiling, blood welling around me. I was sinking, blood and more blood. I lost sight of myself in the mirror overhead.

Why did I do this? Why? Make it stop. I wanted to wake up, but Sue's dope still had me in the darkness of the past. I disappeared from the mirror on Munroe's ceiling and I stepped backward out of another mirror. I was intact, my heart was still in my chest, but I'd given it to a young woman.

Abigail. Perched on the edge of a pink-enameled bathroom sink as I admired myself in the full-length mirror on the back of the door.

"No one can see what you're wearing when they listen to the record," Abigail said to me.

This was before the harvesting. Before Abigail was killed. Our hearts were each other's. We were in the bathroom in our ratty Venice Beach apartment. I was primping topless, and she was bottomless. I was wearing black jeans, trying on different shirts. She was wearing her Sinéad O'Connor T-shirt. Both of us were watching my reflection as I tried to get exactly the right look before heading to the Village Studios for the last night of recording on my EP.

"I'm making myself look good for you," I said.

She batted her lashes at me. Green eyes. Light-brown hair worn to her jawline, shot with several single strands of very premature gray. She liked to give each gray hair a name. *This one is Dad, this one is Mom, here's Sally and Omar and Uncle Ansel,* she'd say, attributing each to someone in her life. *I'm saving the rest of my hair for you, Sid,* she'd say. *You're gonna turn the rest of them gray.* I'd laugh, kiss her round face, her deeply tanned skin. She was my exact height. Her shoulders and thighs were thick and muscled from years of swimming on the Gulf Coast in Galveston, where she'd grown up. She could beat me arm- or leg-wrestling. I liked it, being pinned by her.

"Making yourself look good for little ol' me. How sweet," she said that evening in the ridiculously huge bathroom in our small apartment. We rented it for the bathroom and the proximity to the beach. We couldn't see the water, but we could hear the waves. Before I signed with Munroe, Abigail had paid the rent with what she earned selling her sketches of beach life to tourists on the pier and working at a juice bar on Speedway.

I slipped on a sleeveless red T-shirt with Che Guevara silk-screened on it. I turned this way and that. We studied me in the mirror.

"What do you think?"

She shook her head.

"You don't give a shit about politics."

"It's iconic."

"It's insincere."

I took off the shirt. Abigail hated insincerity.

"You do this for you," she said.

I saw something on my face. A zit? No way, not tonight.

"Look at you," she said, as I leaned close to the mirror to make sure the blemish wasn't a pimple. "It's amazing you have any love left over for me after you slather it on yourself."

False alarm—it was a fleck of dry mascara from my lashes. I started rubbing my hands over my bare chest, like I was smearing myself with oil.

"Mmm, get it all over myself, get that self-love deep in my pores. Good for the skin. Yeah."

She kicked me in the ass.

"Ow. That hurt. That really hurt."

"Want me to kiss it and make it better?"

"Yeah, I do."

She looked me up and down. Sometimes there would be these moments when all she had for me was contempt. This was one of those moments.

"Kiss your own ass."

I tried to play it off, like I didn't see she was genuinely disgusted with me.

"Can't reach."

"You could manage. There's no ass you'd rather kiss than your own. Suck right up and brown-nose yourself. *Yes, Sid, I'd love to kiss your ass, Sid, please, may I?*"

"Why are you mad at me all of a sudden?"

She pointed at the mirror.

"Ask him, maybe he gets it."

I looked at myself in the mirror. Suddenly, I didn't like what I saw. Cocky narcissist. A boy from nowhere and no one. The only thing I had to offer was a talent I was born with, a voice that I didn't have to do anything to cultivate. I was a preening pig. Unworthy of anything good.

"Hey," Abigail said, "don't do that." She made eye contact with my reflection. "I can see where you're going. Don't get dark on me. I didn't mean it."

I hung my head.

"I don't know what I did to make you mad."

"I'm being petty. I want to be at the studio is all. I hate that I can't be there when you record."

"Munroe says I shouldn't have distractions."

"Fuck Munroe."

"Please don't curse."

"Really, Sid?"

"You know I don't like it. I don't know. Heck with it, you should come."

"No. Last night. Don't change it up now."

"I want you there."

"Yeah, but Munroe says."

"Screw Munroe."

"Oh, no you didn't."

We were smiling again. A little rueful, but it was all gonna be okay.

"Really, just come with me. It will be awesome to have you there for the last track. I mean, it's your song."

I was recording "Feel Like Dyin'" that night. With or without an audience, I needed to feel like I was onstage. The right look, hair just so, no zits. Especially when I was going to record the song that was gonna no doubt be my first hit.

"You don't want me there, Sid, not really." She was smiling as she said it. "It's okay."

She pointed at the mirror.

"I'll hang with this guy. Want to hear a secret?"

"Yeah."

"Come here."

I went close to her and she put her lips next to my ear.

"Sometimes when you're not here and I'm missing you real bad, I'll come in here to see you. I'll, like, light candles and burn incense and run the tub really hot, and I'll close the door and strip, like I'm stripping for you. And the mirror fogs over and if I let my eyes lose focus, it's like I see you hidden like a shadow, and I can trace you. I trace your amazing hair, and your eyes and ears and your chin and neck and your skinny arms, your legs and all the way down to the floor, all of you. And I trace your lips last and kiss them before I slip into the water. Then you'll be there with me, and I talk to you, tell you I miss you, and I believe in you, and I know you are going to be a big, big star."

"Now I'm turned on," I said, sliding a hand between her legs.

"You still need to pick out a shirt."

"Give me yours," I said, and pulled it off her and onto me.

I was kissing her, but I was watching us in the mirror. Her lips grazed my ear as she whispered.

"Just remember one thing, Sid."

"What's that?"

"The girl, Sid, remember the girl."

Wait? What girl? Did she really say that?

I tried to remember what Abigail said to me that night. I blinked. And when I opened my eyes I was alone in the mirror on the back of the bathroom door. Abigail was gone. Steam was filling the bathroom. White clouds billowed around me.

The girl. Did she mean Circe?

"Abigail, what do you know about Circe? Why is she important to you?"

Whiteness muffled my voice, and I didn't get an answer.

NINE

I OPENED MY EYES.

It did not feel great. I was on the floor. Whatever Sue had poured into me had apparently melted me. I felt congealed. I sat up and my head punished me for it. I wiped thick gum from my eyes and looked around. No one else was there. It was twilight. My stuff was still in a pile on the divan cushions. I pinned Pegleg Wanda's badges back on to my jacket, checked that my compass was okay, collected my cash and my other stuff.

I tried to remember the last thing that I could remember.

Not Abigail. Not my heart being cut out. Those were way-back memories dredged up by Sue's dope. I needed to remember what I'd said to Munroe. Did I tell her anything important? What did I know that was important? I knew that a girl named Circe was missing and that she had a roomful of mojo up in Sunland. I knew that Munroe was planning something big. I knew she was concerned that some person unknown was also making a big move. I knew my reflection was back. I knew that I didn't know anything useful about what any of that meant or how it was all connected.

Was it all connected? Oh, yeah, it had to be connected.

Deep breath. Quiet my thoughts. Quiet my emotions so I could think as clearly as possible. Quiet. Wait—why was it so quiet? Where was the constant background chatter and buzz of the party? Not there. Listening to the quiet made me remember the last thing I'd heard before I blacked out and went on my internal journey.

My voice.

Munroe had finally given my voice to someone else. It was her prerogative—she owned it. No one had forced me to trade it to her; it had been part of the deal. Why not sell my voice and have my heart cut out? Without Abigail to hear me, I was never going to sing again, love again. Seemed like a bargain at the time, trading a voice I had no use for in exchange for a magical operation that would make it possible for me to find the impossible murderer of my wife, shatter it, and then put myself out of my own misery.

But here I was, still alive. I'd gone so long without finding any sign of Abigail's killer that I'd stopped looking. Now I'd caught a glimpse of the thing on the same day Munroe had handed my voice to someone else. Everything was totally connected.

I went downstairs and stepped out onto the terrace. No one was there. Not a soul or the soulless. The party had been shut down. Unheard of. Never in fifty-odd years had the party been shuttered. There was no last call at the party. I started down the stairs, descending the empty tiers and patios littered with the remains of good times. My eyes caught on something and I stopped.

A compact mirror left on a pool lounger, open, reflecting a hazy evening sky through a film of coke that had been left on its surface. Coke mirrors are reliable mojo sources. It's jangling stuff, wants to go off on tangents, but I wasn't feeling fussy at the moment. I picked up the mirror, wiped my finger across its surface, and rubbed the coke residue into my gums. I am not above such things. I'd save the mojo for later.

Down the stairs to the street, my head as teeter-totter and zigzagged as the steps. Where now? What now? My thoughts vibrated in tune to unknown frequencies, and I had the added impediment of a brutal headache and mental fog from being drugged. I'd had a plan before Sue waylaid me, but it was lost now. Where the heck was I going?

"Where the fuck do you think you're going?"

It was Mustache, one of Sue's CHP manikins, standing in the middle of the street at the bottom of the stairs, hands on hips, uniform crisp, helmeted and wearing his sunglasses.

"Turn around and get back up there," he said. "Munroe doesn't want you running around."

I pointed at his sunglasses.

"Those really make it obvious that you're a manikin. A real cop would take his sunglasses off at night."

"You're wearing sunglasses at night, asshole."

Okay, he had me there. I went for more direct provocation.

"What's it like to know you're not a real boy?"

He took a step toward me and put a hand on his nightstick.

"I'm real, motherfucker. I'm real as a heart attack."

He wasn't real, but his nightstick undoubtedly was, also his gun. Everything a manikin is limned with is fantasy, shatter one and its clothes will shatter with it. Unless they've been replaced with real stuff. Sue would have armed her CHP manikins properly. If he hit me with that stick, it would hurt. Then again, if I hit him with the escape hammer in my pocket, I might break something off of him and get away. I just had to make him angry enough to get a little closer before he pulled that stick.

"Some people call you guys homunculuses," I said, "but I think that's demeaning. A homunculus is a tiny, warty human made from sperm that's putrefied in a horse's womb. It's gross, but still human. Manikins are not human. You're a sham imitation of something real."

He took two more steps, fingers curling on the butt of his nightstick.

"I'm me, motherfucker. I'm the man in the mirror. Just like I always was. Only thing different about me now is I'm left-handed."

This was true. When a manikin is drawn from a mirror, it is an actual reflection of the original person. Someone right-handed has a left-handed reflection, so their manikin will also be left-handed. Everything else will also be reversed. The hairy mole on the right side of your neck will be on your manikin's left. And so on. Go figure.

"You're not you," I said. "You're the reverse image of some pig who liked to admire himself in a mirror. He liked to put on his uniform and quick-draw his gun. You're the remains of some peacock's vanity stamped into a mirror. You shouldn't be walking around, you should be displayed on a shelf with a bunch of china dolls."

"Let's find out how much a china doll can hurt a real boy, motherfucker."

His nightstick whipped out and the tip caught me in the ribs. I folded over and my hand never got close to pulling out my tiny hammer. Served me right, I suppose. Manikin or not, Mustache was a trained law-enforcement officer who knew how to deal with a smart-ass. He raised his stick. This was really gonna hurt.

A mechanical roar out of nowhere. Blinding glare as high beams flashed on. I threw myself backward onto the foot of the steps, screaming on instinct.

"Look out!"

Blur of green and white letters that I was only able to decipher because I knew them so well. FRENCHIE'S CAB CO. Francois's minivan squealing protest, engine at its limit. Mustache had time to turn his head. Crash of glass, plastic, and metal, shower of silver crystal fragments filling the air, light from a streetlamp refracting a million tiny rainbows, a scream like razor blades scraping chipped glass as Mustache expired. His tiny pebbled shards caught in my hair, snagged in the folds and creases of my jacket.

The piles of broken glass you see by the side of the road. *Someone got their car broken into last night,* you think to yourself. Usually you're right. But sometimes it's semi-mortal remains. Why did the manikin cross the road? I don't know, but it got hit by a Prius and it shattered on impact and the driver was so freaked out they drove away as fast as they could and started drinking in the hope booze would erase the memory of the impossible.

The cab screeched to a stop, then backed up, tires crunching in the remains.

"Get in," Francois told me.

I pushed myself off the steps. I combed my fingers through my hair and listened to the tinkle of tiny pieces of Mustache hitting the asphalt. I brushed bits of him from my shoulders. I'd find more later. Like glitter after a children's party, you could never get rid of all of it. I stared at Francois. He looked from me to the stairs that led to the house, worried about pursuit.

"You done grooming? Can we go now?"

I walked around the cab, got in, and closed the door. He put the cab in drive and headed us down the street, front right fender scraping the tire. I stared out the window at trees, cars parked bumper to bumper on the narrow streets, the ramshackle homes of canyon millionaires. It all looked flat and washed-out, a rear-projected background for the driving scene in an old movie. I was lagging minutes behind reality, still at the foot of Munroe's stairs, feeling the impact thrum the air when Francois's cab hit Mustache. That had been close.

"I'm talking to you, Sid!"

I turned my head to Francois. It felt like everything rotated around me.

"Huh?"

"What did you tell Munroe?"

"I don't know."

"Don't give me that shit."

"I'm a little frazzled here. Someone almost ran me over a minute ago."

"Someone saved your life a minute ago. What did you tell Munroe? Did you say anything about Iva?"

That was rich. That snapped me out of it.

"You idiot. You complete idiot. Munroe told me you went to her for a sly before you came to me. She read how hungry you were. She knew you were onto something worth knowing about. She let you dangle so she could see what you'd do next. And you came straight to me. Whatever you're doing, you blew it open from the start. Now I'm caught in your mess!"

Francois jabbed a finger at me. "Fuck!" he said. "You!" His point made, he retired into a sullen silence that matched my own as we dropped out of Laurel Canyon directly into a Hollywood Boulevard traffic jam.

There were the usual tourists and Valley weekenders packing the sidewalks, but there was also spillover from the protest thing that Francois had told me about earlier. I could see clusters of young people sporting badges and patches on their clothing. There were several variations. Some were as basic as Sharpie on a plain white T-shirt or as elaborate as embroidery covering the entire back of a jacket. It looked like the organizers had told attendees to decorate themselves with slashed circles to announce whatever they were personally opposed to.

Francois leaned on his horn. Nothing moved. He put the minivan in park and folded his arms over his chest.

"Fucking tourists."

I rubbed my eyes. The adrenaline of the last five minutes of danger and violence had cut the remaining dope-fog in my head. It was not a pleasant sensation. I was fried.

"You been following me, Francois?"

"No."

"Just happened to be outside Munroe's at a convenient moment."

He turned to face me, traffic gridlocked around us.

"I had this crazy thought after I got rid of your ass. I thought, *Maybe Sid was onto something when he mentioned that Circe is doing theater. Iva won't talk to me, so probably I should cool down and go talk to Sid.* That's the crazy thought I had. So I drive back to your place, ready to eat crow, ask for your help, and what I see is you being marched out by Perilous fucking Sue. That looks like trouble, so I follow you, and she takes you to the party. Nothing else to do then but sit and watch. Then, maybe an hour later, all these limos and party buses start coming up the canyon empty, and then they come back down loaded with party guests and manikins. Leading them all is Munroe in that Silver Ghost Rolls of hers. Some serious shit is going on. Know how many times Munroe has moved the party? Never. But before I can do anything, I get a call from Iva. The last person I expect to hear from. She wants to scream at me because someone has been in Circe's room and moved things around. She's blaming me, wants an explanation. Well, I could explain, but she doesn't actually give me a chance, she hangs up. Me, I have a good idea who was in her daughter's room. So now I really want to have a word with Sidney Catchpenny. Did he leave with Munroe or is he still up at the house? As I ponder, what do I see? Sid in the hands of one of Sue's manikins. What do I do? Not much, just save his ass. What's he do? Yells at me, calls me an idiot, tries to make it sound like his mess is my fault."

Horns blared around us. I pointed.

"You're holding up traffic."

He stuck a middle finger out the window and pulled us into the sluggish flow.

"What's it all about, Francois?" I said. "I mean, I know it's all connected, but what's it all really about?"

"It's not connected, Sid. Get that out of your head. People are trying to get stuff they want. That's the only connection between anything ever. People wanting things."

"What do you want?"

"I want to help Iva find Circe."

"Why?"

He didn't say anything.

"How's she know you in the first place? She told me you helped her with something before. Why make a big deal about hiding that from me?"

Nothing.

"You're acting weird, Francois. Going to Munroe, tipping your hand to her that you're onto something interesting. You could have come straight to me. I mean, yes, I'm not at my best these days, but still. You've been all over the place on this one. Calling me out of nowhere, telling me off, then knocking on my door. Kicking me to the curb and then coming to look for me again. You don't think everything is connected, that's up to you, but the way you're acting, that's connected. That is connected to Iva and Circe and whatever you did for them before. You're acting like Iva has hooks in you. You guys have a thing back whenever it was? Jeez, Francois, is this unrequited love or something?"

"Shut up."

"That's what it is! This is some kind of tragic romance. Were you her knight in armor?"

"Shut up."

"I am seeing you in a whole new light. Francois, the older, experienced lover, and the younger woman. I mean, Iva's pretty young. Look out!"

The cab veered, headed for the crowded sidewalk at Highland, jerked to a stop, whipping me against my belt. Francois grabbed a handful of my jacket, pulled me half out of my seat.

"She's my daughter. Iva's my daughter, so just shut up. Damn. Ow."

He yanked his hand away, started picking silver slivers out of his bleeding palm.

"Some of that damn manikin."

I chose my words carefully.

"Serves you right."

He looked murder at me, bit it back, did not kill me.

"Just shut up with that shit about Iva and me."

He got a tissue from a packet in the armrest, dabbed at his palm, crushed the tissue into a ball.

"I don't know what to do," he said.

I didn't know what to do, either, but I knew what I needed to know. When everything is connected, it's all important.

"You want to go to the Seven-Eleven and get a beer and talk?" I asked.

Francois nodded.

"Yeah, let's do that."

TEN

FRANCOIS got into mojo because of fishing.

The guy grew up in San Pedro, only child of one of the last fishing families to work out of the West Channel. They'd clung to a living down there as the slips were filling with luxury day cruisers and the lanes were taken over by container ships. Bringing in a decent catch depended on more than experience or luck. Fishing is one of those areas that's fraught with superstition and ritual. Whether you're talking about an enthusiast tying flies for trout in Montana or a New England lobsterman, they all have practices and prayers and tokens they put their faith in when nothing else works. It's exactly the kind of environment that courses mojo to a purpose, whether by chance or design. Francois's mom and dad, they knew a thing or two about the racket. Not much, but enough to keep the nets full as often as not. There was more than one curiosity on their boat, *Odyssey.* They leaned on those charms, trusted them to bring them home safe when they pushed out beyond known fishing grounds, taking chances only magic could make pay off.

But mojo is every bit as fickle as a fish.

Francois was nineteen and studying marine engineering at CSU Long Beach when his parents were lost at sea. He dropped out and went looking for his mom and dad. He sold what he had, borrowed more, spending every dollar on chancy curiosities, hoping they would help him find his parents. He never did, but the search led him deeper and deeper into the racket. Eventually it led him to Munroe. By then he was a crafty hand. A guy who got around a lot and heard a lot. He never learned how to manipulate mojo himself, but he could spot the signs that it was being used and he had a knack for knowing more about what was happening in the racket than most people did. He bought and sold information and minor curiosities. He did some courier work, kept an eye on some of Munroe's talent for her, making sure they didn't get into the wrong kind of trouble. He set up jobs for slys and sometimes fenced the goods. On his off-hours, he fished the piers, but never went back onto the water that had taken his parents. Instead he stayed land-bound while plying mojo to haul in every fish he could hook. Like he blamed them for his loss.

I knew all that about Francois, and he knew plenty about me. He'd known Abigail and he knew the whole story about us and how she died. When I turned sly and started searching for my reflection, I needed a source of income to keep the search going. Stealing for a living didn't bother me. I used my quest to justify anything I did.

For a while we were a hot team, pulling off some major jobs. He set them up and I knocked them down. That ended long before Circe went missing. Fourteen years ago, he'd wanted me for something important, and I couldn't deliver. He blamed me for not being able to help when he needed it. I blamed him for not trusting me. Still, I thought I knew Francois better than anyone else. Turned out I didn't know a thing about him. I certainly had no idea he had a daughter.

"A daughter, Francois? If you wanted to blow my mind, mission accomplished."

We were at a strip mall at Santa Monica and Hayworth. The guy in the 7-Eleven kept giving us looks out the window because we were drinking bagged beers in the lot, which we were not supposed to do. I was very excited by the discovery of Ivà and Francois's history. Things were feeling more connected than ever!

"I was shooting blind with all that stuff I said about did you and Iva have a romantic history. I was just looking for some kind of reaction. But daughter? Did not see it coming. Wow!"

Francois held up a hand.

"I have no appetite to explain anything to you right now, Sid. The longer I wait for a space to get a word in, the more I want to leave. So shut up and let me talk."

I took a sip of beer and used my other hand to do a little finger explosion next to my head so Francois could see just how blown my mind was, but I shut up and let him talk.

"I wasn't a good father," he said. "I tried, but it was fucked up from the start. Iva's mom, Laila, didn't want a baby. I did. So right there at the beginning, it was already a mess for the kid."

I didn't like this story. Parents deciding what to do about a kid they didn't want. What can I say? It resonated with my life and made me uncomfortable. I wanted to tune out. But this was about helping Circe, not about my comfort zone. I focused on what Francois was saying, no matter how much it made me feel sick to my stomach.

"Laila and me, it wasn't a serious thing, and she had a career. She was a dancer. Good one. A baby might ruin that for her. At the least, she was gonna lose a year of her dancing life. She wasn't callous. This was hard. A process, figuring out what we could live with. It wasn't just that she didn't want to be pregnant, she didn't want to be a mom. We negotiated compensation. I arranged for an auspicer to lay a course for her career. A pretty standard success and health course. You know how it is with performers and superstition; you don't have to convince them about how mojo works. Anyway, we cut a deal. Iva was born.

Laila took off. What I hear, she had the career she wanted. Me, I had Iva. And I had a plan to keep her safe forever."

He took a long pull from his beer.

"From the moment Laila told me she was pregnant, I got the idea. I knew that Iva's own evolving emotions and my feelings for her could really charge a curiosity. At first I thought I might give her a teddy bear or a doll, something she could have with her every single day of her life. I'd make sure she was never without it. But that shit can get lost or stolen. So then I had this stroke of genius. I'd never give her a haircut, let it grow till it wrapped around her. The care and the brushing, the mamas on the street admiring her, the years of rituals we'd need to keep it clean and free of tangles. Then, when she was eighteen, I'd chop it all off at once and use it to stuff a pillow or have it made into a rope or I don't know. That didn't matter. What mattered was that her hair had to get all the love and attention. I was always on the lookout for her getting attached to a particular book or TV show or toy. I'd get rid of that stuff. I didn't want her investing emotionally in crap. I wanted her mojo going where I wanted it to go. Into her hair. Not for me. I wanted to bank mojo for her. I was gonna have an auspicer course the mojo ahead of her, to make the path of her life safer. What I really did was force her to do things she didn't want to do and took away things she loved. I made her deal with that fucking hair. The hours she had to put into it. The games she couldn't play, the sports. The teasing and bullying. But I wouldn't let her get it cut. No fucking way. Then, when she was fifteen, she came home one day with her head shaved. I went apeshit. I wanted to know where it was. I mean, her cutting it off was an emotional act that would increase the mojo. We could still get something out of it. Except she'd donated it to make wigs for people doing chemo. Gave it away. I flipped. I told her she didn't understand the world and how it worked. Power, I told her, power flows, and the people who know the truth about it use it for themselves and they don't give a shit about the rest of us. To be safe in this world, you have to be willing to use power on your own behalf. You don't give it away. I told her magic was real, and she thought I was crazy as a shithouse rat."

He took a last sip of beer, upended the can, let the dregs run out on the ground.

"She ran away a few months later. Turned out she was pregnant. She didn't want me to know because she thought I'd try to do the same shit with her baby that I'd done with her. She wanted to keep her daughter away from me because she thought I was a crazy, selfish son of a bitch. Kids. So incisive."

"She found you later," I said. "She found you when she needed help. That must mean something."

He crushed his beer can.

"It meant she was in trouble and she was desperate."

"What was her trouble?"

"The trouble was that as bad a father as I was, Circe's dad was a million times worse. Iva was stuck in a thing with him. He was older. Charismatic. She believed in him when they met. As Circe grew, Iva saw what he was really like. But it was a complicated custody. Needed some finesse to get out of it."

"She said it needed magic. That doesn't sound like a custody battle."

"She needed help. I helped. Then she went away. I didn't know where. She made me promise not to look for her. I thought if I did like she wanted, she'd maybe get in touch one day. It worked. Sort of. Took fourteen years, and she only found me because she needed help again. I didn't even know she was in Sunland. When I helped her before, she'd been in Montana. She headed east from there. Last place I thought she'd end up was close to me."

"Why's she living in a compound up there?"

"Because she doesn't trust people."

"Where's Circe's dad?"

"He's out of the picture."

"Dead?"

"Out of the picture. Period."

He was walling up again, told me as much as he was going to tell. Francois had somehow grabbed Iva and Circe away from the dad, so you'd expect the dad to be the top suspect in Circe's disappearance, but Francois didn't want to talk about that. Either he knew it was impossible or he didn't want me to know more about the circumstances. He didn't want me to know more about Circe than I had to know.

I thought of something.

"Hey, Francois, you're a grandfather."

He looked at the sky.

"That I am. And I've barely ever seen the girl."

I walked around the cab and opened the passenger door.

"Let's go to Sunland."

He shook his head.

"Iva's not gonna talk to either of us."

"Not her. I need a cup of coffee. Place called the Plow House. I have an address. Tell you about it on the way."

Here's one for the aspiring philosopher-witches out there. Is mojo a by-product of emotion or is it the stuff of emotion itself? This is important to the fate of the world.

Think about it.

If mojo is a by-product of human emotions, generated through some combination of biology and experience, that means a phenomenon we already struggle to understand, how we feel, has a mysterious component most people don't know exists. But still, you can perceive a cause and effect. I feel something deeply, these feelings imprint on things or people or events, and the strength of that impression translates into a form of energy. Like rubbing your hands together to generate heat. Easy enough.

Now the other idea: mojo as the essence of emotion that's around us all the time, invisible and undetectable to almost everyone. If it's always there all the time, are your emotions yours and yours alone or are we sharing one giant pool of mojo/emotion that is constantly swirling invisibly around us until we open a channel of feeling that draws it into us?

There's more.

If there is a swirling pool of emotion we all share, is it all one thing, one feeling that only takes on substance when we feel it? Do we give character to our emotions because of who we specifically are? Are love and hate the same thing, literally made of the same thing, and they only *feel* different because of our personal circumstances when we draw that emotion from the swirling pool? And if we do draw them into us, what happens after we feel them? Feelings fade or increase or change entirely over time. Love becomes hate, and the other way around. Feelings evolve and often increase, but more often the thing we feel powerfully in the moment will become diluted.

Is that powerfully felt emotion still in us or does it return to the swirling pool? If it returns to the swirling pool, does it get filtered or does it go in there along with everyone else's emotional waste?

Okay then, one more thing.

If there is a shared swirling pool of emotion that we all draw feeling from, is it finite? Are emotions a limited and precious resource? If it is a limited and precious resource and all our felt emotions return to it after we junk them up, does that mean that we are polluting our shared swirling pool of precious emotions?

It might explain a lot.

It might explain the rise and fall of civilizations and how

entire cultures can suddenly seem to lose their ability to work in their own self-interest. It might explain how people get numb to human misery. It might explain the willingness of some people to inflict human misery. It might explain a preponderance of both vitriol and malaise.

Maybe we're sucking emotion from the same limited supply. Maybe there are too many of us trying to use the same precious, limited resource and we're polluting it. But we keep using it anyway, adding filth, until all we feel is the filth.

And yes, it is also possible that the shared swirling pool is infinite and forever replenishing. Always supplying us with the potential to love without limits and to heal all hurts through mutual understanding; it's possible that what I feel is what you feel is what they feel and we are all the same. That, too, is possible. I'm okay with that possibility.

I bring it up here, while Francois and I were on the way to Sunland, because we still thought we were just dealing with a missing girl, but what we were really dealing with was the fate of the world. If we'd known that, maybe we'd have handled things better than we did.

ELEVEN

"ENOUGH OF THIS SHIT, it's time for us to get smartphones, Sid, the internet in our pockets."

We were driving up the Foothill Freeway again, between the Verdugo Mountains and the San Gabriels. There was still the slightest blue tinge in the sky to the west. Midsummer in Southern California. The day never ends.

"This day is never going to end," I said.

"If we had smartphones, we'd know exactly to the second when the sun would set."

Francois was hunched forward in the driver's seat, rocking back and forth like he was urging his minivan to greater speed.

"What are you even talking about, Francois? You hate the internet."

He pointed at the road ahead.

"If one of us had the internet in our pocket, we would be going straight to this Old Barn Theater place and putting hands on this director guy and finding out where Circe is. We'd be doing that instead of driving to some coffee place to buy tickets to a play."

I didn't say anything. Francois was not going to replace his decrepit flip phone, and I wasn't getting any kind of phone at all. He was just pissed because I'd told him I knew where they were selling tickets to the show Circe was rehearsing the night she disappeared, but I didn't have an address for the theater itself. I'd also told him that, yes, I had gone back to Circe's bedroom to look around. Now he was convinced the theater director was behind things and he didn't have much patience for an intermediate step. It was inspiring him to crazy talk about buying phones. Fine. As long as he was obsessing about the theater mentor and phones, he wasn't asking me more questions about what I'd learned so far or what I suspected, and I didn't have to try to tell lies about anything having to do with Circe's room. Which was good, because I had not told him anything that really mattered about Circe's room.

Not a word about the room being awash in mojo. Nothing about the synchronicity of her and me both being Sinéad O'Connor fans. And absolutely not a word about my reflection being there. I didn't want to tell him about that. It was private business. It was connected to everything else somehow, but it was private. Also, I was sure he'd think I was somehow to blame for my manikin being involved. Really, the fewer questions he asked me, the better I felt about everything. I mean, I knew he was still hiding plenty from me so I didn't see any reason to be forthcoming with him.

Francois changed lanes, lining up for the Osborne Street exit.

"You never told me what you said to Munroe."

"She just wanted to give me a bad time."

"About what?"

"It had nothing to do with you," I lied. "Minerva wanted me to go there and pick up a curiosity he bought off her."

"When did Minerva get involved?"

"I told you I had another gig tonight when you called me," I said, very proud of how I made that earlier lie of mine wrap back around and work for me here.

He pulled us off the freeway on the northern fringe of Sunland.

"Bullshit, Sid. You told me Munroe said something about me coming to her for a sly, so I know you were talking about my shit. What did you tell her?"

Okay, so I'm not so clever. Fine.

"You didn't tell me anything so there's not much I could tell her."

Osborne was the old heart of Sunland. A few storefronts. Hardware, pharmacy, saddle and tack, a small bowling alley, three bars, and a diner. Five-bedroom McMansions dotted the foothills at higher elevations.

"But what did she ask?" Francois wasn't letting go.

"She was being Munroe. Everything is a riddle wrapped in an enema."

He laughed at me.

"*Enigma,* you idiot."

"I know what it is. I was making a joke."

"So, what kind of enema did Munroe wrap her riddle in?"

"She had suicide cults on the brain," I said.

Francois stopped laughing.

"What?"

That was an interesting reaction. Was he so interested because it meant something to him or because he didn't understand what I'd said?

"Suicide cults and the end of the world. She brought up both."

He cocked his head like he was listening for some distant sound. A rumor of war.

"In what context?"

"None. Non sequiturs. I came in and we schmoozed and she asked me what did I think about the end of the world."

"She asked about the end of the world and suicide cults? You're sure?"

Francois was very interested in Munroe's mysterious enema.

"Yeah, I'm sure. What's it all about?"

He pulled to the curb outside Plow House Coffee Co.

"Go get the tickets and let's get moving," he said.

I opened the door but didn't get out.

"Gonna need some money."

He looked more murder at me, but handed me a couple of twenties.

"In and out. Hurry."

I got out.

"You want anything? Latte?"

"Okay, yeah, a latte."

"Double shot, skim milk?"

"Yeah. You know how I like it."

I did know. Funny, the things you get to know about people without realizing it. Tiny intimacies. Here Francois and I were, not trusting each other enough to talk straight about all the most important stuff, but we hardly needed to say a word when it came to ordering coffee for the other guy or knowing what radio station to put on or when he just wanted to be quiet. Francois had to know he wasn't fooling me. He had to know I knew he was concealing. Just like I knew he knew I hadn't spilled everything I'd seen so far. We were withholding out of a lack of trust, but trusting that the other one would reveal anything we needed to know before anyone could get hurt. I can't explain that. A friendship is a lot like mojo. Rules and no rules.

Plow House Coffee Co. was in a tiny storefront squeezed between a hardware store and a hobby shop. There was an industrial-strength pole fan standing just inside the door, blowing hard. Their AC was on the fritz and the fan was the best they could do to keep it tolerable. The interior-decorating scheme featured rusted farm equipment mounted on the walls, cable spool tables, and mix-and-match kitchen chairs. A twangy Americana band was playing on the stereo, a couple of people were working on their laptops, a girl was reading *Tropic of Cancer,* and the shaved-headed guy behind the espresso machine had lots of tattoos.

Handbills on a corkboard advertised dog walkers and guitar teachers and yogis. Alongside these items of local trade was one of Circe's *Hapax Legomenon* flyers. Another flyer featured the screaming-mouth motif I'd also seen on her bedroom wall. While that one had been a draft copy with no final caption, this one read YOUR SCREAM IS YOUR VOICE. It had that day's date, but no time and no location. That screaming mouth on the flyer, was that the circle symbol I'd seen all those protesters wearing?

Next to that flyer was a missing-person poster run off a misaligned laser printer, black ink on red paper. It had a blurry picture of Circe and the text

LOST IS NOT GONE—FIND HER

The picture was not one I had seen on Iva's kitchen wall, and I doubted that this poster was her work. The photo was posed. Looking at it, I realized it was blurry by intention. The photographer wanted it to have a journalistic quality. Branches and leaves, out of focus in the near foreground, like the photographer was concealed behind a bush. Circe was a few yards away, crouched behind a tree, as if she'd been spying on or stalking something. She wore black jeans and some kind of oversize black jacket that was held closed by a very long belt or cord wound several times around her middle before looping up over her shoulders and down her arms, its length complexly knotted. A thin scarf was tied at her neck. She was looking at the camera, startled, like she'd heard a branch crack as the photographer carelessly stepped on it.

I unpinned the missing-person poster, show bill, and protest flyer, and went to the counter. I showed the poster of Circe to the tattooed barista. He didn't look up from his phone.

"You know her?" I asked.

"None of your business."

"I'm looking for her. I mean, her mom kind of hired me to find her."

He looked at me, dubious.

"You don't look like a detective."

Smart-aleck kid.

"You ever see a detective?"

"My uncle is a detective."

He had me there.

"I guess you know what a detective looks like."

"I know what my uncle looks like. I mean, he's an insurance investigator. So that's different. Still, you look more like a guy in an all-dad garage band than like a detective. That's not your cover, is it? Like to get teenagers to think you're cool? It's terrible if that's what it is."

"No. I dress like this."

"That's okay, then."

We stood there for a moment. He scratched a tattoo on the side of his neck, a red anarchy *A* inside a black circle.

"So you want something?" he asked.

"Yeah, uh, you're selling tickets to that show."

"*Hapax Legomenon.* Yeah."

He got a small steel cashbox from under the counter.

"How many?"

"Two."

He gave me two tickets.

"Fifty bucks."

I blinked.

"For community theater?"

"It's a whole thing they do up there. Dance, music, theater. Takes a lot of work. I mean, what does art cost?"

I got out Francois's twenties and one of my tens.

"I didn't think fifty bucks."

"Then your priorities suck. Here. See, the artistic experience starts here. You have to come and have a human encounter to get into the show. That action is required. And the tickets are all hand-drawn, each one is unique. When was the last time you bought original art for twenty-five bucks each?"

"So you're part of the show?"

"You're part of the show. Even if you didn't buy a ticket. If you saw a poster for the show, heard about it from someone, you're making a decision to go or not go. You're part of the experience. Making the ritual happen."

"That your idea? The ritual thing?"

"That's Bruce, the conceptual facilitator. You'd say director, but he doesn't like that word. He's helping other people to make the art they want to make within the cooperative environment. I mean, he wants control, but he wants it to feel like there's no control. Circe is the real force for chaos in that dynamic is what I hear."

He handed me two tickets. They were the size of playing cards and made of poster board. Both had the name of the show and the Old Barn Theater, but one was covered in jagged black lines like lightning bolts that twisted and bent over both sides of the ticket, while the other was decorated with black circles, each the size of a dime, arranged in neat rows from top to bottom.

"Circe. She did all the ticket art," he said. "Hundreds of them. Sat over there in the window with her Pods on, drinking double-shot skim-milk lattes and listening to music and drawing for hours without looking up. That was part of the show, too. Performance. Where's the line between the show and life? Ritual and daily shit, what's the difference? We decide what is show and what is real. Art and life, neither one imitates the other, they're reflections. Two mirrors with one thing between them."

Well, that was all eerily on point for me.

"That kind of thinking come from Bruce?"

"That's people thinking and talking with each other and trying to figure shit out."

"So you homeschool, like Circe?"

He gave a violent, single shake of his head.

"I refused to engage in a rigid construct like that. I emancipated myself and created my own life curriculum. But I know that homeschool crowd. That's how I got the job here. My friend's mom owns the place."

I looked at the tickets again. That circle design on the second ticket. Circles kept coming back around and around and around. I was trying to remember where I saw it first. Was it in the set designs on Circe's wall or on a protester's banner somewhere?

"Everything is connected," I said, looking at the tickets.

"Everything is random. Chaos." He touched the tattoo on his neck. "Anarchy is natural. Organization is an imposition. Unnatural."

I held up the ticket with the circles.

"I've been seeing circles a lot."

"Okay, yeah, well."

He pointed at a pie plate and an espresso saucer and the lid of a coffee grinder and his pupil and his nose ring and one of the cable spool tables.

"Circles are all over the place."

I tapped the circle ticket.

"These circles, what do they mean?"

"They're circles."

He closed the cashbox and put it under the counter.

"I mean, it's a *Gyre* thing," he said.

"*Gyre?*"

He pointed at my shirt.

"Okay, that's weird."

"What's that?"

"Your shirt, I just noticed it. Circe always listened to music when she was in here doing the tickets. I asked her what she was listening to, and she gave me one of her Pods. I'd never heard Sinéad O'Connor so she shared the album with me and I checked it out later. Circe said she had it on repeat when she drew. It was part of her artistic process, letting that album flow through her over and over."

"Sid!"

Francois was at the door, arms raised in the universal gesture for *What the fuck is taking you so long?*

"Hang on."

"Now," he said, and went back out.

I started away from the counter.

"Hey," said the tattooed barista. "You really a detective?"

I shook my head.

"Not really. I'm a thief."

"That would be cool if it was true."

I felt bad. Not because the kid didn't believe I was a thief, but because he was an okay kid.

"Look," I said, revealing Francois's two twenties and my ten still in my hand. "I never gave you the money for the tickets."

He looked at me sideways, got the cashbox out, opened it, and checked inside.

"Holy shit. How'd you do that?"

I handed him the money.

"I'm a really good thief."

He took the cash.

"Naw, man, a really good thief would have kept the fifty bucks."

"Everyone's a critic."

He closed the box.

"Sending a thief to find Circe is cool. But I mean, it's fucked up she's missing."

"That's right."

"Sid!" Francois was back.

I flashed the address on the back of one of the tickets at the tattooed barista.

"How do we get here?"

He gave me directions and I went out and got in the van and told Francois where we were headed. He started the van and we drove away from Plow House.

"So," he said, "you got my skim-milk latte?"

I didn't need to tell him no. He could see I'd forgotten. That was okay. I was in a different place for a minute. I was thinking about circles turning into circles into circles. I was thinking about Circe drawing tickets and listening to our favorite album and drinking the same double-shot skim-milk latte that her grandfather liked to drink.

It all meant nothing. It all meant everything. I wished I'd kept the fifty bucks. I felt good about giving it to the kid. It was possible to be and to feel two opposite things at once. I was the bad guy. I was the good guy. Save the girl and steal her room. Rules and no rules.

Anything was possible.

A single streetlamp burned where we left the main drag, heading for the outskirts of a town that was little more than outskirts. A figure wearing a big satchel over their shoulder was standing in the downlight, taping something to the lamppost. Another missing-person poster? Then we were around the corner, and whoever it was, they were out of sight.

Time to see a show.

TWELVE

THE OLD BARN THEATER was an actual barn, half collapsed, subsiding into itself in the middle of a modest citrus orchard.

We were stopped at a gate and asked to show our tickets by a bearded guy with a beer and a traffic vest, and then directed to follow a line of more flashlight-wielding, beer-drinking traffic-vest guys into a parking area along the edge of the orchard. The dirt hadn't been hosed down and dust was thick in the air, shot through with headlights as more cars poured in. We climbed out of the minivan and joined the people streaming toward a clearing around the barn.

Brightly illuminated by strings of lights hung on crisscrossing cables, the clearing was a large swath of bright-green lawn, a good soccer field's worth. Off to one side was the barn. The back of the thing had fallen in sometime in the past, the front still standing. A plywood stage extended off the front. Poles at the downstage corners supported a lighting truss. Upstage, several flats concealed the barn doors that led into the backstage area. The audience was starting to fill the folding chairs that were set up on all three sides of the thrust stage. Behind those, people were spreading blankets and flopping sleeping bags open on the grass. Food trucks had parked across the green opposite the stage. Tacos, funnel cakes, Belgian fries, vegan sliders. A full bar had been set up. A smaller stage hosted a duo of aging hipsters on ukulele and mandolin playing Flaming Lips covers. Some show moms were selling *Hapax Legomemon* T-shirts. Kids ran this way and that, chasing one another, dripping soft-serve ice cream. Every five feet we walked through another cloud of weed. It looked like the event had drawn a cross-section of foothills counterculture from Santa Clarita to Azusa, ranging from hippie grandparents to Millennial organic goat ranchers to Don't Tread on Me off-gridders.

Francois swung his walking stick at the long grass, a man wishing he had something to hit.

"All these people had to buy tickets in person at that coffee place?"

"That's the idea."

"They're all carrying tickets Circe drew?"

"Yeah."

He dug the tip of his stick deep in the grass, wrenched up a clump.

"Someone is working some mojo here, Sid."

I didn't say anything. It was obvious enough. I mean, you'd have to believe in magic in the first place to see it, but assuming you knew something about mojo, it was clear there was an angle in play. Something similar to what Munroe did with the party. But whether the person behind it all was looking to course mojo into an object and create a curiosity or vehemance it directly to some end, I couldn't say.

Teenage stagehands in black were moving scenery around on the stage. The flats were painted with the design I'd seen in Circe's bedroom, that circle made of multicolored cross-hatchings with a black hole in the center. A table was set up a few rows back from the lip of the stage. A couple guys who looked like dads were running through cues on their laptops.

Francois was looking this way and that.

"Any idea what this director guy looks like?"

"Come on," I said, and walked over to the dads running the light and sound boards.

"You guys seen Bruce?"

They barely looked up, scrambling to get their crap together so they didn't do anything to mess up their kids' show.

"Backstage or the bar. Probably the bar," one of them said, flipping through a handwritten cue sheet.

"Thanks."

We walked to the bar, a horseshoe of catering tables surrounding galvanized wash bins that held iced kegs of beer. Another catering table served as a back bar, covered in wine and liquor bottles. Customers walked away with at least two drinks each, like at a baseball game. There were some picnic tables in the food truck area, people eating and drinking, elbow to elbow.

Francois pointed with the tip of his stick.

"That's him," he said.

The guy was hard to miss. Standing at the corner of the bar, he was more than six feet tall, his shoulder-length, thick black hair gone half gray and spilling from a ponytail. He wore multiple necklaces, crystals, and medallions, and a *Hapax* shirt a size too small, the better to show off how he kept himself in great shape despite having cracked fifty. He was holding court with several cronies, sharing some amusing anecdote about something awesome he'd once done, but his real audience was a couple women half his age hovering nearby and shooting looks at him from the corners of their eyes. Twenty-first-century Falstaff in his element.

"Yep," I said, "that's gotta be him."

Francois made a move to push through the crowd, but I grabbed him.

"Hang on. Come over here." I towed him away from the bar, farther down the lawn, away from the brightest lights. "I have a plan," I said.

Francois groaned.

"Fuuuuuck no."

"Listen. Eyes on me. Okay. Over there at the bar, surrounded by his many admirers, you see the undoubted mastermind of all we survey. He's clearly charismatic and much beloved. Over here you have a couple of total strangers getting ready to barge up to him and start asking bizarre questions about magic and a disappeared teenage girl. One of those strangers has a tendency to become violent when he loses his temper. Don't look at me like that, Francois, you hit people. You'd like to hit me right now. Bruce over there is charming his fans, looking to lay some groundwork with the hotties who are young enough to be his daughters. He'll work the crowd at the bar a little longer. But the light-board dads said he was at the bar *or backstage*. So we know he'll be going backstage soon. He has to pump up his cast. Then I bet he does a curtain speech. Uses his fantastic speaking voice, projects so everyone can hear him at the back while he tells them how hard the kids have worked and how they appreciate everyone coming out and how theater is sacred and how it's a ritual."

Francois grabbed my shoulder hard.

"Plan, Sid. Do you have a plan or are you just spazzing?"

I was kind of spazzing. The instant elevation I'd gotten from having my depression erased kept surging through me, making it hard to hold to straight lines of thought. But I did in fact have a plan.

I pointed toward the bar.

"He's gonna go backstage. Means he'll leave the crowded bar and walk around to that dark area behind the barn. You stay here, watch, and follow him when he heads that way. I'll go lurk in the shadows. Then we grab him where no one sees it and we can ask him whatever we want and if you lose your temper and hit him, it won't lead to a riot."

Francois let go of me.

"That's not bad." He looked around. "But I want to get him all the way out of here. You keep an eye on him, follow him when he moves. I'm gonna get the cab. See behind the barn, that road, I can park back there. We grab him and dump him in the cab and take him with us."

"Kidnapping. That's heavy. We could get in real trouble."

"You got a problem with it?"

"Doesn't bother me at all."

He put a hand on my shoulder again, but didn't squeeze this time.

"Keep your shit together, Sid. She's my granddaughter."

"It's okay, Francois. I'm here."

He patted me and turned and trotted away, threading through the crowd.

I looked at the bar. Bruce was charming everyone. He had a spark. I could feel it at a distance. Exactly the kind of inspiring artiste who could fire up a bunch of homeschooled creative kids. I started thinking about those kids. Back when I first started having a plan, before Sue waylaid me and I got off track, I'd wanted to find them and talk to them. Once Francois and I grabbed Bruce, I might not get a chance to circle back to them. But if I expected Bruce to be heading backstage anyway, maybe I could get ahead of him and have a quick talk with some of the cast. I wasn't blowing off the plan, I was shifting priorities.

I walked into a cluster of twisted oaks near the back of the barn. Shadows were thick. I heard excited voices inside the barn, saw the coals of a couple cigarettes flare before being extinguished. I watched a man weave through the shadows away from the barn. Bruce? He walked hunched, with a limp, and his hair had come loose from his ponytail. He'd somehow gotten backstage without me seeing him. But it was too early for a curtain speech. He'd have to return. I still had time to talk to the cast and take a position to ambush him with Francois. Everything was going to work out perfectly for sure. I had this in the palm of my hand.

I slipped unnoticed through a sheet of heavy black plastic that had been hung over a gaping hole at the back of the barn. Exclusive backstage access for Sidney Catchpenny. Gosh, I was slick.

"You're not supposed to be back here."

Oops.

"Yeah, hey, I'm looking for Bruce?"

"You try the bar?"

The guy quizzing me was in his late teens and spent a lot of time in the gym. This was clear because he was wearing short shorts and nothing else and the red backstage lights really showed off every cut of his muscular body. Big darn kid.

"I was at the bar. They said he came back here."

Big Darn Kid shook his head.

"Not here."

We were standing in a kind of entryway between two sheets of black plastic. Nothing here but him and me and a couple of steel folding chairs and a sand bucket studded with cigarette butts.

"I'll wait."

He gave me a frown.

I patted my jacket pocket like I had something important in there.

"I have some stuff for Bruce."

Big Darn Kid rolled his eyes.

"That guy. Yeah. Whatever. He'll be looking for you for sure."

Score one good guess for Sid. Always bet on a theatrical director being into drugs.

"I'll be here," I said.

He gestured at the sheet of plastic behind him.

"I got to go get painted."

"Don't let me stop you."

Big Darn Kid ducked through a slit in the plastic, stepping into brighter lights that were cut off as the plastic flaps closed.

I counted ten, followed, and felt my guts wrench, twisted in an instant knot of nostalgia and envy, remembrance of backstages past.

Young people, dozens of them, jostling about, helping each other into costumes, showing each other funny stuff on their phones, musicians tuning and working the tricky parts of their numbers. Big Darn Kid had two dudes going at him with air brushes, covering him with a pattern of black and red stripes. Costumes were almost entirely black and red with occasional flashes of white and yellow, mostly garage sale odds and ends combined to give everything a rural, postapocalyptic look. There were weapons everywhere. Spears and swords and knives and clubs and guns. Some of them cardboard, some of them real. Giant puppets with papier-mâché heads and cloth bodies mounted on poles dangled from the rafters. Overhead lights were red, while lamps with bright-white bulbs had been set on tables where teens were crowding around mirrors doing their makeup and checking their hair.

"Can I help you?"

Asked by a young woman, seventeen or eighteen, seated at one of the mirrors.

I took the missing-person poster from my pocket.

"I wanted to ask about this."

"What is it?"

I moved closer, unfolding the poster. The girl looked at it, looked at me. The closest kids also looked. "Circe," one of them said. It went around the room, gone girl's name, a whisper passed, silence in its wake, heads turning my way.

The young woman was wearing a black robe. It looked home-made, like she'd dyed bedsheets and hand-sewn them together. Bright-yellow nylon rope wrapped her waist several times and looped around her torso and down her arms, similar to the out-fit Circe wore in the photo on the poster.

The young woman gave a little shake of the head, acknowledging something kinda sad.

"Harry," she said.

"Who's Harry?" I asked.

"Who are you?"

"My name's Sid." I pointed at the picture. "I want to find her."

"I told you to wait out there," said Big Darn Kid right behind me, looking more intimidating than ever with his muscles painted in black and red lightning zags of body paint. He looked at the young woman. "He told me he was Bruce's dealer, Hae."

The young woman, Hae, held out her hand to me.

"Let me see your ticket."

I found my ticket, the one with the circles, showed it to her. She nodded and stood up.

"He's not a dealer. He's a thief."

The universe wobbled under my feet. That was remarkably perceptive of her.

"Uh," I said.

"Thief," the word whispered around me like Circe's name had a moment before. The gut wrench of nostalgia I'd had when I came in was replaced by a hollow pit of dread, an equally familiar sense-memory from my youth. I was about to get beaten up by a bunch of teenagers.

Hae handed the ticket back to me.

"Jan said there was a thief."

What was she talking about?

"What are you talking about?" I asked.

She held up her phone. They all had their phones in their hands. Like a bunch of gunfighters in a saloon, ready to draw and shoot.

"At Plow House, you talked to Jan. He let us know."

The tattooed anarchist barista.

Hae read from her phone.

"*Something gone not found, what searches the dark a thief, don't forget the girl.*"

I had no idea what was going on. Was this regular teen stuff? Was I just super old?

"I don't understand," I said.

"Jan is into haiku," she said.

Oh.

"You knew what he meant from reading that?"

"No. He sent another message right after, saying a thief was looking for Circe."

"Half hour, everybody! Half hour!"

I jumped as a teen with a safari vest, headlamp, and clipboard yelled the thirty-minute countdown to curtain. "Half hour!" they screamed one more time for good measure.

"Thank you, Bernice," everyone said in unison.

Hae turned from me, took a glance at herself in the mirror, sat back down, and started painting her lips yellow.

"We can talk, but I have to get ready."

Big Darn Kid put a hand on her shoulder.

"You need me, I'm right over there."

Hae clucked her tongue.

"Jan said he's okay."

Big Darn Kid gave me a look, shook his head, but went back to getting his body made up. The rest of the backstage kids picked up with what they'd been doing, but eyes kept flicking my way, and nearby ears were tuned to what Hae and I were saying.

"We told the police," she was saying, "but they didn't believe us."

"What did you tell them?"

Hae was done with her lips and was shading her eyelids in a matching color.

"The night Circe disappeared, she snuck out. Cops acted like we'd broken a law because we knew she was sneaking out and didn't tell an adult. Like we should have known what would happen."

"What did happen?"

She had one eye closed as she made up the other.

"Do you not know anything?"

She was looking in the mirror, talking to my reflection. I wanted to ask her to stop it, but I didn't want her to think I was crazy.

"Assume I don't. I'm interested in details."

"Okay," she said, "Circe snuck out, jogged down to Little Tujunga, and we picked her up. Me and a few other kids. I had my dad's car. We drove here for rehearsal, and Circe and Bruce got in another argument."

Ding!

"Argument?"

"Always and forever. Circe was always, like, this is our thing, us, the company, we had this idea to do this show. This class for our schooling. Bruce, as far as she thought, he's a necessary evil."

"Evil, huh?"

"Figuratively evil. Like, the credits won't count for the class if we're not supervised by some individual accredited by the government. Circe wanted the show to evolve on its own, but Bruce said it needed to be formalized."

"Ritualized."

"*Ritual.* Yeah, that's the word. We get that theater is ritual, you have to rehearse and that's a kind of ritual, but he's so rigid about always doing things the same way. Circe hated that. She hates anyone trying to make her do anything. And it was all her anyway, the show. She felt usurped. Her word. Like Bruce was taking her ideas and making them his."

"What kind of ideas?"

"Everything. Doing a mystery play, like in medieval times, but updated, that was her. Doing it as three acts. The *Gyre* of it all. The costuming, the set. She's always having ideas and she's always getting worked up and excited and getting everyone else excited. I mean, I was already a theater nerd, but I wouldn't have started going into *Gyre* or joining Harrow if not for Circe. She was the one who said we should *exvert* our fantasy life. *Exvert* was her word. There would be no show if she hadn't had the idea to invent the class. That's why we all got so upset."

"When she disappeared?"

"No. Yes. But that's not what I mean. That night, Bruce wanted a tech run-through. Run every cue, word-perfect, blocking on the spot. Boring, but normal. Circe, she was saying that the show hadn't been *discovered* yet. She thought we all needed to let loose, do an improv run-through, throw out all our assumptions. Opposite of what Bruce wanted. They really got into it. Bruce is a typical old-white-guy control freak, but he's mostly mellow. Circe got under his skin that night. They were screaming at each other and it got to the rest of us and everyone started yelling, crying, letting it out. Finally Bruce was like, *Whatever, do it your way.* So Circe got everyone together and told us to forget the script and just try to tell the story as honestly as we could. We were all raw by then and mostly just wanted to fuck the whole thing, but we got it together and started this run-through."

She closed her eyes, shook her head, opened her eyes, and looked up, searching for something.

"It was. It was fucking amazing. We were so mad at Circe and Bruce, but somehow all of that anger got turned into this ... energy? The show just came to life. Even Bruce could feel it. And then. And then when it was over, Circe looked at Bruce and was like, *Do what you want now, I'm done.*"

I shook my head.

"Done like how?"

She looked back at herself in the mirror and returned to work on her makeup, shrugged.

"Done like done. Like she had this big journal where she'd

been writing and rewriting the script and doing sketches and designs and lyrics for the songs, right? And we do this amazing run-through she fought for, and then she says she's done and she goes to the firepit we'd sit around after rehearsals, and she throws her journal, the master plan for the whole thing, she throws it into the fire and walks off into the orchard, and that was the last time we saw her."

Big Darn Kid's body makeup had been finished and he'd drifted over to listen.

"It was classic Circe. Get everyone excited and then bail," he said.

Other kids who had been eavesdropping started to chime in, their voices overlapping.

"Major passive-aggressive acting out." "But she's always getting new ideas and obsessions she wants to make happen." "She starts *Hapax,* but she was also going off to do her music and always inside *Gyre* and then she got involved with the Abyss Protest, and whatever else." "She wants you to be totally committed to her thing, but she has like a million things she's doing all at once, so where's her commitment to you?"

Agreement about Circe's fickle nature was general.

Hae was nodding along with what her friends were saying.

"It was like, once we did that amazing run-through, she'd gotten whatever she wanted from *Hapax* and she didn't care what happened after that. It really hurt," she said.

"Did you look for her?"

Hae gave me a look like I was a jerk. Which, yes I was.

"Yes, we looked for her. I mean, we all had shit we wanted to say to her about how she was acting, but we would have looked anyway. I was her ride. Not like I was going to abandon her."

Big Darn Kid pointed over his shoulder, toward the orchard behind the barn.

"She went off into the trees and Harry ran after her but they couldn't find her."

Voices started up again, entwined, finishing for and talking over one another.

"Harry said." "Harry said she disappeared." "They said they found her and walked with her for a while and then." "Gone." "Harry said she was just gone."

Hae nodded, agreeing with what everyone was saying.

"We were all talking about Circe and waiting for her to come back, and then Harry comes running out of the orchard and says she was gone. They're a little kid and they overreact, but it was late and I was sick of waiting around, so a bunch of us started looking for her but we couldn't find her. Then we start getting worried, but she's so stubborn and I thought she maybe decided to walk all the way home. She's done it before. So we drove back up to her house."

Voices again.

"We tried messaging her and calling and she wasn't answering." "Bruce stayed here with some of us to keep looking for her." "We were freaking out." "The roads are dark. She could get hit by a car." "That's what I thought, I thought she was hit by a car." "That's fucked up." "We all thought something might have happened." "I was thinking, *snatcher,* you know. Rape and murder."

Hae held up a hand.

"Don't say that shit," she snapped, and everyone quieted.

"Anyway, we didn't see her on the drive, and we didn't want to go up Circe's road in the middle of the night. I mean, her mom might shoot us or something. Circe always says how crazy her mom is. And, I don't know, we just figured that was it. She got home okay. She didn't answer messages because she didn't want to talk. Fine. Deal with it later. But next day she still wasn't online anywhere. Not even *Gyre.* And then we started getting messages from her mom wanting to know where Circe was. She hadn't come home and her phone wasn't showing a location. That's when we knew it was bad."

She stopped talking.

"I am not crying again. Not tonight. Nope. Not gonna ruin my makeup tonight. Shit."

She was crying. A girl with green hair passed Hae some tissues, giving me a look like the tears were my fault. Which maybe they were.

"Now I have to redo my fucking eyes."

She started redoing her eyes.

"Next we were talking to cops who don't believe that we don't know more than we do, and getting calls and messages from Circe's mom promising we won't get in trouble if we tell her the truth. Like we were doing heroin and Circe overdosed and we chopped up her body and hid it or something. Like we're teenagers so we must be lying. We're not lying."

"I believe you," I said.

"Great. The thief is the one who believes us."

"Yeah, I believe you, and I know you have a show, so I'll be quick because I have like a billion questions, so I'll just keep it to the top hundred or so. Very fast. In no particular order. Who is Harry again? Where can I find them? What's *Gyre*? I've heard that before. What's Harrow? That's a thing. What do you think Circe was most interested in besides the show? Oh, and what's the show about?"

Hae had redone her eyes. She blinked them slowly.

"Ooookay. The show is about the world ending right now. The human part of the world. So in the first act, 'Hope Eclipsed by Black Despair,' Hope is a woman, and Black Despair is our fucked up climate. Hope has a farm that gets hit by drought and flood and fire and finally snow. She never stops being hopeful that things will get better. Things don't, and the world freezes, civilization crumbles."

"That's grim."

"Is it? I wonder why. Second act, 'Death and the Danse Macabre,' is a traditional danse macabre, but where everyone has been shot to death. And Death, big-*D* Death, is a mass shooter. Guy in camo with like eight assault rifles. Third act, 'The Harrowing Call and Demon's Rise,' is rebirth. The remaining people of the Earth who haven't been killed by weather or guns unite in a Harrowing that summons Demon. She consumes everything and births a new Earth. It's all allegory."

"Harrowing?" I tried to pronounce it like she did. The *H* at the back of my throat, emphasis on the second syllable.

She nodded.

"Mass suicide of everyone left alive. I mean, the world is ending, the human world. So you may as well usher it out as quickly as possible to make room for an improvement. That's the Harrow philosophy."

My heart, elsewhere, was really jumping.

What do you think, Sidney? I remembered Munroe asking me. *Is the end of the world nigh? What do you think about suicide cults?* I heard her ask.

"Fifteen minutes!" the stage manager screamed in my ear. "Fifteen minutes to places!"

"Thank you, Bernice," everyone answered, and activity backstage took on a new level of intensity.

"I have to go do my warmup circle," Hae said, standing.

"I still have millions more things I need to know."

"I'm about three seconds from calling a cop."

Hae did not say that. Someone behind me said that. Hae looked past me.

"It's okay," she said.

I turned. Bruce was behind me. Close up, he didn't look as impressive as he had standing at the bar. He was stoop-shouldered and chubby, and his hair was lank and hung all over his face. He looked much less dynamic and much more creepy.

"It's not okay," he said. "Bunch of kids running around in their underwear and this guy, back here."

"Hey, Bruce," I said, "the man I'm looking for."

Hae was picking up a cardboard scythe.

"That's not Bruce. That's Burke."

"I'm Burke," Burke said.

"Bruce's brother," Hae said, as she joined her friends, leaving the makeup area through another sheet of black plastic, heading for the stage. She paused.

"Lost is not gone," she said. "Find her." And then she slipped away, last to leave.

Burke waited a moment, then picked up a prop club, one of the solid wood ones.

"Come on," he said.

Stooped and chubby or not, he was much bigger than me. Then again, I suddenly realized that he had only one arm. His right sleeve was pinned up at the shoulder. And also only one eye. There was a patch over his right eye, mostly hidden by his long hair. Bruce had apparently gotten all the family luck and left his brother with the dregs.

I pointed at the club.

"Taking this backstage security thing pretty seriously, man."

He rapped me on the elbow. It hurt a lot.

"Outside."

I started walking, rubbing my elbow, passed through the black plastic into the little entryway, and there was Bruce, smoking a joint, talking quietly to himself.

He held up a finger.

"Hang on, just running my curtain speech." He whispered a few more lines, did some gestures, bowed to his imaginary audience. "And without further ado, I give you *Hapax Legomenon*." He made cheering crowd noises, waved, bowed again. "That should do it. Time, Burke?"

Burke looked at his watch.

"Twelve minutes."

Bruce shrugged.

"We're gonna start late. It's okay, we always start late. Builds anticipation. The kids get charged up. It's good for the show. Part of the ritual."

He took a final hit off the roach, dropped it in a sand bucket, and turned his attention to me.

"So here's the thing. We here at the Old Barn are very sensitive about backstage access when we do youth productions. We have to be wary about influences. And our usual sensitivities are heightened right now because of the missing-person situation. So when I see an adult chatting up the young people, I get concerned. My first instinct is to call the police because anyone taking that big an interest in our missing person is someone the police want to talk to. But Hae has chosen to engage with you and I want to be respectful of their choices. I'm using gender neutral pronouns. I hope that doesn't confuse you."

"No, I'm good."

"Employing the they-slash-them convention is helping me to rewire the language centers of my brain. I've been doing it for three months now and I'm really feeling the result. It's important work. Once I stop seeing gender differentiations in my mind, I'm going to start eliminating *I* from my speech. The constant favoring of your own point of view, the narrative of the self, is the ultimate form of discrimination. I'm going to pluralize myself, become a *we* instead of an *I*."

"Like a monarch."

"Excuse me?"

I shrugged.

"Kings and queens, they use the royal we. Traditionally. Along with talking about yourself in the third person, it's about the most egotistical thing you can do."

He suffered a momentary loss of bonhomie, flashed a glare at me, then got back into character.

"I don't see it that way, but that doesn't make your opinion invalid."

"I can see why Circe doesn't like you."

That tripped him up again, another crack in the façade, but he smoothed it over, tucking a loose strand of hair behind his ear, slipping on a rueful smile.

"Circe and I had many healthy creative debates, but I have no doubt that they liked me."

"*Likes*," I said. "I'm aggressively using the present tense as regards Circe. Unless you know a reason why I shouldn't?"

His rueful smile became highly unamused.

"Time, Burke?"

"Ten minutes."

"Thank you, Burke." He took a deep breath, drawing his hand up the length of his torso as he inhaled, and pressing it down as he exhaled. "This work we've been doing here, for months now, I don't want to see anything go amiss at this late a stage. I want to remain in this moment so that I can contribute to this final performative element in the art we have been creating. That is the consideration that is preventing me from calling the police. That is the reason I am entertaining the idea of asking Burke to escort you off the premises with no more than a promise from you that you won't come back and won't harass my cast ever again. What do you think?"

I thought for a moment.

"The way you say *my* cast, that sounds awfully possessive. Do they know you think of them as property?"

Burke gave a single disturbing cackle of laughter.

Bruce's face had become pinched.

"Shut up, Burke." He gave me a hairy eyeball.

"Okay. So I'm tense now. A less-than-ideal state this close to curtain. Now I'm gonna improvise some variations on my usual warmup ritual and dispel this tension." He rolled his neck, exhaled. "We are going to take a walk in the orchard."

I held up a finger.

"When you say *we,* do you mean all of us together or is that your paradoxically egoless use of the royal we?"

Burke gave his single cackle again, and poked me in the kidney with his club.

"Come on, let's all go for a walk."

"Yes," I said, "that's much more clear."

I led the way out through the slit in the outer plastic sheet, eyes straight ahead so I wouldn't give anything away. Burke followed me, and then Bruce. And nothing happened. I'd been really sure something was going to happen. I'd been perfectly confident that Francois was going to be standing there ready to whack someone with his rattan stick. I'd been backstage forever. He must have had time to get his cab and drive it behind the barn and come looking for me and overhear us talking and understand what was going on and wait for an opportunity to hit someone. But no Francois.

I stopped in my tracks and looked around.

"Something wrong?" Bruce asked.

"No, nothing wrong."

"Looking for someone?"

"No, nothing like that."

"Maybe I can help," he said. "Let's take a look over there." He led us around the collapsed end of the barn to where the shadows were deepest. I stumbled, picking my way through dirt clods and gopher holes.

"There." Bruce pointed. Something hidden beyond a tangled hump of twisted branches and gnarled trunks where several dead trees had been dumped, waiting to be hacked into firewood. A shape resolved as we came closer. Francois's cab.

Bruce gestured, inviting me to go ahead.

"Open it."

I pulled on the side door handle and the interior light popped on as it slid open. Francois was on the floor between the seats.

"Where the fuck have you been?" he asked.

His wrists and ankles were wrapped in gaff tape and there was a little dry blood on one of his ears, but he was alive. I was glad about that. I'd thought I was about to see a dead friend.

"I was backstage talking to the cast," I said.

"What happened to the plan?"

"I was improvising. I learned some good stuff. And some confusing stuff. Have you ever heard of something called *Gyre*? It keeps coming up."

"While you were improvising, I was following your plan. I drove here, waited for Bruce to appear, and sure enough, there he is. Someone is following him. I'm figuring that has to be you. I make my move, grab the guy, but before I can do anything else I get hit on the side of the head because you are not lurking where you are supposed to be."

Bruce cleared his throat.

"Who the fuck are you guys and what the fuck are you doing here?"

"So you jumped this one, right?" I pointed at Bruce. "And this one was following him and hit you?" I pointed at Burke.

Francois nodded.

"Yeah. Who's that one supposed to be?"

I pointed at Burke again.

"He's supposed to be Bruce's brother. That's what they tell people."

Francois grunted.

"That's rich."

Bruce shoved me and my head banged against the edge of the open door.

"Ow. Don't do that."

He slapped me. Three times, slapslapslap.

"Tell me who you are and what you're doing here."

"Stop picking on me!" I said. Which, I know, not terribly forceful, but being pushed around brings out the picked-upon kid in me and I automatically start sounding like that kid. Probably because I am mostly still that kid.

Bruce smiled.

"What?"

"Leave me alone," I said, still in picked-on-kid mode.

"Okay," Bruce said. "I'll leave you alone. Burke, hit this guy." He stepped aside to make room for Burke to hit me with his club.

"Francois," I said, "did these guys take your gun?"

The word *gun* stopped events in their tracks.

"No, they didn't."

Bruce and Burke had also failed to take my pocketknife. Bruce was a theater nerd and Burke was his broken-down manikin; they weren't tough guys, and they didn't think about searching people for weapons.

I pulled my knife out of my pocket and events started moving again.

Burke raised his club, Bruce reached for my wrist. I opened the unintimidating three-inch blade of my knife and Francois held his wrists out to me. Bruce got in Burke's way. They both cursed. Bruce grabbed my hair and pulled. Burke's club hit me on the back. I slashed with my knife, missed the gap between Francois's wrists, raked the back of his hand, splitting the tape along with his skin. Bruce was yanking on my hair, hauling my head back. Burke hit me again. Neither of them could get to Francois because I was in the way. Francois made a noise as he ripped his hands free of the tape, blood streaming down his fingers.

Bruce grabbed my chin. My mouth was open and one of his fingers slipped inside as he dragged me back. I bit as hard as I could. Burke hit me again, the club landing where my neck connected to my shoulder. Everything throbbed black. Francois pawed inside the armrest console between the front seats.

I was falling backward, Bruce's finger between my teeth. I could feel the scrape of tooth on bone. I could taste his blood. It was gross. He was screaming something. Burke was swinging his club again, but not at me. He was going for Francois. I hit the ground and opened my mouth. The club hit me on the knee as Burke dropped it and lifted his hand up high. Bruce was about to kick me.

"He said to stop picking on him, asshole," Francois said, and thumbed back the hammer on the tiny .32 pocket automatic he kept in the cab in case he got held up.

I hurt. My head hurt. My ribs hurt. My knee hurt and my jaw hurt. My tooth hurt where I chipped it biting Bruce's finger to the bone. But I mostly felt okay.

Bruce was cradling his finger, wrapping it in the bottom of his too-tight T-shirt. Francois ripped the tape from his ankles with his free hand, came out of the cab, rammed his gun into Bruce's ear, and forced him down on the ground.

"Where's Circe?"

I sat myself up.

"He doesn't know, Francois."

He was sitting on Bruce, gun stuck in the director's ear. He picked up a large rock, held it high.

"I'm gonna pulverize your fucking teeth. Where is Circe!"

I was trying to stand. It wasn't easy.

"Knock it off, Francois."

Bruce presented his face for pummeling.

"Do it! Do it!"

"Please don't." That was Burke, hand still in the air. "My finger is going to hurt bad enough."

There was a sharp tink of breaking glass. Burke winced. "Oh, no," he said, and then his middle finger detached from his hand and fell, trailing a little sprinkle of glass, and landed on the dirt. He gritted his teeth. "Fuck, that hurts." Bruce had his right hand up to shield his face from Francois's rock. It was covered in drying blood, but my ragged teeth marks had been erased.

I sat down on the floor of the cab in the open side door.

"He's a leech, Francois. He's a third-rate vehemancer sucking mojo off community theater. He doesn't know anything about Circe."

Francois looked from Bruce to Burke and back again.

"You're pulling a Dorian Gray." He got off Bruce as quickly as he could, as if he'd just realized he was sitting in a puddle of something disgusting. "I've seen some stupid shit, but that's as dumb as it gets."

"He's right," I said. "Everyone knows a Dorian Gray won't last. You can't push all your flaws off on your manikin forever. Sooner or later it comes back on you."

Bruce rubbed drying blood from his hand.

"Mind your own fucking business."

Francois shook his head.

"Idiot. Tell me what you know about Circe."

"I'm not telling you assholes anything. I have a show to start."

Burke bent and picked up his middle finger. As his hair fell to the side I could see that it hid strips of duct tape that wrapped to the back of his head and peeked from under his eye patch.

"How long has he been hurting you?"

Burke shook his head.

"No, it's not like that. He's not hurting me. There's no me and him. We're the same thing. I mean, we're parts of a single entity."

"He tell you that's how it works?" I asked.

Francois poked his gun at Bruce.

"This guy's been feeding you bullshit, manikin. He didn't want to get old or get fat or deal with pain. So he paid a limner to pull his own reflection. Something civilized people don't do. Then he got an auspicer to course mojo from his imperfections to you."

I nodded.

"He created a path to take away the things he didn't want to deal with."

Burke gave his little cackle. Disbelief.

"We're us. He can't hurt me because I'm him. I mean, right?"

"Does it feel like you're him? When everyone is loving him, do you feel that? Or do you just feel it when he has a hangover or stubs his toe?"

Bruce looked at Burke.

"These guys are liars. They want to split us up to make us weaker."

I stood up and gave Burke a little shove.

"You got to get out of here."

"I can't leave. We have to stay together. If I get too far away we'll cease to exist."

"He told you you can't leave because he'll lose the connection if you get too far away. But you can go as far away from him as you want."

"I won't leave."

Francois pointed at Bruce.

"Look, manikin, I'm gonna hurt this guy till he tells me what I want to know. You can stand here and take the damage or you can run away and let him take his own licks for a change."

Burke took a step backward.

"Uh."

Bruce tried to stand, but Francois pushed him down.

"Burke! You can't go. You'll dissolve if you get too far from me."

"He's lying," I said.

"Burke, who are you going to trust? Me or these assholes?"

"Yeah," I said, "the guy who heaps all his imperfections on your head, or us?"

Burke turned and started running.

Francois looked at me.

"How long until I can hit this guy without it shattering the manikin?"

"I'm not sure. But we kinda have to split the difference. If Burke gets far enough away to completely sever the connection, all the bad shit that ever happened to him will land back on Bruce."

Bruce looked back and forth between us.

"That's not true. No one ever said that."

Francois nodded.

"Trust the word of any creepy fucking auspicer who would course a Dorian Gray and you get what you deserve, asshole."

Bruce lifted his hands.

"Okay, fine, I'll talk. I mean, I have no idea who you are or what you want to know, but I'll tell you whatever." He looked in the direction of the barn, where Burke had disappeared. "Just hurry."

Francois spat.

"Where's Circe?"

Bruce shook his head.

"I told you, I don't know. She took off."

"Where would she have taken off to?"

"I don't know. This class, the show, this is the first time I met her."

"He normally does *The Music Man* and *Annie*," I said. "Ask him why he's suddenly doing medieval mystery plays."

Bruce folded his arms over his chest.

"Hey, man, you ever run a nonprofit theater company in a semirural community? See how many tickets you sell staging *Rhinoceros* or *Six Characters in Search of an Author*. You play the hits or no one comes."

I was rubbing my neck where Burke had clubbed me.

"You play the hits to get a big enough audience to course some cheap mojo so you can keep your manikin thralled and yourself looking young enough to get laid by the ingenues."

"I'm living a life in art. I provide live theater to people who wouldn't ever see a play if I wasn't here."

I smacked Francois on the arm with the back of my hand.

"Bet it started when he stopped getting auditions for guest stars on TV. He had a paunch going, had to start dyeing his hair. Look at him, he was a pretty boy in his day. He played the jerk boyfriend on *Baywatch*, that kind of thing. Someone turned him on to mojo and he found out he could vehemance a little. Why not be forever young, he thought."

Bruce was still on the ground, but he did his best to rise to a self-righteous height.

"Guys get a face-lift, pec implants, Botox. No one says shit about that. I use mojo. So what? The industry puts just as much pressure on men to stay young and beautiful as it does women."

"No it doesn't."

"You don't know."

"It's pretty obvious."

"Hey!" Francois stepped between me and Bruce. "Enough with this. Circe. That's what I want to know about. What Sid asked. Why the sudden change from crowd-pleasers to this weird shit you're putting on tonight?"

Bruce looked again to where Burke had run off, chewed his lip.

"He won't go far. He's never been more than a hundred yards from me. He won't leave."

Francois handed me his gun. "Shoot this guy if he does anything," he said, and picked my knife up from the ground. "Little experiment. I'll poke a hole in you and let's see if it heals. If it doesn't, he's gone."

Bruce scooted away from Francois.

"No, it's cool. The play. The kids wanted to do something historical, cultural. For homeschool. They wanted to knock out three requirements with one class. That's all they cared about. I planned on *Romeo and Juliet*. It's the one Shakespeare that will bring in the local audience. But then Circe started talking about how they should do something that had historical resonance, but also mattered to them and their times. At first I tried to steer things back where I wanted them. I didn't want to do some experimental shit that no one would come see. I have to keep the mojo flowing to stay."

He waved a hand at himself.

"To stay like this. Anyway, the kids loved Circe's ideas. Even the musical-theater geeks got into it. She's like that, someone kids want to follow. She had this concept all in her head. So I decided to go with the flow, let the kids guide the process."

I laughed.

"Yeah, specially when you realized that the mojo the kids would pump out doing something like that would be sweeter than what you'd get from an audience coming to see Shakespeare at the Old Barn."

Bruce was rubbing his middle finger where I'd bit him.

"I think this might be starting to hurt, man."

Francois kicked his ankle.

"Circe had all the good ideas. And then what?"

"Your asshole friend is right: I saw how good the mojo could be. But it needed to be controlled, channeled. Every rehearsal she had something new. Changing constantly. I'm an actor first, not a vehemancer. I need the mojo to be focused as it's developing, I need it to have a shape or it's hard for me to gather the big lode on the night of the performance. With Circe always changing things, I could feel the mojo growing wild. It was like she wanted it that way."

"What are you saying?" Francois asked Bruce, waving the knife back and forth. "Are you saying she knows how to course mojo? Are you saying she's in the racket?"

Bruce was clutching his middle finger now, wincing.

"My finger really hurts. I think, I think Burke might be getting too far away."

"Did you say Circe is messing with mojo?"

"I said it was like she wanted the mojo around the show to

be wild. But it might just be she's a wacky artist kid who has too many ideas and doesn't know how to take fucking direction from someone with decades of experience. I was telling her that we couldn't keep adding new things all the time. But she'd have some idea and tell everyone and they'd be into it. So all the historical costuming becomes that *Gyre* stuff, and then the tickets have to be sold in person. I mean, I have a website for that shit. But it had to be her way. And then."

"What?"

"And then she disappeared, man. And it all settled down and got easier. I mean, whatever you think, I'm not an asshole. I hope she's okay. But my job got a lot easier without her around."

He looked down at his hand. Blood seeped from the reopened wound.

"Oh, no."

I nudged Francois.

"Ask him about *Gyre*. What's *Gyre*?"

Bruce was looking toward the glow of the lights at the barn.

"*Gyre*? It's. Um. That game, the game they all play online. The whole third act is from *Gyre*."

"'The Harrowing Call and Demon's Rise,'" I said. "That's from a game?"

"I have to get the show going. That how I make it happen, the curtain speech, that's my part of the ritual."

We heard rising crowd noises, a loud round of applause, music.

He stood up. "That's the first cue. They're starting without me. They can't. This doesn't feel right." He started looking around, like something was missing. He opened and closed his hands like they should be full. "It should be thick right now. Where's the mojo? Ow! Shit!"

Blood was starting to flow freely from his finger.

"I have to find Burke." He coughed, bent, clutched at his neck. "Burke!"

I took a step back from Bruce.

"I think his manikin is getting out of range."

Francois made a face.

"Grim."

Bruce looked at us.

"No. It's okay. I just need to start the show from the top. Do my speech. But. But where the fuck's my mojo?"

I opened the cab's passenger door.

"Let's get out of here. I don't want to see it when all the crap Burke was carrying comes back to this guy."

Francois shook his head.

"Dorian Gray deals always end the same way."

Bruce turned, started toward the barn.

"Burke! I'm coming, Burke! Don't run away from me! I can make it better than it was!"

Francois and I got in the cab. He started the engine.

"What an asshole."

He eased us through the trees to the dirt road that ran behind the barn. I looked back and saw Bruce's lurching silhouette stumbling toward the stage lights. Then it was like something hit him in the side and he was thrown to his right. Something else struck him from above, and he bent double. His limbs thrashed, a puppet on tangled strings made to dance. The accumulation of discomforts and injury, the wear of decades, all heaped on him in instants as the mojo course he'd aimed at his manikin collapsed. I'd heard about this kind of thing, but never seen it myself. I was glad we'd left. It was a grim way to go. He might deserve it, but I didn't want to see it up close.

THIRTEEN

WE WERE BOTH QUIET as Francois drove us out of the orchard.

Through the trees, I could see the stage washed with throbbing tones of red and orange. It was the first act. "Hope Eclipsed by Black Despair." The world was cooking under a brutal sun.

I got a tickle of curiosity and slid my compass from its pouch. It was weird. Bruce had said he couldn't feel his mojo, but my compass needle gave a regular pulse of light that indicated a steady course flowing away from the theater. The mojo was going somewhere, and someone had to have set that course for it. I pocketed my compass and thought about Hae's and Bruce's stories of Circe being the creative force behind the show. Its mojo might be coursing to her right then, an entirely natural by-product of her being the focus of the show. Whoever had grabbed her might have wanted the mojo from the show all along. I didn't think it was as simple as that, but someone had for sure back-doored Bruce and coursed that mojo away from him.

Francois took us onto paved streets and we left it all behind, but still neither of us said anything. I don't know what he was thinking about. Probably he was chewing on the possibility that Circe knew something about mojo. Being her grandfather, he'd have strong feelings. The mojo racket is hazardous and rough. You don't need to be a shortsighted fool like Bruce to run afoul.

A lot of the danger of being around mojo is the people it attracts. Power corrupts and attracts the corrupted.

I turned my thinking to Burke, to manikins in general. Not everyone's mirror reflection is strong enough to be drawn by a limner and become a manikin. That's a big reason the celebrity manikins at Munroe's party have such great fidelity; it's a by-product of the vanity and egotism produced when someone has basked in the constant regard of millions of adoring fans. The mythologizing that follows the death of the famous only makes the limner's job easier. But Munroe's celebrity ghosts were bou-tique products drawn from difficult-to-acquire mirrors that had hung on the walls of the living subjects' private spaces. Those famous faces had great value to her as attractions at the party, but limited applications otherwise.

Mostly people treat manikins like toys or cheap labor. Like Minerva's 1980s toughs, Dak and Neil. Detailed enough to be capable of independent thought, but not so much that they have a clear idea about who or what they really are. *Fogged* is the word that gets used for half-cast reflections. Anyone in the racket can spot a fogged manikin from a mile away.

Why was I thinking about manikins? Why did I care so much?

The girl, Sid, I heard Abigail saying to me, her voice repeating in my ear from my doped hallucinations earlier in the evening. *Remember the girl.*

"That's right, I'll focus on the girl," I said out loud.

"What the fuck are you talking about?" Francois asked.

"Nothing. Talking to myself."

"You better be focusing on the girl. That's the whole point."

"I am. Find Circe. Laser focus."

"Your laser focus said we should come up here because Circe going missing was about the theater, but all we got was kicked around by a lame-ass Dorian Gray."

"Sure, Bruce isn't the bad guy we're looking for, but we got lots of good information."

Francois pulled to the curb. We were back in Sunland, a few blocks from Plow House.

"I don't even know where I'm going," he said, and killed the engine. "Shit! Fuck!" He hammered the wheel and the dash and punched the roof. "Where the fuck is she?" He slumped, opened the armrest storage compartment, and started rolling a cigarette with a few flakes of hash. He lit it, took a drag.

"What did you mean we got good information back there? Did the kids you talked to have anything useful to say?"

I put my hands alongside my eyes, like blinders.

Francois blew some smoke.

"What are you doing?"

"I'm framing my thoughts." I was. I was trying to get my many, many thoughts to fit into a simple picture. It did not work.

"Circe is a strange and unusual kid. She is special in some way that may have something to do with her dad, but you don't want to tell me about that, so let's move on. Whatever would make someone want to kidnap Circe, it has to do with mojo. You don't have to like that, but that's what's up. Munroe maybe knows something. Remember, *end of the world*, she said to me. *Suicide cults,* she said. The kid I talked to backstage told me what the show is about. Wait for it. Ready? It's about the end of the world and how it is reborn after a mass suicide of the surviving people. When I mentioned suicide cults before, you reacted like I'd pinched you. But don't explain anything to me. It's more fun for me to figure it all out myself. What else? *Gyre!* There's some online game called *Gyre* that Circe is into and she used it for the show. You heard Bruce mention that. Iva told me Circe was into theater and online gaming. I fixated on theater because so many mojo-heads get a cheap fix off doing plays. Online gaming didn't sound like a thing because mojo and the internet don't mix. But maybe it's connected. I'm telling you, it's all connected."

Francois took a long, hard drag, blew a thick plume.

"It's not all connected." He flicked his ash out the window.

I looked out at the street. The only businesses still open were Plow House and a bar across the way. A few people were smoking on the sidewalk in front of the bar. Someone carrying a big shoulder bag came down the street and started talking to the smokers.

"Do you think Circe was messing with mojo, Francois?"

He stubbed his hand roll in the ashtray.

"She doesn't know anything about mojo."

He was wrong. It didn't mean he was outright lying, it just meant he didn't want to believe Circe was involved with mojo. But I needed Francois to give me more.

"Iva knows about mojo," I said. "I mean, she acted like she wanted not to believe in any of it, but she knows. You told her about it when she cut off her hair. And she called you for help when she needed to get away from Circe's dad. That had something to do with mojo. How long ago was that? Circe might have seen something back then or Iva might have said something to her."

"Circe wasn't even two. And Iva would never talk about mojo with her. As far as she's concerned, I fucked up her childhood because of mojo. And she's not wrong. She'd never let Circe get exposed to the shit."

He shook his head.

"It has to be Munroe," he said.

"What about her?"

"She's our next stop."

I didn't want to see Munroe.

"We don't even know where she is."

"I can find out. She can't move the whole party without making a splash."

"I'm thinking about this game Circe is into, *Gyre*. Games can be a thing. World Series of Poker, a lot of mojo has been raked off of that one. We should go talk to Bob or Klarnacht or one of their crew. They know everything about gaming."

"I'm not wasting time in that geek's mom's basement. It's Munroe. I want to know what she knows."

"You can't front Munroe, Francois."

His lips drew back from his teeth like he was about to take a bite out of me.

"I can front anyone I want!" he screamed.

"Okay," I said, because it seemed like the only thing I might say that wouldn't make him bite me.

He stared at me, waiting to see if I'd say more. I opted for a long, nonconfrontational look out the window so Francois wouldn't think I was trying to stare him down. I watched the person with the shoulder bag who'd been talking with the smokers. They were now walking across the street and into Plow House.

"I'm gonna get some coffee," I said, opening the door.

"Double skim-milk latte," Francois said, his voice still drawn tight.

"I know."

He took out his flip phone.

"I'm making calls to find where the party is. Don't be long."

I closed the door and walked down the street and into Plow House. Not much had changed. I waved at Jan.

He looked at his phone, checking the time.

"Show over already?"

"No. I made a choice to alter the artistic environment by leaving early."

He smiled.

"Yeah, it's not for everyone. Kind of unstructured. Circe thinks art requires a lack of consciousness on the part of the people creating it. I don't buy it myself. I think she just wants to be different."

"Circe's not like that, Jan."

I didn't say that—someone else did.

Jan looked past me to a person sitting at one of the cable spool tables.

"It's not a crime to enjoy getting attention, Harry. I'm not ragging on her."

Harry looked no more than thirteen, chunky, shaved head under a black watch cap, pierced lower lip, thick mascara, black leather motorcycle jacket, white painter's pants, Ethel Cain T-shirt, and a red ribbon tied like a choker around their throat. They had a cup of tea and a scone; a large satchel stuffed with a thick sheaf of paper was on a chair next to theirs. They were the person I'd seen talking to the smokers across the street.

I took Circe's missing-person flyer from my pocket.

"You've been putting these up?"

They placed a hand on the satchel, as if they thought I might confiscate the contents.

"It's not illegal to put up flyers."

Jan tipped his head at me.

"He's not a cop, Harry, he's a thief. He's trying to find Circe. Like hire a criminal to find a criminal."

Harry took a good look at me.

"Circe isn't a criminal."

"I know. I'm just good at finding things that are hidden."

"Why are you trying to find her?"

"Her mom asked me for help." Technically true, even if she later told me to get away from her.

"Oh," Harry said, with a deeply felt verbal eye roll. "Iva."

"Can I sit?"

"I told everyone everything already. No one believes me."

"I believe a lot of weird stuff."

The tip of their tongue poked at the hoop of silver in their lower lip.

"You can sit."

I took a seat.

"Thanks. You followed Circe when she took off that night?"

"Yeah."

"But you didn't see where she went?"

"No, I saw. Like I told the cops and everyone else, I knew she was upset and I wanted to, I guess, make sure she was okay? I followed her because everyone else was being a dick to her. And me and Circe, we have a different connection. I caught up to her in the trees, okay? I say, *It'll be okay, everyone's just worked up.* And she says, *It doesn't matter, I'm done with this anyway.* Then she starts walking, heading toward backstage. I thought she was gonna get her stuff from back there and take off, like she was quitting the show, but then she was gone."

They shrugged.

"That's it."

I made a rewind gesture with my hand.

"*Gone.* Tell me how that worked."

"I don't know. Like, I was two steps behind her, and she went through the curtains. We have these plastic curtains backstage, and I came through right behind her. And she was gone."

"Gone from backstage?"

"Yeah."

"Where you guys have the makeup mirrors?"

"Yeah."

"Can you? I want to know. Um." What did I want to know? "Can you tell me about Circe?"

"What part?"

"Whatever you think is the most important thing about her."

"That's easy. Circe isn't afraid of anything. She's free to do anything she wants, say anything, go anywhere, because she's not afraid of what might happen or who will say what about her or whether the cops will catch her or if Iva will put her on restriction or anything at all."

I imagined being fearless like that. I couldn't, really.

"That's pretty amazing."

"It's why we're friends. I mean, it's a small thing, but she didn't care what anyone thought about her hanging out with a seventh grader. Most of them didn't want me around. That line people cross when they get to be fifteen or sixteen and they become embarrassed about having been kids and they don't want to be reminded. Assholes. But Circe didn't care."

"You never saw her afraid of anything, ever?"

"Never."

"What about her dad?"

"She talked about Iva all the time, never her dad."

"What did she say about Iva?"

"I don't know. Iva is a mom. There all the time, nosy, wanting to be involved. Caring. That's what parents are like, yeah? Other people's parents. Some parents don't care at all. Iva's the kind who cares too much. Circe loves Iva, she just wants her own life is all. That's why *Hapax* is so important to her."

"But she's got other things that are important to her, yeah? Like *Gyre*."

They sat up a little.

"*Gyre* always. *Gyre* everything. You inside?"

Uh.

"I'm not sure."

They shook their head.

"You're not. That's okay. You sort of look like you might be. But it's okay."

"How do you play?"

"You don't play *Gyre*. It's not a game. Not like that."

"What is it?"

"It's where you go. It's the other place."

"Like one of those big online games. What are they? Massive, fantasy online global gaming things."

"No. Not that. I mean, yes, *Gyre* is that, physically it's that, but it's also a thing you enter into. There's nothing there, just information on servers, but you go into it. You go into nothing and find yourself. Find your real self. I can't explain. It all sounds dumb when you try to explain. There are rules. And there are no rules. If that makes sense."

I was having the very uncomfortable feeling of being on the verge of becoming fictional. Was I in Harry's story or were they in mine?

"Harry," I said, "can I ask you something?"

"Okay."

"Do you think everything is connected?"

They broke off another piece of scone, dug a raisin out of it, and put it in their mouth, chewed slowly.

"I like your shirt," they said.

"Circe's favorite album," I said.

They nodded.

"Why did you ask that, about everything being connected?"

"It feels that way to me sometimes, and I got that everything-connected feeling while you were talking about *Gyre* and what it's like. Why do you ask?"

They picked up another piece of scone, put it down.

"It's something Circe says sometimes. *Everything is connected,* she says."

Oh. Oh, man, I was having a very hard time not popping out of my skin.

"Tell me about that?"

An engine rattled outside. Francois was done waiting for me.

"Actually," I said, "I have to do something else." I looked at Jan. "Where's the bathroom?"

"The door at the back there."

I went to use the bathroom, talking to Jan as I crossed the café.

"Can you make a double skim-milk latte for the guy about to come in? He'll be looking for me."

"Sure. I'll tell him you're in the john."

I opened the bathroom door and looked inside. "There's no mirror, Jan."

"I thought you had to take a leak, not fix your hair."

"Is there a back door?"

"Down the hall. What do I tell your friend?"

"Tell him I'll meet up with him later."

"Where?"

"I don't know yet. He'll pay you for the latte. Thanks."

I went out to the alley, circled the block, and came out on the street in time to see Francois going into Plow House. I ran across to the bar, a place called Winston Flats, and paid for a beer so I could use the bathroom. This one had a mirror. I closed and locked the door behind me, and I never came out.

FOURTEEN

I WASN'T DITCHING FRANCOIS so I could do something nefarious.

I was ditching Francois because he was going to force me to go with him to Munroe and that might get me hurt and it wouldn't get us any closer to Circe. Also, as long as Francois kept hiding stuff from me, he was getting in my way. I couldn't solve this mystery and get some of the mojo in Circe's room and make everyone happy if he kept protecting some buried secret. Man, was he invested in keeping me in the dark. It smacked of denial. Francois wanted to avoid the truth of something as much as he wanted to keep it concealed from me.

But me and Circe, we had a connection. I was really starting to relate to that young woman. At first it was the whole Sinéad O'Connor thing, but now it was getting deep. *Everything is connected,* she had said to Harry. I mean. If ever I had needed more evidence that everything was indeed connected, there it was.

Be like Circe, I told myself. *Be fearless.* Easier said than done.

Francois would forgive me for ditching him once I'd found his granddaughter and helped him heal the wounds of the past with Iva. They were going to have holiday dinners together and send birthday cards back and forth. I'd be like a weird uncle, eccentric but lovable. I was going to be part of the family. Francois knew what family meant to me. Before I was a thief, before I was a sly, before I knew anything about mojo, before all that,

Francois was the guy who my manager kept around to drive musicians back and forth to things they couldn't be late to. He and Abigail really hit it off. They got each other. Francois was with us a lot.

He was there the night Abigail was murdered.

He knew, Francois knew, what family meant to me.

He'd driven me home from the Village Studios the night I recorded "Feel Like Dyin." He was coming in to have a drink with me and Abigail. Long past midnight, swollen moon. Abigail would be up, night owls that we were. She'd be waiting to hear how the final session had gone. How it had gone was weird. Magical and weird. I'd been on fire. I nailed everything on the first take, but Munroe kept pushing for one more.

I'd been singing over recorded tracks that we'd laid down earlier; the session musicians were gone. But she sent Francois to pull them out of whatever beds or bars they were in.

One more, Sidney, she said. *A live one with your blood and guts all over it, baby love. To make you a star forever.*

That was Munroe, always reaching higher. She got the band back, passing out cash, promising it would be one take. Gold or garbage, that was all she wanted.

Spill your blood on this one, boys and girls. Like this.

And she'd taken a razor blade the engineer had been using to cut lines of coke in the booth, slit her thumb and dribbled blood in the studio, tiny droplets on my guitar and Krysta MacGuire's drum kit and Aja Kijm's Moog and Olaf Harper Fennimore's bass. I couldn't say no to that, taking the blade from her, cutting, mingling my blood with hers. The blade went around the studio, everyone adding their drops to ours. We were all into the dumb devil rock vibe of it. Only Francois pulled a sour face, seen through the glass of the booth as he shook his head and went outside to wait for it to be over, while Munroe hurried us into place so we could count it off at the stroke of midnight.

Like it was a ritual or something.

Munroe turned down the lights in the booth and I saw myself reflected in the glass. I wondered if Abigail was seeing me like this, singing her song, knowing I was a star before anyone else knew it. I thought about everything she had said to me earlier that night, in our bathroom, entangled. She'd whispered secrets. Her lips at my ear, a breath of words, the slightest vibrations passing from inside her mouth to inside my ear.

The girl, Sid, remember the girl.

Was that what she said?

It didn't need to be worried about. There was plenty of time to figure it all out. What mattered was that I was going to be a star. My blood was sprinkled on the altar of the Village Studios and I was going to be a star. We nailed the take. I didn't even stay for playback. I grabbed Francois and made him drive me home. I wanted to see Abigail, I wanted to share it all with her. I wasn't going to worry about whatever it was she'd been trying to tell me. That was for later.

Our apartment was half the upper story of a rambling old beach house that had been split into a quadplex. Stairs ran up the outside to a tiny landing and a door that opened into a kitchen with a two-ring burner and a dorm fridge. When the owners divided the house, they'd done little more than put drywall over doorways to partition the place. By luck, we'd gotten the unit with the original master bedroom and bath. We had a dinky kitchen, a stretch of hallway, the big bedroom, and the oversize bathroom with the enormous tub that had convinced Abigail we had to live there. Coming home from the studio, I ran up the stairs, banged open the kitchen door. I had a bottle of Jack Daniel's in one hand and a cheap bottle of Champagne in the other.

Start packing, baby, I hollered. *We're moving to the Chateau Marmont.* That's what I thought would be happening next. Stardom, money, rock-'n'-roll clichés. Oh, how I was looking forward to those rock-'n'-roll clichés.

No answer.

I could hear Sinéad O'Connor, "Never Get Old," coming from the turntable in the bedroom. I went down the hallway. The walls were covered in Abigail's pencil drawings and watercolors. Taped and tacked up, floor to ceiling all down its length. Faces, faces, faces. Abigail rarely drew anything but people. A bus driver from our westward trek, the Elvis minister who married us in Las Vegas, a Black Superman from Hollywood Boulevard, a blissed-out skater from the pier, customers at the juice bar, random tourists who she'd sketched and failed to entice into buying their portraits. Munroe was on those walls, and Francois. But mostly they were me. Dozens of pictures of me, awake and asleep, pensive, smiling, clothed, nude—infinitely pleased with myself. They fluttered as I walked past them, a papery round of applause.

The bedroom was empty. Our cheap turntable sat on top of a battered dresser, cranked loud, set to auto, repeating the side over and over. The bathroom door was ajar, candlelight flickering in the gap. A bottle in each hand, I used my shoulder to nudge open the door. Three candles in Smucker's grape jelly jars that she'd rinsed the labels from. Abigail was addicted to Smucker's grape jelly, spreading it on toast, dipping french fries into it, dolloping it on vanilla ice cream, eating it with a spoon straight from the jar. Four more candles guttering in overflowing pools of their own congealing wax on mismatched tea saucers from a flea market we'd gone to at Melrose Trading Post. Incense, sandalwood, had burned to ash, its dry spice mixed with a too-flowery lavender from Abigail's favorite bubble bath. Her flip-flops were on the floor, where she'd kicked them off, a single yellow plastic daisy decorating the strap on each one. Abigail had painted the claws on the feet of the huge tub with her own preferred burgundy nail polish. I'd expected to see her on the toilet, as unembarrassed as a cat. Or maybe putting on makeup, something she often did when she was bored, spending an hour making herself closeup-ready and then washing it all off and starting over on another look. She'd been about to get in the tub when I'd left several hours before. I didn't expect to see her in the water. The door swung open, and I saw nothing that I had expected.

For a moment I thought I was looking at a mirror. Somehow I had forgotten that there was a mirror at the far end of the bathroom on the wall behind the tub. Sea-green tiles on that wall—Abigail had painted a school of fish on them. Smiling fish swimming in a line, bubbles rising from their gills, paused in their progress to contemplate a fishhook that dangled from above. The hook was baited with a dollar sign. But half the fish were hidden now, blocked, somehow, by myself. I was standing in my own way, across the room. Had Abigail moved the mirror from off the back of the door and put it over there? No. No, she hadn't moved the mirror. I was standing here, at the door, and I was also sitting there, on the edge of the tub. I perched there, leaning, one hand gripping the rim, knuckles white, one hand in the water, deep. My hand had been plunged in the water long enough for my sleeve to become soaked to the shoulder as water leached upward. I was pale—even in the candlelight, I could see how pale my face was.

I was dreaming.

I was having a dream where I was myself and saw myself at the same time.

Something was in the bathtub. Something was under the water. The surface was scummed with the oily residue of bubbles that had subsided hours ago. I could see the water was cold. There was a shape underneath that cold pallor. How could the surface be so still with my arm thrust through it? I must have reached into the water long ago and remained unmoving as the water stilled around me. How long? Candle stubs cast reflections on the water, making it hard to see what was submerged. I took a step into this dream. *Abigail?* I said. The song changed in the bedroom, the next track on *The Lion and the Cobra* starting to play "Troy."

I saw what was underwater.

Glass broke—two bottles hit the tiled floor and exploded.

I looked up at myself. I pulled my hand from the water, upsetting the stillness. I stood up. One word. A question. *Why?* I asked. I reached toward myself. One of us reached toward the other. I reached with my right hand, I reached with my left hand. Our fingertips touched. Mine dry and mine dripping. *No,* I said. *No!* I screamed. I ran, I shoved myself out of my way, I ran to the bathtub, I ran to the door. I fell to my knees and looked into the water. I swung the door closed and looked into the mirror on its back. Traceries on the glass, faint smears where someone had drawn in fog with a fingertip. I reached into the water, trying to bring life back to the surface. I pressed myself against the mirror, trying to find a way through it. My hands found her, I leaned into the tub, my face went into the water. I held her close, pulling her to me, nothing ever so heavy. There was broken glass under my knees. At the other end of the room, the mirror would not take me back. I crashed my forehead against it. The mirror shattered, pieces of my reflection falling. I pulled her up from the water. I couldn't pull her out of the tub. I knelt there in the broken glass, keeping her as close to me as possible. I wouldn't let her go. I wouldn't let her go back into the water. The mirror was broken. I looked at myself. Now I was the one next to the tub, now I was the one standing at the door. *Wake up!* I shrieked. At myself, at her. I opened the door and I ran, through the bedroom, down the length of the hallway, my portraits flapping as I ran past.

I was alone. I wasn't dreaming. Me and Abigail. But Abigail wasn't with me anymore. She was as gone as the other I was. As gone as if she had run away with me down that hallway.

Francois found me. He saw me run out of the apartment, pushing past him as he came up the stairs. Then he came into the bathroom and found me there, my arms full. He helped me get her out of the tub and put her to bed. He turned off the turntable. Francois was there and saw and knew. I told him what she'd told me earlier, when she was warm and in my arms, before I'd left her there.

The girl, Sid, remember the girl, she'd said to me. That was what she said. Wasn't that what she said?

There was more; there had to be more. Police, yes, and questions. Time of death, yes, and my time accounted for. Munroe called, yes, and her lawyers. My story, yes, and how I was counseled to amend it. *They won't believe you, Sidney, and it will complicate things.* The story of having seen myself was changed to having seen *a man.* But she believed me, Munroe, yes, when I told her that I had seen myself. Francois told her about me running from the apartment before he went inside and found me there. Munroe believed and promised me, yes. She promised me she could explain. I wanted explanations. I wanted more. I wanted to find myself, catch myself, kill myself. I was done singing—I'd never open my mouth for song again. Munroe had answers for that, too, yes. If I'd never use my voice again, then I could offer it in trade. If a long hunt to find myself was all I wanted, she knew a way I could have it. There are infinite ways you can come to believe in the impossible. My world broke to pieces and I could never have it back. I could believe in anything because nothing mattered to me.

I'd never get over it, I thought at the time. And I was right: I never did get over it. But still, time fades it all. Beastly time, washing out all the color, crumbling the sharp edge of detail. Memory dulls, as do the feelings. Chase your own tail for a few years, and then a few more. Lose your way. Me chasing my tail or my tail chasing me?

The years slipped past and then caught up to me until I went into a mirror in the bathroom of a bar in Sunland, and was spat out of the black mirror mouth of a laughing goblin onto the floor of someone's mother's basement, looking up at a bunch of people who'd been sitting around the same table playing Dungeons & Dragons for forty years.

FIFTEEN

AXARADA, scarred and dishonored paladin, had been hacking the heads off orcs for weeks, and she was fed up with it.

"If I see another orc," she said, "I swear this on a stack of Tolkiens, if I see another orc, I am going to change my alignment to chaotic evil, go straight to Pennmore's throne room, kill that asshole, and take the crown."

Lehlynol, elven thief, another outcast, ignored Axarada's complaints. They'd quested together for many years, and he'd heard all this before.

"I think this door might be trapped. I want to check it before I pick the lock."

Their boon companion, Undon, the warrior priest, was searching the orc corpses.

"I'm gonna search the orcs for chips. Because since none of you will pass me the chips, I am reduced to searching headless orcs for chips."

Klarnacht, the mage, rummaged in a chest full of cassettes, looking for anything they hadn't listened to a million times.

"I'm gonna play *Synchronicity* again. No, I'm not. How about some nice, relaxing Molly Hatchet? Blondie? These tapes are cursed, has anyone noticed? If I look at them, just look, I instantly hear the entire thing play in my head in a flash. Every note and lyric, total Memorex moment. It's like I'm the deck and the tapes are playing on me." Klarnacht was, as usual, totally stoned.

The voice of the gods spoke through their intermediary on the material plane, their avatar come to interpret their rules and dictates. Bob, Master of All Dungeons, dispensing answers and wisdom to the supplicants.

"I don't like orcs, either, Axarada, but a certain number have to be killed every year. Hew away, roll your twenty-sided and don't complain unless you want to DM. The door may or may not be trapped, Lehlynol. Just make a damn decision. People make decisions all day long. I'm deciding not to throw anything at you while you decide whether to check for traps. Meanwhile, the longer you wait, the more orcs are coming from their nest in the catacombs and Axarada's arm is going to get tired and you will be overwhelmed and all die and have to start new characters. The chips are on the coffee table, Undon. They will always be on the coffee table. The coffee table will always be on the other side of the room from you. The bowl will never be on the game table because it takes up too much room. Go get chips, put them on a paper towel, and eat them. Klarnacht, if you try to play Blondie I will send a beholder to turn you to stone."

The avatar of the gods turned his baleful gaze my way, his eyes magnified behind thick lenses, his once-dark, curly hair a gray halo about the crown of his head, his chinos stained with the orange powder of many Doritos, his ElfQuest T-shirt faded by the long passage of years.

"And, Sid, if you're gonna fall out of my goblin mirror without an invitation, the least you can do is take over a nonplayer character."

He carefully unclipped a piece of graph paper from a three-ring binder and held it up so I could study the handwritten attributes.

"Here. She's a ranger. Claims she's half elf, but Lehlynol doesn't believe it. She guided them to the Tombs of Hiveret, said she heard a rumor that one of the Jewels of Enlightenment might be in there. The gang doesn't know her alignment yet. She may be a spy. I can give you her backstory. You don't have to stay all night, just play her while you're here."

I knew better. Bob and the gamers were okay, but the campaign was sticky. Sit down to play for a couple hours and next thing you knew, a week had passed. Time did strange things in Bob's mom's basement. It was like a faerie hill. Go in for a quick revel and come out to find that the princess you'd meant to wed has grown old and died.

"No thanks, I'm in the middle of something."

Undon pointed at the bowl of Doritos on the coffee table.

"Little help, Sid?"

I tore a paper towel from a roll on the table, used it to grab a handful of chips, and took them to Undon, a heavily bearded fiftysomething, eternally dressed in Birkenstocks and Grateful Dead T-shirts.

"Okay," Lehlynol finally said. "I'm checking for traps." Also in his fifties. Bald and clean-shaven, bespectacled, slightly built, dressed for a business-casual Friday at a tech company. He picked up a twenty-sided die and prepared to roll.

"No," Bob said, "it's a hidden roll."

"You never said a hidden roll."

The other players groaned.

Bob held up a die.

"Forever and always, it is a hidden roll when you detect traps." He rolled the die, hiding it behind a laminated cardboard screen covered in tables of numbers and pictures of dragons facing down parties of adventurers. "You do not detect a trap," he said.

Lehlynol chewed his lip.

"How confident am I?"

"Fairly confident."

"Well, that doesn't help."

Axarada, the only woman at this middle-age sausage party, wearing yoga pants and an olive drab T-shirt that read RESERV-ISTS DO IT ON THE WEEKEND, was squeezing a tension ball hard enough to make the muscles in her forearm jump into sharp relief. "If you want to be sure, use your detect-traps wand."

"I don't know how many charges it has left."

"Then you can't be sure."

"What if it's trapped? My hit points are low."

"Drink a healing potion."

"I only have six."

"I'm putting on *Synchronicity*," said Klarnacht, fiddling with the stereo. "It's appropriate, seeing as how Sid just showed up."

The tape wasn't rewound to the beginning. Klarnacht hit play and "Every Breath You Take" started up mid-chorus. Sting's voice was too low, intoning rather than singing, sounding like he was the victim of demonic possession. The tape was stretched from overuse, but none of them seemed to notice. Klarnacht, long-haired, carpal tunnel braces on both wrists, a Zildjian T-shirt, cutoff jeans, and combat boots, kept malformed time on his thighs. The others began singing under their breath, matching every distorted syllable.

Every smile you fake
Every claim you stake
I'll be watching you

It was creepy, but everything was creepy in Bob's mom's base-ment. They'd been playing the same Dungeons & Dragons cam-paign since junior high. The game was a variation on Munroe's party, a mojo churn. But unlike Munroe's party, the mojo cre-ated here didn't get used anywhere else. This crew was in an emotional feedback loop. The mojo of the game swirled about the game, fed the game, produced more of itself, and repeated. Most people assumed they were banking mojo for a purpose. But the game was the game's only purpose. Bob and the others wanted to play D&D, that's all.

When they were kids, they dreamed about living in a fantasy world. If they couldn't actually be transported to magical realms, the next best thing was to spend all their time inside their imaginations with their friends. Playing the game made continuing to play the game possible. The mojo they coursed from and back into the game shaped itself to allow the game to perpetuate. They received a small inheritance here, a modest legal settlement there, unlikely windfalls constituted the majority of their incomes. They all lived in the house together, Bob having taken ownership when his mom died years ago. The game was played every day. They'd wanted something when they were in junior high school, found a way to make it possible, and became trapped inside it until it was questionable whether they could stop playing if they wanted to. The inertia of the mojo sustaining the game might not let them leave.

The music suddenly squelched, sped up, squeaked, and ended.

Klarnacht slapped the stop button on the tape deck.

"Shit, not *Synchronicity*."

The deck's door eased open and he gently withdrew the cassette, trailing a mess of tangled brown magnetic tape.

"I told you to clean the heads," said Axarada.

Klarnacht used the tip of a number-two pencil to pick the tape free from the player.

"It's not the heads, it's the tapes. Stretched tapes get eaten. We need to get new tapes. Or a Bluetooth speaker. We could listen to whatever we wanted."

Bob shook his head.

"No Bluetooth. It'll mess with the mojo."

Klarnacht freed the cassette from the machine and began using the pencil's eraser to spin the little white-toothed wheels that spooled the tape.

Outside the basement, they used phones, computers, all the stuff. And they had interests beyond D&D. Although those interests were comprised almost entirely of other games. All games. From bridge to strategic military board games to classic eight-bit console video games to Band Hero and Dance Dance Revolution to Monopoly to World of Warcraft to Uno and tic-tac-toe, they played. New games arrived every day from around the world. They crammed them on every shelf upstairs, stacked them on the floor against the walls, filled the garage. Card tables were set up in every room with in-progress games laid out. They played one another, they played solo against themselves, they played online and on their phones and through the mail. Some games they ordered, some were sent to them by designers to be test-played and critiqued. Along with the games came tertiary streams of information. Geeky vibes and signals that were embedded in the designs of the games, the rules and concepts. The global network of gamers communicated in low-affect subtleties. There was no idle social chitchat with their fellow players; conversation always centered on the games themselves. These five master players gleaned freaky wisdom from new variations in backgammon strategy emerging from online players in Cyprus or the sudden popularity of Boggle in Thailand or a fad for canasta among millennials in the Twin Cities region.

"Sid." Klarnacht looked at me. "Does Bluetooth interfere with mojo? Has anyone ever told you that you have to put your phone in airplane mode so it won't mess with their mojo?"

"I don't have a phone."

"Weirdo."

Bob took off his Coke-bottle specs and rubbed his baggy eyes.

"It's not a matter of signals, it's a matter of forms. We can't disrupt the forms in my mom's basement. Are you like a doppelgänger of Klarnacht? Because the only logical explanation I can think of for us having this conversation after all these years is if you are actually an evil doppelgänger who has been sent here to disrupt our mojo and kill the game."

I leaned over and whispered to Undon.

"How long you guys been at it?"

He whispered back, giving me a faceful of Doritos breath.

"Thirty hours straight. We're quota-gaming. Bob's getting testy."

Bob heard us.

"Yes, I am getting testy. I seem to be the only one invested in keeping this game going. I guess that makes me the bad guy. I seem to be the only one who wants to remember that we have to fulfill a basic quota of dungeon crawling."

Axarada squeezed her ball.

"The quotas are dumb, Bob. No one believes in the quotas except you."

Bob put his glasses back on.

"Believe them or not, they exist. When we first started playing D&D we fought orcs and goblins and rescued kidnapped maidens and collected treasure and magic items and killed a dragon at the end of every dungeon. Those are the forms. You guys can roam all year long, have interesting, character-rich encounters, solve complicated riddles and puzzles, and battle strange new creatures, but eventually we have to do the quotas. That means spiked traps and hidden doors and mysterious hermits and, yes, it means killing orcs. It also means no Bluetooth speakers in my mom's fucking basement. Now can we play the game?"

"What about replacement tapes?" I asked. "New old stock. You could listen to the same music on tapes that aren't worn out."

Klarnacht loaded his one-hitter pipe.

"That would be awesome. Bob, come on, do you even remember what 2112 sounds like when it's not warped?"

Axarada raised her hand.

"I vote yes."

Undon did the same.

"Aye."

Bob narrowed his eyes as me.

"Why are you here, Sid? Your timing is suspect. Coming in and offering to help update our tapes. That's not like you."

"I'm a helpful guy."

"No you're not."

I shrugged.

"I need some information."

"So you want to trade information for tapes?"

"Something like that."

Undon ate his last chip and wiped chip dust from his hands.

"What do you want to know about, Sid?"

"*Gyre.*"

I didn't have a pin, but I am certain that if I'd had one I could have dropped it onto deep-pile carpet and heard it clearly.

Bob pressed his fingertip down on the pointed tip of a pyramidal four-sided die.

"We don't use that word in my mom's basement."

"Is there somewhere else we could go to talk about it?"

"It's time for you to leave, Sid."

Time for me to go? In the normal course of things I'd have to struggle to shut them up about any random game I mentioned. Love it or hate it, they would engage in lengthy discourse about hangman, if it came up.

"I'm not asking you to play the thing, I just want to know something about it."

"Go online, you'll find plenty."

"Online isn't my strong suit."

"That's your problem. My problem is orc quotas."

"I'm gonna use the Chronosphere to stop time."

We all looked at Klarnacht as he put his tiny pipe between his lips.

"Twenty minutes. Full freeze, everything in a one-mile radius so we don't have any orcs piling up on our asses."

Bob clenched his teeth.

"You can't do that."

Klarnacht took a hit.

"Man, I'm chaotic neutral, I can do whatever the fuck I want."

Undon stood and stretched.

"Great. I'm getting something to eat besides chips."

Axarada followed him.

"I need to take a leak."

Lehlynol chewed his lip harder.

"I don't know, Klarnacht, do you think you should? You can only use the Chronosphere a limited number of times."

Klarnacht headed for the stairs.

"That's not your concern, Lehlynol. Your concern is deciding what the fuck you're doing about that door before time starts moving again." He looked at me. "Come upstairs, Sid. We can talk about that thing you mentioned. I want those tapes."

Bob looked from one of us to the next, making eye contact with each.

"I am starting a twenty-minute timer. Exactly twenty minutes. When time restarts, you four be ready to crawl some fucking dungeon. And you, Sid, be gone." He pressed a button on his digital watch. "Time stops now."

Time didn't stop. Bob controlled a lot in his mom's basement, but even a dungeon master's power has limits.

SIXTEEN

KLARNACHT led me out to the front porch.

We were in Hancock Park, the old-money residential neighborhood in the heart of Los Angeles. Lawns sprawled in front of big houses set far back from wide streets. Bob's mom's place was larger, older, and shabbier than its neighbors, a white elephant that the homeowners' association would have liked to see restored and updated to the current codes. But the game's mojo had a way of rebuffing any legal efforts that threatened its home. Motions filed were lost, plaintiffs were relocated to Decatur by their employers. Over the years, residents on the street had developed a blind spot, choosing not to see Bob's mom's house. It was safer that way.

A full moon was rising, swollen and yellow. It felt too close. A great, glowing, dead eye, watching us. Not a happy thought. I tried to unthink it.

Klarnacht stepped off the porch and took a deep breath of non-basement air. He'd grabbed his phone as we exited the basement. He kept glancing at it and giving the screen thumb taps and swipes as we spoke.

"Can you really get those tapes, Sid?"

"*Gyre,* Klarnacht, what can you tell me?"

He took another deep breath, bent at the waist, almost touched his toes, came up short, stood straight.

"What have you heard?"

"Nothing before tonight."

He tucked his one-hitter in the corner of his mouth.

"Seems like it should be on your wavelength."

"I don't think I could name more than a couple of online games, man. I'm not exactly the demographic for that kind of thing."

He dug his lighter from his pocket.

"No, man, I don't mean *Gyre* should be on your wavelength like it's a game. I mean I thought you'd hear about it because of all the other shit."

This was not helpful.

"I can't do vague and allusive right now. Aside from the fact that time isn't going to stay frozen forever, I am a broken calculator trying to compute a quadratic equation, except all the numbers have been replaced with random words clipped out of an Arabic dictionary composed by an ethnocentric Western European in the nineteenth century."

He turned the flint wheel on his lighter a couple of times.

"What?"

"Internal focus is a challenge right now so I need external clarity. Simple. Small words. Declarative sentences. Please."

"I'll do my best."

He struck a flame, put it to the end of his pipe, took a lung-buster hit, held it for a moment, and exhaled a huge cloud.

"It's not weird that you don't know about *Gyre* as a game. It's one of these cult deals. Launched a few years back by an independent developer. Very down-low. People had to find it on their own. Indie games are like indie bands. Fans are more invested in something they think they discovered first. *Gyre* fans are very committed, and they don't like tourist players."

I already wasn't liking the sound of this.

"Are a lot of people playing?"

"So, like, that's all relative. The very biggest games, they have hundreds of millions of active accounts, a million to tens of millions of players logged in at any one time. *Gyre* has two or three million accounts globally. A few hundred thousand doing it live when it's peaking. But those are huge numbers for an underground game that has no corporate backing, no advertising, no merch, and doesn't distribute though the big streaming companies. The game is donation-based, pay what you want. And players must be generous, because running something like that is expensive. The creator had to have found some kind of financing for development, but the whole thing, like where it comes from, who made it, how they made it, is all shrouded, man, mysterious as hell. That's part of the appeal for a lot of people. You starting to understand why I thought you might have heard of it?"

I understood. A game launched in secret, attracting independently minded people who had a sense of ownership and commitment. Fierce devotion to an object of obsession. A couple of million players. Mystery-shrouded. Normally, I'd say someone was manufacturing a curiosity of some kind. But making an internet curiosity would be pointless.

"Okay," I said, "but what is the game? I mean, are people shooting things or collecting things or what? How do you win?"

He took his one-hitter from his mouth, shaking his head.

"Wrong idea. I'm saying the word *game* because we need to say something. But then the associated assumptions come in. Play. Goals. Levels. Points. No, not that. *Gyre* is not a game. You can't win. There is no winning. People don't play *Gyre*. *Gyre* plays them."

That didn't sound good.

"You're gonna have to explain."

He gave the back of his neck a hard squeeze.

"Indie games. It's a quadrant of human experience for some developers. They want you to have to live something. Like, you are the parent of a baby with a terminal disease, twelve months old. You see medical charts, hear doctors' voices. A baby's gurgle. Heart monitors. Make choices. Course of treatment. What to say to your family and friends. You and your spouse talking in bed at night. These are the components of the game. That's a real example."

"Why would anyone want that?"

"Because it's art. Experiential. Emotional. This is a niche. Gaming does not have to mean win or lose. Debates rage. I have opinions. Never mind. *Gyre*. How does it work?"

He gave his phone a long look, nodded, and carefully tapped out a message. He looked at me, exhaled, and pocketed his phone.

"Okay, Sid, here's what it is. Before you can really enter *Gyre*, first you solve puzzles. Moral dilemmas are posed to you. You meet Hitler when he's a child, you have a gun. A mother is giving birth and something goes wrong, and you can save only her or the baby. Your suicide will cause misery to your family, but save the lives of ten strangers. What do you do?"

"This is part of the game?"

"This unlocks the download. No wrong answers, but you have to make a choice for each. Dozens of propositions like that. You haven't started playing, and *Gyre* is forcing you to make life-and-death, morally conflicted choices. When you finish that, an encrypted file installs on your device. All platforms supported. Now you open *Gyre*. What is this thing? What does it look like? First, you have to read a shitload of text. Like first-generation role-playing computer games. *Zork* and those. But with animated sequences knitted into it. Not three-D computer animation. Hand-drawn, primitive. Childlike, almost. But beautiful. Each one ends with a frozen image that you can navigate. You click this and that, guided by clues in the text you've read. There's music."

He paused like he was listening to something.

"Drums made from hollowed stone. A three-stringed lute tuned to the scream of some kind of bird. A six-foot flute carved from the bone of an extinct monster. Those are the instruments.

The music is insinuating and jarring. Like a tune is being whispered in your ear on the floor of a steel foundry."

"I'm having trouble picturing this."

He pointed both index fingers at me.

"Imagine a wall of text. You try to read it. Unintelligible. It looks like English, but it doesn't read like English. You have to read this wall to proceed. Try again. Words begin to make sense. It's English in a phonetic dialect. Your brain adjusts, translates. Not good enough. You have to speak it aloud into your microphone. English spoken at the back of the throat and in front of the teeth. You get cramps in your tongue when you speak it. It's a big wall. Finally, tongue in knots, you succeed. The wall opens, you enter Gyre, an eternally demolished city at the heart of a world."

This was getting creepier and creepier.

"How common is that? A game making you do something in the real world?"

He blew through his pipe, clearing the chamber of ash, sounding a high, hollow note.

"Not common in gaming. But typical in life these days. Phones, Sid, the internet. Drugs, if you prefer. Rewiring our brains, yeah? Social media installs new codes of behavior in you. Creates appetites, needs you never had before. Requires physical actions. Feedback and contributions. You want likes, you must feed the machine what it wants to eat. Take pictures, make physical gestures, say words. You feed yourself to the thing."

"Are we still talking about *Gyre*?"

He tucked his pipe into his hip pocket.

"Social media has norms. Fashions. Fads. *Gyre* has philosophy. A belief system. To be in *Gyre,* to be successful and live in *Gyre,* you have to believe. You can't negotiate the world, you can't understand its workings, you can't communicate with inhabitants and other players if you can't grasp the belief system that underpins the world."

"How do you learn?"

"The basic text is on that wall you have to translate before you enter. The rest you learn by spending a lot of fucking time online. Invested. Investing. Deciding what you believe. Which side you're on."

"There are sides?"

"It's a religion. There are always sides."

"There are gods."

"Only Demon."

"What's that?"

"She lives in a huge hole that the city of Gyre is built around. The Chasm. Nothing mythic about it. Demon, the creator of the world, is at the bottom of the Chasm. Sleeping."

He looked down, kicked the cracked concrete path that led from the sidewalk to the front door of the house that he rarely ever left.

"You think much about the end of the world, Sid?"

The end of the world. That old thing again.

"Generally no, but lately it's been coming up."

"You think it's happening?"

What's a chronic depressive to say to a question like that?

"Not like I can do anything about it if it is."

He laughed, unamused. Rueful. He was still looking at the ground.

"Lot of that feeling going around." He looked up from the ground. "How important is all this, to you, Sid? What you're asking me?"

I thought about Circe's room. The pull of that mojo. Release from despair. I thought about having an auspicer lay a course to bring some of that mojo into my Sinéad O'Connor shirt so I'd always have it with me. I thought about being better. And I thought about the girl. Circe. The possibility that she could be found. Helped. All was not lost.

"More important than anything for a long time. I haven't been alive for a long time. And maybe I can be again. I don't know."

Half his face smiled; the other half did not join in.

"Okay, then. Ask me about Demon." He pronounced it in the manner he'd described, in front of the teeth, back of the mouth, sounding like the tongueless hunchback in an old horror movie. Not in a silly way.

Something tickled me. Unpleasantly. Back of my throat. Faint invitation to puke. What was it, that feeling?

"Okay. Tell me about Demon."

"Demon," he said, that same pronunciation, a correction, an instruction.

I let my mouth hang slightly open, tried to freeze my tongue, pushed the first syllable to my lips, swallowed the second syllable.

"Demon," I grunted, feeling the nauseating tickle grow stronger at the back of my throat. "Tell me about her," I finished, a sense of disproportionate relief filling me as I returned to my regular speaking voice.

The unsmiling half of his face joined the smiling half. Briefly. And then the whole face collapsed.

He nodded at the house.

"We all tried it. New game. Of course we all tried it when it launched. Undon, Lehlynol, Axarada, they dropped it at the wall. It made them bored, anxious, angry. Respectively. Emotional reactions are typical. Bob and I stuck with it until the wall opened. Bob shut it down right after that. Deleted the app. Scoured it from his memory. His laptop's and his own. Forbade mention of *that abomination*."

The night pulsed. The midsummer humidity pressed close. The crickets and traffic, constant background in an L.A. night, grew distant. Stars, scant and dim above Los Angeles, trembled. Fear was a scent. Acidic and fecal.

"I stayed inside it a little longer," Klarnacht said. "I wanted to know more about what was going on." He looked side to side, gave a slight sweep of his hand, encompassing something, everything. "Whatever this is, all of this. Our world. It may or may not be crashing and burning. If it is, I don't know what to do about it. But." He moved his hand, shaped his fingers into a spearpoint, and drove it down, penetrating into something. "In there. *Gyre*. It is certain. Demon is rising from the Chasm. The world is ending for sure. It's a cycle. Once every couple millennia or something, Demon rises from the Chasm and destroys her creation. It's all her. She makes the world from her flesh and then is exhausted and hibernates. Then she wakes, hungry, and consumes. Once she's eaten her fill, she sleeps again. But she doesn't eat everything and everyone, there are remnants, so civilization rebuilds on the ruins of what came before, over and over again."

The night had closed tighter. It was just the two of us in darkness and mist. I felt pressure. My ears popped. There was a pull. Something was tugging at me, stirring in my guts.

"I think we should stop talking about this right now," I whispered, afraid of the unseen.

Klarnacht stepped closer to me.

"You said it was important. Don't worry. I'll hurry. I really want those tapes, Sid. I need to change something. Anything." His voice threatened to break, danger of tears.

"Listen," he said. So I listened.

"*Gyre* was launched with the clock of the world set to midnight. The brink of Demon's rising. Everyone who plays knows for certain that the world is going to end. Nothing ambiguous. But they also know that they can change what happens. It is a powerful feeling. Two camps. Guild and Harrow. Guild is urban, technocratic. Steam engines and gunpowder and electricity.

Harrow are nomadic northlanders. Swords and magic. Guild has a plan: kill Demon; ambush her when she rises; end the cycle. Harrow have always fed Demon, coming to the Chasm before she rises, throwing themselves to her. Nourishing her as she wakes. To them, the cycle is natural. The world must end to be reborn."

I felt muck welling inside me. The mire of my depression. As if the change in pressure were drawing it up from where it had sunk below my surface. It climbed in and around me. I would be submerged. I couldn't live like that anymore. I lifted my face, feeling I'd soon be choked if I didn't keep my mouth clear. What was happening?

"I can't," I said. "I can't breathe."

Klarnacht was panting as he spoke.

"Almost done. You said you needed this. Right now, *Gyre* is tearing itself in half. Guild and Harrow. A final battle is being fought. It will end when Demon rises. She will die or consume the world again. After that, no one knows. The game ends forever or restarts or changes into something new. Whatever it is, every single player can influence the outcome with their actions."

He leaned close, his face bent to mine.

"Anyone can change the fate of the world."

Still the muck rose. It clotted around everything I wanted. There was no point in wanting.

"Stop," I gasped.

"I'm tired of all this, Sid. Being where I am and what I am. Aren't you? I want to be able to change something. Anything. But only if it's something real. Even if it's just the fucking music in Bob's mom's basement."

I gagged, felt vomit rise.

He stepped back from me.

"Reject it, Sid. You have to make it go away. Make a choice."

Klarnacht stepped backward into the darkness, was swallowed by it, leaving me alone.

A choice? There were no choices. I was immersed in clay. There was no way to break free. I'd made this trap for myself. I'd lived it and I couldn't blame anyone else. It was my fault. All my fault. Abigail. I'm sorry. It was all my fault.

The girl, Sid, remember the girl.

The girl. Reach for that. There is nothing else worth doing. Try to save the girl if not yourself.

I moved. Wrenched myself forward a step.

"No," I said. "No more. Stop."

Another step. Darkness winked away. The world was back. The humid midsummer night. Crickets and traffic. Klarnacht standing in front of me, taking a big hit off his pipe.

"What?" I said. "What was that?"

"That," he exhaled, words riding on smoke, "was *Gyre.*"

I still felt weighed down by my existence, but the weight was lifting. I hadn't been dragged back to the full depth of the depression that Circe's room had lifted me out of, but something had tried. The course of mojo in that room had buoyed me. Now something else had almost taken me back under.

I spread my arms, filling them with whatever had just happened.

"That wasn't a game. That was a course. Talking about *Gyre* drew us close to a serious course of mojo."

Klarnacht nodded at the big old house.

"Now you know why Bob erased it from his memory and banned discussion."

Yeah. Bob wouldn't want that course anywhere near his D&D campaign. Courses were like waterways. The stronger ones drew the weaker ones into their stream. Everything he and the other players had built could be wiped out, all their mojo pulled into the greater course running through *Gyre*. The mojo being drawn from the devotion of its players and taken to . . . To where?

No. It made no sense.

I dropped my arms.

"The only place for the players' mojo to go is into the internet. All that *Gyre* mojo will drain to where no one can use it. Who would do that?"

Klarnacht did a little flourish with his pipe, a wave of a wand.

"Someone who hates mojo."

I touched my shirt. Abigail's shirt. The fragile reservoir that housed what was left of her. The slightest feeling of Abigail. Ghost traces left behind from her having loved that shirt so much.

"Mojo can't be destroyed," I said, thinking out loud. "It's like matter and energy. It can change states, but it can't be destroyed. If someone had a reason to want to get rid of it, all they could do is try to make it unusable."

Klarnacht nodded.

"Put it where no one can get their hands on it."

I thought about what it would mean if all the mojo circulating in the world were to be sucked away. The major courses of mojo that ran like invisible rivers, guiding the most common desires of people in the racket. Good fortune, good health, wealth, power, and safety. Those courses influenced events small and large around the world. Power behind the power we think we see every day.

Would getting rid of mojo be a return to a natural state we had before someone, some wisewoman or whoever, figured out how to use it in the first place? Or would it be a perversion of order and stability in the world? It almost didn't matter. The immediate result would be a tidal wave of instability that would wash through every facet of life and throw everything into chaos.

I laughed. I don't know why. Too big an idea to do anything but laugh at it.

"It's not possible."

Klarnacht nodded and shrugged, a man willing to allow for all kinds of possibilities.

"I think so. Yeah. Probably not possible. But, you know, a couple of million people play *Gyre*. And because Demon is rising, most of them are in there right now, tonight, deciding the fate of a fictional world that they love. The emotional reaction when that end comes, whatever it might be, is gonna release a lot of energy, man."

"If this was a real danger, people in the racket would know more about it."

"Did you know about it?"

"I've been out of it for so long I barely know which way is up. People in circulation would know."

"They know something is riled, Sid. The major courses are turbulent. People in the know think someone is trying to lay a big new course. Who and why? That's what's being asked. But the internet? No one in the racket can imagine someone purposely laying a course to send mojo into the internet. And no one is going to listen to a guy like me with some crazy idea that even I don't really believe is possible."

He wasn't wrong. People in the racket depended on received wisdom. We learned what we learned about mojo from one another. Tradition ran deep. Superstition and calcified beliefs. We believed in rules and no rules. Mostly the rules. Everyone was pissed about how much mojo was dumping into the internet, but no one was doing anything about it. No one was thinking about the possibility that there might be someone who'd want to send it all there. People in the racket had a secret path to power. They didn't want to share it or see it change. And they didn't think much about how it might be changed by anyone who played by rules different from their own. That would mean someone outside the racket knew more than they did. And how the heck could that be?

So, could a cult online game be developed into a curiosity that set a course pulling the mojo generated by the intense emotion of its couple of million devoted players, and then dump all of the mojo it produced into the internet, therefore establishing a course that was strong enough to draw more and more mojo along with it? All without anyone in the racket knowing that it was happening? Maybe? But still, it couldn't pull all the mojo out of the world. That was impossible. I thought.

"I don't buy it," I said. "I don't buy a game as a doomsday device. No game could generate the depth of feeling you'd need to build a course that strong."

Klarnacht pulled at his lower lip, thinking.

"*Gyre* speaks to people, Sid. Powerfully. Especially these kids growing up with trauma after trauma. It's wearing them out. I have a niece who's exhausted from caring. Floods and fires, politics, racism, sexism, nuclear weapons, genocide, extinctions, pandemics, mass migrations, refugee camps, food scarcity, economic collapse, and the constant pressure to look cool online. I'm not even joking about that last one. It's huge. She's worn out from caring and feeling powerless at the same time. *Gyre*, a place she can go where she can truly influence what happens. She's all in. She wishes she could live in Gyre and stop caring about the real world. I have a hard time thinking of a reason why she *should* care. You know?"

He glanced at his phone.

"Meanwhile, as the world is falling apart, I'm doing my part by killing fucking orcs." He took a last look at the moon and climbed the steps. A prisoner told that his time in the yard is over and he has to return to his cell.

"Ever think about leaving the basement?" I asked.

"Not really. I wouldn't know what to do out here." He put a hand on the door. "Something is happening with *Gyre* for sure, but I don't think it's a global conspiracy to end magic forever.

That's just a D&D player's take on something normal. Normal for us, I mean."

"Yeah. You're probably right. Make a list of the tapes you need." Thinking about the tapes, I remembered something he'd said in the basement right after I arrived. "Hey, what did you mean about *Synchronicity*? When you put that tape on, you said it was appropriate because I showed up."

"Right. Um, some people called looking for you right before that."

"Who?"

"Uh, Shingles. She wants you to call her. Seemed kind of synchronous, the timing. She calls and you come through the mirror."

"How'd she know I was coming here?"

"I think she's been calling a lot of places looking for you."

"Can I use your phone?"

"Come on."

I followed him back inside and he pointed down a hall.

"I have a dungeon to crawl. You can use the landline. It's in the den."

I started down the hall, stopped.

"One more thing about *Gyre*. Do you know anything about the maker?"

Klarnacht was at the basement door, setting his phone on a little table where they had to leave anything that couldn't have been in Bob's mom's basement before 1984.

"Not much. Young guy, they say. Lives in L.A. somewhere. Has a kind of compound. Keeps a low online profile and refuses to say anything about *Gyre*. Rumor is, he spends a lot of time inside it. There's a kind of legend that if you meet his avatar it will send you on a quest. Complete the quest and you can meet him, the designer. In the real world. Could be true or could be internet legend bullshit."

"Thanks, Klarnacht."

"No problem. We who are about to slay salute you." He gave a tired smile. "Maybe I should stop playing. I have all the mojo I could ever use. There has to be something else I could do with it besides this. I just don't know what."

"Ask your niece, maybe."

He scratched his head.

"Funny. I never thought of that."

"Klarnacht!" Bob's voice coming from the basement. "Time is starting with or without you!"

He shook his head.

"Voice of the gods." He chewed his lip, started to say something else, then changed his mind.

"What?" I asked.

"Nothing." He shrugged. "Just. Be careful out there, Sid."

He stepped inside the basement door and closed it, sealing himself and his friends in their time capsule.

Why was it like that? I wondered. Why were so many of us stuck? Minerva in the eighties, Iva in her ravine, Bruce to his manikin. Even Munroe, draped in chunks of actual amber, was caught up in her party and the manikin ghosts she drew to haunt it. And me, wearing my dead wife's shirt, stalking her killer—a literal reflection of who I was thirty years ago. Why were so many of us who lived close to mojo mired in our lives? Was it the mojo or was it us? We got into the racket so we could get things we wanted, so we could move toward something, but even the ones who got what they wanted seemed to never stop trying to achieve the same thing, relentlessly pursuing more mojo to course to our own benefit. But was it really to our benefit?

We were supposed to be using mojo, but was it maybe using us?

That was the gamers getting into my head. They were caught in an obvious trap of their own making. Play the game to make the mojo so they could play the game. That wasn't me. Nothing was playing me. I wasn't stuck. The course in Circe's bedroom had pulled me out of my depression. I could move and act and think how I wanted.

Do something, Sid. Make something happen. Now!

The phone was shaped like Ms. Pac-Man. I lifted the top of its head and called Shingles.

"Hello?"

"Shingles, it's me."

"Sid!"

"Yeah, me."

"Where have you been? I called and called your place."

"I'm not there."

"Where were you? Are you okay? How are you?"

"I'm fine."

"You sure?"

"What are you talking about?"

"I want to see you. I'm at that place where we saw that movie that you said was worse than being entombed. You know what I'm talking about?"

"*Citizen Kane.* Unwatchable."

"You're an idiot."

"It was like watching Orson Welles masturbate."

"It is literally on every single list of the best movies of all time."

"Best movies about Orson Welles jerking off."

"What's your favorite movie?"

"That's not the point."

"Remind me."

"Irrelevant to the topic at hand."

"*Knight Riders,* yes? A low-budget flick about medieval reen-actors who joust on motorcycles."

"Budget isn't relevant to the quality of cinema."

"You revel in being contrarian."

"I do not."

She laughed. She exhaled.

"I'm glad you're alive, Sid," she said.

"I'm glad you're alive, Shingles. If that's what you want, I mean."

"You remember the place I'm talking about?"

"Sure."

"Come there now. I want to see you."

"Why are we talking about it like we can't say the name? Is the CIA bugging you?"

"Come now. Quickly."

"Sure. Could you maybe use your phone and get me one of those rideshare things?"

"There are no rideshares. I mean, the traffic is insane. All the drivers are tied up taking people downtown to the protest."

"What is it about, anyway? What are they protesting?"

"Everything."

"They're protesting the universe?"

"More or less. Just get over here. It's not far. I'll get you a scooter. Hang on."

"Not a scooter."

"It's the best I can do."

She used her phone to find an electric scooter, told me where it was, and gave me a code to unlock it.

"I hate those things."

"Grow up."

"On a scooter, sure."

"Pretend you're a knight in shining armor riding into battle."

"Orson Welles jerking off, Shingles. Every time you watch *Citizen Kane,* you're participating in Welles pleasuring himself."

"Goodbye, Sid. See you soon, Sid. Can't wait, Sid."

She hung up.

SEVENTEEN

THE SCOOTER Shingles had reserved for me was a few blocks away.

The streets seemed dark despite the moon. Humidity was gathering around the globes of the streetlamps, shrouding them and limiting their reach. It never used to be humid in L.A., but it was becoming the new normal. The clammy air was a constant reminder that Circe and her friends were right to be creating plays about the end of the world. I thought about ill humors carried in the atmosphere, poisoned airs that could pollute one's spirit. It was nonsense, but it was also entirely possible. If mojo was indeed a free-floating, invisible, and intangible element, that meant we were passing through it at all times. Awash in magic without knowing it. And since mojo has the character of the emotion it is created by or associated with, it also has the feel of that emotion.

I thought about the feeling I'd had of being sucked under the muck when Klarnacht was explaining *Gyre*. Whatever kind of course was running through that game, its feel was pure misery. Hopeless desperation. It had run close to us for those few moments. Merely talking about the game put us near the current. Usually you needed a ritual to put you in sync with an existing course. You could stumble into one randomly, like Circe's room, but that's not what had happened outside Bob's mom's house. Thinking about it made me ill at ease.

Or was something else making me unsettled? Wait—was I being watched?

An engine roared behind me and I remembered that I'd ditched Francois. He was going to slap me around good for that. Then a mid-1980s Lincoln Town Car limo jumped the curb and cut off my path, and I recognized that I was in much deeper trouble than being chastised. A door swung open and I was grabbed and slammed into the side of the Lincoln, air knocked out, arms stretched across the roof.

"Check him for mirrors," someone said.

"Hey, Lloyd," I managed to gasp.

"He doesn't carry mirrors," Minerva called from inside the limo. "Just get him in the car."

I was shoved face-first into the back of the limo, pitching onto the floor between luxuriously upholstered facing seats. People climbed in, Lloyd and Dak, both making a point of stepping on me as much as possible as they took their backward-facing seats and the limo bounced off the curb and headed slowly down the street.

"Your face, Sid," said Minerva, looking down at me from the forward-facing seat, "you have something on your face."

I touched my face.

"Just a little blood. I bit my lip."

"Wipe it off. I want a nice clean face to carve off your skull."

"Grim joke, Hillary."

"Not a joke."

I heard a ratcheting series of clicks and looked at Lloyd as he opened and closed a green plastic box cutter.

My mouth was very dry.

Dak raised his hand.

"Mr. Minerva."

"What?"

"I get carsick sitting backward like this. Can I maybe sit on your side?"

Lloyd snapped the box cutter closed.

"Shut up, Dak."

Minerva shook his head.

"So rude to your help, Lloyd. It doesn't pay in the long run. Not for a guy like you." He pressed a button and the smoked glass that sealed off the passenger compartment slid down. "Let's pull over for a moment, please," he said.

I looked at the driver. I could only see the side of his head from the floor, but I knew who it was.

"How you doing, Neil?"

He pulled the limo to the curb and turned his head toward me.

"Fuschk yoush," he slurred. He had to slur because half his teeth had been knocked out and parts of his cheek and jaw were shattered. Epoxy had been slathered over that side of his face to keep it from chipping away.

"Sorry about hitting you," I said.

"Fuschk yoush," he said again.

Fair enough.

Minerva pointed at Dak.

"Go up front."

"Thanks." He opened the door, closed it, circled, and got up front with Neil.

"Take a seat, Sid," Minerva said. "I want to see that face. Enjoy it in its natural environment for as long as possible."

"Sure."

I climbed off the floor and onto the seat next to Minerva.

"Over there, Sid. Next to Lloyd."

"No," I said, pulling Francois's pistol from my pocket. "You go sit next to Lloyd."

I'm sure Francois intended to get his gun back from me when he told me to point it at Bruce, but distractions abounded. It is a lesson of sorts—not to hand things to a thief. Stuff has a way of finding its way into our pockets.

Minerva took a very deep and exasperated breath and moved over to the backward-facing seat next to Lloyd.

"You didn't search him?"

I waggled the little .32.

"In fairness, Hillary, you told him to just get me in the car."

"I'm going to kill you, Sid."

"Is that a threat you should be making right now?"

He gave me a long look.

"You're not a killer. Never have been."

"Guns are dangerous in anyone's hands."

"Sure. But I know you won't shoot unless one of us tries to jump you."

Lloyd slitted his eyes.

"I'll jump him."

I raised the gun again.

"Take it easy, guys. How'd you find me?"

Minerva laughed.

"You don't have many friends, Sidney. Finding one to sell you out is a cheap proposition."

I thought about how displeased Bob was about having his game disrupted.

"Bob?"

Minerva shrugged.

I shook my head.

"You got here awfully fast."

He nodded.

"We were in the area already. I had a little mojo coursed to speed me toward you."

Lloyd got a sour-lemon look on his face.

"That was my idea. Coursing mojo to lead us toward him was my idea."

Minerva tsked.

"It's a poor employee who tries to claim credit from his boss, Lloyd." He looked at me. "You get my bone from Munroe, Sid?"

"She said it wasn't yours. Looks like I was right that you just wanted to dangle me in front of her to cause trouble and see what happened."

"So what happened?"

"What do you think about the end of the world, Hillary?"

He didn't say anything.

"Suicide cults? That mean anything to you?"

"You're talking nonsense, Sid. I don't even know what language you're speaking."

Funny thing was, I believed him. There wasn't a glimmer in his eyes, nothing to suggest anything I'd said had meaning to him. Maybe he really had just sent me to Munroe's to shake the tree and see what fell out.

I could play that game.

"Speaking of faces, I saw an interesting one earlier today."

He shrugged.

"Okay."

I pointed at my face.

"Ironically enough, considering your grim threats, I saw my own face today. Imagine."

He smiled, Mr. Nonchalant.

"You're right, Sid," he said, blasé as heck. "That is interesting."

"You're not surprised?"

"Why would I be?"

Lloyd laughed.

"You're an asshole. Sidney Catchpenny, asshole extraordinaire that doesn't know fuck about fuck all."

Minerva casually reached over and flicked Lloyd on the nose hard enough to produce a sharp smack of finger hitting skin.

"Shut up, Lloyd."

"Man, I've told you not to do that."

Minerva did it again, stared Lloyd down, and returned his gaze to me.

"Are there questions you want to ask, Sid? Anything you're curious about regarding this apparition you saw manifest this afternoon? Maybe I can help. Maybe I can solve a mystery for you. Despite this stupid situation you've gotten yourself into, waving a gun at me, maybe I could still help. You can see that Lloyd is becoming more and more of a pain. I'm just about ready to get rid of him entirely. Instead of me cutting off your face, we could move your account over to a new page of the ledger. Come work for me full-time. Five years indenture. Exclusive. I say, and you do. To sugar the deal, I'll tell you anything I might know about your manikin. To accept my offer, all you have to do is shoot Lloyd in the head and then give me your gun."

Was I tempted? Was I desperate and selfish enough to consider for a moment the possibility of killing another human being so I could get what I wanted? Yes I was. I was desperately tempted. Did that temptation reach as far as my gun hand? Did it twitch in Lloyd's direction? No, no it did not. Which isn't to say that it never would have, just that events moved ahead of any impulse that might have tickled my trigger finger. Because shame on Lloyd for not searching me to see if I was armed with anything more dangerous than a piece of bicycle chain, but also shame on me for not remembering to tell him to give me the box cutter when I brandished Francois's pistol. Now I was vividly reminded about the box cutter as he swung it up from alongside his thigh, the blade ratcheting to full length as he screamed.

"Fuck you, Hillary! Fuck you, Hillary! Fuck you, Hillary!" The blade sinking repeatedly into Minerva's neck. A pulsing stream of blood painted Lloyd's face as he continued screaming. "Lock the doors! Lock the fucking doors!"

Too late for that. I was already moving to my right, left hand scrabbling across my body to find the door handle as I tried to keep the gun pointed toward Lloyd. I felt the handle under my fingers and yanked, opening the door before the locks could chunk down.

Lloyd screamed again. Nothing coherent. Pure rage as he pulled the box cutter from Minerva's neck and threw himself across the limo's interior. I overcame any hesitation I might have had left about shooting him and pulled the trigger. Because I was falling out the limo door, I missed Lloyd, but I did get him to rethink coming out of the car to kill me as I fell to the ground and scrambled backward.

"Drive!" he screamed. "Fucking drive!"

The Lincoln lurched, spun its rear wheels, spurted forward, glanced off a Mercedes at the curb and sped up the street with Lloyd hanging out the open door.

"I have your heart, you fuck! I have your fucking heart!" were his parting words.

Then it was quiet.

The moon shone down. No front doors were opened by the curious, but they'd be calling for help. Police and armed private security would be zeroing in. I ran across lawns, staying close to privacy hedges and trees. Watchers would be reporting gunshots and a speeding limo. For the moment, Lloyd had more to fear from pursuit than I did. Then again, if Hillary coursed a little mojo for luck when they went out hunting me tonight, it might still be flowing. It wouldn't take much to send a police cruiser into a traffic jam caused by the protesters that were flooding the city.

I had to assume the worst. I had to assume that Lloyd was not going to be shot down by a squad of trigger-happy LAPD officers, that he would make it back to the Sunset Strip in one piece and assume proprietorship of Minerva's holdings. Including my heart. But I could also safely assume that he didn't have the combination to Minerva's safe. The only place that combination would be was inside Minerva's head, and that head was lolling on a severely punctured neck. It would take Lloyd some time to untangle the course of security mojo Minerva had woven around his safe, but once he had it open, the list of horrible things he could do with my heart was nearly endless.

EIGHTEEN

I FOUND SHINGLES at the Hollywood Forever Cemetary, robbing a grave.

She had two familiar faces with her, Wendell Which and
Horace Hoo, a married couple of auspicers who had an antiques
shop in West Hollywood and worked as groundskeepers at Hollywood Forever on the side. They could be mistaken for any
happy couple who shared a penchant for capri pants paired
with checked vests and hand-painted silk ties. The only thing
that separated them from any other eccentrically stylish shop-
keepers was their interest in picking through the coffins of the
recently deceased.

"Hey, Sid," Wendell said, looking up from down in the grave
they were excavating.

Horace was clearing earth away from the side of the grave to
keep it from tumbling back in.

"What's up?" he asked.

"Hey," I said, not feeling very conversational after seeing
Minerva's throat sawn through. I coasted the last few feet on the
paved path before I dismounted and ditched the scooter.

Shingles was down in the grave with Wendell. She dropped
her shovel, boosted herself out, and ran over to me. She threw
her arms around me, gave me a tight squeeze.

"You're okay."

I tried to shrug, but she was holding me too tightly.

"It was tense, but yeah, I'm okay."

She pulled away, looked at me.

"What was tense? Is that blood on your face?"

"It's not mine."

"That's not reassuring."

"I had a run-in on my way here. Minerva."

"Is he after you?"

"Not anymore."

"You sure?"

"Pretty sure. I'm gonna sit down." I perched on the side of a headstone. "It's been a weird night."

She hunkered down in front of me and put her hands on my knees. She was wearing gardening gloves so she wouldn't get blisters while she dug up graves.

"How are you, Sid?"

"I'm fine," I said. Clearly not fine.

In addition to her gloves, Shingles was wearing denim overalls embroidered with a pattern of lilies, and a straw sun hat with a yellow ribbon tied in a bow around its crown. Shingles, despite working at a suicide crisis line and being a necromancer, is a singularly upbeat and sunny person. The fact that her disposition is largely the product of an especially clever application of mojo is beside the point. Shingles wants to feel good, so she uses mojo to help her feel good. Her relentless good humor is simultaneously infuriating and literally infectious. It is hard to feel bad when you are with her, which is one of the reasons why I sometimes don't want to be around her. I am suspicious of my emotions when I'm with Shingles. It feels like cheating to have someone else's good mood lift you up. I'm not saying there is anything healthy about my point of view—I'm just sharing it.

She smiled her irresistibly cheery smile and pulled a bandana from her back pocket, dabbed at the sticky drops of blood on my forehead, and I went inert. The adrenaline that had flooded me when I thought I was going to die in the limo swirled out of my system. I was crashing.

"Why is there so much dying?" I asked her.

Shingles stood, put a hand on my elbow, and drew me to my feet.

"You guys mind if I take a walk with Sid?" she asked Wendell and Horace.

They waved us on our way.

"We'll get the casket open," Wendell said.

She slipped her arm through mine and led me to the path.

"Let's go look at the movie," she said.

We wandered down the path. It was quiet in the cemetery. Los Angeles's background traffic noises had the quality of wind in treetops, punctuated by the occasional angry blast of a horn. The only other sounds were our feet on the gravel and dialogue from the movie, amplified and indistinct, drifting to us from across the grounds.

I tried to remember what I was doing there.

"You going to tell me why you were looking for me?"

Shingles gave my arm a squeeze.

"Because of all the suicide stuff."

"I'm not suicidal. Not more than usual. I mean, I had a bad patch, but it's over."

"Not you. I'm talking about everyone else's suicide stuff."

She unhooked her arm from mine and tugged off her gardening gloves.

"The hotline these last few days, we've been getting hammered. Never had this kind of call volume before. Lots of people are thinking about killing themselves. Our locality is going haywire. Off the charts."

She took off her hat and scratched fiercely at her scalp. She had a punk shag—once naturally pitch-black, but recently bleached blond in defiance of encroaching gray.

"It's like all these people are becoming suicide-curious."

She put her hat on and looped her arm through mine. Up ahead, I could see the flicker of the movie playing on the side of a mausoleum. An audience was spread across a small plaza near the cemetery's main entrance, sitting on blankets and lawn chairs. Cinespia, the outdoor movie show at the Hollywood Forever Cemetery, was a scene not unlike the Old Barn Theater. It was a side hustle that Wendell and Horace ran, commissioning a vehemancer to peel off some extra mojo from the audience.

Shingles sat on a bench. I joined her.

"We're getting calls from all kinds of people. The majority of them have some kind of history of depressive disorders. But it's not like they're on the verge with pills or a gun or a razor in hand. It's, well, more like they're suspended. Waiting for something. It's like they're anticipating a signal or a sign that's going to tell them it's time to do the deed."

"What kind of signal?"

"I don't know. Ideas like that can be weirdly contagious. It happens, rashes of suicide in clusters. Twos and threes, a half dozen. But this is much bigger. Like, waaaaay bigger."

She took off her hat again, fiddled with the ribbon.

"I thought I better call you."

"Why?"

"A wave of contagious suicidal thought is hitting Los Angeles, Sid. I thought you might get caught in it and kill yourself, that's why."

Something amusing happened in the movie. Laughter rippled across the audience. Funny stuff on the screen. Funny stuff in my life. But my funny stuff wasn't the kind I was laughing at. A wave of contagious suicidal tendencies? I could imagine it. With very little effort, I could almost feel it. The thick tide of *Gyre* mojo that had wanted to take me under, down, away. Forever.

The city of Los Angeles had a population of just under four million people. Following global trends for the developed world, probably about fifteen percent of those people had some experience with major depressive disorder. That meant six hundred thousand of them had gone though some period of their life that lasted weeks to months to years when they had felt useless, hopeless, worthless. For some it had been a onetime occurrence, for some it came and went with troubled times, for some it was chronic and they never fully escaped. I imagined those people being caught in the *Gyre* course if it were to grow into a forlorn wave fed by the emotions of its obsessed players.

Six hundred thousand people.

My breath shortened. A chill climbed my spine and pierced my brain. Did Lloyd have my heart? Was I dying? No. Too soon. He couldn't have it yet. Thinking of Lloyd, I saw his face covered in Minerva's blood. I saw Minerva, red bubbles foaming from the punctures in his throat, and replayed a wet whistle that I hadn't known I'd heard as he was dying. I saw my reflection, perched on the edge of the bathtub, holding Abigail under the water. The reflection doubled, and I saw it standing over me in Circe's bedroom. It doubled again and again, then fractured and shattered. I saw Iva, weighted with fear, her daughter gone. I saw Bruce and Burke revolving around each other, broken and breaking. Sue's snaggled grin. Munroe's red mouth, gaping always for more. I saw the theater in the orchard, the young people capering on the stage, Hope and despair and the end of the world.

I laughed. I didn't want to, but I laughed and laughed. Shingles was staring at me, hand on my arm, asking me what I was laughing at. I tried to explain, forcing the words out, giggling all the time.

"People waiting for a signal to kill themselves? That's funny. Everyone says everything is not connected, but you're telling me about people waiting for a signal to commit mass suicide and I'm supposed to think that's not connected to what I'm already working on? You don't know the details, but trust me, it is all connected. And then, on top of that, what movie is playing tonight? *The Big Sleep*. Philip Marlowe is wandering all over Los Angeles, trying to do something very simple, help this *girl* who's in trouble. But that case keeps tangling with other cases until everything is hopelessly confused. People want to tell me it's not all connected, but I'm telling you that I know it is all connected and I'm going to figure out who is doing what and I am going to fix it."

Shingles put her arm around me and took her bandana out of her pocket again and started to mop my face. Somewhere in explaining everything, I'd stopped laughing and started sobbing.

"Shhh," she said. "It's okay," she said. "It's not your job to keep people from killing themselves," she said. "That's not why I told you about it," she said. "I only told you because I've been scared for you," she said.

Me keep people from killing themselves? Why would Shingles think I'd care about something like that? Please. Sure, she'd known me for a long time. Sure, she'd known Abigail. Sure, they'd worked together at the juice bar in Venice. But that still did not explain why she would begin to believe that I, of all callous and selfish bastards, would be brought to tears by the thought of masses of faceless people I'd never met contemplating suicide. That was not my problem. Really, what did anyone else's suicide have to do with me?

The girl, Sid, remember the girl.

"You don't have to worry about me thinking I have to save other people," I said. "I have my own problem right now. Lloyd Fonvielle has my heart."

She pulled her arm free of mine and stood up.

"That creep has your heart? You have to get over there."

"I have time before he has it in his hands. There's this other thing I'm doing right now. It's more important."

She put a hand on either side of my face.

"Sid, I'm not saying that whatever you're working on is not important. I'm saying that you won't be able to accomplish your goals if Lloyd eats your fucking heart."

She had a good point.

"Shingles," I said, "I want to try to explain to you why it's so important, what I'm doing, but I'm having a hard time explaining it to myself. Somehow, everything I ever cared about, and everyone I ever cared about, and everything that is happening right now, this instant, tonight, all of it is connected in a way that can only mean that either I am the center of the universe or that the gods are super invested in messing with my head. So, as much as I want to outwit Lloyd and rescue my heart so he can't play kickball with it, before I can do that, I have to figure out where do I go next to solve everything that's happening. I'm not crazy, so I know I'm not really the center of the universe and I know the gods don't care about me and I know nothing is predestined, but I also know that there is somewhere I need to be."

Shingles held up a finger to hush me, and then pointed back in the direction of the grave she'd been digging up.

"Lady in that hole, Sid, she was a hundred and three. House-cleaner. Worked from when she was a little girl until she was eighty-six. Cleaning houses. Put five kids through college like that. She had eighteen grandkids. Nine great-grandkids. True matriarch. People get all uptight about necromancers, but dead people and their lives and all the love and regret and hate and all of what comes to them when they die, that doesn't belong in the ground, clinging to a corpse. I was going to take her life's mojo and course it into something simple and useful. An old cast-iron pan that Wendell and Horace could sell in their shop. A pan that would never burn anything, never have to be seasoned, food would never stick to it. No one would ever drop that pan on their toe. Simple and useful and quietly beautiful and full of magic. Just like that old lady. But how about instead of that, me and you figure out a way to use that load of mojo to fuck with Lloyd and get your heart back?"

She stopped rubbing my neck and offered me her hand, beaming light and sunshine and hope for a new day.

"You ready?"

I stared at her outstretched hand. An invitation to turn away from the mess I'd made in the hours since Francois had first called me. A pathway to doing something as basic as saving my own heart. I covered my face with my hands, sure of only one thing.

"The girl, Shingles," I said, pulling my face from my hands and looking up at her. "I have to remember the girl."

Her smile wavered.

"That was a long time ago."

"I'm not talking about Abigail."

"I know what you're talking about, Sid."

"No you don't. Here. It's here. Look at this." I was trying to find the missing-person poster from Sunland, but I suddenly seemed to have nothing but homemade handbills in my pockets. *Hapax Legomenon,* some random gig flyer, one for the protest. "Not this, not this. Wait. This one, look." I found Harry's poster with Circe's picture on it and showed it to Shingles. "This girl."

"What about her?"

"I'm trying to find her."

"Why?"

That question again.

"Because this girl, Circe, she's connected to all this suicide stuff. The question is why. Why? And what? If I can find her and figure it all out, it will connect to the rest of it. The people, your callers who are waiting for a signal. Somehow, Circe is part of that signal."

Shingles heaved a sigh and pulled her smile back on.

"You're kind of freaking me out, Sid. But. How can I help?"

"I gotta go. I know where I need to be."

"Where?"

"I need to find out more about her. I'm gonna need a mirror."

She nodded.

"Let's see what Wendell and Horace have around here."

"This is highly irregular, Sid," Wendell said as he sorted through keys on a big ring clipped to his belt.

"Expensively irregular, Sid," Horace said, leaning against the gate of a mausoleum, arms folded, giving me a dubious eye-balling.

Wendell found the key he was looking for and unlocked the mausoleum gate.

"To be clear, we are only doing this because we love Shingles." Horace stepped clear as the gate swung open.

"To be clearer, we are only doing it because we love Shingles and because she's coursing the dead old lady's mojo for us at no charge if we do you this favor."

Wendell gestured, inviting us into the mausoleum. He beamed his flashlight into the darkness.

"There it is."

I walked into the echoing chamber and took a look at the mirror. It was small, polished silver, set into the marble face of a crypt.

Wendell swept a hand near the mirror is if presenting a prize on a game show.

"Mrs. Zanuck specified the mirror. She wanted to be able to check her lipstick after kissing her husband goodbye when she visited." He aimed the light at dozens of ancient dry lipstick smears on the crypt door. "She was a devoted spouse. Very romantic."

I eyed the little mirror.

"You got anything bigger?"

Wendell shot the flashlight in my face.

"It's a cemetery, Sid, not a department store."

I raised my hands.

"It's pretty small. I mean, getting out of something like this, okay, that's one thing, but going into it is uncomfortable as heck."

Shingles nodded at Wendell and Horace.

"You guys go on. I'll be right there."

Wendell gave me a pat on the shoulder before heading out.

"Good luck, Sid."

Horace tipped an imaginary cap.

"Don't get lost in there."

Shingles waited for them to leave, took her gardening gloves from her pocket, and started to pull them on.

"I meant what I said before, about it not being your responsibility to try to save a bunch of people who might kill themselves."

I nodded.

"I feel the same way."

"But it would still be an amazing thing to do, Sid."

She walked out of the mausoleum and closed the gate. The lock snapped shut, and she pressed her face to the bars.

"Who knows, it might even make you feel better about being you."

I watched her yellow ribbon bobbing along until it disappeared in the darkness, and turned my attention to the mirror, trying not to think about the likelihood that I might blow myself up if I got this wrong.

Once you get past the handful of unbreakable rules, like no time travel and no coming back from the dead, mojo can be directed toward any goal. Provided you can conceive and believe in it, provided you have enough mojo to do it, and provided you can handle the necessary mojo without blowing up. I mean that literally. Blowing up because you've taken on more mojo than you can handle is a thing that can happen. Picture a bag of microwave popcorn left in too long, swelling until steam splits the seams, and blackened, half-popped kernels covered in grease fly everywhere. Now replace that image with someone's head and the contents thereof.

Grim.

This is relevant because willing yourself into different physical dimensions so you can shimmy through a mirror that is too small for you requires not a little risk. To do it, I was going to have to make myself smaller. Or at least make myself look smaller. Fortunately, I had the coke mirror I'd grabbed on my way out of Munroe's, and it had a slight sheen of mojo clinging to it. Just enough, I hoped.

The vanity mirror on the crypt was fixed in place, so there were a limited number of angles of reflection that would work for me. I spent a few minutes propping the coke mirror on different plaques and vases, judging angles back to the Zanuck vanity mirror until I could see that they were reflecting one another, creating a diminishing tunnel. The reflections in the coke mirror were, of course, smaller than those in the vanity. The problem was that this wasn't a straight sly, but a two-fold.

A straight sly goes from one place to another, requires only one mirror on each end, and doesn't ask for a huge amount of imagination or belief in order to picture success. The more complicated the sly, the more mojo it requires and the harder it is to pull off. And also the more mirrors you need. You have to create new spaces in the reflections, seams, and cracks that only appear when you get the arrangement of multiple mirrors just right. A good sly is like a human protractor; they know all the angles. I knew I had a good angle for this sly, but then again, I'd had good angles for every complicated sly I'd attempted for the last fourteen years, and I'd blown every one. That was the knock on me. I'd been reduced to a straight sly. My depression had sunk me so deep that I doubted my ability to do anything right.

I hadn't attempted a two-fold sly for a long time. Bad things could happen. A mirror could snap shut on me and clip off my toes or a hand or my head. I could mis-fold into a volcano. I could become lost in an endless, dimensionless non-space of anti-existence. I might emerge into the Oval Office and be tackled by Secret Service agents and imprisoned for life. Still, a two-fold sly like this shouldn't have given me pause. I knew my destination. I'd slyed there recently. I just needed a second mirror to help fit myself inside my primary mirror. The less I thought about it, the better.

So I stopped thinking and did the thing.

I ducked below the angle of reflection between the two mirrors, and then stood up straight into the middle of it. Now I was reflected down the twin tunnels in both mirrors. The next bit is where it gets weird. I turned toward the coke mirror and backed away from it toward the vanity. My reflection in the coke mirror grew smaller. Once I was standing next to the vanity, I could see that the coke mirror held a tiny me that was multiplied into a series of ever-tinier me. I focused on just the first tiny me. I was looking at blank space and a little compact mirror with a smudge of coke in the upper right corner and a tiny me standing in the middle of it. Behind me, the vanity mirror held a reflection of the tiny me bounced from the coke mirror. I began to pantomime climbing into the vanity mirror, and my tiny reflection did the same thing except that it was facing the vanity, reflecting the front of my body. I mimed climbing into and through the vanity, and the tiny me in the coke mirror did likewise.

And then I fell.

I fell into tiny me.

I fell and then I was standing in front of Mrs. Zanuck's vanity mourning mirror and it was very large. Much larger than tiny me. It was the easiest sly I could imagine. Just step through a huge mirror with no stooping or wriggling necessary. How nice. And that is exactly what happened. Tiny me stepped into that little vanity and emerged as full-size me at my destination.

I tumbled onto Circe's bed for the second time in the last several hours, except this time I didn't see my manikin. This time I hit the mattress feeling more victorious than I had in many years, right up until Iva stuck the barrel of her twelve-gauge shotgun in my ear.

NINETEEN

"I AM GOING TO BLOW YOUR FUCKING HEAD OFF," Iva said.

She sounded very serious. I searched for some compelling piece of information that would keep her from killing me.

"I know where Circe is!" I said.

She pulled the shotgun away from my ear.

"Where is she?"

I scrambled backward away from her, cramming myself against the wall at the head of the bed.

"I'm sorry. I lied. I don't know where she is."

Iva jabbed the barrel of the shotgun at my face.

"You fucker! Don't fuck with me!"

"Please don't shoot me! I don't know where she is, but I know she's alive. She's in the middle of something terrible. She's being used by someone who needs her for something. I don't know who. But she isn't *gone*, Iva. She is somewhere. We can find her. We can save her."

"From what?"

"I don't know yet. Something to do with mass suicide. If you'll talk to me, maybe we can figure it out."

She twisted the shotgun like she was thinking about drilling it into my forehead.

"Suicide? *Suicide?* Shit! Shit!"

She yanked the gun away from my face.

"Get out of my daughter's bed. I don't want to talk in here."

I got up and we left Circe's room and went to the kitchen, where we'd talked that afternoon. Iva set the shotgun down on the seat of an empty chair next to her, far out of my reach. She looked at me and then at the corkboard on the wall, the many photos of Circe.

"Where's Francois?" she finally asked, looking at the pictures of her daughter.

"I don't know. I ditched him."

"Good."

I scratched my ear. I could still feel the impression of the shotgun barrel.

"I can try to tell you what's happened since I was here. It will sound crazy. I'll do my best to keep it straight but I'm a little wound up."

"It will sound crazy, you say?"

"Yes. Um. Well. Francois told me you know more about this kind of stuff than you maybe let on when I was here before?"

"Uh-huh."

"So maybe it will sound less crazy than it would for someone else?"

"No. I think all this shit is crazy."

"Me, too."

"What else did Francois tell you?"

"He's your dad."

"Take off those stupid sunglasses. I want to see your eyes."

I took them off and she looked at my eyes.

"Francois tell you about Circe's dad?"

"He just kept saying her dad doesn't matter, he's not part of this."

"That's almost right. He's not part of this, but he does matter."

I folded my sunglasses, opened them, closed them, set them on the table.

"You and Francois, whatever the problems between you. Why all the secrecy? I mean, he wanted me to help. I came here to figure out if I could get a bead on Circe. That was the point. But he won't tell me anything. You know about mojo, but act like you don't want to believe in it. Why pretend? Why lie?"

She made fists, pressed them to the sides of her head.

"Because I don't want that shit in my life."

She pulled her fists away, springing her fingers open, like she was trying to yank something out of her head and get rid of it once and for all.

"I just didn't want this to be what I knew it really was. Fuck. As soon as Circe was gone, I knew. But I wanted her to just be missing. Run away. Something the police could deal with. I wanted it to be something normal. I wanted all that fucked-up, scary weirdness to be over. I wanted it to not be Francois and his shit. That shit he put me through growing up. Trying to make me into his lucky charm."

"He told me he was trying to lay a course to keep you safe."

"It doesn't matter what he said he wanted. That shit ruined my life. He twisted it around me and it changed my life. Whatever I might have been or done, I didn't get to find out what that would have been because he had my life in the knots that he tied with my fucking hair. I wanted *my* life, not his magic-charm life. I tried to get away and it only got worse. Finally, finally it was me and Circe alone. I needed it to be real, our life, free of that shit. So, yeah, when she disappeared, the last thing I wanted to think was the word *mojo*. I would never have called Francois if I hadn't seen that thing. Smelled that ghost. Once that happened, I couldn't deny it. Circe disappearing had something to do with mojo. Fuck. I called Francois. He said he had someone. The same guy who helped us when I had to get Circe away from her dad. Years ago. Well, shit. You were supposed to be the help. You were supposed to have helped us before. I thought you knew everything already. So why explain all that to you? But now I find out that you don't know anything. What game is Francois playing with me? Fuck it. What do you need to know before you wave your magic fucking wand and bring her back and leave us alone?"

I pressed fingertips into the outside corners of my eyes. There was a faint crust of salt from the tears I'd shed in the cemetery. I wiped it away, shaking my head.

"I don't know why Francois lied about me helping you guys before. I'm doing my best to help now. But I have to know more about Circe and you and her dad. I need to know everything you can tell me."

She still had Dizzy the bat in her cargo shorts. She pulled it out and spread it flat on the table.

"Did you grow up knowing about it, mojo?" she asked me.

"I came to it later. I saw something impossible and needed to understand. And then I wanted to be able to do something impossible. It made believing easy for me."

She shook her head, stroking Dizzy's wings.

"It's always been a part of my life, but I still have trouble believing in it. I didn't know for a long time what it was, but there was always this thing going on in the background. Francois's rules about my hair. That kind of thing. He had so many rules. It came to a head when I was a little younger than Circe and he tried to explain it to me. Mojo. My first thought was, *Oh, shit, my dad's insane.* Then I wondered, *What if it's true?* I didn't know what was worse. Him binding me up with that shit without my permission or him being crazy. But whatever it is that a person needs to fully believe, I don't have that. Imagination. Blind faith. Part of me still thinks it's all tricks. Like my whole life, Francois has been manipulating me because he's insane. That, or I'm crazy. Either of which makes more sense than magic being real. And then something happens and I. Fuck. I *feel it*. Like in there, in Circe's room. That pull in the air when you step inside."

She folded Dizzy's wings around its body like a blanket.

"If I had felt that before she disappeared, I would have

grounded her for life. If I'd had any idea she was involved with that shit. But I didn't. Probably there were plenty of signs. But like I said, most of the time I want it to not be real."

"You know for sure she was messing around with mojo?"

She flashed me a look that reminded me she had a shotgun in arm's reach.

"Are you listening? This is supposed to be your area of expertise. Has she been fucking with that shit? Has she been doing witchcraft?"

I looked at the corkboard, the photos. I realized there were no pictures of Circe before she was about two. She was alone or with Iva in all of them. She had a standard expression she seemed to put on for the camera, a flat smile that said she was barely tolerating having her picture taken. It started as a child and deepened as she became a teenager. She had her mom's cheekbones, forehead, and mouth, but her hair was straighter and her skin lighter. The eyes were from someone else.

I looked at Iva.

"Yeah, I'd say she was messing in the racket. That feeling in her room, that doesn't happen by chance. But it can't be all her. It's too intense for a kid. That kind of mojo, that's an experienced hand at work. Circe would have to be involved, but she's being used, for sure."

"You know by who?"

"No."

She tucked Dizzy under her chin, rubbed it against her neck, thinking, but not saying anything. I reached across the table and touched one of the photos on the wall. Circe, maybe nine or ten, on horseback. Jeans, cowboy boots and hat, T-shirt for some kind of summer camp. Just a kid.

"Iva, I'm not a guy who normally helps people. I've got an angle in this. The mojo in Circe's room, I want to tap into that. But I don't want anything bad to happen to her. And something very bad is going on. I think I can help you, but I have to know the history. Whatever you've been hiding from, I need to know what it is."

She looked at the picture I'd touched.

"I really did think it was over. I thought I got her away from it in time, and it couldn't touch her. I made myself believe what I wanted to believe. Is that irony? I don't know. I wanted the past to be done forever, so I made myself blind to so many signs of trouble that I should have seen."

She picked up Dizzy, rubbed it against her lips, seemed to come close to cramming it into her mouth like a gag as she struggled to get her words out.

"I don't. Talk about this. I did. Something once. I don't. Talk about it."

She bit her lips closed, made a humming sound. Mouth full of regretful bees.

I unpinned the photo of Circe on her horse and set it on the table in front of her and she opened her mouth and all her breath scraped out of her lungs.

"Please, Iva," I said.

She refilled her lungs and stuffed Dizzy back in her pocket.

"Suicide," she said to me. "You brought up suicide before."

I waited for more, and she nodded to herself, acknowledging something she'd wanted to pretend wasn't there.

"What do you know about suicide cults?" she asked.

TWENTY

CIRCE was born into a suicide cult.

Her dad was its leader.

"I didn't know that, of course," Iva told me. "He was just an old hot guy I'd see down at the beach with my friends. Not old-old, but I mean, I was fifteen and he was about thirty. So he was a lot older than me. Had that straight-edge vibe. Lean, ripped, always clean-shaven. He was balding, kept his hair buzzed close. He'd do these super-intense workouts. One-armed push-ups, planks that went forever. He'd go in the water and swim straight out until you lost sight of him and be gone so long you were sure he'd drowned, then he'd come bodysurfing back in. He was so over the top. Clearly in love with himself, showing off. We made fun of him, me and my friends, but we were always checking him out. We called him Hot Rasputin because when he wasn't working out he was preaching. He didn't scold or tell people they were damned or anything. He'd encourage people, talk about potential, how the body was a container for potential and everyone had it and could let it out. He'd do gymnastics and feats of strength. That's what he called them. Standing backflip, rip a phone book. Circus stuff. Demonstrating potential. He'd do that and tell stories. He had all these tattoos. Pictographs. That's what he called them. He tattooed himself. Each of them had a story from his own life. So he'd tell a story about a tattoo of a stick-figure boy with a stick-figure dog. This really sad story about his dog dying, but him realizing it was still alive in him. He got a good crowd. Tourists, beach people. He had fans. Kids, mostly, a handful that showed up to watch him all the time. They'd hang with him and join his workouts and listen to more of what he had to say when the performance was over. Like it was inner-circle stuff. We watched sometimes, from a distance. He never wore anything but these black trunks, from morning to night, no matter how cold it got. My friends gave me a bad time because they said he was into me. They said he was always checking me out. We made cradle-robber jokes. They were right, he was into me, but not because he liked young girls. I mean, he liked young girls, but with me it was the other thing that he was interested in. It was swirling all around me, the stuff Francois had done. Mojo. It was supposed to be protecting me, but instead it attracted Circe's dad. Crispin. That was his name."

I knew the type she was describing. Charismatic. Good at pulling in an audience. Not unlike Bruce at the Old Barn. Might be a busker, might be a fakir, might be a street-corner preacher. Low-rent vehemancers pulling mojo from audience reactions, scant amounts that basically float up into the air. Mostly harmless. But Circe's dad, Crispin, he was more than that. More and worse. Far from harmless. He was an animancer, taking mojo straight out of the hearts of the people who admired and loved him.

"So he had his eye on me, yeah. And then I had my showdown with Francois. We were always fighting by then. He was trying to control everything I did. He wanted every element of my life to add up to something. It was worse than my friends whose parents were on them about their grades and building a college résumé. Because I didn't know what it was about. His rules for my hair were so crazy. Not just that I couldn't cut it. The way it was brushed and washed and how I wore it. Like it was almost a religious thing. Which it sort of was, but I didn't understand that yet. When you're little, you do what your dad says and it seems normal because it's all you know. Then later it feels restrictive. You want to do things your own way, like get a fucking haircut. Then you're a teen and you realize how creepy it is. One night I had had enough. I ran away. Stayed a few days with this boy I was seeing. I wasn't planning to leave forever, I just wanted some space. I cut off all my hair. To show I could control my own body. Francois found me. He saw my shaved head and he completely lost his shit. He was raving; I mean for real. I couldn't understand. He was talking about something called mojo. Blurted all this crazy shit. I thought he was maybe on drugs. Then, he must have seen how freaked out I was. He tried to calm down. He wanted to explain how the world wasn't what I thought it was. How everything I thought I knew about how the world worked was wrong. He wanted me to understand that magic was real. Magic was probably the only actual real thing there was in the universe."

She dropped her face into her hands and stayed that way for a while.

"I mean. Fuck," she said finally, and lifted her face again.

"So right there I realized my dad was crazy. Had to be. Except. Except that it connected to things I felt. I couldn't disbelieve it entirely. But either way, he had no right to do that to me, raise me like that, make decisions about what path I'd follow. I got out of there. I went to the beach. I was there, crying because I was bald and my dad was crazy, and someone asks me if I'm okay. Crispin. He's standing there, like out of nowhere. And I kind of nod, even though I am obviously not okay. And he nods at my head and says he loves my new look. *You look ready for action,* he said. *It suits you.*"

She shook her head.

"Fifteen-year-old girls don't control much. No one pretends that they do. Asserting yourself at that age, you make some dumb choices. I thought my dad was crazy or he was an evil wizard. I didn't want him to be in charge of me, I wanted to be in charge of me. So I proved I was the boss of me by fucking an old guy I barely knew."

She went to the sink and filled a glass with water from the tap.

"After that, I was there at the beach with Crispin as much as I could be. My friends were worried because I started hanging with his inner circle. They said I wasn't acting like myself. I said they wanted me to be weak and reliant on them. Francois knew something was happening, that he was losing me. What matters? What do you need to know? Circe matters, right? Okay, I got pregnant. That was that. Once I knew, I told Crispin, and he was so happy. He really wanted our baby. That made me want it. But I couldn't stay with Francois and risk he'd do to the baby what he did to me. Be crazy, do magic. Real or unreal. Crispin had a place in Montana. I went with him. Our caravan. Us and a couple of cars with his new followers. On our way to Montana to work on his ranch and learn to unleash our potential. A family. Shit."

She sipped from her glass.

"There's no surprise here. It went down like you think it did. There were seventeen of us, including the followers he already had up there. He started letting us in on the secrets of our potential and its source. The cycle. I'd just turned sixteen, pregnant by this guy, uprooted, surrounded by people who worshipped him. Literally. So I believed. That's what you do. You're growing a baby inside you. Without him, these people, your family, you have nothing. So you believe. You do your chores, tell the seven stories to one another. You join every dawn and dusk, the rising and the falling, the cycle. You join at the Chasm."

"What?" I asked. But she ignored me, talking faster and faster, trying to get it out.

"Holding hands around that hole, old mining pit at the center of the compound, looking into it, searching for Demon."

"No, wait. What?" I said, but she still ignored me.

"Circe was born at the edge of that hole. She was the child Crispin said he'd waited for. He had a son who had been the special one before her, but now it was Circe. I didn't know why. I should have known why. What I knew was that Crispin, my love, my leader, my fucking guru, he was saying that our daughter was *the dawning and the night*. I mean, fuck yeah. My daughter was going to usher in a new age. Crispin still hadn't revealed that part to us. She was a year old when he told us the secret of releasing our potential. It came out in death. We were going to use our lives to bring Demon into the world, remake it, that was our true potential. I mean."

She reached for something that wasn't there, her hand grasping at the air as if the item she wanted kept fluttering from her grasp. I knew how she felt; everything was flying farther from my own grasp the more she told me. Demon?

She latched on to her thoughts, pulled them back down.

"How did I miss it? Because he kept saying *potential*. Of course that was just another word for it. He was like Francois. He was into mojo. That's what it was all about. Him wanting me, wanting a baby with me. Because I had it all over me, that shit. Mojo. Francois had put it there, and so it was in Circe, too, like an infection I'd given her. Only worse, because Crispin was also using the stuff. Crispin was, I don't know, brewing mojo from all his believers. And he was pouring it into Circe. These little circles of adoration he'd direct, all of us passing Circe around to love her and respect her and contribute to her potential. She was the vessel for Demon, he told us. We'd all kill ourselves, feed our potential to Demon, and Demon would rise from the Chasm as Circe. But Circe had to die first. She had to go down the Chasm before she could come out of it. He was planning to throw my baby down that fucking hole. Then we'd follow her, after drinking a libation. Poison. Then the new dawn. New world. Seeded by us. That fucker. That insane fucker. He was going to sacrifice all of us and then suck it all up, the emotion, the suffering. It was

Francois again, but worse. Our suicide cult was supposed to fix
the world, but it was just a way for Crispin to power up and go
to the next level. He was going to kill my baby to make it happen. And I didn't leave."

She gagged. Tried to take a sip of water but spat it up. The
glass fell into the sink and broke. She took hold of the edge of
the counter.

"I knew. He was raising my daughter to commit. Suicide.
And. And I didn't. I didn't leave."

She jerked back and forth on the counter, wanting to rip it
loose. The frenzy passed through her. She dropped her arms
and stood there shaking.

"It was my fault that I was there with my baby. But I still
didn't leave. Not for another year. Seven was Demon's special
number. Crispin said it wouldn't be time for sacrifice until we
were seventy-seven in all and Circe was seven years old. I told
myself that I had time to figure out what to do. But what I was
really figuring out was what I believed. He didn't make it sound
like a happy thing, sacrificing our child; he cried while he told
me. We were going to be martyrs. He told us it would be hard,
but it was to save the world. You don't unplug this shit from
your brain. I went crazy. I felt like I was literally being ripped
apart. I wanted to die so I wouldn't have to figure out what was
true. Because it was awful, whatever the truth was, it was awful.
I would have killed myself if not for Circe."

She came back to the table and collapsed into her chair.

"It went like that for a long time. And then one day I was in
the garden. Circe was next to me. She was almost two. She was
mimicking me digging, making a little hole. We had chants and
songs we sang as we worked. About the cycle. What Crispin
called 'the gyre of life.' A few others were in the garden singing.
I thought I was silent, but someone said it was good to hear
my voice again, and I realized I was singing aloud. There I was,
doing my chores, singing the cycle. Demon rises and falls, we

fill the Chasm, she rises again. Like it was normal. I felt almost normal, and I hadn't noticed that I did. Circe dug her hole and put a black rock in it and said something. She hadn't said any clear words yet, just sounds that might have been words. But right then she said a word. She put the rock in and said, *Demon*. Then she took the rock out, then she put it back in and took it out, and put it in. And the whole time she said it over and over again. *Demon*. She was learning the cycle. She was being raised to know who and what she was and what she would be asked to do. I saw it then, so clear. When she was seven, when the time came, she'd be a total believer. She'd stand at the edge of the Chasm and jump into it so she could save the world. That night I ran. I took Circe and I ran away, and I got caught. Crispin said I could go. *Betrayal and disbelief are your burdens,* he said. He had me taken off the compound and left by the highway. But he kept Circe."

She ran fingers through her hair, pulled it hard, and let go.

"I walked awhile till someone picked me up. Trucker. A family guy with a teenage daughter. Concerned for me. He dropped me in Wolf Creek. There's a gas station and a motel. He gave me a handful of change from his ashtray. They had a pay phone at the Exxon there. I called Francois. I told him some, enough. He told me to get a room at the motel, said he'd call and pay for it with a card. I went to the motel. Once I was in a room, I called him again. He told me he needed to know everything I could tell him about the compound. Where it was, the layout. I talked him through it. I told him he could find it on Google Maps and see for himself. He said he needed to hear the words from me. I knew it was mojo stuff. I didn't care. That's why I'd called him. I told him they had lots of guns. We all shot up there. We had to hunt to eat. Also, Crispin wanted us to be able to *repel invaders*. Francois didn't care about the guns. He said he was sending someone to get Circe. He said this person might as well be invisible. I didn't want to know more. The only other thing he wanted to know was where the mirrors were. Any mirrors."

She gave me a look.

"You know about that kind of thing."

What was I going to say? She'd seen me fall out of her daughter's mirror less than an hour ago.

She shrugged.

"Yeah, you know. Anyway, there were mirrors. One of the barracks was mirrors all over. The gym. You know. Crispin and his body? He had us all working out. Mirrors on the walls so we could appreciate ourselves. He encouraged us to study our physical selves and recognize the illusion. He wanted us in there, but most of us hated working out. Really, it was mostly him pumping iron with a couple of his bro apostles. I told Francois and he got mad about it. He asked if we always used the same mirror. That was weird because he was right, when we worked out, we always had one mirror that was ours. Crispin didn't want us working out in front of one another's mirrors. Francois made me tell him which one was mine. And that was all. He knew what he needed to know. He said to wait. He was coming for me."

She stopped talking. Looked at me. Frowned.

"Are you okay?" she asked.

It was a strange thing for her to ask in the middle of her incredibly messed-up life's story, but I guess it was the look on my face right then.

"You look like you want to throw up," she said.

I did feel like throwing up. I was adding things together. Circe's age now and back then. The passage of time in between. Fourteen years. The same span since Francois had come to me desperate for my help. The span since I'd been unable to help him and our friendship had broken. The same fourteen years that I'd been becalmed in life. Long time drifting.

I needed to hear the rest of what Iva had to say, but some of it I could now figure out, and some of it I knew from experience. I knew that after talking to Iva, Francois had gone to get the canniest sly in the business, the most reliable thief around, who also happened to be his friend. He'd gone for me. He'd needed me to get his granddaughter away from her dad, a man who planned to lead her to suicide and reap mojo from her death.

My friend needed a sly to pull an important job, but I'd been in the middle of a depression. Deep in the hole of myself. It was near the anniversary of Abigail's death. That time of year was always a struggle. When Francois showed up with a job, I snatched at it. Anything to crawl out of myself. But he took a second look at me and said he'd find someone else. He didn't trust me when I was *in self-pity mode*. I begged him to let me help. He tested me. Told me to show him I could pull a two-fold sly. He told me to show him I could rig a crossover in the room, setting up two facing mirrors, entering one and exiting the other one at the same time. It's a parlor trick, but it's insanely difficult. You have to be able to step around yourself in there. If you muff it, you bump into your own body and get knocked off angle. It's a cocky piece of showmanship, a flash move that slys learn to impress one another. Slys get sliced in half if they blow a crossover. Or, in my case on that day, they just ram their heads against the glass and get a bunch of cuts because they're so shaky they can't find a crease to slip through. Francois looked at me while I picked slivers from my forehead and told me I was pathetic and I'd wasted his time. He'd walked out to find someone who could do the job.

At the time, I knew I deserved it. His contempt. I was worthless and I'd let him down. As much as I've wanted to kill myself in my life, I don't think I've come closer. Not right after Abigail died, not in all the years since. I sat on the floor of my apartment and used my fingernails to pry a blade of glass out of the mirror I'd broken with my own stupid head. I made the first cuts, two long slashes down my forearm. They were shallow and I needed to cut them deeper. I dug the tip of the glass blade into the first cut, ready to retrace it, make it permanent. I caught sight of my face in that blade, blood on the glass, blood on my face. If I died, my reflection would still be alive. I'd die, but the me who killed Abigail would still be out there. Bitterness saved my life. A streak of meanness. I didn't kill myself, but I still thought Francois was right to think I was worthless. It took a long time for me to start feeling different. Francois had turned his back on me. He'd needed help, sure, but so had I. I'd been in pain, desperate for friendship, and because I couldn't help him steal something, he'd abandoned me. That's what broke our friendship. When we'd both needed each other the most, neither of us was there to help. It was only in Iva's kitchen, once I'd heard her story, that it came clear to me.

I could guess at what happened after Francois left me that day. He needed a sly, so he went to Munroe. Probably she connected him with Lloyd. He was the young ace then. It would have been a heck of a sly. About a thousand miles, unknown territory, no time to scout. All those mirrors in one room, Crispin's gym, that would have created some confusion. A lot of cross angles and multiple reflections. Tricky tricky. Lloyd was a creep who was looking to eat my heart, but thinking about what he must have pulled off to save Circe, I found a little respect for him. And once on the other end, inside the compound, Lloyd still had to find Circe, snatch her, and run back into the mirrors. That would have been a straight jump to somewhere nearby, wherever he planned to meet Francois and do the handoff. But before he ran, probably right when he got to the compound, Lloyd would have found the mirror that Iva had used when she worked out, and he'd have shattered it. That would have been part of the contract with Francois. Crispin had obviously been setting up his followers to cast reflections. After they all killed themselves, he could keep those mirrors and have their manikins limned. He'd have a batch of servant-followers to do whatever next messed-up thing he had planned. But Lloyd handled it all, and he did it clean. Got Circe out, handed her off to Francois. And then Francois took his granddaughter to his daughter at the motel in Wolf Creek. Meanwhile, I'd probably been in an emergency room getting my wrists stitched up.

I felt a wrench of jealousy. Lloyd had helped Francois when he needed it most. He'd done a slick sly and saved a baby girl from an evil bastard. Lloyd had been the hero. I hated that.

Iva filled another water glass and offered it to me.

"You want this?"

I shook my head.

"I'm okay," I lied. "Better finish the story."

She looked at the pictures of Circe on the wall.

"I was in that motel room for two days. Francois called a couple of times to ask more questions. I had this idea that he'd be going in himself with a team. A magic squad. All of them wearing Harry Potter's Cloak of Invisibility. It was the worst two days of my life. And then, he knocked on the door and he was there with Circe."

She started crying, tried to talk, couldn't. I waited a minute. She got her breath back and started again.

"Francois said Crispin would be coming for me. He said I needed to come back to L.A., where he could protect me and Circe. I was like, Fuck that. I blamed him, you know. I'd never have caught Crispin's eye if I hadn't been stewed in Francois's magic in the first place. I was taking Circe away to someplace brand-new. I wanted to get all that mojo crap off of her. But he was right, Crispin would come after us. I thought about calling the cops, some kind of anonymous tip about the compound. There were illegal guns up there, and I wasn't the only underage kid having sex with Crispin. But those people, they'd been my family for two years, and I didn't want them to get hurt. I just wanted to run. Francois gave me money and a car. I told him not to try to find me. I made him promise to leave us alone. I think he knew that his best chance to ever see me again was to leave us be. I was so scared. I didn't really believe I could get away from Crispin, but I had to try. Four days later we were in Alabama, running, heading for the tip of Florida. The farthest away I could think of. That's when I saw the news reports. *Mass suicide at cult compound in Montana*."

She pressed the heels of her hands into her eyes.

"I felt so. Fuck. So relieved."

She took her hands away.

"Once Circe was gone, things must have gotten unstable there. I think Crispin probably told everyone it was a sign or something? It was time to do the ritual, the cycle repeating, the gyre of life. Drink the libation and jump in the Chasm. He'd be last. But of course he wouldn't jump. He'd stay to, whatever, collect the magic from them and then run away. But he didn't do that. He killed himself."

She wiped a few last tears from her eyes.

"They had burned everything first. The compound was ashes. That's how the bodies were found. Some folks out riding near the compound saw the smoke plume. Fire crew went up, but there was nothing to do except wet the embers. Took a while for a search party to get organized. Dogs smelled the Chasm. The bodies down there. It took time to ID everyone. I waited and waited, and when they said that Crispin was among the dead, I broke down. Pure relief."

She opened her hands and stared into them as if they were full of an incredible gift she never expected to receive. Then she closed her hands and looked at me.

"Do you remember this? When it was on the news?"

I remembered a bit. The usual swirl of tabloid fascination that surround cult deaths. But there had been no standoff with the law, and no survivors to tell the tale or explain their actions. I recalled it as being a bit of a mystery. Who were these people and what radical beliefs had driven them to this sad end? But I'd had no reason to think about it myself. And the world had seen more than enough misery in that last fourteen years to make this little story fade from popular memory.

I tipped my head.

"I don't remember much."

She nodded.

"No one really knew we were a cult. Out there, off the grid in Montana, everyone minded their own business. We hunted and fished and grew our own food and had septic and propane. We were like a lot of people up there. Some maybe knew it was religious, but they didn't know what the religion was. At the end, no one was left alive to talk about Demon. And no one knew who or how many people had been in the cult. Not for sure. So no one knew I'd run away, no one knew to look for another girl and a baby in that hole. I wasn't missed. I barely existed. I got exactly what I wanted. Clean start for me and Circe. No identity at all. We'd be new people, get away from the shit that had been put onto us by Francois and Crispin. I don't know what I thought we'd do. How we'd live. For a while we bounced around. It wasn't good. I had a friend here, from high school. I got in touch with her, told her what had happened, without the magic. She was at community college, living with friends, but they partied too much and she wanted to study for nursing school. So I came here. Sunland. I was able to become me again. I got a copy of my birth certificate. I got work here waitressing. Got some assistance for being a single mom, put Circe in preschool. Took night classes in web design. I wanted a job that would pay well and that I could do at home, freelance. It all worked out better than I could have expected. I told Circe I got pregnant when I was a teenager. The dad was some kid who didn't want to have a baby. I told her my dad kicked me out. I told her we were all we had. I learned coding, got good at it. I make a nice living. Out in the foothills, it's a little like Montana. People mind their own. I got lucky in a lot of ways."

I could imagine that. Mojo twists tricky around a life. The stuff Francois had put around her had been warped when it got tangled in Crispin's junk. Once Iva was on her own, the charms on her might have had a chance to smooth her path for once. Or it may have just been that things went her way because they went her way. Did it matter?

She spread her arms, taking in the room, the house, the land around.

"I got us this place. Secured it. Dug in. Felt safe."

She stopped talking, looked over her shoulder. Like she thought something might be there. There was one more shoe to drop. I knew that. Something was missing. Because there we were at the kitchen table, with cameras and alarms and guns. There had to be a reason. She knew what I was waiting for.

"They were one short," she said. "When they pulled the bodies from the Chasm and they counted them all up, there were twenty-three. We were seventeen when I got to the compound, more came in, and we were twenty-six at the end, counting me and Circe. There should have been twenty-four dead. No one but me knew that. Everything had burned. No bunks to count, nothing like that.

"They didn't show pictures of the corpses on TV, you know. They'd poisoned themselves and jumped down an old mine shaft and sat in there for days. IDs were hard to make. The police and whatever, they tracked reported runaways and missing persons. Used fingerprints and DNA. People who had family members who had disappeared into cults could call a hotline. Some IDs came quick, some took years. I followed it all. Once it was tallied, once I could sort out the ones they knew for sure and the ones they didn't, I could figure out who was missing. It was Crispin's son. Circe's half brother. The one

who'd been declared Demon's vessel until Circe was born and
displaced him. He was missing. He disappeared like we did. I
guess I mostly hoped he was in that mine shaft and they missed
finding him. The more time passed, the more that seemed
likely. That or he couldn't figure out how to live in the world
by himself. Cult kid, how would he survive alone? I convinced
myself he was dead. I didn't think about him when Circe disappeared. I willfully did not think about him. *Not that,* I told
myself. That was impossible. But now you tell me that Circe
must have someone influencing her, using her. And I can only
think about him. That boy. He was just a little younger than me.
Eleven or twelve when I got to the compound. His father used
me, and now *he* might be using Circe. But I don't know what to
do about it. I don't know where he is or how to find him. I don't
know anything. I'm lost. Circe is lost and I can't help her. I'm
frozen. I hate it. I hate this."

There was a question I had to ask.

"When you told me Circe was doing theater, you also mentioned games."

Iva looked blank, no idea what I was getting at.

"Okay?"

"You know anything about that?"

She half laughed.

"The games are like weeklong fads. Everyone plays the same
thing for a few days and then it disappears."

"Recently."

"A fantasy game. Role-playing? She doesn't answer questions.
What's that you're playing? A game, Mom. Why? Is this like theater? Do you people mess with online gaming?"

"No. The internet traps mojo. That kind of gaming isn't a
thing in the racket. But. Um. I just. I don't have a, a kid. So I
don't understand some things. What a parent knows about their
kids and what they don't know. Is it easy to miss big things?"

She had no idea where I was going. I barely knew where I was going.

She frowned.

"Basically, you go from knowing what their poo feels like in your hand, to living with a stranger who keeps secrets from you. What is this about, gaming and your lack of parenting experience?"

I was dizzy. It was that light-headedness you get when you are close to the thing you most want. You can feel success at your fingertips. There may be work left to do, but you sense victory at hand.

"Gaming, Iva. Ignore the parenting thing. It's all about the game Circe plays. I know. The boy, brother, Crispin's son. I know where he is."

Her hand flinched toward the shotgun on the chair next to her.

"Where?"

"No, I don't know exactly where, but I can find out. I know the people who will know. I know who he is. I know what he's doing. I know why he wants Circe and I know that he has to have her alive. He won't hurt her. There's time. I got it. I got this!"

Iva's fingers curled tight, tendons bulging. She was looking to dig them into something fleshy.

"Where do we go? Where is he?"

"Iva, this is going to suck. What I tell you next. The game that Circe has been playing. It's called *Gyre*."

Her fingers clutched, twitched open, closed.

"What? So what? What?"

She got it and didn't get it. Her brain was trying to skip over what it knew.

"*Gyre* what?"

"It's a fantasy world. A whole thing, a society. A game about a world with a city at its center called Gyre. And in the middle of Gyre is a hole called the Chasm. And at the bottom of the hole is Demon."

Her hands opened, fingers bent far back, like she wanted to let go of everything and fly away.

"Oh. I see. Yes. I see." She closed her eyes. "Carpenter. That's his name. Circe's half brother. Carpenter. A game. He turned it into a game. What the fuck?"

"Crispin's group, the cult, did it have a name?"

She shook her head.

"No one from outside ever knew it. It was sacred. No one outside the compound ever knew any of our beliefs."

"What was the name?"

Her mouth started to shape it, stopped.

"I've never said it out loud. I wasn't allowed to back then. And after it was over, I never wanted to. It feels like calling out to something."

"I think I can say it for you."

"No! Don't do that. I can tell you. Harrow was our name. We were Harrow together. Until we weren't anymore."

TWENTY-ONE

CIRCE was a curiosity.

It had started with Francois when he set out to turn Iva's hair into a curiosity. That father and daughter ritual, shaped by love and resentment, directed the mojo they produced into Iva, but it was contentious stuff. Like a teenager, it was chaotic potential, still unresolved when Iva became pregnant. All that unresolved mojo Iva was carrying, it would have found a focus in her womb. Then Crispin coursed all the emotion and religious feeling produced by his followers into his daughter, using her as a repository.

It didn't end there.

When Circe was snatched by Lloyd, everything the Harrow felt about her and the loss of her, it coursed to her. When Crispin led them to their Chasm, everything they felt, all the accumulated emotions and the mojo of their lives, it was guided back to Circe by the course he'd created. When Crispin decided to die, his own undoubtedly extravagant supply of mojo flowed toward his daughter. When the bodies were discovered, when the news broke and a nation's fascination was briefly directed to this mystery, when the families of the dead were informed of their losses; it all got caught and carried on the strongest course that related to those feelings, a stream that led to a reservoir. Circe.

It was still happening.

The global gamers who were decanting themselves into a

fantasy digital world of Gyre and the Chasm and Demon and Harrow, what those players felt for the game, the potency that bled out into the real world: That mojo wasn't all going into the internet to be lost forever. Some of it was being drawn by the course Crispin had cut years ago, pulled into that stream, joining a torrent, filling Circe.

I wondered if he'd known what he was doing, Carpenter, the half brother, when he created the game *Gyre*. Did he build it to generate mojo? Did he have a plan for it? He must have. The real question was whether he knew that the mojo from the game would course to his sister. Had he always planned to kidnap her, or had he realized what was happening and grabbed her out of necessity? And what exactly did he plan to do with all that mojo?

My best guess, based on how that *Gyre* mojo had felt when it had grazed me earlier in the night, was that his plan involved mass suicide. Carpenter turns his dad's cult into a game, which becomes a source of mojo, which is coursed toward a culmination of the religion he grew up in and thought he would lead, until his sister was born. He had once been Demon's avatar, destined to embody her, and now he intended to reassume his role by creating a new major course that would pull people toward mass suicide.

It made sense. I mean, it made no sense at all, utterly mad, but it totally made perfect sense. Everything plugging into everything else. It was all connected.

I asked Iva to take me to Circe's room, and as carefully as I could manage it, I explained everything.

"That is total batshit," she said.

I spread my arms, floated them as if on the current of mojo in the room.

"Do you not feel that?"

She shook her head.

"I don't mean that I don't believe you, I mean that it is batshit crazy. He's batshit, Carpenter. He's insane. Obviously. Okay, I believe you. Now what? You said you can find out where Carpenter is. Do that."

I clapped my hands, rubbed them together, turned myself in a slow circle, taking in the details of Circe's walls. A mastermind marshaling his resources and concocting his perfect plan. Except I had no plan. My understanding was sprinting way ahead of my capabilities. I needed to focus on one simple task, one element, something that I could use to begin to figure out exactly how to save Circe and how to walk away with as much of this tidal wave of mojo as I possibly could. Also, I had to find my reflection and shatter it. Wait. My reflection. How did it fit in?

Something squeezed my heart. Not in a figurative sense.

I made a noise somewhere between a groan and a scream. Pain launched an attack on my body, spearheads shooting from the dead center of my chest. One lanced down my left arm, one ran its point directly up into my brain and through the top of my skull, one made some impossible bends that corkscrewed through my sinuses and out of my nose. The pain overcame me and I collapsed. I couldn't breathe. My mouth was wide open and my tongue was jutting and my eyes were rolling around and trying to pop clean out of their sockets.

It went on and on and on and on and on for about maybe three seconds.

Eternity.

Then it stopped and somehow it hadn't killed me. My body unclenched itself and I recovered the ability to breathe. Although it took a few attempts for me to remember how to do that without swallowing my tongue.

Iva hadn't had time to do anything but watch me be in agony. Now she edged over and looked down at me.

"Are you?" she asked. Apparently uncertain about what else she wanted to know.

I wrapped my arms around my chest, hoping it wouldn't hurt me again.

"I have to go right now," I said, and started trying to get off the floor. I failed, and held out a hand toward Iva. "Little help?"

She didn't seem to love the idea of touching me, but got past her aversion, took my hand, and helped me to my feet.

"Are you . . . ?" she asked again. "Okay?"

I shook my head.

"No, I'm not. A creep has my heart and he's sending me a message that I better go see him right now or he's going to eat it."

"Eat your heart?"

"Not literally, but close enough so that it will be awful and I'll die."

"So he doesn't actually have your heart."

"No, that part is literal. He has my heart."

She was still holding my hand, but now she let it go and took a step away from me. I couldn't blame her. No one should hold hands with a guy without a heart. We are unreliable by nature.

"I gotta go," I said.

Iva shook her head.

"What do I do if you die? How do I find Circe?"

"I'm not gonna die," I said, totally unsure if it was the truth. "I'm not gonna die and I will be back."

Iva came close to me again.

"I think promises mean less than shit in your world."

I didn't say anything. Because, I mean, she wasn't entirely wrong.

She came closer still, very.

"But you promise me anyway. Look me in the eyes and promise me you're going to find Circe and bring her home."

I looked her in the eyes and mentally crossed my fingers.

The girl, Sid, I heard Abigail whisper to me. *Remember the girl.*

I uncrossed my imaginary fingers.

"I am going to find Circe and I am going to bring her home. I promise."

Iva searched my eyes for something that I doubted she could find there. Honesty, reliability, worthiness. But she seemed to find enough of a trace of it to give her some kind of assurance that I could be, I don't know, trusted?

She broke eye contact and gave me a little space.

"I'll walk you to the door."

I pointed at the mirror over Circe's bed.

"No, Iva. I have to go by the express route."

She made a face.

"I hate seeing that stuff."

"Turn around?"

"No. I'll still feel it. Go. Save your. Heart. And then save my daughter."

She didn't look at me again. Just turned away and walked out of the room and closed the door behind her, leaving me alone.

I gathered myself. It didn't matter that I'd been through this mirror that same day, and that my reflection had also been through it; there was enough mojo in the room to turn it into a six-lane sly freeway. I took a last look around. I was thinking bad stuff.

But my options were few.

Somehow Lloyd had gotten Minerva's safe open and now he had my heart in his hands. If he wanted me dead, I'd be dead. What he wanted was me in front of him, so he'd given it a squeeze to make sure I knew who was in charge. It could be that the only reason he wanted to see me was so he could watch me die with his own beady eyes. Whatever his intentions, I was going to have to prove to him that I was worth more to him alive than the brief moment of pleasure he'd receive by sucking away my life's mojo, mortifying me, and playing croquet with my heart.

Fast talk was not going to work. I wouldn't be sucker-punching his manikins and running for it. The only thing that might keep me alive was if I had something to bargain with. Something to trade. And what I had was exactly zilch.

TWENTY-TWO

MINERVA had a back door in the storage room behind his shop.

It was a way for the slys he did business with to drop in unannounced. But even when you deal regularly with slys, you want to take precautions regarding how freely you let them come and go in your place of business. Accordingly, the back-door mirror into Minerva's storeroom was mounted at floor level inside a locked closet with a lowered ceiling. You had to crawl out of it, press a buzzer, and wait there on your hands and knees until someone let you out. It was not a popular point of entry.

I was expected when I crawled through on this occasion, so I was spared waiting in indignity for someone to answer the buzzer. Instead, Dak and Neil grabbed me by my hair before I had quite crawled out of the mirror and dragged me from the closet into the storeroom where Minerva had kept the overstock from his storefront before he was killed with the box cutter that Lloyd was now waving in my face.

It was crusted with dry blood, and several of the little sectional blades must have snapped off inside Minerva's neck, but it still had more than enough of them to be able to do a similar job on me. Lloyd was emphasizing this point by ratcheting the remaining blades up and down and feinting at my eyes.

"I still got some razors for you, Sid! See? See?" he said, and jabbed me, sending the tip of the cutter into my face an inch below my eye, deep enough for me to feel it rake my cheekbone.

I gave a shriek that must have been satisfying enough for him to give Dak and Neil a signal to let me go. I guess I was giddy with pain and terror because otherwise I can't explain why I didn't immediately start begging for my life. Instead I got all smart-alecky.

"Yes, you have more knife left, Lloyd. I see it. Have a party, you creep. All praise clever Lloyd and his bloody stump of box cutter. He killed once with it, and he can kill again. Mighty is he."

He kicked me in the balls. Because Lloyd. I curled up on the floor like guys do.

"Bring him over here," he said to Dak, who took a double handful of my hair and wrenched me across the floor to a little display they had arranged.

"Take a look, Sidney." I was still in fetal mode so he had to jam the toe of his boot under my chin to lever it away from my chest and force me to look at what he had set up for my amusement.

It was my heart, in its jar fortunately, balanced precariously on one pan of an old-fashioned set of scales that looked as though Justice were meant to carry them, but Justice was not around. The counterbalancing pan of the scale was loaded with a tall stack of VHS cartridges. I could see by the titles that these were undesirable overstock. *Vision Quest, Cobra, Kiss of the Vampire*—those were some of the movies in whose balance my life was being held.

Lloyd tapped the end of the box at the top of the pile, causing it to slide an inch, imparting the slightest wobble to the scales.

"You like movies, Sidney? How about *Red Sonya*? Here, I'll get it off the shelf for you." He gave the box another tap, harder, and it slid off the pile. The wobble of the scales increased alarmingly.

"Lloyd," I said. I had to wring the word from my throat because it was still clenched around my testicles where they had lodged after he kicked them.

"Speak up, Sid. I can't hear you. If I can't hear you, how do I know if you're begging for your life? If you're not begging for your life, how can I enjoy this?"

My heart was pounding in its jar. It was going to shake itself off the scale. I was going to kill myself. Absurdly, surrealistically, I was in danger of scaring myself to death.

Lloyd inspected my thudding heart.

"Are you going to have a heart attack? That would be the best and the worst. Don't do it, don't die. I'm gonna rake off your mojo first. Then I'm giving your heart to Neil as a gift because you fucked up his face."

Neil shook his head, took a step back from the scale and my heart.

"I don't want anything to do with that, man. I'll beat the guy up, but I'm not messing with someone's heart."

Dak raised his hand.

"Me, either. I'm not into it."

Lloyd looked like he wished he had a hammer.

"You two are the weakest pair of manikins I've ever seen."

Dak had his hands on his hips.

"It's not about who's tough or not. That heart shit is gross."

This dispute between employer and employees had given me a chance to clear my nuts from my throat so that I could get a few words out.

"Lloyd, hey, you really don't want to mess with my heart. That would be bad for business."

He was still glaring at his sidekicks.

"Shut up, Sid."

I didn't shut up.

"You got Minerva's safe open. I don't know how you did it so quickly, but bravo. You now have one of the most valuable sets of assets in the racket. A couple dozen hearts from top slys. Banked with Minerva because he was utterly reliable. Most of these slys will probably be happy to continue doing business here. That is as long as they know that new management isn't the kind of creep who starts pulling hearts from his lockup and playing games with them."

"Fuck you," said Lloyd, flicking *Ladyhawke* off the stack of tapes. It hit the floor, skidded, and slid out of its cardboard sleeve. The jar slipped a few millimeters over the edge of the pan. It stayed there, my heart swinging in an unstable parabola.

"I got into the safe because I know the combination, asshole. Hillary didn't want to do anything when he could have someone else do it for him. *Open the safe, Lloyd. Take a shit for me, Lloyd.* Reliable? He was slack. Him and his useless eighties sideline. Let me tell you about reliability. I'm bringing in an auspicer to pull the mojo from all this eighties shit so I can re-course the walls around this place, seal up any cracks. Then I'll close the storefront and focus entirely on banking. Security is going to be tighter than ever. There won't be a sly anywhere who won't want to bank with me. As for you, everyone knows you're a useless fuckup. No one gives a shit what happens to your heart."

He gently flicked the bottom tape of the stack. *Xanadu.*

"You got a counterargument for me, Sid?"

He cocked his finger, ready to send *Xanadu* flying.

Did I have a case to make regarding the relative value of my heart? No, I did not. I'd given it scant regard myself for thirty years. Hadn't I been tempting this fate every day since Sue pulled my heart out of me and dumped it in that jar? Not just a miserable death wish, but also a pathetic death hope. After all, I knew magic was real and the universe was probably an illusion. Dead was dead and resurrection was impossible even with mojo, but that didn't mean death was the end. I'd never been able to send myself into that undiscovered country to take a look and see who might be there, but that didn't mean I didn't wonder about it. Let my heart go and I might find myself somewhere else. Abigail with me.

It was possible. It was really and truly possible.

And Lloyd was right. No one would care.

He gave *Xanadu* another tap. The scales swung.

"Last chance to beg for your life, Sid," he whispered.

Stay quiet, and make an end of it all. That was the easy thing to do. But no. I'd made a promise.

"I brought you a payment," I said. "Top stuff. Very, very clean."

He didn't look at me, focused on edging the tape another millimeter.

"Where is this payment?"

"I dropped it in the closet when your manikins grabbed me."

"Dak, take a look."

Dak bent, reached into the little closet with the mirror inside it, found what I'd brought, looked at it. "It's a record," he said, "Sinéad O'Connor. *The Lion and the Cobra.*" He shook his head. "I don't know this one."

Lloyd's desire to knock *Xanadu* off the scale was palpable.

"It's from after your time, Dak." He chewed his lip. "Fuck," he said. "Fuck," he said again. Because once was apparently not enough to express whatever frustration he was feeling.

He put out his hand to take the album from Dak.

"If this is bullshit, Sid, I am going to do something mean."

He yanked his compass from a sheath on his belt, popped the cover, and glared as the needle did as I knew it would, shining bright and steady and strong, pointing directly at the cover of Circe's favorite album.

Would Iva have let me take the album if I'd tried to explain my need? Perhaps. I don't know. But I'm a thief. It was easier to just steal the thing once she'd left me alone in Circe's room. I'd make up for it later. I mean, if I lived, I'd make up for a lot of things later. Once Iva had her daughter back, I didn't imagine that she'd be sweating a stolen record. No harm, no foul. But I still felt pretty cruddy about the whole thing.

Lloyd snapped his compass closed. He was frowning, looking

from me to the album and back again. He nodded at Dak and Neil.

"Stand him up."

The manikins grabbed me from either side and hauled me to my feet.

"Hillary knew it was worth letting me slide on my rent," I said. "I always come through with something good sooner or later."

Lloyd laughed, a low honk that I'd never heard before. I didn't like the sound of it.

"Is that why he kept you around, Sid? You dumb shit. You don't know anything."

"Okay, I'm dumb. But that album is still prime."

He fanned himself with the album.

"It's hot, for sure. Someone's been loving on it hard. And it reminds me of something."

He pulled my jacket open, revealing my T-shirt, same picture as the album cover in his hand.

"Some kind of coincidence, Sid? Or you playing a game on me?"

He pulled his compass out again, popped the cover. It hummed as he held it close to my Sinéad O'Connor T-shirt. He took a step back and moved the compass, holding it between my shirt and the album. The hum grew, as did the glow shining up from the compass onto Lloyd's face as a nasty smile grew there.

"You holding out on me? Got a matched pair of curiosities here. You gonna slip me the album, then use the shirt's mojo to home in on where I lock it up so you can steal it back? I mean, it's not a bad play, but it only works if you're alive."

I was looking at the glow coming off his compass.

"No, they're not a pair. Solid curiosities, both of them. But it's a coincidence, the Sinéad O'Connor thing. No real connection."

He closed his compass.

"Bullshit. That shirt and that record go together."

He snapped his fingers at Dak and Neil.

"Get it off him."

I'd always sworn that if anyone tried to take that shirt, I'd do something appalling to them. But my options for appalling actions were currently limited. Lloyd being Lloyd, he'd forgotten that the last time we were together I'd had a gun. I still had it. But the manikins were on either side of me and Lloyd was right next to my heart. The gun felt like a bad call in the circumstances. I needed to get out of there, and it seemed like Lloyd was willing to entertain the idea of letting me go. I just had to give him my most precious possession. Life sometimes. I mean, really.

Dak and Neil started to jerk the jacket down my arms.

"You'll rip the shirt. Let me take it off!"

They looked at Lloyd and he shrugged.

"I never knew you cared about anything that much."

I took off my jacket, started to lift the hem of the shirt.

"This is a deal, yeah? You get the album and my shirt and you let me go and stop messing with my heart."

"Take off the shirt, Sid. Then maybe we can talk."

I took off the shirt. It felt like peeling my skin. He put out a hand. I folded the shirt, placed it in his hand. How much laundering to make it clean after that? He gave it and the album to Dak.

"Lock 'em up."

Dak took my shirt and Circe's album and left the storeroom. I bent and picked up my jacket and put it on, buttoning it over my bare, scarred chest.

"So it's a deal, yeah?"

Lloyd pointed at my heart.

"I'm gonna have an indenture drafted, Sid. I want your services for five years. Exclusive."

"I don't have time to stick around to sign that."

"Okay. Ten years. You come back tomorrow to sign. That or I get butterfingers with your heart. Agreed?"

Indentured to Lloyd. Yeah, there are fates worse than death. Did I have options in that moment? I did not.

"Agreed."

He honked that awful laugh again.

"I'm gonna make your existence miserable. It's gonna be awesome how awful I'm gonna treat you. Just the absolute best. Oh, man. I'm gonna have you both."

More honks of creepy joy.

"You are such a fucking idiot. Get out of here, idiot. But when I call, you come running."

"I don't have a phone."

He jerked his chin at Neil. "Go get him Hillary's old phone. He'll love that."

So, yeah, at least I got a phone out of the deal.

TWENTY-THREE

I EXITED TO THE ALLEY behind the storeroom, walked up to Sunset, and discovered that the protest traffic from downtown had backed up all the way to the Strip.

It felt like a street festival. Friday night. The old clubs. Rainbow, Whisky, Viper, Roxy. Traffic jammed tight. Protest caravans chugging toward downtown. Revelers from the Valley, Inland Empire, OC, forcing their way west. Everyone looking to abandon their cars. Parking in loading zones, in front of hydrants, bus stops, cramming the curbs on the restricted residential side streets. People walking because it was faster than driving. Buzzing excitement. It didn't feel like Armageddon, it felt like anticipation. Phones out, shooting the scene. It was like a blackout or an earthquake. Without the riots or the falling buildings. People felt that something was happening. Something different. They didn't know what it was, but I knew. I sort of knew, didn't I?

Where was I? What did I have? What did I know? What had I promised? Who was looking for me? What had I lost? What was I trying to find? It all swirled for a moment as I tried to grab on to one thought that could guide me.

Carpenter.

I needed to find Circe's half brother, Carpenter. The only living person besides Iva who knew anything about the Harrow cult's mythology. The only one who could have turned it into a giant online ritual masquerading as a game. I had nothing to trade for information like that. The only thing I had was leverage. I'd been sold out by someone I thought I could trust. All I could do about it was turn a table and hope for the best.

I hefted Minerva's old phone. It required considerable hefting. It was, of course, an eighties-era mobile. A black plastic brick with an antenna. A Motorola X-something with its guts removed and replaced with the essentials of a simple slab phone that was compliant with current cell standards. Minerva hadn't carried the thing around himself—he'd kept it on his desk for laughs. It was huge and inconvenient, but it was prepaid.

One of the benefits of never having owned a cellphone myself is that I remember phone numbers. I dialed, it rang for a long time, and then Klarnacht picked up.

"Who is this?"

"It's Sid."

Silence.

"You there, Klarnacht?"

"I'm here. Your caller ID says Marty McFly."

"I'm using Minerva's novelty phone. He's obsessed with *Back to the Future*."

"You're with Minerva?"

"Were you expecting a call from Minerva?"

"I'm not expecting any calls, Sid. I mean, I had to stop time again to pick up. I thought it was an emergency or something."

"Minerva is dead."

Silence again.

"Ask you a question, Klarnacht?"

"I got to get back to the game, man. We're in the middle of a thing."

"The orcs will wait. I wanted to ask what Minerva was going to give you for selling me out."

Silence. I filled it again.

"I asked about synchronicity before. About why you mentioned it when I showed up? You said *people* were looking for me. Plural. But when I asked who, you only mentioned Shingles."

"Don't make a thing out of this, Sid."

"All that phone fiddling you were doing while we talked. You were bargaining with Hillary Minerva."

"I barely know the guy, man."

"Won't be getting to know him any better now. Your deal died with him."

"Fuck. Fuck."

"Pretty important, I guess, whatever he promised you. It'd have to be. I mean, you and me, we're not tight or anything, but you're known as a trustworthy guy. I don't think you'd risk that rep unless it was for a major payoff."

"I don't need payoffs. I told you, I don't know what to do with the mojo I have."

"Exactly my point. Why would you need extra mojo from Minerva? You wouldn't. Unless something is sucking your mojo away."

"Listen, Sid."

I did not listen. I kept talking.

"If only I knew of something you might be doing that could be draining away your mojo. Then I would know why you sold me out to Minerva."

"Just shut up and listen."

"You're still playing *Gyre*, Klarnacht. You are eyeballs deep in that mojo vacuum. It is sucking you dry, and once you're empty, I'm guessing it will start to drain the campaign and Bob and the others. No heaps of dead orcs will stop that."

Silence. I didn't need to fill it. It was eloquent enough on its own.

I knew something was wrong about what I'd felt when the *Gyre* course grazed me outside Bob's mom's house. Just talking about it shouldn't have created that intense of a connection. If the course was that strong, that easily drawn by casual invocation, everyone in the racket would know about it. Internet game or not. It only made sense if the course was running strong nearby. If someone was engaged with it. It was obvious in hindsight. Klarnacht had never quit playing *Gyre*. He must be in deep. Deep enough that the mojo from the D&D campaign was in danger of being swept into the course.

He broke the silence first.

"It just. It means so much to me. I feel like I'm doing something real. I know it's pretend. I know it's taking something from me. But in there I feel like I matter. I feel like I make a difference. Out here, there's nothing out here, Sid. I want to stop. I think about it all the time. But I'm afraid I'll feel even worse. So I keep going. Demon is rising."

Hiding from reality was my thing, so I felt for the guy. But I still needed what I needed.

"I want to meet the creator of *Gyre*."

"Sid, I mean. I can't. I mean. I don't know."

"You told me there's a way to meet the guy. Don't try to tell me now that you haven't figured it out. You're one of the supreme gamers in the world, man. And that *Gyre* course is running right alongside you. You're into that thing as deep as can be. You know where the guy is. I need to meet him. Tonight."

"I found him, yes, but in *Gyre*. I don't know where he really lives."

"You said he's local. Get me an address."

"It doesn't work like that. To find the guy, the creator of *Gyre*, you go on a quest. It's really fucking hard. Every step. Every text you find and have to translate, all the puzzles you solve, your successful interactions with characters. All of it is a ritual. All of it binds you closer and closer to the course you felt when we were talking. But if you take the final step, translate that last text and actually meet him. I mean, people go into that house, his house, and they don't come out, Sid. I mean, I think I'm the only one to find him and not go inside."

He was all over the place, spilling it in a rush that I couldn't follow.

"Slow down. Explain all that to me."

"The quest is to find a fragment of the Ruination Crown. Demon's crown from another age. Broken and lost. Dorky dork dork. Right? Yeah. Each fragment has two pieces of information. A special kind of QR code and a unique piece of text. Each fragment is different. Scan the code and you get the location of the creator. The real location, I mean. When you go, you show the code and recite the text and you're admitted."

"You get to meet the guy for real?"

"I think so. But I can't be totally sure because everyone I know of who has gone to meet *Gyre*'s creator has disappeared."

"Disappeared to what extent?"

"Entirely. Characters erased as if they never existed. But also, the same for the real people."

I laughed. Not amused, more like gut-punched. One little pathetic, scared laugh.

"These people, Sid, the ones who have completed the quest, they're fanatics. If they've been disappeared, they were probably willing. They're so far inside *Gyre*, this guy would be almost a god for them."

"*Almost* a god?"

"Demon is their true god. The creator of *Gyre* is more like her instrument on Earth. These people, seekers, they'll do anything to serve her through him. You still want to know how to find this guy?"

"I do."

"The QR code is encrypted so that it can't be sent or copied. Best I can do is give you the address and teach you the song."

"What song? You said I had to recite a text."

"Sing a song. Same thing."

"I can't sing."

"It doesn't have to be pretty."

"No, I mean I cannot sing. Physically."

"I wouldn't worry about it. You show up without the code, it doesn't matter how you sing, I doubt they'll let you meet him. What they will do with you, I don't know."

"Don't worry about me, I have a magic word to get in."

"I'll teach you the song, then."

Klarnacht sang me a song from *Gyre*. It wasn't long. And as strange as it was, I didn't find it hard to memorize. Darkness encroached as he sang. The course of *Gyre* drawn by one of its believers singing in its language. Ritual and intent. Each of these interactions bound me closer to the course. I tried not to think about that.

"You want to sing it back to me?" he asked when he was done.

I didn't have any idea what would happen to me if I tried to sing anything at all. Better to save it for the show. Whatever that turned out to be.

"This guy, Sid. Do you think he really wants to get rid of all the mojo in the world?"

I didn't know what I thought.

"Get rid of it or use it to do something terrible," I said.

"I told you Demon is rising in *Gyre*. Whatever he wants to do, it's happening tonight. You gonna stop him?"

"I guess that's what I'm maybe trying to do. I don't know for sure, man. But I better go and do it."

"Sorry I sold you out to Minerva."

"It happens."

We hung up.

He'd given me the address. I should have been surprised about where it was, but I wasn't. I mean, everything was connected. So discovering that this god on Earth, Circe's half brother, was to be found about a mile from where I was standing seemed perfectly in keeping with how reality was functioning on that particular night.

He had a castle in Beverly Hills. I could walk there in twenty minutes.

TWENTY-FOUR

GREYSTONE MANSION was a sprawling twelve-acre estate built by Ned Doheny for his wife Lucy.

In 1929, five months after they moved in, Ned was shot and killed by his aide, Hugh Plunkett, who then shot himself. No wonder Carpenter bought the place from the city of Beverly Hills. Murder-suicide was perfectly on-brand for him.

Like all the residences in the neighborhood, the Greystone was hidden by walls and landscaping. All I could see of it from the street were the terra-cotta tips of chimney pots. There was an iron gate and a stone gatehouse at Doheny and Loma Vista. It looked like the kind of place Sherlock Holmes would be called to in the middle of the night, except that instead of being cold and foggy, it was balmy and humid.

At the foot of the driveway I took out my compass. The needle made an audible pop as it resolved, gave the hum of a plucked bowstring, and pointed at the chimney pots, the tip lancing beyond the rim of the compass as if seeking to launch itself. Not the read I'd expected. This close to the nexus of the bad guy's evil scheme, I'd thought the compass wouldn't know where to point. I assumed Carpenter would have courses running every which way. Some for protection, some for luck, some to spread the incipient despair that was making people suicidal, and a scatter of background radiation coming off the collection of curiosities I assumed he'd have stockpiled. This read was zeroed in, like all Carpenter's mojo was coursed into a single curiosity.

If I was right, if Circe was a curiosity herself, my compass might be reading her. I thought about dungeons and oubliettes, dank places of forgetting. I thought about Circe discovering the game *Gyre*. Iva believed that the girl didn't have any conscious memory of her father or of the Harrow cult. How much does anyone really remember about their lives before they were two? But maybe Circe hadn't been so ignorant. What if she'd had an inkling of her patrimony, and what if she'd used the internet to learn more? Once she started playing *Gyre,* she might have had an idea of who was behind it. Even if she didn't know about her half brother, she'd want to know more. I imagined her becoming a seeker, one of the obsessives trying to find the creator. I imagined her finding a piece of the Ruination Crown, taking it here, and disappearing. Carpenter might not have had to hire a sly to kidnap Circe; she might have delivered herself to him.

"This is private property," someone said to me from the darkness.

I looked around, but didn't see anyone.

"We have armed security in the neighborhood," the voice said.

It was coming from an intercom set into the stone wall a few feet away. A camera lens peered at me.

"I'd like to come inside," I said.

A light popped on next to the camera lens.

"Take off your sunglasses," the intercom said.

I took them off.

"You don't know me," I said.

"Do you have something to show me?" the intercom asked.

"I know a song."

"Let's hear it."

I started to recite the syllables Klarnacht had taught me, wrestling with pronunciation and the odd popping noises he'd made deep in his throat.

"You're supposed to sing it," the intercom said.

I hadn't sung a note since I sold my voice. I knew there would be a price to pay if I tried, but I didn't know how high it might be. Could be everything I had left. Whatever that was, and whatever it was worth, I wasn't ready to lose it.

"I can't do that."

"Goodbye."

"Wait," I said. "I'll try."

Once upon a time, opening my mouth to sing was as easy as breathing. Without effort, something beautiful would spill out of me. What would come out now? A lung? I looked for a way out of this test, but Circe was on the other side of that gate, and the only way I could open it was to do something impossible.

I began to sing the song of *Gyre*.

Gravel and razor blades and drain cleaner bubbled up my larynx. My tongue swelled to twice its size and my teeth bit it and my gums bled. My eardrums were lanced by venomed spines. My lips dried and split and blood ran down my chin. It went on and on. And every moment, I could feel the course of *Gyre* pulling close to me, drawing my depression to the surface, tugging at my own thin trickle of mojo. I couldn't hear the sounds I was making, I could only feel the pain they caused me.

Batter my body, I thought. *Cut me and kick me and break my bones. Just leave me my spirit. Don't drown me in despair again,* I silently begged.

It was leaving me; the glimmer and shine I'd taken from Circe's room was dimming. Bleak, gray, muddy nothing was crawling over my skin. There was no reason for this. No reason for anything. I spat out the last unintelligible lyrics of the song and three of my teeth came out with them.

"Thank you very much," I gasped. "There will be no encore."

"That was terrible," the intercom said.

I held up a finger to ask for a moment's grace, still recovering. My throat was unshredded. I'd not chewed my tongue to ribbons. There was no blood on my chin, I could hear just fine, and I had all my teeth. Depression licked my heels, but it was back at bay. I could see a reason to live.

"I'm out of practice," I explained to the intercom.

"You've never been to *Gyre*. How did you get this address? What do you want?"

"Let me in and I'll tell you."

"I'm calling armed security. They are very aggressive."

It was time to use my magic word.

"Circe," I said. "I'm here for Circe."

Hiss of intercom static.

"You better come inside then," the intercom told me, and the gate began to open.

I put my hand under my jacket and touched my scars and reminded myself that Abigail's shirt was gone. My touchstone. Shingles had coursed it for me long ago, secured that little bit of Abigail that clung to the warp and weft, directed the mojo into a modest charm of safety. It was the closest thing I'd had to armor. Dubious knight outside the villain's castle. I felt exposed. I felt unprepared. I felt inadequate. But also, bitterness filled me up.

This girl, Circe—why was she suddenly my problem? I didn't even know her. It was very clear right then that I was making a huge mistake. I shouldn't be there doing what I was doing. I should be going after her mojo. I was a thief with a thirst for blind vengeance. I should go steal as much of the mojo in Circe's bedroom as I could and then use it to find my reflection and drop an anvil on its face. But instead of doing what should come naturally to me, I'd traded away my last trace of Abigail and sold myself to the biggest creep in town, and now I was about to try to face down the insane architect of an online death cult, and a cadre of his most devoted followers.

Why?

The girl, Sid, remember the girl.

Abigail's voice in my head. But she had never said that. She couldn't have. She knew nothing about Circe. What had she really said to me?

I felt the presence of something impossibly huge. It eclipsed everything, its dimensions making it unknowable. It was somehow inside of me. I had no idea how I could contain something so vast. Big enough to blot out anything I'd ever want to see.

I knew what it was. It was always there. I had pretended that it wasn't. I knew why I cared about Circe. I knew why I kept hearing Abigail urging me on. But I didn't want to know. I didn't want to understand. I didn't want to remember the unforgettable. I took deep breaths and told myself none of it mattered. It was all in the past. It wasn't happening right then. I told myself I didn't care.

It was a lie. I cared. I cared. I cared.

The gate was open. I walked through it. Remembering.

The girl. Our girl. Our long-lost girl.

TWENTY-FIVE

ABIGAIL was pregnant when she was murdered.

I was in the bedroom one day, picking a new song from my guitar. The windows were open. When the breeze was onshore it would blow us the sound of the waves. They were whispering around the room that late afternoon, filling it with the hint of the rising tide. I had a gig that night, and then we'd be going to Munroe's party. We'd been going to the party ever since I'd had my debut and been invited up to the house to meet Munroe. Now, about a month later, we were regulars and I was Munroe's client.

Life was very good.

I was writing a song. Munroe wanted more songs. I sat on the bed, leaning into a pile of pillows shoved against the wall, and I wrote a song about just exactly that moment. Waves, pillows, sun lowering toward the horizon. Odd to think how at peace I was in the moment.

I heard a loud gasp. Shock.

I stopped plucking the strings of my guitar.

"Babe?" Abigail was in the bathroom. She didn't answer me. "You okay?"

"Yeah," she called. "Fine."

Something felt wrong. I got off the bed, bare feet, sand on the linoleum floors. There was always sand on the floors. The bathroom door was ajar. I pushed the door open. Abigail had her hands braced against the edge of the sink, staring down.

"You okay?"

She looked at me, stunned by something.

"I think I'm pregnant," she said.

There was a pee stick on the sink. She picked it up, showed me a blue stripe.

"What's that mean?" I said.

She picked up the pregnancy test instructions, held the stick against the picture of a positive test. Blue for pregnant. There were two more tests in the box. One at a time, she peed on both of them and we watched as blue lines appeared.

What's that mean? I'd asked her.

That was the best I could do when she told me she was pregnant. Silly manchild.

Neither of us said anything else until we had the three positive tests lined up on the sink. We stood side by side, looking at them. Abigail put her arms around me.

"We're having a baby," she said. Shock gone, replaced by something else. She was so happy. The wind shifted, pulled. The bathroom door swung shut behind us, the mirror on the back of it reflecting her happiness and my dismay. But we didn't see that. She leaned her head against my shoulder.

"You gonna write a song about this, superstar?"

"Undoubtedly," I said, and kissed the top of her head.

But I never did.

Who was the first person I told that I was going to be a dad? Munroe.

We were in her lounge late that night, just the two of us. Abigail had gone home from the party, driven by Francois. I'd stayed. There had been other people there when I came up the spiral stairs, but Munroe had sent them away.

"What's eating Sidney tonight?" Munroe asked, slipping behind the bar. "Come tell your secrets before they fester."

I'd sat on one of the barstools while she mixed a margarita for me. My gig that night had been flat. I'd been distracted. I was nineteen and I was going to be a dad. Here's what I knew about being a dad: Dads don't raise their children. If they're like my dad, they abandon their kids when they're born. If they're like the dads of a lot of the group-home kids, they hurt their children. I'd never had a single thought about being a dad myself. But I had known that Abigail wanted to be a mom.

I drank a couple of Munroe's margaritas and then I told her. I thought she'd drop me right there. Rock-star dad was not a concept that was likely to sell a ton of CDs.

"Yeah," I said, "so here's a funny thing. Abigail is having a baby."

Munroe's hands shot to her face, covered her mouth, and she let out a delighted squeal.

"Sidney!" She lunged across the bar and wrapped her arms around me, spilling my drink on us both. "That is fantastic. Congratulations. Oh, honey-doll sweetie. What amazing news. When? She's not showing at all. Is that why she went home? Is that why you're worried? Do not be worried. I am going to make sure you have exactly what you need. I know the most amazing baby doctor." She let me go and took my face between her hands. "This is going to be tremendous for you."

All I had been able to do when I got the news from Abigail was ask her, *What's that mean?* Munroe was ecstatic. Her enthusiasm for becoming *Auntie Munroe* was utter showbiz bull crap but somehow endearing. Even to Abigail.

"I guess mothering her clients isn't enough for her," Abigail said with a smile. She didn't mind Munroe's pushiness, not if it came with a doula to the stars and an extensive prenatal herbal nutrition program. As for my fears that becoming a dad would abort my infant career (the child that I really wanted), Munroe scoffed.

"Don't be dumb," she told me. "Young dad with your voice

and your hair, with Abigail holding your babe in arms in the wings? That, Sidney, will look hot as fuck."

Most fairy tales could only aspire to a happier ending.

Of course most fairy tales are bloody and grim.

Abigail was a little more than three months pregnant when I was recording the last track for my EP. She'd had a checkup that day. I didn't go. I'd been once, met the baby doctor. Once seemed like enough. I had songs to write, gigs to play, recording sessions. I mean, my career was more important than ever. My wife was having a baby. Once Munroe had assured me I was still going places, I'd become pretty okay with the idea. I imagined a version of being a dad where I got to introduce my kid to all my favorite music and teach them how to play guitar. A little buddy who I could be a super-cool role model for. I hoped they'd have my hair. I hadn't even remembered about the appointment that day. Abigail had been home for hours, and I hadn't asked the one thing that anyone would have asked. She sat on the bathroom sink while I got ready to go to the studio to record "Feel Like Dyin," waiting for me to remember, to ask her the question. We were flirting and teasing and I thought it was all good, and then she got testy with me, and I still didn't remember where she had been that day.

I think she let go of it then. I think she decided that I was the guy who she'd married, no better or worse. I think she decided that me asking wasn't important. What was important was for me to know what she had learned that day. So she whispered it in my ear while we were making out.

"It's a girl, Sid," Abigail said to me, "we're having a girl."

I'd forgotten that she was finding out if it was a boy or girl that day. I was shocked for a moment by this reminder of the reality of what was happening. The baby was no longer *it*, the baby was *her*. I was pierced by terror. An icy shiver that came up from my gut and forced words from my mouth.

"Are you sure?" I asked her.

I could have meant, *Are you sure it's a girl?* But she could tell by my tone what I was really asking. *Are you sure you want to have this baby?*

"Of course I'm sure," she said. "Sid, I want this baby."

I shook my head, instantly denying her understanding of my words.

"No," I said, "that's not what I meant. I want it, too. I mean, are you sure it's a girl?"

I smiled at the misunderstanding and wrapped her in my arms and looked at myself in the full-length mirror behind her. It saw me for what I was. It saw me as I thought, *Babies don't always get born.*

It was just a thought.

The baby might not come. I might not have to be a dad. Women miscarry all the time. It wasn't a wish. But it did make me hopeful to think it. Then that flash of hope soured and turned my stomach, and I looked away from my eyes in the mirror. But it had already seen me, and what I had hoped for. *It's a girl, Sid,* Abigail whispered in my ear, *we're having a girl.* And sometime later, while I was off recording and worrying about what being a father would do to me, my reflection, the product of all my vanity, came out of that mirror and drowned her and our baby.

Why had I been asking myself why I cared so much about Circe? Why was this young girl I'd never met getting under my skin? Why did I need to save her and return her to her mother? Why did I keep hearing Abigail tell me, *The girl, Sid, remember the girl?*

Now you know.

Now you can see me for what I really am.

TWENTY-SIX

I CROSSED THE GROUNDS of Greystone Mansion.

It occupied a high point, overlooking all it surveyed in traditional lordly fashion. Flood lamps faced away from the mansion, revealing anyone who approached while keeping the building itself in shadow and appropriately sinister. The driveway bent around the house, leading to a path and stairs that climbed to a veranda. A gallery of arched French doors glowed with cold flickers of bluish light that suggested an active poltergeist. There are, by the way, no such things as poltergeists. Although meeting Carpenter felt a bit like meeting the ghost in the machine.

Inside the nimbus of the floodlights, I could see a silhouette framed in one of the arches, waving me toward an iron-bound wooden door at the end of the gallery. I turned left, walked up more steps, and stood in front of the door, an instant away from coming face-to-face with someone who had constructed a supernatural suicide meme that was programming thousands to kill themselves before the next dawn. I realized that not only did I have no real idea what on Earth I planned to do, but I was also very scared. I mean, this guy was fantastically dangerous. Maybe I was making a huge mistake walking up to his door and knocking on it.

"I should probably leave and think about what I'm doing," I said to myself.

"Are you talking to yourself?" said the young man who

opened the door before I could decide if I really wanted to knock on it.

"Uh," I said. Always ready with a snappy comeback.

The young man was in his late twenties. Skin so pale it almost fluoresced in the blue glow behind him. Long blond hair drawn up in an intricate topknot, long beard twisted into a short braid that jutted from his chin and was decorated with a large onyx bead at its end. He wore white denim cutoffs, no shirt, and no shoes. The lean, taut build and V-shaped torso of an under-wear model or a professional fighter. Roughened red skin on his palms and white pads of scar tissue on his knuckles and face said fighter, not poser.

He looked tough. I was glad I still had a gun.

"I'm here for Circe," I said.

He was very good at being still. Only his eyes moved as he listened, only his mouth when he spoke.

"She's not here."

He took a step back, opening the door wider. Graceful in every movement.

"But you should come inside."

He was standing in a high-ceilinged entryway. Wood arches, stone walls, and floor. It opened to a vaulted great hall behind him. I could see that the blue poltergeist light was being cast by several super-high-definition screens mounted on the walls. Chairs, couches, stools, cushions were scattered around the floor. People, shadows of people in the blue lights. Something was on the screens. Movement, icons, drawings, maps, text, numbers. There was music that sounded like it was played on stone instruments. Flat and unresonant. Dozens of voices whis-pering and coughing up oddly shaped syllables. The patter of hundreds of fingertips tapping out commands onto screens.

Creeeeeeepy.

"You can try to leave if you don't want to come in," the young man said.

"*Try* to leave?"

He raised an arm—it might have been ivory carved for an anatomy lesson. He pointed behind me at the grounds.

"People get lost. It becomes confusing. Once you come up here, you're one place. Back there is somewhere else. Turning around can be disorienting. People end up wandering around until they fall over. You might do better than most. You know things. That's clear."

"I know your name," I said.

"You should come inside."

"Your name is Carpenter."

He smiled. A guy who just found something pleasant and unexpected.

"You really are an interesting guy, aren't you?" His arm was still raised, pointing over my shoulder. He sighted along its length as if aiming at something. "I don't think you'll want to leave now. He's here."

I didn't hear anything behind me.

"I'm here for Circe," I said again.

"She's not here."

"I don't believe you."

His eyes ticked back and forth a few times as he thought that over.

"The only way to be sure is to come inside."

"I don't want to."

"Why?"

"Because everyone who goes in there disappears."

"I like how honest you are."

"I just want Circe."

"Last chance. Come inside or deal with what's out there."

I didn't move.

"As you wish," he said, and started to close the door.

I heard something behind me. Pad of foot, a breath.

"No," I said, and threw my shoulder into the door, forcing myself inside.

Carpenter made way for me to enter, then closed the door quickly, slamming it shut, shooting a bolt.

I leaned against it, exhausted, seeking support.

"What's out there?" I asked.

His lips might have twitched, but it was hard to tell because of the beard.

"Just what you brought with you."

"So nothing," I said.

"Mostly nothing. But this guy is in here," he said, tipping his head so that his beard braid pointed at something next to me. Something that moved.

I spun.

A shadow stepped into the light. Five or so years older than Carpenter, more heavily muscled, black shorts, cave-painting tattoos covering his darkly tanned skin. Cropped dark hair and a prematurely bald bullet head.

"Where's Circe? Where's my daughter?" he said, coming straight at me.

Carpenter put a hand on the other man's chest.

"Take it easy, Dad," he said to the man. "He doesn't know anything."

The man looked confused, growled, turned, and wandered off down a hall into darkness, talking to himself.

"Where's Circe? Where's my daughter?"

Carpenter shook his head at the man's receding shadow.

"Manikins. Some are better than others."

I watched the manikin fade into darkness.

"Crispin," I said.

Carpenter looked closely at me.

"You know an awful lot about my family."

"Hardly anything, I think."

He smiled again, lots of even, white teeth.

"It doesn't matter. Pretty soon we'll all be learning together."

"About what?"

He pivoted toward the great hall.

"You came inside. Have a look around."

I followed him. Several dozen people were spread out around the great hall, their gazes lifted toward the wall screens or down at pads, phones, or laptops. All of them had headphones clamped on their heads or buds poking from the swirl of their ears. The sounds of shifting bodies, keys being tapped, fingertips patting against screen surface. And the voices, mutter and hiss, the warped dialect of *Gyre* pronounced from the back of the throat and in front of the teeth. These were fluent speakers of the tongue talking to other players around the world. Hundreds of thousands of them, as many as three million. Klarnacht had said their world was at its final moment of crisis. An unequivocal end day. Demon rising and forces marshaled to battle. The Guild fixed on killing their god, Demon, and the Harrow coming to aid her rising and begin a new cycle of destruction and rebirth.

It sounded super dramatic and geeky cool, but the reality on screens was a little less so. The massed seekers in the hall were breathing and occasionally moved and spoke in their alien language, but otherwise they might have been dead, preserved in attitudes of gaming. There was an IKEA countertop next to the walk-in fireplace, a microwave, water cooler, bins of snacks, and refrigerator. The seekers were mostly young, only a few past thirty. The vibe was that of an especially groovy shared workspace. They were segregated into two groups. On one side of the hall they were all wearing yellow T-shirts that read TEAM GUILD—NEVER MAY SHE RISE. On the other side of the hall they were wearing red T-shirts that read TEAM HARROW: SHE RISES—WE FALL—SHE RISES.

The action on the screens was not the whirl of amazing

computer-generated visuals I'd expect from an elaborately imagined game set in a rich fantasy world. It was, as Klarnacht had described, text-and-image-based. Written descriptions of the scenes at hand, choices available, actions to be taken. The text in phonetic English, the pronunciation Gyre-ese. Sometimes the text would rearrange itself, the letters warping, lengthening, bending, shifting into simple pictures and animations, all rendered in a primitive pictographic style that reminded me of the tattoos that covered the Crispin manikin's body. Sound effects and the music of *Gyre* accompanied some of the animations. I watched what I assumed was the ring-shaped city of Gyre as it was sucked into the Chasm it was built around, and then a new version of the city build itself on the bones of the old one. I saw a map of a continent sketch itself into being, and a tribe of stick figures pour down its face from the north. I saw a procession of robed shapes delivering bodies into the tributaries of seven rivers. I saw airships battling one another, cannonballs flying between them, one plummeting in flames into the sea.

I realized that some of these images were being created as I watched. Some of the seekers were drawing on their pads and then activating those drawings in *Gyre*. It was a game that asked you to learn its language, sing its songs, talk to it, and solve its puzzles, then draw your actions and put them into the world. I wondered how much of *Gyre* had been created by Carpenter when it first launched and how much had been built and written and sung and spoken into the online world by the seekers in this room and the adherents all over the world. It was the single largest mojo ritual I'd ever heard of.

It was beautiful.

A work of deeply personal art that had drawn a following, who had then elaborated upon it and made it larger and more inviting and somehow deepened it. I had never seen anything like it. It had built a community, and I understood why it was so vastly important to the people who were inside of it. It was their world, and they wanted to save it. They just had vastly different ideas about what that meant. I was moved by the humanity of it.

I was also, not incidentally, totally scared out of my pants. These poet/artist/gamers were contributing to a course of mojo that was probably going to lead them all to suicide and generate a global wave of chaos, and they had no idea what they were doing. What could I do to stop it? What could I say to Carpenter to change his plans? Whatever his actual plan may have been.

"So, that's *Gyre*," I said.

Carpenter kept walking, leading me across the hall.

"No," he said, "not really."

I was confused.

"That's not *Gyre* these people are playing? Doing? Whatever you call it."

He stopped in the middle of the hall, turned to me, placed a fingertip against his forehead.

"Gyre is up here. Which is the point. Gyre, the world Gyre, not the game, exists, but it's in here, in my head. The trick is getting it from here"—he drilled his fingertip deeper into his forehead—"to here." He pulled his fingertip away from his head and pressed it against mine. "Those things"—he waved an arm at the screens—"those are tools for helping to translate Gyre from where it is now to where it is going to be."

I looked at the seekers, finders of the fragments of the Ruination Crown. If someone made a movie about zombies playing video games, that's what it would have looked like.

"For a bunch of people who gave up their lives to see the face of a god, they don't look very happy."

"They didn't give up their lives. They didn't give up anything. Their lives aren't here. I know you know better than that. Is this life, what we're all doing? Is *this* even here? Me and you and what we're looking at and talking about, is any of this here?"

The secret of my ability to sly, to do magic, was based on

being able to forget that there was such a thing as reality. So I answered as honestly as I could.

"I don't know."

"You're looking for Circe?"

"Yes."

"Yes. And that guy by the door with all the tattoos, I called it a manikin. You know what that is."

"I do."

"Yes. You know what it is and you also know where it came from."

"I can guess."

That amused him, for some reason.

"You can guess. I like that. Tell me."

"It's a reflection of Crispin, your father. It came from a mirror that was in a gym in a cult compound in Montana fourteen years ago. You either limned it yourself or had someone do it for you."

"There, see. You know impossible things that are possible. You know the world isn't what it looks like. So if it's not what it appears to be, if this is all fake, what really is here? What have you seen in your life that you know for certain is real?"

I thought about stepping into a mirror. I thought about what is(n't) on the inside.

"Nothing," I said.

"Exactly," he said. "I think I can change that. I think I can replace all that nothing with something. Come on."

We walked to the far end of the great hall and he led the way up a staircase that swooped and curled to a gallery that overlooked the hall on one side and was lined with windows looking down on the city on the other.

"Let's sit."

There were window seats set in the recessed casements. He settled in, elbows on knees, close to me, intimate conversation.

"You look different," he said.

"From what?"

"Before."

"Maybe it's the light up here."

He looked down at his hands, his face hidden.

"The light," he said, and I saw a tear splash on one of his scarred knuckles. He looked up.

"I'm not going to help you. You won't get what you want. The same thing that happens to everyone is going to happen to you. You're going to cease. You can't help Circe this time. You never could. This started long before you became involved. Before I became involved. The only difference between myself and anyone else is that I can see. And tell. That's what I can do now. I can tell you everything."

I was looking at the tiny tearstain just under his eye. This was not the confrontation I'd expected. It made me keep saying the first thing that came into my mind.

"You seem so incredibly earnest. I can't tell if you're pretending," I said.

"I can't do anything about that. Okay. You want to find Circe."

"Yes."

"What do you think is happening?"

There was too much happening for me to be able to understand what I thought was happening. Better not to think too much, better to just spit it out as fast as possible.

"You kidnapped your little sister because all the mojo that is associated with your father's cult and most of what has been generated by people playing your game is coursing to her. I think you're some kind of vehemancer. You can pull mojo off your game as if it were a live event, like a party or a concert. You need that mojo to complete a major course that will pull people's emotions into its current. I think that current runs toward despondency and suicidal thoughts. I think you are trying to complete what Crispin started. I think you designed a game based on his religion so you could reap the mojo that came out of its players, and to bait Circe into the open. I think Circe is your real problem. Because no matter how hard you try to course the mojo from the game, the bulk of it is flowing to her. You have to have her if you want to complete what your dad started. It's a massive ritual. Crispin began it, Circe got caught in it, you designed a game to extend it, and now you aim to finish it by compelling your gamers all over the world to kill themselves, which will deepen your misery course and draw I don't know how many thousands and thousands of other people so they also commit suicide. That's what I think. But I am going to save Circe and I am going to stop you."

His eyes were bottle-green. Whites shot with red. He hadn't been sleeping.

"Well," he said. "You are right about a few things. But wrong about everything that matters. Start with none of this was ever about Crispin. It was always about me. I was the one who saw the shadow of Demon and knew what it meant and followed that meaning to understanding. I felt the presence of Gyre. I dreamed the truth and shared it with Crispin. And then he messed it up."

He placed a hand on my knee, gave it a reassuring squeeze, like I shouldn't be bummed about being so wrong.

"I don't want to bad-mouth my dad, but his beliefs were haphazard. Mostly he believed in himself. Whatever fit the idea of Crispin being awesome was integrated into his mythology. I told him about Demon when I was so young I didn't have the words I needed. I knew that the world I saw was fake. I had to stare into truth for a long time before I saw Demon's shape. But I told Crispin what I had discovered. He had some followers then, a little clan, but he was preaching about being your best self, having great abs, eating clean, loving you for being you. He was collecting their mojo and using it to make himself cooler. *Kind of a half-assed self-improvement wizard.* That's how he described himself later, after he started preaching about Demon. As if he'd been on a path from one thing to the other all along. But all he did was pick and choose from what I told him. I never claimed I was Demon's avatar. I never said anything about his followers leaping into the Chasm. I told him that there was a vast cycle of rising and falling, a process that would take time and hard work. He didn't actually believe any of it. He just thought it was a great mythology he could use to frame his own story, a way to get his followers more invested in *him*. He was a paranoid schizophrenic with grandiose delusions. His illness made it impossible for him to grasp the truth I was trying to tell him. That was part of the problem for us as father and son. You know how it is, dads can't admit their kids might know more about something than they do."

Carpenter leaned away from me, turned, and put the side of his head against the window. It was dim inside the manor, brightly floodlit outside. He cast hardly any reflection.

"I never thought I was *the one*, but it still hurt when he replaced me with Circe. On a father-to-son basis. And it had larger implications beyond my hurt feelings. Crispin didn't see how he was investing Circe. The irony was that she wasn't special at all, not to Demon. None of us are special to Demon. But Crispin made her central to the cult's beliefs, and that act fulfilled what he was saying about her. She wasn't a real avatar any more than I was, but she did become a locus for the cult's mojo. That made a mess of things and I had to do something about it. I mean, all sons, I do believe this, all sons think about killing their dads."

Carpenter took his face from the glass.

"Crispin was never going to kill himself when the rest of the cult did it. I knew he wouldn't. And I certainly wasn't going to kill myself. There was so much to do. That's why Circe being taken away from us was such a big deal. She'd already become a powerful reservoir. Without the mojo she was harboring, my path forward was going to be nearly impossible. Once she was gone, I had to act. Crispin was freaking out. I told him we should go to the Chasm and look into the depths and see what Demon had to say. It was a cheap trick. Well, he peered into the darkness and I pushed him in. He smashed his head open and died right away."

His eyes had grown unfocused while looking into the past, but now he brought them back to the present.

"You already know this part, don't you? Did Iva tell you this?"

"No. I mean. You know I talked to Iva?"

"You'd have to if you were going to grab Circe. Crispin and the mirrors in the gym, you know about all that. I assume you know most of the rest."

"Right. Yeah. Okay. No, I don't know this part. I don't think Iva knows it. The details."

"My bad. She was gone for this part. She couldn't tell you."

"I'll hear it. It fills in a lot of blanks for me. If you have time."

"Yes. Time and light. Yes. I have those. For now. I won't ever tell it again, that's for sure. Yes. I pushed Crispin in the hole, he cracked his head open. Done. The rest of it: I told everyone it was time, and that Crispin had sent me to gather them and show the way. All I really had to do was point a flashlight down the hole so they could see he was already in there. It was. It was intense. These people taking the poison. Some of them jumping in, some asking others to throw them. I'll never forget it. Not until I cease. The hardest part was physical. Getting all the mirrors out of the gym before I burned the compound. All but one. You know about that. The one broken mirror."

"The mirror Iva sat in front of."

"Yes. Iva and Circe both. Shattered. That told a tale, didn't it?"

"I guess it must have?"

"It did. It did. You know, I first saw signs of Demon in a mirror. When I was a baby, Mom would set me in front of one to keep me entertained. My first companion was my reflection. A child's imagination is so potent. I imagined my reflection reaching from the mirror and taking me by the hand. It took me by the hand and led me through. And I saw. You know what I saw. Yes?"

I thought about a child. How old? Two or three. I thought about that child's reflection being drawn, limned, coming through, and somehow pulling him inside the mirror. I thought about a child seeing that expanse of un-existence with no training or frame of reference. What would it do to their mind? Would that child's consciousness shed all limits or would it be broken and driven insane? Was there a difference between the two? The answer was in front of me, telling the story of what had happened.

"I know what you saw."

"I've never stopped seeing it. I have to concentrate to see what everyone else sees." He moved his fingers, a tiny ripple of movement. Reality, barely worthy of being waved at.

I didn't like his story. Who would do that? Who would put their infant child in front of a mirror until they could limn its reflection, and then slip the child into the mirror to look at oblivion?

"Your mom did that to you?"

Carpenter's hand came up and covered my mouth, his fingers squeezing.

"You don't want to bring Mom into this. That won't help anyone." He took his hand from my face and stood up.

"You think I want to make a bunch of people kill themselves, drive people to throw themselves down a metaphorical Chasm. You think it's a bigger version of what Crispin set up with his followers. But I am not Crispin, I'm not interested in making myself more awesome."

Something had started to seethe inside of him as soon as I mentioned his mom. I didn't care. I wasn't seething, I was just upset. I stood up. I didn't want him standing over me. I wanted to be toe to toe. The best I could settle for because he was too tall for me to be eye to eye.

"You are doing all this so you can raise Demon. Bring your deity into the world. But, look, raising Demon is crazy. Because she does not exist. It is impossible because Demon is not a real thing, and bringing Circe and all her mojo here can't change that, and that is the real truth."

He leaned his face very close to mine. Now we were eye to eye.

"I don't need Circe here. That's irrelevant. I don't need people to kill themselves. They are irrelevant." He turned from me and walked to the railing at the other side of the gallery, and pointed down at the seekers. "This is what matters. What they decide. The battle they are fighting inside *Gyre* is all that matters. Look."

I went over, but I stood well away from him. He had a history of pushing people to their deaths.

"Look," he said again.

I looked. His seekers were playing his game.

"Okay."

"There are almost three million of them in there right now. In *Gyre*. Fighting for their lives. For Demon and against her. Around the world. *They* are the ritual. I'm not coursing anything. I don't have to. I only have to wait. My part comes last. Look with the eyes you have when you go inside the mirrors."

I looked. I let myself remember the world was not there. The trick with my compass. The trick that let me pretend a mirror was a gateway. A trick. But not a trick. Rules and no rules. This side and that. Mirror and reflection.

It's a girl, Sid, we're having a girl.

The girl, Sid, remember the girl.

How one thing can become another thing. How the thing

you cannot live with becomes what you will allow yourself to believe.

I looked.

And I saw.

"It is all the same nothing," Carpenter said in my ear. "There is no real world. There is no game world. What we do here we can do there. What happens in there matters as much as what happens out here. No there. No here. Demon doesn't distinguish, because there is no difference. It's all hers and her."

"Oh, no," I said. "You can pull mojo out of the internet, can't you?"

He gave me the congratulatory pat you give a dog when it sits.

"That's it. The words you're using are all wrong, but that's it." He leaned against the railing. "How the players feel about their characters' lives matters as much as what they feel about themselves. The mojo building around the war inside *Gyre* is as great as the mojo that would build around any war. Demon won't rise no matter what happens in there. She doesn't have to. She's already here, as is the world Gyre itself, just obscured by the nothing. Gyre is the real world. I have a map of it. *The map*. I'll show you. I've been working on it since I could hold a crayon. It's what I showed Crispin, trying to make him understand Demon. He only took what he wanted. But it was a whole world I was trying to show him. The world I saw in my mirror when I was a little kid."

He nodded at the screens on the walls below us.

"That's the pretend version. The best I could do. The gamers are fighting and dying right now; characters they've spent years developing are dying. Mojo is pouring from them into the game. Pretty soon, Harrow are going to break into the city of Gyre and throw themselves down the Chasm to Demon. I haven't created a suicide course to make people kill themselves.

That's just a feeling bleeding from the emotions inside the game because the game is becoming more real. The game is the avatar of the reality hidden behind the illusion we see. All I will have to do in the end is use the mojo I have collected to peel away the final illusions. The false world you see around you will dissolve."

He spread his arms.

"Gyre and Demon will replace this. I am making Gyre. I am replacing this fake world with a real world. We will all have real lives with true meaning. Everything I need to do it is in my map. It will focus and supply me. Come on, I'll show you. What's that?"

"A gun," I said. I'd taken out Francois's pistol and I was pointing it at him.

"What for?"

"I think I should shoot you, Carpenter. You can't make the world go away and replace it with a fantasy realm that you invented. You will fail, but you will also make a fantastic mess. I can't imagine how much a plan like that will junk up everything. Maybe it's not your fault that you're so screwed up. But I don't know what to do except shoot you."

"You don't pay a lot of attention, do you?"

"I'm doing my best to understand."

"Not what I meant. Dads."

"What about dads?"

"Behind you."

Not again.

Patter of bare feet, strong hands, my wrist twisted, thumb splayed, pain dropping me to my knees. The Crispin manikin had my right hand forced back, arm levered up. The pain that came out of my wrist met more pain in my shoulder, and the rest of my body went submissively limp in the hope that the pain wouldn't go any further. Gun hit the floor. All through it, a voice repeating its sad mantra.

"Where's Circe? Where's my daughter?"

No, not a voice. Voices, several voices in a disjointed chorus. Did Carpenter say *Dads*?

"Let him go," Carpenter said, picking up the gun.

The Crispin manikin released me. I cradled my throbbing arm and turned and screamed one of those half-strangled screams that you force out from deep inside a nightmare.

There were seventeen Crispins, all closing in on me, all saying the same thing.

"Where's Circe? Where's my daughter?"

Carpenter stepped between us.

"He doesn't know. He barely knows anything."

I was shaking my head at the crowd of manikins.

"You can't do that. No one can do that."

Carpenter sounded exasperated with me for the first time. Like I'd not been listening to him at all.

"You can do anything. The limits are yours, not the world's, not Demon's. The mirrors from the gym at the compound: Crispin spent more time in front of them than anyone else. And the followers didn't reflect themselves anyway, they reflected what he wanted from them. It wasn't that hard to find him in all the mirrors. I took them with me. I didn't want to be alone in the world." He offered me his hand. "Come on, get up. I want you to see the map. I worked on it for a long time. It's really cool and I won't get to show it to anyone else after tonight."

So I got up and went with him to see his really cool map, followed by the shuffling herd of his father's many reflections, each of them fogged in its own special way. Most of them had cracks. One was missing its nose, another had a splintered chin, many were without a few fingers. I was guessing they'd be fragile. Multiple manikins was a new concept for me, but Crispin's vanity would be diffused among them, making them prone to faults and fractures. Only one of them, the one I'd first seen in the entry hall, appeared entirely intact. I looked at their hands, all those missing fingers, and then at Carpenter's profile as we walked side by side. The little white scars crisscrossing his cheekbones and the bridge of his nose.

"Do you fight your dad's reflections?"

His hand went to a scar on his ear, a notch in the lobe.

"We spar. And please don't say anything about the psychology of me fighting with my dad after I killed him. It's not anything you could really understand."

He stopped walking at a double door, and a couple of Crispins stepped around us and opened it, standing to the sides like a surreally Freudian praetorian guard. Battered reflections of the father Carpenter had murdered. I followed him through the doors into what appeared to be his office/library/dojo. The walls, except for one with huge windows facing the L.A. sprawl, were lined with floor-to-ceiling bookshelves. The stock looked old and smelled musty. Probably it was the same collection that Doheny had bought by the yard when the mansion was built. Most of the floor was covered in sweat-stained mats, glittering where glass powder from broken manikins had been ground into the fibers. There was one of those wood sparring posts with holes bored into it and dowels shoved into the holes so Carpenter could toughen himself up by beating on something harder than his dads. There was a desk, massive, old, and oaken, cluttered with the typical workstation junk of this century. A desktop monitor, two laptops, a few pads, and several phones. Game action from *Gyre* was displayed on several of the screens, a few were switched off, and the rest were scrolling a constant stream of notifications. Next to the old desk was a modern standing desk, upon which rested a single huge book bound in some kind of graphite-colored synthetic cloth with a metallic sheen. No text on the cover, just a black circle, clean and symmetrical. Three task lamps illuminated the book, the only light in the room other than the active screens on the other desk.

Carpenter placed a hand on the cover of the book.

"I don't show this to many people, but I think it will mean something to have you look at it. It's an instinct. Because of our history. The Circe connection. All of that. What do you think?"

I didn't know what to think.

"I'm not sure what you're talking about."

Crispin raised his hands, like he was willing to humor me on some lesser point of contention.

"That's okay with me. But come take a look."

His enthusiasm made me wary. I felt like I was about to trigger some kind of trap. A bomb would go off, a poison needle would poke my finger, a Slinky snake would spring out and startle me into a heart attack. I opened the book. He called it a map. But the map was a life's work, child to adult, the record of a life and a whole world.

The first pages were little more than kiddie crayon scrawls, blotches and crooked lines on scrap paper. But these quickly evolved into rudimentary maps that might have been in a pirate movie. X marks the spot. Those improved. Topographical shading was added, color codes, legends, compass rose. Marginalia and footnotes began to proliferate. A mature cartographer's hand developed. A map of a globe spiraled across two pages like the skin of an orange peeled in a single coil. Continents and archipelagoes. Index of countries, cultures, census data. Sociological notes. Illustrations of national costume, details of primary industries, accounts of wars and treaties. Religion. Demon. City maps. Gyre. All roads led to Gyre. The Chasm. Painstaking detail of the rim of the abyss at the center of Gyre, the seven rivers that poured into it, the known depths that had been plumbed by intrepid geologists and archaeologists. A world between two covers. When Carpenter called it a map, he didn't just mean geography. It was a map of every aspect of Gyre the fantasy world, *Gyre* the game, and the Gyre mythology. As much a manual and encyclopedia and bible as it was an atlas.

Here was the world Carpenter planned to put where ours used to be. Once he destroyed our world.

No biggie.

I really should have shot him when I had the chance. That had been a mistake. Now I was going to have to do something really cool. The map was obviously the gargantuan curiosity my compass had pinged from outside. That's where Carpenter stored all the mojo he was taking out of the game, and it would be essential when it came time for him to erase reality.

Clearly I had to steal it.

TWENTY-SEVEN

IT IS SOMETIMES EASIER to want to steal something than it is to actually steal it.

"What do you think?" Carpenter asked, standing at the old desk, flicking screens with both hands, checking his feeds, following the process of the war raging inside his fantasy world.

"I think it's a little sad," I said. "It makes me sad to think of you spending your life on this. I don't know why." I closed the book.

He was still fiddling with screens.

"What have you spent your life on?"

"Nothing that's ever mattered."

He stopped fiddling, looked at me.

"One thing mattered. That's more than most people can say. Circe mattered."

Past tense. I took a step toward him.

"What's that mean, she *mattered*? She still matters."

He turned away, walked to the windows looking down on L.A.

I followed him.

"Circe still matters," I said again.

"Sure she does. She matters like you matter. Very similar. But it's what's already happened that matters most." He faced me, gave me a kind smile. "Thanks for looking at the map. Do you know the next part, yet?"

I ignored the question.

"Tell me where Circe is."

Feet shuffled around the room.

"Where's Circe?" the Crispins said. "Where's my daughter?"

Carpenter tipped his head at the window.

"She's out there. I'll use her when I'm ready. Like I'll use you now. Demon rises, we fall, Demon rises. You joined the ritual. Coming here, singing the song of Gyre. Listening to my story. And now you touched the map. Hardly anyone touches it. Between the past we share and our new connections, your mojo will go right into my map when you die. You are quite the curiosity. And I've got you coursed."

My mouth was very dry. Hairs on my neck stood on end. My heart hammered in its jar. I felt like I was going to pee myself. The way he'd told me his life story, that was a ritual. He'd been incorporating me into his course. He was going to kill me for my mojo.

And Circe. It didn't matter to him that all the mojo surrounding the cult had coursed to her, it didn't matter that so much of the mojo around *Gyre* coursed to her. When he needed it, he could get at it. All he had to do was kill her and the mojo of her life would course to the next most natural path. Through Carpenter and his map. He was going to kill me. He was going to kill Circe. I was about to die.

Fear and confusion overflowed my mouth with questions.

"Why haven't you asked anything about me? How I got here and stuff? I thought it was egotism, but something else is happening here. Why do you keep acting like I should know something that I don't? I think there's been a mistake. What do you mean, *the past we share*? What past? We don't have a past. Are you sure you want to kill me? Don't. Don't kill me. I don't want to die. Not now. Sometimes I do, but not now. I don't want to die like this. Like *this*. Like who I am. I want to do something first. I can do better. I really think I can do better."

"You will do better," he said. "You're going to help bring the true world to light."

"Where's Circe?" the Crispins were saying. "Where's my daughter?"

Carpenter was looking at me. The Crispins were behind him, encircling us. I could see how I was to die. He was going to have his dads beat me to death. That's how it's done in the racket. Mojo is folded on mojo. The thief who came to steal his sister and who played with his map would be killed by the reflections of the father he murdered. A perverse series of connections, a ritual sacrifice. I could see it. Carpenter was stepping back, making way for the seventeen manikins. I still had the window breaker in my pocket. Designed to help trapped motorists escape from their crashed cars, would it help me to escape from this mess? I might break a couple of them, but not all.

"Where's Circe?" they kept saying. "Where's my daughter?"

Carpenter was watching, waiting to capture my mojo. It wouldn't rush out of me in a stream of colored lights and wind. It would be as invisible and intangible as ever, but it would become unmoored. Left alone, it would flow to my heart, but now Carpenter had set a course to take it to his map.

I mean, at least Lloyd wouldn't get it? No, not enough of a silver lining.

The Crispins shuffled closer.

"Where's Circe? Where's my daughter?"

I'd backed as far as I could, flat against the window. The Crispins closing on me.

And then I stole the map.

Impressive, yeah?

I was the only one to see it. From the corner of my eye I saw a shadow whip from nowhere. Carpenter and the Crispins couldn't see it. It was behind them. They couldn't hear it. It was silent. But something changed in the room. They saw my eyes shift, this way and then that. Carpenter spun. Both of us looked to the same place. The tall desk under its trio of bright lamps. The white surface of the desk. Empty.

The map was gone.

"Where's Circe?" The Crispins were still closing on me. "Where's my daughter?"

"Not him!" Carpenter screamed, composure cast off. "Not him! *Him!*" Pointing at the double doors that led to the gallery.

Not me. *It.* In the doorway, paused for a moment, looking back at us, map under its arm. Smiling at me. Did it wink? Black suit, gray shirt, pink striped tie, red oxfords, no socks, fantastic hair slicked back. Stealing the map I wanted to steal, but couldn't. Me. It. My reflection. There, and then gone. Running down the gallery.

"Him!" Carpenter was still screaming, running to the door. "Get him! That one! Him!"

The Crispins finally understood that there was another him. They turned, ran, streaming out to the gallery, pursuing the other me.

Carpenter turned to me. Actual me. Real me. Boy, did he look mad.

"There are no mirrors in this house. None. You brought a mirror in here." He started to walk toward me. "You. You're not even you. He's you. You're not pretending that you don't understand. You don't understand."

He had that right.

Carpenter yanked one of the thick dowels out of his sparring karate dummy pole thing and came toward me.

"You dropped a mirror for him. Where? There's no other way for him to sly away."

I didn't wait for him to get closer. I pulled my window breaker and used it for its intended purpose. I smashed the window behind me, jumped out, and stumbled across a broad balcony.

I windmilled my arms, skiing on pieces of broken glass, headlong toward a stone balustrade. More glass breaking behind me as Carpenter followed. His feet were bare. Maybe he'd slash open a major artery in his foot and bleed to death. Are there any major arteries in the human foot? Probably not. I was off-balance. Trying not to face-plant. There were bushes on the other side of the balustrade. I planted my palms, swung my legs up, vaulted into space. I was not going to clear the bushes, I was going to land in them. I hoped for no thorns. I looked down. Oh. Those weren't bushes, they were trees. The tops of trees. The ground was quite some way below. I went into a treetop. Branches crackled and snapped, scratched and snatched at me. My clothes were snagged, then let go. My left arm hung in a fork, wrenched, twisted loose. I folded across a thick branch, a kick in the gut, stopped falling, spun headfirst over it, flipped, fell some more. The backs of my knees hooked another branch, and it bent, spilling me down its length. Leaves slapped my face, and yanked my amazing hair. Coming out of the canopy headfirst, I was swung upside down like a pendulum, my shoulder slamming into the trunk. I grabbed, hugging the tree. My legs kicked, trying to find something to wrap around. Nope. I skid-slid down, my face and neck rashed by the bark. The ground was there, thick roots bunched up, hard as rocks. I let go of the tree, tucked my head, took the impact on my shoulder, flopped onto my back with a huge knuckle of root jammed into my spine.

I was alive.

It hurt.

I didn't know if I could move. I tried. I could move.

I ran.

The canopy of trees hid me from above. Once I broke cover I'd be easy to spot, and I didn't want to test whatever confusion of mojo Carpenter had coursed over the grounds to keep people from getting out. Nothing was crashing down through the branches overhead. Carpenter had declined to throw himself after me.

I came to the front of the house. The terrace and the row of French doors that looked in on the great hall. I could see the seekers in the blue lights of the screens inside. They were all mortified. Their mojo had already been coursed into Carpenter's map. That's why he'd dropped the bread crumbs to bring them here in the first place—so he could draw off their mojo and begin building his major course. Big things start small in the racket. Always.

Some Crispins were in the great hall looking for my reflection. The seekers stayed focused on their battle for the fate of Gyre. They had nothing else. Carpenter entered the hall, leaving bloody footprints behind him. Raging. He hit a switch and all the screens died. Now the seekers were disturbed. He was shoving, ordering, enlisting them in the hunt. Seekers were prodded into search parties, dispersed through the mansion, each group accompanied by a Crispin. The front door opened and a pack of seekers and their Crispin came out and began to spread across the terrace.

Where was my reflection? Carpenter was wrong about me bringing in a mirror, but somehow it had slyed into the sanctum sanctorum of the mansion. And it looked more and more like it had already slyed back out. I didn't know how it got inside, but it could have accomplished the escape by bringing mirrors with it. It would have needed at least two because they'd have been small and it would have had to do a two-fold sly to make itself tiny. I still had no idea how it could sly at all. Manikins weren't supposed to be able to use mojo. Then again, no one was supposed to be able to pull mojo from the internet and Carpenter was doing that. No multiple manikins, but Carpenter had done that, too. He'd said it made no difference what was in his game and what was outside his game. Everything was nothing.

We project everything onto the nothing. The world doesn't have rules, we do.

Rules and no rules.

Rules we make up.

It was difficult to see inside now that the blue light of the screens had been extinguished. But I knew what was in there. And I could see now how my reflection had slyed in and how it had slyed away. Very slick.

Could I do the same? Sure I could. If a fake me could do it, I could. I could get away from here. Without his map, Carpenter was stalled for the moment. I could get away and go find Circe. Where was she? I still didn't know. Where the heck would I sly to? I needed an angle. I needed. What? What did I have to work with? I went through my pockets.

Two of Pegleg Wanda's band badges were my only mojo. Notebook and pen, keys, giant phone, pieces of paper. Here was Circe's flyer for the play. That was over—she hadn't been there. Here was her flyer for the Abyss Protest. Maybe she was there. I knew where to find some mirrors downtown. I could sly there. Then, what? Look for her in a crowd of hundreds of thousands? Another piece of paper. What? A flyer for a gig. Where'd I get that? I remembered the Melrose punk at Munroe's party shoving it into my hand. It was old-school cut-and-paste evoking the golden age of photocopied gig flyers. It announced a special engagement, midnight tonight at the Echoplex. Munroe presents for the first time, a new band:

PENNY CATCHER

I laughed. Bitterly, but I laughed. Munroe and her sense of humor. A joke meant only for me. She'd given my voice away, and given me a tweak when she named the act she gave it to.

Oh, well. The guy, whoever he was, might have my voice, but he'd never have my hair. I crumpled the flyer. That's where she'd moved the party, the debut of her "new" act. Not my problem right now. Except. Yes, well, except.

Except everything is connected.

I unfolded the flyer. Why tonight, Munroe? After thirty years, why debut my voice tonight? And also Adam's rib. My voice and that rib. Quite a load of mojo. People were bringing out the big guns tonight. You only unloaded the big mojo to do big things. To lay a major course or to change an existing one. Munroe had known suicide was in the air. She'd brought up suicide cults. Francois had told me that she knew he had a daughter and a granddaughter. She'd brokered him the sly who snatched Circe from Crispin's compound. Lloyd. You can't bring mojo anywhere near Munroe without her knowing about it. She knew. She had to know. She had to know that Circe was a curiosity. She had to know the kid was being charged with mojo flowing from *Gyre*. She was obsessed with the mojo she was losing from the party, the share that was pouring into social media and the internet.

Did she know about Carpenter?

How could she not know about Carpenter?

She knew.

She knew it was possible to pull mojo from the internet. But she wasn't like Carpenter. She was limited by her understanding of how it all worked, the rules that bound her and limited what she could do. She needed a ritual that would unleash a flood of mojo to cut a new major course that would pull mojo out of the internet and run it back to her. Events were her specialty, the emotion pumped out at live events. That was her gift as a vehe-mancer. The same way she'd launched her career and laid her first big course at Altamont, that's what she meant to do again. Only bigger than Altamont, where four people died, the deaths adding to the mojo of the event itself and to its legend.

Bigger. Worse.

She knew about Carpenter, she knew about *Gyre*, she knew that the suicide mojo in the air was leaking from the game. And she planned to use it for her own ends. One night only. Midnight tonight. My voice. The Adam's rib that had been carved into a knife by a Satanic coven. So much mojo, but more is always good. The course she was laying would lead to death, suicide. The gig would become a new legend, a national tragedy. An audience all taking their own lives at the same show. *Why?* the pundits would ask. No reason anyone could see. So many opinions, a feedback loop of attention that would keep the emotion of the event alive. But to hammer it home, to make sure she got the deaths she needed, she wanted a final element in the ritual. A sacrifice to push it into motion. A high priestess of suicide.

Circe.

I'd been right in the first place. Munroe was the bad guy. She knew it all and she was behind it all. Finally I knew where I had to go, and I knew how I was going to get there.

The seekers who had come outside were leaving the terrace, pouring over the grounds. Their escorting Crispin was staying close to the mansion. I'd have to take a chance. I filled my hands and I ran from the darkness under the trees. The front door was still open. Seekers were wandering the house and the grounds. The Crispin at the edge of the terrace heard my footsteps and turned.

"Where's Circe?" he asked as he started to run after me. "Where's my daughter?"

At the Echoplex, I could have told him if I'd had breath to spare. *It's a club. She's at the Echoplex, in the clutches of my former manager. She's being spread on a metaphorical altar so she and her mojo can be sacrificed. She's being induced to kill herself with a knife made from Adam's rib while some nobody sings with my voice. It's bananas,* I could have told the poor, sad thing, *but it's all true!*

I ran inside, turned, rammed my aching shoulder into the back of the heavy wooden door, and shoved. The Crispin's arms thrust inside and were smashed off at the elbows as I slammed the door shut. Running again, into the great hall, a band badge in each hand. Devo in my right. Roxy Music in my left. The dead screens on the walls. Each of them a dark mirror.

That's how my reflection did it. Slying in through one of the blank screens in Carpenter's office. Slying out through one of the many screens elsewhere in the mansion. Black mirrors. Rules and no rules. I avoided phones because I hated the feeling of carrying a mirror that looked back at me. But I never thought about it as literally a mirror. If I could remember to forget the world existed, I could remember to believe that a screen was another kind of mirror. It was just a different kind of impossible. Like Carpenter had said. It was all the same nothing.

Carpenter. There now, above me, on the gallery. I'd hoped to have a moment or two to think this through. I knew the Echoplex, I knew its mirrors, but I didn't relish a sudden leap into a crowded club. Leap. Crap. Those big screens were high on the walls. Carpenter was pointing at me. No, he was aiming at me. Francois's little automatic. That's why guns are stupid. You carry one and someone else ends up aiming it at you. Screens on the walls. Something to climb. The only thing tall enough was the kitchen counter next to the hearth. A screen was mounted directly over the hearth.

BANG! KRSH!

A bullet hit something, but not me. What had that sound been? *Krsh*? Did he shoot a Crispin? Was there a Crispin in the hall? No. Screen, he shot a screen.

BANG! KRSH!

He shot another screen. Carpenter had figured it out. He was shooting screens to keep me from getting away. Easier targets to hit than I was, but there were a lot of them. Run faster. I was going to have to jump onto the counter and then into the screen over the hearth. I could do that. Normally I could do that. Battered by a tree and everything else that night, I was going to have trouble doing it.

"Get him!" Carpenter screamed. Who to? Oh, there they were. Four Crispins and several seekers running in through the arches.

I jumped. One foot on the countertop. Wobble. Second foot on the countertop. Run some more. Just a few steps.

BANG! Scream.

Someone screaming in pain. Not me. A seeker who'd been coming at me. Why'd Carpenter shoot a seeker? Yes, got it—he was aiming at me and hit the seeker. Sorry, seeker. Other seekers close. Two Crispins.

"Where's Circe? Where's my daughter?"

BANG!

I jumped, flung myself at the screen, arms outstretched, hands filled with the badges filled with mojo. It wasn't a screen, it was a mirror. There I was, my dark shadow-self diving at me. It wasn't me. It wasn't there. Nothing was there. A bullet was in the air. I could see it reflected in the mirror-screen. Which would hit the screen first, me or the bullet? No. There was no bullet and no screen. Nothing ever anywhere. Nothing to go through, nothing to leave behind. No me.

I was free.

I could do anything.

I was gone.

TWENTY-EIGHT

THE HARDEST PART ABOUT SLYING is that you have to find your way.

You don't just think of where you want to go and step into one mirror and walk directly out of another one as if they were the front and back of a two-dimensional slab. When I say that there is nothing inside, I mean that as literally as one can mean it. What I mean is: There is *something* inside, but it is *nothing*.

Perilous Sue had a theory.

She explained it to me when I was studying with her. She'd taken me to an architectural salvage place in Silver Lake. A warehouse. The kind of place where interior designers and set decorators can dig through stacks of vintage bricks or barn timbers or bins of glass doorknobs. She'd led me to the back, where the mirrors were. Hundreds of mirrors. Hung floor to ceiling, piled on tables, dangling from the beams.

"It's like subatomic physics is what it is, Catchpenny," she said as she stopped in front of a row of funhouse mirrors. "Like how we're all mostly nothing, right? Us and the whole entire universe, we're mostly empty space, is what they say." She walked down the line of warped mirrors, her reflection stretching, widening, corkscrewing, shrinking. "What I think we're doing is taking advantage of all the empty space. Like what I imagine is finding a crack. I put my eyeball up to it and look inside. What's that I see? Why it's nothing at all. Let's have a gander, I say to myself.

No problem, because this crack I'm peering through is mostly emptiness itself, right? Yes it is, Catchpenny. So I can fit through it with room to spare. Now I'm where all the space is, inside. Inside what? Is that what you're wondering, Catchpenny? Come have a look," she said, and waved me over to stand shoulder to shoulder with her in front of a double mirror. She pointed at the one on our right. "Do you figure, Catchpenny, that you could sly this one?"

I shrugged. I'd just been learning then and I hadn't slyed anything without an escort. Sue herself.

"I reckon you could, my dear. You're ready. You could go right in, slippery as an eel. And come out here." She pointed at the mirror on the left. "No distance. Easy as. Only watch out." She took hold of the frame, closed the mirrors with a smack so they were sandwiched front to front against each other. "What would happen then, do you think? If you'd gone in the one intending to come out the other? Just keep going around and around? Be stuck inside forever, perhaps?" She moved me to another mirror, stood behind me, fussing my hair. "You do have such gorgeous hair, Catchpenny. Look at you. Charming brat. Woebegone Byron, that's you. Too bad about your voice. I did like to hear you croon. None of us can stay what we were after we fall into the racket." She smiled, displaying her horrid teeth. Always a shock for her beautiful lips to part, revealing the snaggled rows, twisted and pitted. "I had a lovely smile once. Traded it away like you and your golden tonsils. We get what we get and we don't get upset, that's what one tells the kiddies."

She stepped back to the closed double-fold mirror and opened it again.

"No, lover, space inside is not the trouble. Slip through the crack, find yourself in all that emptiness that fills the universe. *I could be bounded in a nutshell and count myself a queen of infinite space,* if I may be allowed to paraphrase the Bard, *if it were not that I would run out of time.* Time is the stickler, Catchpenny. You could wander in there to your heart's content, if you still had a heart, and if it weren't that you'd run smack out of time. Here now, let me have a look."

She unbuttoned the top of the plaid shirt I was wearing, standard grunge of the era, and looked at the scars she'd carved into my chest a few months before.

"Those are healing nicely. Quite lickable to my eyes. Start here," she said, placing a perfectly manicured nail at the end of a squiggle of scar, "and follow where it leads." The pink tip of her tongue had slipped between her magnificently awful teeth. "Fancy some strange, lover? Very strange, I mean."

She knew she didn't have to ask. Did I want some strange? I wanted anything that blotted out how I felt. I wanted anything ugly or dumb or dangerous. I wanted to be drunk on all the strange in the universe. Lose me in meaninglessness. My wife was dead. My unborn daughter would never be born. Make me not care. Make me stop feeling bad. Make me stop feeling. I was hardly the first heartbroken jerk to start screwing around with someone who was obviously very, very bad for them.

Sue's tongue found the scars she'd cut with her knife, followed them, ran up my neck and into my mouth.

"Let's see what's inside it all, Catchpenny," she'd said, and leaned into me.

I fell back, kept falling. Falling as she opened the mirror behind me. Falling inside the nothing, her fingers opening my jeans. Her leather pants were skintight and had buttons down the back. I popped them open and she squirmed snug leather down her hips.

Something somewhere cracked.

"Time's catching up, Catchpenny. We'll have to be fast," she said, straddling me, "but not too fast, lover."

She smiled and I slid my tongue over her teeth. Nothingness cracking open around us as time ran down. Both of us getting off on the risk of being erased. One does not generally hang about in the Vestibule for a casual screw. That's a move best left to daredevils like Perilous Sue.

That was then, decades past.

Now was now, and I had to sly in a hurry.

I was gone from Greystone Mansion. And like Perilous Sue had explained long ago, space was not an issue. Nothing was inside the mirror, which is also a way of saying that everything was inside the mirror. Everything but time. You don't go in and come right out. You go in and wayfind your way out. How to find your way in nothing? That, as I said, is the hardest part.

You walk into a mirror. You are in the Vestibule now. You must orient, and then you must wayfind. All around you is flat gray that has the depth and sheen of dozens of panes of glass stacked together until they reach the edge of opacity. You need directions so you can get someplace.

You look over your shoulder. You decide, That will be *behind*. Now you need *forward*. You turn around. There is no left or right for the moment, no up or down, no cardinal directions. For the moment you only have *behind* and the movements of your own body to give you a sense of where-ness. You want solidity beneath your feet, so you make that *below*. But when you look the opposite of below, you decide you want options, so you make that also *below*. Now, if need be, you can walk on that below as well as the one your feet are on.

You need cardinal points. *North,* you decide, looking one way; *south* is the other way; *east* is this way; and *west* is that way. As you orient, the endless silvered nothing around you begins to take on hints of definition, as if a giant invisible hand were applying faint streaks of charcoal. A crossroads at the heart of a vast labyrinth of corridors. Leaving the final two choices. *Here,* where you are, and *there,* where you want to be.

You scan the surfaces of the resolving corridors that twist and kink off into the distance, looking for a hopeful hint of light. The notional twinkle of your destination. That's *there.* You walk *forward,* aiming for the glint. You turn *south* and then *west* and then *west* again and then you lose the twinkle for a moment and then you have to move to the other *below,* inverting the Vestibule. The mirrored corridors seem to rotate, flip, disconnect, and rearrange as you navigate.

Crack.

There it is, the first flaw, hairlines in the surfaces of the mirrors. The Vestibule is folding. The mojo you used to enter is running out.

Crackckcklickckckck.

The hairlines thicken, multiply, start to stretch fingers toward you.

You run, racing the cracks that spread everywhere, fracturing *behind, left, right, north, east, south, west,* and *here,* converging on *there.* Your goal. Everything is collapsing back into glassy gray nothing and nowhere. The cracks open, split wide, and anything that might be anything falls into the cracks, leaving nothing that could be something. You see the glint of *there.* You dive. Cracks hit the glint, your exit shattering. No choices.

Jump through the dark, as cold, icy shards of emptiness pepper the back of your neck and the Vestibule closes and locks behind you.

TWENTY-NINE

I CAME OUT OF A MIRROR into the usual scrum of activity in an overcrowded coed john at a packed club.

Men and women waited for a stall to free up, checking phones, doing key bumps of coke, fixing makeup, heads bobbing to the DJ mix that vibrated through the walls. I'd wanted to go to the Echoplex, but I'd needed to aim for a specific mirror. I'd been to shows there and knew the bathroom layout. I had to risk a public entrance and hope for the best. The best in this situation was that I knocked someone over and clipped my chin on the edge of the sink as I belly flopped onto the floor. For most of the people who caught a glimpse of the action, it looked like a guy had gotten rowdy and shoved someone. For a couple of people who saw the whole thing, it looked like reality was broken. I had no time to help with their existential crises.

I jumped up and began pushing my way out. Which then led to a bunch of people yelling for security to do something about the jerk coming out of the bathroom. The call for security from the bathroom patrons was picked up spontaneously by some of the clubbers outside the door. People were pointing at me, waving hands over their heads to get someone in authority to pay attention.

The Echoplex was the bottom level of a building that had its façade up on Sunset. Floors and ceiling painted black, the walls alternating stripes of blood-red paint and gold wallpaper. A big disco ball slowly rotated over the stage, speckling the walls and bodies with white light. The situation in the club proper was not fire marshal–approved. Munroe was cramming them in for her big event, but the authority figures were starting to notice some unrest. I jumped up to get a look over the crowd and saw bodies homing in on the ruckus I'd caused. Munroe's manikins. A couple of bodybuilders, a few bikers and assorted toughs, all looking like they were fresh from central casting. I could lose them in the crowd. I was worried about the real security. Perilous Sue was at the elbow of the bar at the back of the club, a half head taller than anyone around her. Her mismatched eyes were tracking her staff, making sure there was no serious trouble that might need her personal, vicious attention. I took advantage of my lack of height and slight build, ducked low, and started to bob and weave, looking to split the defenders and surface elsewhere.

Being in a music club is a fraught affair for me. The musical part of my life lasted little more than a decade from when I first found an old guitar in a closet at the group home to when I sold my voice to Munroe. The part of my life where I had both Abigail and my voice is a shrinking fraction of all my years, but somehow it is able to eclipse everything that has happened since then. Imagine it. I've become a wizard-thief. I use arcane powers to slide myself through mirrors into impossible places and steal magic artifacts. I have parted the veils of existence and seen and walked in the nothing that is the only true reality. But I still fantasize about being a rock star, and I can't get over the first girl I ever loved.

Depression is dead time. Null emotional space. You adhere to the thoughts that make you feel the worst, infantile and ineffectual. I'm sure there are plenty of depressives who are able to move forward with their personal growth, maturing and learning about themselves. I, however, have never been one of them.

My depressive cycles have been emotional comas during which I played and replayed the greatest hits of my worst moments. And I have been depressed for years and years and years. Know what I see when I let myself look in a mirror? What I really see, the deepest mystery that is revealed in my own reflected eyes? I see a man who can't grow up.

But moving on, there were lives to save.

These people, these partygoers and music fans, their faces under-lit by their phones as if we were at a séance in a horror movie, in just a little while they might be dead by their own hands. Those were the stakes. Munroe's maniac musical suicidal party tour. One night only. That was the key. Munroe would only get one shot at this ritual. If I could throw a monkey wrench into the night, that would knock her ritual off-kilter. But with all the huge mojo flying around that night, a monkey wrench could cause terminal widespread chaos. Was there anything more specific I could try, besides just pulling a fire alarm?

"What the fuck do you think you've been doing?" hissed the owner of a hand that grabbed the back of my neck and shook me. "I'd kill you right now except there are witnesses, you little piece of shit."

Tobacco breath tickled my ear. Tobacco and hash breath.

"Francois, hey, you're here. Perfect."

His hand squeezed harder.

"Do not pretend you planned to meet me here."

"I told the barista at Plow House I'd meet you later."

"You snuck out on me."

"I forged ahead to take advantage of a lead."

He twisted me around to face him. I've heard the phrase *tears of rage,* but I had never seen them shed before that moment.

"Stop it. Stop acting like you know what you're doing. You're playing games with my granddaughter's life. You've got a bead on some mojo in this, and that's all you care about."

We were pressed together by the crowd, both of us whispering at maximum intensity.

"I care about Circe, Francois. I do. But it's bigger than that. These people here, they're all in danger."

"From who?"

"Themselves. But they don't know it yet. I can't explain it all right now. But it's Munroe! She grabbed Circe! She's the villain!"

"Munroe has Circe?"

"There are a few loose ends, but it's all connected."

"You are so terminally fucked up. It is not all connected."

I grabbed Francois's arms.

"The girl, Francois. *My* girl. I didn't forget. I remember her all the time. Always. Please. I think I can do something. Now. To make it better. I can do better this time."

He jerked his arms free.

"Back off," he said.

In the past I'd made Francois mad enough to voice his desire to end my life, but I'd never been afraid that he might really hurt me. When he told me to back off, murder was in his eyes. So I backed off. Or I tried to back off, but as soon as I moved away from him, I bumped into someone.

"He's not talking to you, lover," the person I'd bumped into said. And I realized that Francois wasn't even looking at me. His eyes were aimed above my head. Someone tall was back there. Someone tall and frightening. I was making a bad habit of being caught unawares.

"Hey, Sue," I said.

"Back off," Francois said again.

I felt Perilous Sue shift behind me, her arms wrapping around my waist, a palm coming to rest warmly on the point of my left hip, her other hand holding something.

"You curious to see Catchpenny's insides, Francois? I've seen them myself, but maybe you'd like a peek."

I looked down. Her right hand held the blade that had cut out my heart, the flat pressed tight against my belly, the tip at the bottom of my sternum.

Sue was tall enough in her boots to rest her chin on the top of my head. I could feel her breathing fast, excited. Perilous Sue's nickname cuts two ways. She is a dangerous woman, a hazard to be avoided, and also she loves danger and violence. I made a joke once that she should really be called Jaded Sue because she spent most of her time being spectacularly bored by everything.

"I could give a shit what you do with that guy," Francois said to her.

Sue's head shifted, as if she were nodding a greeting to someone.

"Fry that guy," she said.

"Oh, no," I said.

"What?" Francois said.

A CHP officer had appeared behind Francois, the ponytailed partner to the one that he'd run over outside Munroe's. There was a flash of blue-white, a sharp crack, tang of ozone. The crowd shifted hard. Voices of concern raised and rippled away from us and faded.

"What was that?" "Move back." "Sorry." "Firecracker." "What?" "Some asshole." "Set off a firecracker. Or something."

It was a few seconds' worth of action. That zap from the taser Ponytail had pressed into Francois's back. The spurt of rictus tremor that juttered though him. The frightened startle that ran through the audience and died. Then it was done.

Ponytail hoisted Francois, and the crowd made way for her, letting her remove the old guy who had passed out in the heat of the club.

THIRTY

"I AM DISAPPOINTED with you, Sidney," Munroe said to me in the office of the Echoplex.

Like the offices of most small clubs, it doubled for liquor and merch storage and would have been crowded with one person seated at the single desk, let alone packed with myself, Munroe, Sue, and the still-unconscious Francois dumped in a corner. Munroe was closest to the door, holding it open a crack, her attention split between her disappointment in me and what was going on in the club.

I ignored her disappointment, having a different set of priorities.

"Remember, Munroe, how you asked me what I thought about the end of the world and suicide cults? I have an answer for you now. I don't like them. I think they are bad ideas."

She kept her eyes on the door crack. One hand on the knob, the other hand holding her phone.

"It's eight before midnight," she said. "Where is everyone?"

Sue flicked her phone screen.

"Twice capacity, and more trying to get in. Breathless with anticipation. Squeeze in another body, the place might crack open."

Munroe didn't like that answer.

"There should be a riot outside. I've put everything into this show. It's the most secretly anticipated concert in forever. People have been waiting for it without knowing what they were waiting for. Why aren't there more?" She looked at her phone, swiped, and scrolled. "Why aren't we trending higher?" She pressed her eye to the crack of the door. "More. Bigger. More. I need live bodies. Emotion. Mojo in the flesh. Where is everyone?"

Sue played with her phone some more.

"Traffic is a snarl. That protest is the only thing out-trending us. But it's a different crowd. Political. Dour. Not who you want here. Not the cool kids."

I waved my arms over my head.

"This is wrong! What you are doing here is wrong! How can you two just? No! No! Stop it! Munroe, you can still stop this!"

Munroe closed the door, turned to me.

"What is it that's on your mind, Sidney?"

"Suicide!" I screamed. "Mass suicide!"

Munroe looked at Sue.

"That, at least, seems to be working."

Sue tapped her phone.

"It is a trending topic across platforms, dear."

"Of course it's trending!" I was really raving now. "Suicide is all anyone can think about in this town."

Munroe was wearing pleated white slacks with a broad alligator belt, a gold watch chain looping from her pocket. A double-breasted vest revealed a purple lace bra worn Madonna-style without a shirt.

She tapped a fingernail against her chin.

"Start a rumor in the crowd that the show is being canceled. Get them restless out there."

Sue began tapping her phone.

"Munroe, please," I said. "I know you're pissed about your party slipping away. The internet sucks, we all agree. It's made everything worse. You spent all those years creating a fantastic spectacle at the party, entertaining people, giving them something. All you asked for was their attention, and now they want to pay attention to something else and it's costing you. Times change. Look at travel agents, look at taxis, look at TV and retail stores and the porn industry and politics. The internet ruined them all."

Munroe raised a finger to silence me.

"Shush, Sidney."

But I wasn't being shushed.

"You don't need to replay Altamont. People don't have to kill themselves so you can keep the wolf from your door. The wolf is nowhere near your door, and you know it."

Sue leaned over and bit my ear. Blood squirted. She hissed, an animal threat, then opened her mouth and let me go, wiping her lips with the back of her wrist.

"Little respect, lover. Our lady said shush."

I shushed, a hand to my bleeding ear.

Munroe had forgone her usual hunks of amber in favor of a few loops of thin gold chain that lay across her collarbone, a charm dangling from each one. A heart, a moon, a dolphin, and a gun. She played with the heart.

"I bought something of yours tonight, Sidney. I was shocked to hear it was for sale, doubted its provenance at first, but here you are without it, looking positively naked."

I touched the *V* of my bare chest at the top of my jacket.

"My shirt?"

Munroe shook her head.

"*My* shirt. It came as part of a set. Rare chance. Locking them up for safekeeping seemed the best thing. But I knew someone who would love that shirt, so I gave it as a gift."

I imagined someone else wearing Abigail's Sinéad O'Connor shirt. I tried to stop imagining it. They'd course off the mojo, use it for something dumb and selfish, erase the last feeling of her.

"Lloyd had no right to sell it. He was supposed to hold it in trust."

"He didn't see it that way."

"I'll buy it back."

"With what, Sidney? You have nothing but debts and enemies."

"I do have something valuable, Munroe."

"Please?"

"Knowledge. A trade. But not for my shirt. I tell you what I know, and you stop what you're doing. Deal?"

"What do you know, Sidney?"

"Deal?"

"You don't know anything."

"I know that mojo can be coursed directly from the internet. Right now. Your plan, creating a new major course to change the rules, you don't have to do that. No one has to die. I met someone. He knows how to do it. This guy, he understands how it works, so he can help. I can introduce you. He's mad at me now, but that can be fixed. Listen to me. All I want is that you don't make people kill themselves. And also give me back my voice. I never really wanted to sell it. And I want my heart. You can get it for me. That's all. I'll introduce you to a guy who can pull mojo out of the internet, put the world on a platter, and all I want is to save some people. I deserve a few scraps for trying to do something nice, don't I? My voice and my heart. That's all. And, and, and I want my shirt back. Please."

Sue spat some of my blood.

"Want me to remove him to some other place? Trouble is all he does."

Munroe shook her head, stepped over to me. Her eyes were magnified by the huge round lenses of her glasses.

"I'm sorry everything is so hard for you, Sidney. Honey, baby, you should have been amazing. None of it was fair. All of us who know you, your friends from the long ago, we know you were battered by fate. Abigail. Tragic. The baby. I don't dare think about it or I'll fall apart right here. I tried to talk you out of all this. I know you don't want to remember how it really happened, Sidney, but I tried to persuade you not to sell your voice. You, honey, you insisted you didn't want it. Sue remembers."

Sue shrugged.

"Never wanted to sing again, he said. Without Abigail there was no point in it. Revenge was all he wanted, cold-blooded as possible. Ways and means for getting it, he wanted. You tried to talk him away from it, Munroe. Don't fault yourself."

Munroe tucked a loose lock of my hair behind my ear.

"I told you, we all lose. We all lose everything in the end. I told you to let your art heal you. There would be other loves. You and Abigail barely knew each other. Terrible to say, but it probably would have ended sooner than later. If you'd kept your voice, you would have seen the world, been adored, had all the things dreams are made of. You would have gotten over Abigail. But you didn't want that. You wanted to wallow, Sidney. You barely knew the racket existed, but you wanted in. You insisted that I buy your voice for enough mojo to pay Sue to take your heart and teach you to sly."

Sue clucked her tongue.

"Told you it wasn't a life for you, Catchpenny. But try to tell a boy anything. We couldn't. Nineteen and certain he knows the way of the world. Suppose we're all like that at that age. We were, weren't we, Munroe?"

"Yes, Sue, we were. But we were made sterner than soft Sidney. I should have said no, but I couldn't. Not to him. And it's never gotten better for you, has it, Sidney? No voice to cry with, no craft or career to follow, no way to move on and get better. Just blunder and bluster in the same circles, looking for your own tail, finding nothing."

I shook my head.

"I'm not chasing nothing. I saw it. I saw me. Twice today."

Sue gave a little sigh.

"He was a glorious little thief while it lasted, our lad Catchpenny."

Munroe smiled sadly.

"He was, he was. When it had a point, when he thought it would get him somewhere. Steal his way to revenge. But look at him now. Even his best friend doesn't want him." She nodded at Francois. "Think of what he's hidden from Sidney."

Sue clucked.

"Fair is, Monroe. We've all lied to and kept secrets from lover boy for years now."

Munroe nodded.

"For his own good. He'd have ruined the only thing he had going for himself."

Sue chuckled.

"*Going for himself.* That's some wit, dear."

Munroe put her hands on my shoulders, tender and reassuring.

"The point, Sidney, baby honey, is that I know it has been hard for you, dreadful. I know you have suffered in life and been challenged by your mental health. You've become all but useless to everyone, and it is your own fault. Hard truths. You are underfoot. I don't know what Francois was thinking when he went to you this morning, but I'm sure he regrets it now. He was in a panic. Mistakes were made. I did my best to keep you out of trouble. You deserved a little mistreatment for being a pest, nothing more. All you had to do was stay put. Instead, you've been blundering all over town. Sidney. Listen now: You have no knowledge to sell. You're delusional. The internet is a pit. The engineers and those Silicon Valley insiders have made their monster and we all have to live with it. Do you think they didn't know what they were doing, Jobs and Wozniak and Gates and the others? Do you think the world was changed as much as their toys have changed it without mojo being coursed? They were all in the racket. They knew what they were up to. They created a mojo sinkhole with a course that only they can tap. Their elite coven laid a major course that will last generations. No one else can get at it. End of story. Anyone telling you they can tap mojo from the internet is selling bridges where they don't exist."

She took her hands from my shoulders.

"Power, Sidney, always and forever, power. If you have it, others try to take it away. The only way to protect what you have is to get more power. I know it's sad and circular and pointless, but we are talking about life, honey baby. Pointlessness is the name of the great big game. Now, I hate to make you feel worse than you always do, but I don't know anything that might cut the fog in your head other than honesty."

"No," I said. "But suicide. And. And all that. Your evil plan."

She took a very deep breath, patience at an end.

"My plan, my *evil* plan, amounts to finally doing what I've been avoiding doing for years. I am launching my own social media platform. 'The Party.' I reinvented live events in the seventies and rested on my laurels. Long enough. I'm going to show these Generation-Zs what influence is."

I might as well have stepped through a mirror. Which way was up? There were no directions and nothing made sense. No, wait, I think I understood something. Could I have heard that last part right?

"So, wait," I said. "Your big plan is to release an app?"

"I may not be able to pull mojo out of the internet, Sidney, but I can direct it toward my own app. If I make people love the app enough, that will give me the mojo I want. Sure, yes, okay, most of it will go into the fucking internet, but I'll get my cut. Tonight we have our first big event. Premier my new star and do an exclusive onsite download of The Party for early adopters. It took a lot of mojo to draw the attention I need, and I'll burn more tonight, but when it's over I'll be bigger than ever. *Rebranding* is what it's called, Sidney. The suicide vibe is just color, part of the act, the legend people will be telling. No one is going to be offing themselves."

I guess I understood what she was saying, but compared to Carpenter trying to erase the world and replace it with Demon Land, it seemed pretty weak.

Sue held up her phone.

"People are restless, dear. We should start the show so they can shoot their videos and post."

Munroe fanned herself.

"Flop sweat before a debut. Never fails. Come on, Sidney, you should see this."

Sue tucked her arm through mine.

"Best enjoy the show, lover. You're going on ice after this."

She was towing me toward the door. I looked at Francois, still unconscious.

"I'm worried about Francois," I said.

"Don't waste kind thoughts on him," Sue said. "He's played you against yourself all these years, he has."

"What?"

Munroe jumped up and down a few times, getting pumped.

"Don't confuse him, Sue. He can barely remember who he is right now."

Sue pulled me closer to her.

"Trials, Catchpenny, that's what we were made for, trials and tribulations and grabbing at what we can get in between them. Come see the new new."

Munroe led us out. A roped-off aisle took us up a few steps to the Echoplex's modest VIP area at the back of the club. Two café tables and a few chairs on a raised platform with a wobbly brass rail. The music on the PA was pure bass, hammering out a dance beat that was felt rather than heard. The disco ball over the stage spun. The crowd was packed in a single surging mass. Phones were held high, glowing screens panning to shoot the dangerous giddiness.

My brain was static on an old TV screen. Whirling dots, spinning, colliding, tumbling in senseless patterns. I couldn't get a grasp on anything that I'd been certain of just minutes before. All was uncertainty.

Francois was working against me?

Munroe had no idea that mojo could be taken from the internet?

She wasn't trying to make anyone commit suicide?

A social media app was her plan?

The Party?

How could so much trouble be caused by something so lame?

The house lights went out, but one spot remained on, aimed at the disco ball over the stage. Speckles of light swam over everything, like my thoughts swam in my head. The bass pushed against me. Then a silence that made you feel the keening of damaged nerves in your eardrums. Then a synthesizer, distorted piano notes picked at random, like a kid plunking; a tune resolved. I recognized that tune. Where had I heard it before? A drum machine, a simple beat. Then baseline. A Hammond organ joined in. Finally a voice.

My voice.

My song.

Light dawning onstage. Not a band. One silhouette surrounded by a horseshoe of keyboards. Laying down a melody, rhythm, looping it all together, layering. Lights rising, the keyboardist singing, in a trance, my voice coming from her throat. Her face. There were her mom's eyes, chin, cheekbones. Her hair was bound close to her scalp, woven with red twine, and tinged fuchsia from a faded dye job. Black fatigue pants cut off at skater length, red cowboy boots with red-and-black-striped tube socks sticking up from the shafts. Black leather motorcycle jacket jingling chains and studs, vested with a red denim jacket that had the sleeves razor-bladed off. Red ribbon choker with a hand-painted ceramic disc, black with a red screaming mouth. A bone sharpened like a knife, hanging from a chain: Adam's rib. And my Sinéad O'Connor T-shirt, *The Lion and the Cobra*.

Circe.

Singing the song I wrote for Abigail, with my voice.

Because of course.

THIRTY-ONE

When I get close enough to you
To feel you breathing
I can smell the smell of you,
And my heart stops beating.
Take me down, take me down, take me down my love
I feel like dyin whenever you're around
I feel like dyin whenever you're around.

I don't lie to myself, I just selectively remember the past in a way that makes me hate myself less than I might otherwise. Isn't that normal?

Yes, I had wanted to sell my voice. Munroe was telling the truth about that. She did try to convince me not to do it. She wanted a hot young star, not a voice in a box. Or wherever she kept it. I was never clear on that. And yes, I wanted my heart cut out and locked away outside my body. I told myself it was so I could find my reflection and destroy it. The truth was that I hoped losing my heart would keep me from hurting. Yes, I chose to never leave the past. I anchored myself to myself. I said I was trying to find a copy of myself to kill, but I was the one who wanted to die.

The things people want.

Iva wanted her daughter back.

Francois wanted Iva to forgive him.

Carpenter wanted to replace the world with a fantasy.

Munroe wanted more of what she already had.

I'd wanted to get my hands on some mojo. I'd wanted to help Iva while I helped myself. I'd wanted to find Circe. I'd wanted to save lives from pointless death. I'd wanted to stop selfish people from warping the world to their own ends. I'd wanted to do something that would matter. I'd wanted to feel better. I'd wanted to be better.

Now I just wanted to know what the heck was really going on.

"Your voice suits her, don't you think, Sidney?" Munroe asked, leaning close so I could hear her over the music.

It was absolutely my voice, and it did suit her, but Circe sang it in the higher register, working in the overlap between countertenor and contralto, rising more freely into falsetto than I had. I wondered if it was hard for her to stay at the top of my range or if it was a natural result of my voice transplanted to a young woman's larynx. Was that where it was now, my voice? Had she been physically altered by mojo or was there an invisible course of the stuff running in her throat to allow my voice to flow through her?

It didn't matter.

There she was, onstage, singing my song with my voice. Killing it. I'd written "Feel Like Dyin'" as a rock ballad that Elvis might have crooned. Circe had reinterpreted it as 1980s techno emo. It was cool.

Munroe leaned against me, shoulder to shoulder.

"Things come together sometimes, honey. I never knew what to do with your voice. It's fantastic, but it needs the right package. It sat at the back of a shelf. Then Francois came to me fourteen years ago and told me he needed a sly. You had let him down, he said, when he needed you most. *Tell Munroe every-*

thing and she'll see what she can do, is what I told him. The words stuck in his craw, but he got them all out. Imagine, Francois a grandpapa. I was so tickled. Sue sized up the job, said it could be done, but it was a chancy piece of work. The kind of tricky bit you had been best at. Needed your carelessness. Your death-wish daring. But you were sidelined in misery, honey. Oh, wait, here's my favorite bit."

Circe had come to the high point of the song, a stab-into-my-head voice, a final cry. She drew it out as the walls of music that had been building around her crashed down, a shriek not of desire but of anger. *"I feel like dyin!"*

"Sidney," Munroe said. "That girl has it. Of course all the mojo doesn't hurt."

She was right on both counts. Circe had charisma, all the presence her friends had talked about, and she also had the magnetic sparkle that came from being draped in mojo. Adam's rib on a chain around her neck, my shirt, and the current that flowed to her from her family's crazed history.

The song ended, but Circe didn't give the audience time to react, bridging straight into a Sinéad O'Connor cover, "Jerusalem."

Munroe continued her story.

"Sue was the one who had the spark for how to grab Francois's treasure. She'd been working with a protégé. I viewed it askance myself, not a healthy relationship, but Sue can't be told anything. She said her boy toy could handle the thing. We settled up some odds and ends with Minerva and took the chance."

It was news to me that Sue had tutored Lloyd and that he'd shared her bed. I didn't like to hear about it now. More vanity.

Munroe always read me easily; she saw my hurt feelings.

"Don't take it personally. A thing needed to be done. As far as my needs were concerned, I got a sharp new sly, and I got my first peek at baby Circe. The little thing was already awash in mojo. I had a moment of weakness, I will admit, when I thought about spiriting her away for myself, but if you lay your courses with care, opportunities will come to you. And so it was. Circe reached out to me a couple years ago, the dear thing. Showed up at the party, just like a certain hungry boy I once knew. Her with a ukulele and a thin voice full of feeling. She could hardly be heard over the bustle of the party. I'd never have known someone new was singing if it hadn't been the way the crowd hushed to lean closer and listen. She was singing "Never Get Old." Another Sinéad O'Connor fan. I saw right away that there was mojo glowing around her, and I knew right away who she was, even though I hadn't seen her since she was a wee thing in a sly's arms. It started to tickle me then, this idea. I didn't know what it was yet, but it was there. Tickle, tickle, tickle."

She tickled her fingers into my side.

"Sue had been telling me forever that I needed to stop complaining about how the party was losing mojo to social media and do something about it. Well, it takes mojo to make mojo. A special event and a new star, a ritual live event to help set a new course for myself to pull mojo and attention to my new app. The Party. So much of it is technical; I don't understand it all myself. But talent and stage presence I know. Your voice with Circe. The sacrifice you made, the melancholy flavor of the mojo in your voice paired with her backstory? Oh, my. Wait until it leaks out, and it will leak out soon, that this new viral sensation is the survivor and heir of a mysterious suicide cult. Sidney, your song is finally going to be a hit. 'Feel Like Dyin,' sung by the suicide sweetheart, is going to top all the charts. And all that mojo is going to gush right into the new course I'm laying. Circe, the dear thing, has been as helpful as could be. Ready for her moment in the spotlight; she wants all the truth of her life out in the open. She'll do anything to get away from her mom. That is the heart of the matter as far as she is concerned. Getting away from her mom. Teenagers and their parents, nothing ever changes."

Circe slammed into the end of "Jerusalem," leaving space for the audience to react, and they reacted. I'd brought down the house a few times, had them in the palm of my hand so they clapped and hollered and whistled and stomped their feet. But nothing like this. Munroe had plotted and planned and connived to bring mojo coursing through the Echoplex that night. She'd used all her experience and skill to put Circe at the cross stream of tragedy and pop. There in the Echoplex, those hundreds of people crammed in would be able to say they had seen Circe's debut, they had been there the night Munroe fed the magic girl to the world's hunger for sparkly hot new things.

They ate her up.

It was a metaphorical feeding, but it wouldn't stay metaphorical. And it wasn't the masses who would tuck into this particular treat. Munroe was coursing mojo to and through Circe, but that wouldn't serve her own hunger. She was using Circe as a conduit for the attention and emotion that galvanizes a new star. Once she had Circe established, Munroe would change the course of all that mojo, bringing it to herself. Not just the mojo she had invested, but everything Circe had of her own. That was the invisible print on any contract made with Munroe. It was true that I'd asked her to take my voice and help me lose my heart so I could chain myself to one moment in my life, but it was also true that if I'd stayed on my rock-star path, I would have been another morsel on her table.

"Let her go, Munroe."

The words were my thoughts, but it wasn't my voice saying them. It was Francois standing at the top step of the platform, shouting over the raucous adulation. He must have been hard-pressed to find a weapon in the office where he'd been left. He held a stubby knife a bartender would use to slice wedges of lime. Sue was between him and Munroe. He had no hope of anything, and I had no way to help him.

"You can't use her like this," he yelled. "I won't let you." He raised the knife, but he was barely looking at Munroe, his eyes pulled to the stage, where his granddaughter was leaning into the microphone, a hand raised to acknowledge the crowd and ask them for a little quiet.

Sue's hand had darted inside her jacket, emerging with the blade, held like a magic wand that cast spells of death.

"Don't kill him, Sue," Munroe said.

Francois didn't hear her, lost in seeing his daughter's daughter.

"*Thanks,*" Circe was saying, her amplified voice cutting through the din of the crowd.

Francois was pointing at me.

"Did you know about this? Is this some fucking deal of yours, giving her your voice?"

Sue gave a little wave of her blade.

"Catchpenny knows less than nothing, Francois. We've been halfway to telling him about how you replaced him, and he still doesn't see light."

"*Thanks,*" Circe said again. "*Tonight is really special for me. Being here is amazing for so many reasons. It's magic, right?*" The crowd cheered. "*Right?*" she said again. "*You can feel it, can't you?*"

She was laying down a beat on her synthesizer as she spoke, thick and ominous, building, grinding.

Francois was shaking his head.

"Circe wasn't part of the deal, Munroe."

Munroe ran a hand over the side of her head, slicking her hair where a few strands had come loose.

"Don't make this about yourself, Francois."

"*It feels like anything is possible, yeah?*" Circe was saying. "*And it is, it really is. This world, it's not what it looks like. It's not what they tell us it is. Something else is on the other side.*"

Munroe looked at the stage.

"I don't like the patter. She was supposed to play four songs before she said a word."

"*We don't have to be here,*" Circe said. "*We can decide not to do this. We have options they don't want us to know about. We have a way out of all of this.*"

Munroe was out of her chair, stepping to the edge of the platform, ringed fingers wrapping around the brass rail.

"What is she talking about?"

I felt ice and darkness gathering. Forebodings of misfortune. Not for the first time that night, I suddenly knew I'd been wrong about everything. I grabbed Munroe's wrist.

"Pull the plug. Cut her off. The mojo you coursed, take it back now."

She tried to pull her arm away from me.

"I can't turn it off like a tap. And I don't want to. This is my night."

I pointed at the stage.

"It's her night. We all got it wrong. It's her night."

Circe fingered a quick riff on her keyboard.

"*You don't have to be here. You can be somewhere else. This world is all wrong. We can do better. I have a song about what I'm saying.*"

The crowd wanted to hear the song.

Munroe was shaking her head.

"What song? I know all her songs." She looked at me. "She has your songs. What is she talking about?"

I tried to get her to look at me, to understand what she had done.

"She's the suicide sweetheart, Munroe. You said it. You did it.

She's talking about suicide. She has her father's mojo and now she has yours and she's going to use it to finish what her dad started. Pull the plug."

She wrenched free of me, looking at Francois.

"Does he know what he's talking about?"

Francois was staring at Circe, shaking his head.

"He's crazy. Her only problem is you."

Sue had taken out her phone.

"Whatever her game, dear, people are into it. Her accounts are exploding. Everyone is tuning in." She glanced at Munroe. "I think Catchpenny has the right inkling. Say a word, I can shut her up right now." Her arm rose, knife poised to be thrown.

Circe pointed at the audience.

"*Okay, I'll sing it. But not here.*" She smiled, riding the energy of the crowd and the looping, layering steamroller of techno gloom she was building on her keys. "*There should be more of us for this to be right. A lot more. You find me. We can sing together. Change everything together. Yeah? You want to do that? Yeah!*"

Yeah, they wanted to do that. The walls vibrated with how badly they wanted to do it.

She pulled a phone, showed it to them.

"*Follow me to find me, yeah? Okay. Let's go!*"

She lifted her arms as the disco ball above the stage took a sudden whirling lurch and a pair of arms stretched out of it, followed by a head and torso, spinning as the ball spun, hanging out of it upside down like a kid with their knees hooked on the highest bar of a jungle gym. Rotating, face coming around as the hands grabbed for Circe's, took hold, and lifted her.

Me.

Me.

Me.

Me.

My reflection distended from the mirrored bottom of the spinning disco ball, lifting Circe from the stage. I heard voices saying things that made no sense and did not connect to anything. Everything happened in a stutter of images and words. Random frames in a disjointed movie with a fractured plot.

"What is he doing here, Sue?" I heard Munroe say.

Francois screaming, "Circe, don't trust him!" Clambering off the VIP platform.

Sue frozen, stunned by dismay. "Clay?" she said, and I could see the confused question mark floating over her head.

Munroe jerking the brass rail back and forth, threatening to pull it loose.

"Stop him!"

Sue's arm whipping forward. "Clay," she said again, a mourning, as the knife spun from her hand in an arc over the audience, skimming the pipe-tangled ceiling, flying toward the stage. An impossible throw guided by magic. Sue never missed her mark.

And me, I'd already dived over the brass rail of the VIP platform, directly onto the packed audience. Hands came up, arms instinctively lifted, and for a few seconds I lived one of my rockstar dreams, surfing the crowd as they pushed me away, each of them trying to get rid of this jerk who had just landed on their heads. I rose and fell, surging with the crowd as they lurched toward the stage for a better view.

There was Francois, trying to claw his way through the bodies between him and his granddaughter as I was surfed past him.

There was Munroe, heaving on the rail, watching her dreams running away from her.

Sue, eyes following the path of her knife as it spun toward the stage.

And my reflection, twisting, dangling from the mirror ball, snatching the suicide girl, hauling her up and away. Circe rose and began to spin with the ball, revealing, as she rotated, the hand-stitched patch on the back of her red denim vest. A black circle, encompassed by the words I'd come to recognize.

SHE RISES—WE FALL—SHE RISES

I rolled, listed, was pulled down, lifted up. A last gasp and last look.

Knife slicing toward the stage.

Circe rising, pulled up and away and into the nothing hiding inside the mirrors that coated the disco ball, leaving behind the astonished and delighted hush of an audience who had just had their collective jaw permanently dropped as Perilous Sue's knife, thrown sure but a moment too late, smashed into the mirror globe, shattering it instead of my reflection.

And then the roar. And then everyone heading for the exits, ready to find Circe and to follow her all the way to the end. And me hitting the deck, scrambling on hands and knees, doing my best not to be trampled. People were jammed at the doors, back-washing, spurting out in jets. People were climbing onto the banquettes along the walls, getting above the mob. I saw someone go down, saw three people help them to their feet. It was chaos, but it wasn't a riot. Security manikins were helplessly trying to quell the exodus. I didn't look behind me, keeping my eyes on my goal, the stage. If Sue was following me, I'd know about it when I felt her hand. I boosted myself up on the stage. I wasn't the only one. Audience members were up there, phones out, shooting the scene, talking, searching accounts, looking for Circe. The hint she had given them.

Follow me to find me.

They needed to find the right social account to follow so they could discover where she'd land next. I could have told them where to look. *Gyre,* I could have said, but I wasn't going to pass out any hints that would speed these kids to Circe. The word would be out soon enough. Plenty of people would have clocked the patch on the back of her jacket and realized that she was into *Gyre;* they'd be looking for her account and posts.

Someone would figure out where she wanted them to go to hear her song, and they would spray that information across the social-verse.

I had a different kind of following in mind.

I squeezed between the kids who lined the edge of the stage. Circe's keyboards had been kicked over by her flailing boots as she'd been spirited away. The stage itself was randomly mosaicked by hundreds of tiny square mirrors that had scattered when Sue's knife hit the disco ball and sent it crashing down. The remains of the ball, a crumpled mirror sphere, was at the center of the glittering spread, Sue's knife jutting from it. I began to walk the perimeter of the arrangement, stepping carefully between the fragments, doing my best not to disturb the lay, moving quickly, picking out a path toward the broken ball of silver glass. Care must be taken, but there was no time to spare. I saw itsy flickers of myself as I walked over and among the tiny mirrors.

The broken disco ball was like my mind and my thoughts in that moment, fragmented and scattered, each one a cracked piece of something else, all of them reflecting back at one another. Nothing to hold on to. No time to think, no capacity to hold a clear thought. My eyes skipped over the random pattern on the stage while my thoughts skipped through the random patterns in my head. I was looking for something. What was I looking for? I felt it without knowing for sure what it was. I'd know it when I saw it. I'd recognize it when I knew it. I'd see it when I saw what it was.

Answers.

Was I sure about what I thought was happening? I'd been wrong more than once that day and night. Several times wrong. Was Circe the bad girl, after all? Mad, bad daughter of her mad dad, and sister to even madder Carpenter. It sure seemed to run on that side of the family. But what about me? My reflection, I mean. Maybe it was the bad guy. Maybe I'd misinterpreted what

I saw. Was Circe bringing the suicide circuit to a close of mass death so she could enact her own version of Crispin's dreams? Had I seen my reflection come to her aid? Or had I seen it kidnap her?

I walked through the tiny broken mirrors on the stage. This pattern. Something was in it. Dozens of minuscule reflections looking back at myself. My thoughts skipped from image to image.

Perilous Sue's dismay. *Clay?*

Munroe, furious at what she saw on the stage. *What is he doing here, Sue?*

Circe, don't trust him, Francois had screamed.

Something resolved for me in the scattered mirror fragments. My reflection's name was Clay. And Sue and Munroe and Francois all knew it. They all knew *it*. They knew my reflection.

I'd reached the broken disco ball, its bits and pieces flung wide. I stood where Circe had stood, the center of a mojo whirlpool. But it was draining, flowing, following Circe. It would be gone soon. What should I do next? I had to follow Circe so I could do something. Stop her or help her, I didn't know which. It didn't matter. You can't follow someone in the mirrors. That's a rule.

Rules and no rules.

I stood in the swirl of Circe's mojo, looking into all the dozens of tiny mirrors spread around me. Tunnels inside tunnels inside tunnels. What was I doing? I was making new rules to get where I wanted to be. I reached toward the smashed disco ball on the floor, my hand stretching toward my hand. I touched the ball and fell forward. My hand in my hand, my arm slipping into my arm. My face, etched into a grid by the little cracks between the tiny square mirrors. Here it came. Here I was. There I was going. There I went. I was nothing.

Inside the Vestibule.

I wasn't supposed to be able to follow. I didn't think about that. I thought about Circe. Where she'd gone and how to find her. Don't think about it. Do it. My rules. I began to orient before I was fully inside. Only my goal mattered. I just had to place Circe, and I would go to her. It would work. It should work. I really hoped it worked. One shot. Go!

"Sid!"

I felt a hand on my ankle, the piece of me that hadn't yet fallen into the disco ball. Someone had grabbed it. Sue? I'd left her knife jutting from the side of the ball. I was floating free in the nothing. I needed somewhere to stand.

Below, I thought, creating it with that thought and then hitting it hard. I stood on it, hauling my foot the rest of the way inside before Sue could slice it off.

"Sid, pull me in."

I looked *down.* It was Francois, the top half of him, his hand wrapped around my ankle, desperate. From the waist down he was a gray indistinction, shadow beneath stacked panes of thick, cloudy glass. If he let go of me or if I kicked him loose, he'd be snipped in half. The half with me would be gone, the half back there in the Echoplex would kick and bleed and then be a mystery for cops and coroners to solve.

My broken thinking wanted to reassemble into a single thought. A clear idea. One thought that was vastly important to me. A lie that was lodged at the heart of my life without my knowing it had been there.

"Who is Clay?" I asked.

Francois was shaking his head, trying to climb up my leg, out of the mirrors. But I had not oriented *above*; there was no up for him to climb to.

"Pull me in. Sue's coming."

I looked *behind* him, into the vagueness of the shadow of the world. Lines, a stick figure, coming closer. Sue.

Francois was a distraction. He'd make it harder to follow Circe. I could only use the mojo that had flowed in with me, and it would drain more quickly if I had to anchor Francois to myself. He'd lied to me for longer than I knew. I didn't even know what the lies were.

"Please, Sid."

Stick-figure Sue was thickening, closing. With one good yank she could dislodge Francois and rip him in two. She knew all the tricks, Perilous Sue did. She'd taught me well, but kept secrets for herself. She could wayfind in any unmapped territory. Bored by the very idea of slying for the sake of stealing knickknacks, she'd only plumb a mirror for a thrill or a kill. When Sue deigned to walk into nothing, it was to steal a life.

Francois grabbed harder on my ankle.

"I'm sorry, Sid," he was saying. "It was Sue's idea to use your reflection. I was desperate."

His fingers slipped as Sue pulled on his legs. I grabbed his hand, our fingers tangled together. I tried to pull but didn't have the Vestibule fully oriented. I strained to pull him *forward*, but that was a direction that had no meaning relative to him. I needed *above* to pull him up from *below*.

"He's not you, Sid," Francois said, face red, hands white. "Don't think he's like you. He's different. He."

A sudden heave on his legs jerked him. Our fingers slipped but didn't pull apart.

I looked away from him. I tried to orient *above* so I could pull him up to me. I couldn't focus. I kept thinking about the lie I was living in. I couldn't concentrate. I laughed.

Francois dug his nails into my palm, grunted.

"Are you fucking laughing at me, Sid?"

I tried to stop, but couldn't.

"What do you think they're seeing back there? Is Sue hugging some disembodied legs sticking out of a broken mirror ball? I mean, what a show they got tonight."

Francois coughed, gripped harder.

"Don't, don't make me laugh. Ahgh. Shit. Shit."

"Francois!"

"She stuck me, man."

Forgetting the world and the nothing, I remembered how to orient, found *above* and held desperately to the hands of my friend, both of us pulling. A heave and lurch and Francois was with me, falling to me, but not against me because there was no *sideways*.

Face-to-face, but only for a moment.

"Find her, Sid," he said. "Keep her safe. Shit, this hurts."

I looked *below*. Sue's knife was stuck through his calf, her hand wrapped around the hilt, blood running over her fingers and down her straining forearm. She was pulling herself in. Sue and her tricks and her ways. Her other hand appeared, a fist punching through the invisible border between nothing and something, fingers closing on Francois's thigh as her face, teeth bared, emerged like a swimmer surfacing for air.

"Don't dare hurt him, Catchpenny," she screamed.

I felt her weight add itself to Francois's. He slipped from my grasp, his arms around my waist. Sue dropped back below the surface of nothing, except for one hand and the knife in Francois's leg. He was still fully inside the Vestibule with me, but just barely.

He looked up at me.

"Help Circe," he said.

Sue's hand twisted the knife. His face twisted with pain.

"I'll take care of this," he said.

And let go of me.

No. No. Please, no.

I reached for him. But, letting go of me, he was already gone.

I was alone.

Every-nothing began to crack open around me.

Out of mojo, out of time. Cracks split empty space and shot

at me like crooked black bolts of lightning. That was okay. I was where I needed to be. I chose a direction and destination and made them the same thing. Gave it a name.

Circe, I called it.

I reached for it. A hand found mine, pulled, and there I was, standing above myself, still holding my hand, as I fell out of a mirror onto my back.

THIRTY-TWO

MY REFLECTION STOOD OVER ME.

It had taken my right hand in its left, an awkward grasp that twisted both our wrists. I was on my back, at its mercy. I tried to remember what weapons I had. I'd lost Francois's gun and my knife and my window smasher. The only heavy item I was carrying was Minerva's phone, buttoned inside my jacket. There I was, my enemy literally in hand, and I didn't have anything to hit it with.

So I hit it with my fist.

Punching left-handed from my back, I swung as hard as I could. Decades of rage and misery and desperation were in my fist. I swung at my own face. One of my hands holding its hand, I was about to crush its head with a single blow. This could never have ended any other way. And what would happen to me in the next instant? After my last sliver of reason for living was gone, what would I do? I didn't care.

My fist made contact. With predictable results.

Swinging with my left hand, flopped on my back, I missed its face and slugged it in the elbow, hurting my hand and striking its funny bone. It flinched and made a funny-bone face and we let go of each other so I could rub my bruised knuckles and it could massage its elbow. My moment of furious culmination dissolving into pathetic slapstick. What could I have really expected? It was my life after all.

"What is he doing here?" I heard someone say, and realized that I had been hearing voices since my reflection pulled me from the Vestibule. Loud voices raised in argument, and also crying.

"Why is everyone in my room?" the voice, very angry, wanted to know.

I'd been unable to look at anything but my reflection until the sting of my clumsy punch knocked me back to sensibility. Now I could shift my eyes and see where I was. Circe's room. Again I had come out of her mirror and flopped onto her bed. My reflection was standing next to the bed, holding its elbow, blocking my view of half the room.

"Get him off my bed," the angry voice said. "I want everyone out of my room."

The crying I'd been hearing started to heave and gasp as the crier tried to talk through their tears. "Yuhr hrr, yuhr hum, oh, oh, thuhnk yuh, yuhr aluhv," the crier said.

Angry voice was still angry.

"You have to let go of me. Enough, okay?"

I sat up on the bed and finally saw what I'd hoped to see. Circe, with Iva wrapped around her, sobbing, squeezing her daughter as hard as she could, rubbing her face in Circe's hair.

"Mom, you have to stop."

Iva did not stop, not until Circe said, "Let me go, Mom. I have to get out of here."

Iva drew her head back to look her daughter in the face, sobs choking off.

"You're not going anywhere."

Circe was trying to wriggle free of her mom's arms.

"People are waiting for me."

"People can wait."

"It's important."

"You explaining to me where you have been and what you've been doing is important."

Circe gave a hard twist to break free.

"Don't pretend like you don't know."

"How would I know when you never tell me anything? You are not leaving this house until you tell me what you have been doing."

"I'm trying to make something, Mom. I'm in the middle of it and it is really important and you are fucking it up."

"Everything is my fault, as usual."

"Don't get all fucking victimy."

"Don't drop f-bombs just to make me angry. I know you can curse, you don't have to show off in front of other people." Iva waved her arm at me and my reflection, the other people in the room, and looked at us for the first time. Her eyes went from one to the other, an expert double-take. "What the fuck?"

Circe folded her arms over her chest.

"Now who's dropping f-bombs?"

Iva was shaking her head.

"Why are there two of you?" she asked my reflection. "Have there been two of you all along?"

I raised my hand.

"I think you mean to be asking me that."

Iva covered her face with her hands.

"This fucking shit."

Circe rolled her eyes.

"Right, Mom, like you don't know anything about any of it."

Iva still had her face in her hands, her voice trembling, a hint of an earthquake of anger ready to break loose.

"Circe, you do not want to use that tone with me right now. Not after you've been doing what you've been doing."

"What have I been doing, Mom? I thought you didn't know anything about it."

Iva pulled her face from her hands and pointed, one index finger jabbing at her daughter, the other aimed at me and my reflection.

"You've been fucking around with that stuff!"

"What stuff, Mom? Say the word, for fuck sake."

Iva swung her arms around, pointing this way and that, trying to take in the multiverse and all its mysteries, contradictions, and annoyances.

"Mojo! You ungrateful brat!" She dropped her arms. Her top blown. "After I tried to protect you. Give you something normal. Keep you away from that shit. You go out and jump into the middle of it. Bring it into our home. All I wanted was for you to have what I never had. I just wanted you to have a chance for a normal life."

Circe stared at her, unmoving except for a slight cock to her eyebrow as she said, "You call this normal?"

Iva's eyes narrowed.

"What is that supposed to mean?"

"I don't know, Mom. I mean, you moved me around so much when I was a kid I never had time to make friends or finish a grade at a school. I had like a hundred different last names and addresses. Was that normal?"

"Don't exaggerate. It wasn't that many names."

"When we did settle down, you wouldn't let me go to a regular school even though I wanted to. When I make friends you say you have to *vet* them. You actually do some kind of hacker background check on their families. How normal is any of that? You act like you don't have a family, like you were spontaneously generated from the atmosphere. Pretty normal, uh-huh. We live in a compound with cameras and alarms and guns everywhere. Yeah, all the normal people live like this. You treat me like a prisoner who you're trying to brainwash into thinking that a jail is the normal world."

Iva opened her mouth, closed it, shook her head.

"I'm not that bad," she said.

Circe planted her hands on her hips.

"Fine, Mom, you're great, and my childhood has been perfect. Now I really have to go. Just give me my stuff so I can get out of here and finish what I started."

Iva lifted her hands and turned her face away, over it all.

"I don't have your stuff, and you aren't going anywhere."

"This is really important!"

Iva turned her back, and went out the door, heading down the hall.

"Then it should be important enough to explain it to me," she called back into the room.

Circe looked up at the ceiling in adolescent disbelief.

"Oh. My. Fuck. Mom. You are being so stupid right now."

"Calling me stupid isn't helping anything, Circe," Iva said from down the hall.

Circe stiffened her arms, made fists, and stomped out the door, following her mom.

"Mom, just give me my fucking stuff!"

Leaving me alone with my reflection. I rubbed my fist, glared at it, fixing my eyes at the spot just above its nose. I was going to grab its hair and drive that spot into the corner of Circe's dresser.

It smirked.

"What're you staring at, asshole?"

I came off the bed, aimed myself at the thing that killed my wife, and it casually tucked its hand inside its black jacket, produced a small, flat automatic pistol, and I had a change of heart and stumbled to a halt in front of it.

It eased the door shut and leaned its back against it, the gun at its side, its presence a sufficient deterrent.

"Moms and daughters. Better for us to stay out of that."

Its free hand went into its jacket and came out with a pack of Dunhill Red cigarettes and a small silver lighter. It expertly one-handed a smoke from the pack and lit it.

"Since when do you smoke?" I said. "I never smoked."

"Yeah, well that's the point, Sid," it said, and blew a tidy smoke ring. "I'm not you."

I eyed the gun, and took a seat on the edge of the bed. It was uncomfortable sitting there, waiting, hearing Iva and Circe arguing as they tromped around the house. My reflection had cigarettes to pass the time. All I had was secondhand smoke. I made it through half a cigarette before I had to say something, anything, the first thing that came to mind.

"So," I said, "you and Perilous Sue are a thing."

It flicked ash.

"You have a problem with that? Never mind, I know you have a problem with it."

"I don't have a problem if you don't have a problem."

"Yeah, right."

It smoked. I coughed, pointedly.

"I'm not putting it out," it said.

We stopped talking. I made it another eight seconds.

"So, people call you something."

"They call me by my name."

"*Clay*. Like made from. Like a golem. Whose idea was that? Sue's?"

"It's Clay, like short for a Claymore mine. Because I intend to blow shit up."

"That's dumb."

It dropped its cigarette butt and ground it into the floor.

"Your stupid fucking face. I can't believe I have to stand here and look at your face."

I shrugged.

"It's your face, too."

It made a face. I mean, it made a disgusted expression.

"I do not have your face." It pointed at itself, drew a circle around its face. "This is mine. We are not the same. I know your face. The first thing I remember ever in the world is how happy it made me to see your face. I hate you for making me love seeing your face. I was nothing but a craving to see your face. My sensation of existence was being forced to love you as much as you loved yourself."

I looked at the floor. I didn't want to look at its face while it scolded me. I didn't want to lose my cool and attack it while it had that gun. Until I could be sure I had a way to smash it, I had to stay cool. Eyes on the floor. But I couldn't keep my mouth shut. That would be asking too much of myself.

"Don't blame me for being here," I said. "I never wanted you."

It laughed, bitter, forced. Like I probably would have.

"I'm all you wanted. More you. You, you, you. You can't pretend with me. I was made out of your want. More of yourself, that's what you wanted. A universe made of Sid so that you would be the undisputed focus of everything that existed."

I didn't want to look at it, but now I was too mad not to look at it. Blaming me for what it was. I couldn't take that.

"No," I said. "I didn't draw you out of a mirror. I'm no limner. It wasn't me. You know, you were there; it wasn't me. It was. Her. Abigail was the one who wanted you. Not you. Wanted me. To be there. You can't tell me, because she told me what she did. She looked for me in the mirror when I wasn't there, she traced me in the steam from the bath. You were the one trying to get out. You were the one looking out and making her feel like she could reach me that way. Do not blame me for what you are. I know what you are. I know what you did."

"What *I* did?" it said under its breath, almost like it was trying to remember. It looked at me. "I will tell you what I did," it said. "First, I'm going to tell you what I saw. Once I could see anything but your face, feel anything but love for you, the next thing I saw was this girl. This very funny, beautiful, very messed-up, very sad girl. Once I saw her, she's what I wanted more of. But I didn't get to choose what I saw. I could only see anything if you were there. That was like a condition, an illness. I couldn't *be* unless you were there. But what I wanted for myself was to see this sad girl. Of course most of the time when she was there, you were standing in the way and I had to love you whether I wanted to or not. Imagine having love, feeling love, imagine someone being able to force that on you. Oh, man. Not cool, Sid, not cool. What I saw, when you and that girl were together, was how little you knew her. When you looked at her, what you saw was what you wanted to see. You saw the girl you wanted her to be. That girl, the pretend girl you had in your head, was strong, independent, didn't give a fuck, and could take care of herself no matter what. Most important, Sid, she could handle it if you ditched her. She could handle it if you weren't around while she was having a baby. But the real girl you were living with, who loved you as much as I had to love you, she was barely hanging on. She'd been that way for years. She was hustling drinks in a bar when she met you. She was so desperate to have something, someone, to not be alone, she hitched herself to this stranger with a guitar and followed him to Los Angeles. She married this guy who had nothing but a nice voice and good hair. She needed him so much, she tried to hide everything from him. She didn't want him to know why she'd run away from Galveston. She didn't want him to know about how her parents couldn't deal with her *problems,* how they'd put her in a hospital, in a facility. She didn't want him to know about the times she'd been on suicide watch, about the way it sometimes felt like she had someone else living in her head, someone who took over her thinking. She had to be strong to survive, had to be able to take care of herself, but anyone who really looked at her could tell she was hanging by a thread. Her toughness was a front, anyone could see it. She needed someone to help her, but she was afraid to ask for help because the guy she loved thought she was a tough Texas broad and he liked her that way. When she found out she was going to have a baby, she didn't know if she was more happy or more scared. She wasn't scared of having the baby, she was scared she was going to lose her guy. She knew he wasn't into being a dad. She thought about getting rid of her baby. But she couldn't. Anyone could see all of this, if they could see past themself. It was hard for me, with you in the way, but I saw it. The way she was looking at you while you were looking at yourself, and the way she changed what was on her face when you bothered to glance her way. That told the story, man. No matter how much I wanted you to look at her and help her, I couldn't stop loving you. But she was the reason that I knew I was me. The way I felt about her, how I could see her in a way that you didn't, that told me I wasn't just there to love your face. I had more than that. I was more than that. I was something of my own. That night, I was there that night, watching you."

It began to ape me. Me from back then. Preening, posing me. It primped its hair, turned to look at itself over its shoulder, did my little dance of self-admiration. A perfect imitation of who I'd once been. Man, it really nailed me.

It dropped the imitation and became itself again, poised and languid and cold.

"I watched you loving yourself that night. At the same time, I watched her sitting on the sink, talking to you as if you were paying attention to her. But you were hearing what you wanted to hear. You were hearing her be strong, a boss. You were letting yourself believe she had it all under control, like she knew what she wanted. You pretended it was a slipup when you asked if she was sure she wanted the baby. That was no slipup. You were telling her what you wanted. *Get rid of it,* was what you were saying. *Get rid of it or I'll get rid of you.* You throw this pity party for yourself over and over, feeling guilty for not wanting a baby. You won't admit what you really wanted. You wanted her to deal with it and leave you out. If she wanted to keep the baby, she'd have to deal with that without you. She was strong enough, you told yourself. You needed her more than she needed you, you told yourself. You think she didn't know? She knew. You went off to record your song that night and left her alone. And she knew she was alone in the world, man. You weren't going to be there for her."

It took out its cigarettes, then stopped moving, looking at its hands, gun in one, Dunhills in the other.

"Do you remember being born?" it asked, shaking its head. "I do." It fingered a cigarette from the pack, slipped it between its lips, and put the box back in its jacket. It lit the cigarette, held it between forefinger and middle finger and forgot about it.

"She ran the bath. The room filled with steam. The mirror clouded. That was the first time I was there without you. You had put so much into the mirror that night, it was the last part of you that I needed so I could be something without you. But she made it happen. She wanted you with her so much. But she wanted you to be the person she'd always needed you to be. She drew me on the glass. She drew the you she wanted to be with. She kissed me. The tub was full and she got in. She'd had some drinks. Do you remember? You don't. You didn't care if she was drinking with the baby. So she'd had some drinks. She was hearing the bad voice in her head, the voice that hated her. She took a pill. Just one, to shut up the voice. I watched. Her eyes closed. I watched. She slid, and her eyes opened and she sat up. I watched. She knew she was falling asleep. She knew she should get out of the tub. But she didn't know why she should. She didn't think anyone would care. Probably, she thought, everyone would be happier if she did nothing. Especially you. Her eyes closed. I screamed. I made a face like someone screaming and tried to make a noise, but I'd never made a noise. I tried to reach for her. But I'd never moved. Her head rolled to the side. Her eyes opened again. She looked at me. She saw me. She smiled. Her eyes closed. She slid down in the tub. Water washed over the top, spilled on the floor. Water washed over the tiles right to my feet. I was screaming and pushing. I was clawing my eyes out. I wanted to stop being there. I wanted to see something else. I think she died then. She died, and she coursed to me. Her love, it coursed into me, and there I was. I was on the other side without knowing there was another side. I was what she wanted. I lifted her out, her face. But I couldn't look at it like that so I put her back in the water. I sat there and held her hand under the water. For hours. Until you came back. I didn't understand anything. I didn't know what was happening. I felt like I was in a million pieces. When I saw you, I knew I was trapped in something mad. I ran away. I had to get away. I didn't even know what I was running from."

It remembered its cigarette and took a drag.

"That's what I did," it said. "What you did was make up a story about it all. One that was tragic, that made you feel bad about yourself. But not too tragic, and not too bad. Just tragic enough and just bad enough that you could still make yourself into a hero. Sad boy sacrificing his voice and his heart so he could look for a murderer with his own face. Okay. Here I am. Let me help you. Turn around."

I turned around.

There I was in Circe's mirror.

There it stood behind me, smoking.

"If there's a murderer in this story, he's in that mirror right now. You tell me who it is."

THIRTY-THREE

TWO SAD, homeless teenagers running away from their pasts meet in a West Texas honky-tonk.

They don't know anything about anything and no one has ever cared about them. They dig each other, and with nothing else to hang on to, they hang on to each other. *I give it a few months,* you think. But turn it into a myth or a legend or a ritual, and it could last a lifetime. Someone might live in it forever, letting themself forget what was hard about it. Erasing the fights they had about where they should go next, how to pay for the bus tickets, who was going to dive in the next dumpster for something to eat. Blurring the memories of breaking into cars to steal a purse or a suitcase. Someone might remember only the sound of waves and an oversize bathroom, and forget rats and cockroaches. Someone might forget the mornings their young wife was paralyzed with depression and had to be cajoled into going to work at a juice shop, where she'd spend the day being hit on by boardwalk creeps and tourists. Let yourself live in a myth long enough and you could entirely forget the feeling of being trapped in a relationship that was making you feel worse about yourself when you were just starting to think you might be special.

No matter what tales you spin for yourself about how special it all was, you can't unfeel what you felt when you found her dead. The sickening and unwanted sense of relief. Now you'd never have to choose to leave your wife and your unborn baby. The choice had been taken from you.

Your problem became how to live with yourself after you felt that.

Having a mission would help. Like, what if you hunted down the guy who killed your sad, young, beautiful wife and your unborn baby? What if it was like a magical quest that required you to give up your dreams and debase yourself by becoming a thief? Pretty noble, all that. No one could ever accuse you of being callous and selfish and uncaring if you did all that.

Selling my voice, throwing it away for no good reason. Having my heart cut out. Leaving myself no way back. *I* did that. I became a thief. I wasn't doing it because I wanted to chase my reflection and get revenge. I wasn't doing it because it was the ultimate romantic sacrifice. I did it because I didn't deserve to have my voice or my heart anymore. I wasn't chasing or seeking anything, I was punishing myself for what I had felt. Abigail was dead. Whether she'd been murdered or had just slid sadly alone under the bathwater, she was dead. And the first thing I felt was relief.

I could have spent the years between then and now singing songs. Singing songs might have made someone feel good. Singing songs wouldn't have hurt anyone. It might even have made something better than it was before I sang. I could have been singing songs. I might have made something a little better for just one person in some tiny way. All I had to do was be honest with myself. Look at myself in a mirror. Learn to live with who I was. I could have sung my way through it all, and maybe made something beautiful out of the stupidity and loss.

Instead. Well.

Instead, my life.

My heartless, thieving life.

THIRTY-FOUR

I LOOKED AT MYSELF in Circe's mirror. There I was. Nowhere to hide.

It stood behind me, smoking.

Not it. Him.

Clay stood behind me, smoking.

I turned back to him. He wasn't me. He wasn't a mirror. He wore cool suits and terrible shoes and carried a gun and smoked English cigarettes and used swear words. He was on a secret mission to blow stuff up. He was in cahoots with Circe, deep in the machinations of some master plan to junk up the world. I was none of those things. His cheeks were dry. My cheeks were slick with tears.

"So, Clay," I said, "what have you been doing all these years?"

He took a drag, blew smoke.

"I thought you'd never ask, Sid." He looked up, thinking for a moment, looked at me, shrugged. "I guess that mostly I've been doing my best to not be like you. Long story short? I ran out of the apartment and freaked out for a few weeks. I was a newborn. We, people like me, from where we come from, we don't know everything you people know. You *casters*, you stand in front of a mirror and this thing happens on the other side that you know fuck all about. So what's in our heads, memories, life details, whatever, it tends to be random. I knew a lot about

you and your life and Abigail, but I didn't know what life was.
I lurked around Venice for a while. I even came back to the
apartment. You were gone. I poked around in there. I felt like
I knew most every item, but I also knew I'd never really seen
any of it before. I took some stuff. An armful of your junk that
I thought made me more like me. Man, did I blend into the
Venice scene, wandering the streets with a bag of random stuff.
It took a couple of weeks for me to understand things. Things
like three-dimensional space and gravity and light and darkness
and breathing and weather and sound and the rub of my skin on
my own skin and blinking. I didn't know anything about reflections and mirrors and mojo. But, like you, I knew that someone
named Munroe knew some weird stuff and had hinted at it with
you. I didn't know how to find people. I thought I could say,
Munroe, and that would make something happen. I guess I did
that a lot. I was a crazy guy shuffling around the streets saying
the same name over and over. *Munroe, Munroe, Munroe.* Well,
you know the racket, it's a small world. I got noticed. By then,
Munroe knew what had happened. She knew you saw yourself
kill Abigail. Pieces got put together. Munroe heard about a guy
with great hair walking around Venice saying her name, and she
sent Sue to find me."

He stopped talking, took a drag, and inspected the coal at the
end of his cigarette.

"I'm not sure of the timing on all this. You'd probably know
better than me."

He stopped talking again, and I realized he was asking a
question.

"I'm sorry, what do you want to know?" I asked.

"So. Were you already hanging out with Sue? Right away,
after Abigail? Or was it later?"

It was surprising how awkward this was.

"Soon after. Right after she." I put a hand to my chest, where my heart should be. "After she took care of this for me. We were around each other a lot. She was teaching me to sly. Things just kind of happened with us. Not for too long. I couldn't take it."

"You dumped her."

"We weren't like that. There was no dumping. It just stopped."

"Did she stop it?"

"No. I mean."

"Who called who last?"

"Uh."

He took a drag.

"You ghosted her, Sid. You never said a word to her about cutting it off."

"Why is this a thing?"

He shook his head.

"It's a thing because there I was, an actual gibbering idiot, lost and bound for a grim ending, and this person comes up to me on the street and says hello to me. Stranger, but her face rings a bell. You'd met her at Munroe's so I had some idea that I knew her. She says she can explain why I'm so confused. I was mostly still trying to be you at that point. What I knew and felt almost all came from you. Remember what you felt for Abigail and the baby, Sid? That's what I was feeling. I thought me and you should be together so we could comfort each other. Who else could understand what we were going through? But Munroe wanted me iced. I was just another curiosity as far as she was concerned. She wanted to have me in her collection. Sue tucked me away at her place in North Hollywood. Mostly I was alone. Looking in the mirror, wishing I could figure out how to see you. Crying about Abigail. Being miserable. Sue would stop in when she wasn't doing Munroe's bidding. We'd talk about the world, about people I thought I knew because of your memories, about what I'd been watching on TV. I watched a lot of TV. She'd look at me sometimes while we were hanging on the couch watching *Seinfeld* or something, and she'd say, like,

You really are different. She meant different from you, of course. Then something changed. She came in one night drunk. She came in my room, woke me up. She had a hammer. She was saying how Munroe wouldn't let her break the original so she'd have to settle for breaking the copy. That was the night she figured out you dumped her."

"Wait," I said. "Sue didn't care about me. I was just fun for her."

"No. You were a big deal. Rejection hurts. Being cut off with no explanation. She was hurt and wanted to hurt you back, but you were showing your potential as a sly so Munroe backed her off. I was the next best thing. It was an important moment for me, Sid. It was the moment when I first really knew that I could be my own person. She was standing there with a hammer, eyeing me like I was a china teapot, and I said to her, *I'm sorry he treated you like that.* Could have been my last words. But she lowered the hammer and said, *You didn't do anything.*"

He pointed at himself with his cigarette.

"*I* didn't do anything." He pointed at me. "*You* did it. That's when I really started to get the whole I-and-you thing. Anyway, Sue climbed into bed with me. It was a drunk thing, she was thinking about you. She left right after, and that was all for a while. I was crazy for her, but she had to work some stuff out. Fucking a manikin is a kink for most people. She didn't care about it being taboo, she just didn't like the idea that she'd be using me as a substitute for you. That was beneath her. We worked it out eventually. But she never was comfortable making it public. Partly that was Munroe's fault; she didn't want anyone to know she had me. You were a big-time sly then, and she thought she could use me if she ever needed to leverage you. So me and Sue were on the down-low for years. That changed when Francois needed someone to grab Circe for him. That's the job that made my rep. But I guess you've figured all that out by now."

No, I had not figured it all out. I was still trying to wrap my head around the idea of my reflection being in a long-term relationship with Perilous Sue. It took me a moment to catch up with what he was saying about Circe.

"No," I said. "Lloyd rescued Circe."

"No," he said. "I rescued Circe. Because you couldn't."

Clay and Sue talked a lot. Like lovers do, they talked about their histories and their dreams and what they wanted from the world and how great they thought each other was. This was an odd exercise, as Clay was still sorting himself from me. Listening to him talk about what it was like to become self-aware while being essentially nonexistent, Sue realized he might have some perspectives on slying that she could use. She counted on knowing that side of the racket better than anyone. After a few years, Clay asked to be taken into a mirror. Like he wanted to see the house he'd grown up in. Sue obliged. When they came out, he felt certain he knew how to get back himself. He tried, but a reflection can't sly. A reflection has no mojo and can't use mojo.

Rules. And also, no rules.

I was slipping by then. I'd lied to myself, saying I was on a heroic quest, and years after Abigail's death I was having troubling holding on to that lie. Truthfully, I was on a running-away-from-myself quest. You can't have it both ways. You can't be the hero and a coward at the same time. To me, it felt like I hit a bad patch. I couldn't make anything work, and I didn't want to try very hard to fix that. It was a major depression, but it wasn't chemical, not entirely. Somewhere inside my brain, I'd figured out what I was up to. Running away instead of questing. My sacrifice was pointless. My reason for slying, for becoming a thief, it was all pointless. A depressing, if only unconsciously acknowledged, conclusion. It felt like my depression came from the outside, an attack, but it was all my own.

Then Francois needed my help rescuing Circe and I was incapable of helping because I was useless. So Francois went to Munroe, and she figured Lloyd for the job. But Sue had another idea. Actually, it was both her and Clay who had the idea. They'd had it sometime before, but couldn't find an angle on it. Theoretically, any reflection should know more about how things work in the Vestibule than any sly. Take a reflection like Clay, who'd been tutored by Sue, and cast by a top sly like me; it figured they'd be able to pull off some astoundingly tricky multifold shenanigans.

If, and only if, you could get past that rule about reflections not being able to use mojo.

Sue and Clay had an idea about that, too. They pitched Munroe. Lloyd was an uppity independent contractor. Why take a broker's percentage of what Francois would pay Lloyd when you could pocket it all yourself, and maybe replace your fading star sly at the same time? All it would take, Sue told Munroe, was a little capital, a phone call to Hillary Minerva, and a bit of minor coursing to redirect mojo away from my heart and into Clay.

They didn't know if it would work, but if it did, it would open a lot of possibilities. Munroe agreed to cover the costs with Minerva, and they set a course that directed my heart's mojo to Clay. It made twisted sense when I thought about it. Rituals are often made of formal gestures and conceptual associations. Clay might not be me, but he was as close to me as one could be. The mojo skimmed from my heart was a similar step of removal from myself. It reminded me of voodoo dolls and effigies working in reverse. Instead of punishing the original by destroying the copy, they gave the copy my power. But that doesn't mean I went unpunished in the process. Fourteen years of drain on my mojo. All the years I'd struggled against myself to get my act together. It really had been a struggle against myself. They stuck a siphon in my heart and slowly bled me.

With the tap in place on my heart, Clay attempted to sly from Minerva's office to Munroe's place. Success. Then they tried a few experiments and discovered that he couldn't use mojo from a curiosity or have it coursed to him from any other sly's heart. Only my heart served, only my mojo. Rules and no rules.

So there it was. Clay could ply both my trade and my mojo better than I could. And everyone knew about it except me. Lloyd and Minerva, Sue and Munroe. That made me feel lame. Like a tool. I was a tool. And Francois knew. That made me feel confused. Hurt. Mad. Francois. Hanging off me, Sue's knife in his leg. Letting go of me in the Vestibule to keep Sue from pulling herself inside. Blink. Gone. Now I'd never get to tell him how pissed I was at him. Or thank him for saving me.

I flopped back on Circe's bed and covered my face with my hands.

"My life is a joke," I said.

"So's everyone else's."

"Mine's not funny."

"That's your fault."

I uncovered my eyes, wishing they were cannons.

He shrugged, impervious.

"You're a sad, pathetic fucker who wallows in misery, Sid. Don't blame your life on me because I used your mojo. You being stuck, that's your own doing. Shit, I've kept you afloat. If I wasn't around slying my ass off, Minerva never would have let you coast on your back rent so long. I made use of your heart while you were letting it rot. I know you have depression, but that doesn't make you less responsible for your life. As for Abigail, well, hey, man, you may want to be the hero or the villain in her story, but you're not either. You can't steal what she did from her. I was there and I can't say for sure what her intentions were, other than wanting not to think for a few minutes. I don't know if she meant to kill herself or was just careless and sad. You didn't do anything to her. Fuck sake, you were messed-up kids. Of course you didn't know what you wanted or how to take care of each other. In the end, Sid, the worst thing you did, the only thing you did, was say something shitty about not wanting a baby. The rest of it after that was you trying to make it all about you. Vanity. So, yeah, there's nothing funny about your joke of a life. Not a giggle to be had. I wonder if you have any intentions of doing something about that now."

I now knew more about myself than I ever wanted to know. But you don't have all your assumptions about your life ripped up in front of you and come to terms with it in an instant. He could have been lying about everything. That's what I wanted to believe. But I was looking at myself in a painfully, absurdly literal way. I didn't like what I was seeing or hearing, but I was staring myself right in the eyes, and I knew I was telling the truth.

I imagine that my heart, just at that moment, if seen in its jar, would have looked like a deflated balloon. I can't say I was numb, because I did feel something. But I didn't recognize what I was feeling. I just knew that I was very tired.

"What are you doing here, Clay?" I asked.

"The best I can."

I got off the bed.

"Why are you in the middle of this mess? I'm vain? Listen to all the superior crap coming out of you, like you have all the answers. So give me the answers. Why are you here in the middle of this? You're mad at me, you want revenge for having to be someone's copy. Okay. But why do you have to screw with this kid's life? What are you doing here?"

He stepped close.

"I'm finishing what I started."

"When? Started what?"

"The girl, Sid? Remember? The girl? Circe?"

Uh.

He pointed at the mirror.

"First job. Rescue the girl. She wasn't even two years old, Sid. I told you that what you felt about Abigail, losing her and the baby, I felt that. I had to watch and couldn't save her. I lived with that, never got past it. So years later Francois needed help to save a little girl. You think I just wanted to fuck with you? Fuck with your heart? I needed to save the girl. It could have shattered me, using your mojo. Going into a mirror by myself, that could have been it for me. I risked it because I had to. And I did it. I found her. I picked her up and held her close and ran as fast as I could to get her out of there. That weird kid saw me, her brother, Carpenter. He chased me. I had to take her into a mirror, Sid. Not knowing if I could. I had to risk losing her in there. I held her so tight. When I came through into that motel room, handing her to Francois was one of the hardest things I'll ever do. I had to let her go, but I could still keep an eye on her. Munroe thought she owned me like the rest of her manikins. But every job I did for her was a chance to get back in the Vestibule, and every time I was in there, I searched for Circe. It wasn't that hard. It's where I'm from. I know the lay. I started talking to Circe. She was maybe five when I found her. I peeked out from a doll's mirror. She still carries it. We talked. I'd check in on her and tell her stories. She knew I was real, and she knew she couldn't tell Iva about me. When she got older she understood it wasn't normal, a friend in a mirror. But she already knew there was nothing normal about her. I was able to answer questions she couldn't ask her mom. You can't leave a kid like that to figure out mojo alone. I told her the truth about her family history, mojo, me. When she wanted curiosities for herself, I helped her get them. And when she wanted to try to change the world, I told her I would help. I guided her to Munroe. The lady thought she was running the show, planning to use Circe to set a new course for her party. Launch a fucking app? Lame. We were a kid and a manikin. Munroe could never believe we had plans of our own."

"What are those plans? Exactly what?"

He smiled. My cockiest smile. I knew it from the old days, when cockiness was my default expression.

"Blow. Shit. Up," he said.

"No," I said.

"Try to stop us," he said.

"Are you smoking in my room, Clay?" Circe said, coming through the door.

"Sorry." He lifted a foot and crushed his cigarette out on the sole of his shoe.

Circe had a phone in her hand, fiercely working the screen.

"It took me forever to get this room set up just right, Clay. I'm trying to get my mom to hand over my stuff and you're dumping ashes on the floor."

"I didn't move anything."

"You're not supposed to be in the room. Get out of the room. Out!"

She stood aside, waiting as Clay and I went into the hall and waited just outside the open door.

Circe looked at her phone.

"So close," she said, tapping. "These people. Some of the comments. Do they think? No, they don't. Okay. We still have time. It won't last forever, but we have time to make it happen. Okay. So first things. Got to put this back."

She pulled something from the hip pocket of her cutoffs. A black handful of plush. Her bat, Dizzy. The intimate family curiosity that had helped to manifest the scent ghost, kicking off this crazy deal for me. Circe took it to her bed and carefully tucked it in with a few other stuffed animals, her hands moving confidently as she arranged them and straightened the covers.

"Iva finally came across with this. So that's one piece back in place. I don't even know if it matters now. I mean. No, I do know. Everything matters. It's all connected and it all matters.

Now is not the time to start questioning. It matters. It works. It will work."

She was talking to herself. Looking at herself in the mirror over her bed, giving herself a little pep talk.

"You got this. You have this nailed. You're a superhero goddess. Rule everything. It's yours. Okay, next piece."

She went to a satchel on the floor, opened the flap, and hauled out Carpenter's map, his book, the master-plan atlas of all of Gyre. She looked around the room, and took it to where a cluster of her own sketches were pinned on the wall at floor level. More of her Gyre circles, more screaming mouths, more dark Chasm pits. She opened the map to the first page, Carpenter's original babyish crayon scribble of Gyre, and leaned it against the wall.

"That should work. I mean, it would be working now if everything was where it's supposed to be."

She turned, and walked back out the door straight to me. Taller than me by a couple inches in her cowboy boots, she looked down into my eyes.

"You," she said. "Mom admitted she had Dizzy, but that's all she has. So that means you stole it. Tell me now where my Sinéad O'Connor album is. I need it to make all this other shit work."

THIRTY-FIVE

THE ALBUM.

I'd been so absorbed with Clay, I hadn't thought about the album or how the course in Circe's room was missing. No more mojo flow in there.

"I don't have your album," I said.

"Mom told me you were here. I know you took it. Give it back."

I raised my hands.

"I said I do not have your album." I lowered my hands. "I didn't say that I didn't take it."

"Where is it?"

That was the rub, where the album was. But only I knew how bad that rub was. I'd stolen Circe's album because I needed something to swap with Lloyd. Now it turned out she couldn't finish her plan without it. The extent of my smug satisfaction could not have been measured in that moment.

"I will consider telling you where the album is if you explain to me what you are doing. Because I think you are trying to break the world."

Clay, I'd somehow forgotten, still had a gun.

He shoved me into the wall, pressed the barrel against my neck.

"The album connects everything. It ties Circe to me to you

to Abigail to me rescuing Circe. It ties her to your voice and to the show tonight, it ties her to Munroe. The album is half of everything she's doing. The other half comes from her dad and his cult and her brother and his fucking game. That's the map. But she needs the first half to make it all work. She needs all the mojo that's been coursed into her life. She needs it tonight. So where is the fucking record?"

"Nothing connects her to Abigail. To me. Nothing but you."

He leaned his forehead into mine, our faces pressed together.

"It's Abigail's record! I told you I took shit from the apartment. I took her record. Did you think it disappeared? I took it. I kept it for years. Listened to it constantly. Did you think it was a coincidence that Circe is a Sinéad O'Connor fan? I gave her the fucking record!"

A matched pair, Lloyd had said when he took a compass read off the album and saw it vibrate with my shirt. Abigail's album. Abigail's shirt. Loaded with decades of my mourning and Circe's dreams. I got it now. The connection between my own mythology, the story of my love and loss and sacrifice, and how it linked to Circe's mythology. Her twisted childhood, her father's religion, her brother's game. Munroe said when Circe came to the party that first time, she sang "Never Get Old." That wasn't an offhand choice. Circe knew it would resonate and get Munroe's attention.

Was nothing random? Was nothing unconnected? It seemed not.

"Clay," I said, "get your stupid gun out of my neck because if my wife's album is that important to your plans you can't shoot me until you know where it is."

Clay screamed, a ragged cry of anger and frustration. I had the length of the scream to wonder what a bullet would feel like, and then it ended and he stepped back, taking the gun from my neck.

"I don't want to shoot him. I want to shoot him. I don't want to shoot him."

Circe squeezed his arm.

"Clay? Are you cool?"

He shook his head, waved his gun at me.

"This is harder than I thought it would be. Facing him is messing me up more than I thought it would. I have to smoke a fucking cigarette. Take this."

He handed her the gun and pulled out his cigarettes. His hands were shaking.

"I don't know what I'm feeling, I don't know what I *should* be feeling," he said, lighting up.

I exhaled loudly.

"I'm glad it's not just me."

Circe pointed the gun at my foot.

"Where's my album?"

I shook my head.

"You don't know how to use that thing."

She gave me an eye roll.

"It's *my* gun. I gave it to him."

Right, yes, Iva told me that Circe liked to shoot. One of her hobbies, along with theater, music, scenic design, gaming, and casting spells to disrupt the natural order.

"I'm not telling you where the album is until I know what you want it for, and also I want my shirt back."

I zipped my lips. I actually drew my fingers across my lips like I was zipping them closed. It felt like the thing to do in that moment.

Circe aimed the gun carefully at my foot.

"Circe! Do not shoot him in the foot. And you, the twin, yes, you. Put out that cigarette. You may not smoke in this house." Iva had appeared at the end of the hall. At the end of her rope. As were we all.

"Mom! I'm almost done!"

"Circe! I gave you Dizzy and you said you'd be right back to finish explaining. This is not explaining."

"I lied, Mom. I was planning to get my album from him and go back out my mirror, but he's being an asshole about it."

I raised a hand.

"Your daughter is doing something gargantuanly destructive. I know you love her, but I think you got her out of the cult too late. I think she's programmed for suicide and she's going to try to get all the people at that protest downtown to kill themselves so she can raise Demon."

Iva looked at the ceiling.

"Holy fuck."

"It's not like he's saying, Mom."

Iva looked at Circe, held up her hush finger, and came down the hall.

"Give me the gun."

"There isn't time for all this. It's a mess out there and it's going to get worse if I don't do something about it."

Iva grabbed Circe's wrist in both of her hands.

"If you try to leave this house you will be dragging me with you. I am not letting go."

Circe offered the gun to Iva.

"Stop being so dramatic, Mom."

She nodded to Clay.

"Come on. It looks like if I want to stay out late I'm going to have to tell my mom where I'm going and who I'm meeting and what time I'll be home."

Iva took the gun.

"You fucking got that right," she said.

Circe walked away, heading for the kitchen.

"Fast, Mom. Minimal questions. Because, seriously, if I don't finish what I started, it will terminally fuck up the world forever and ever."

THIRTY-SIX

Hi, guys, my name is Circe. You maybe know me from my other accounts. I post about theater and art and stuff I like. I *Gyre*. Harrow. And I've been making music. You maybe saw some of the videos I shot and dropped the last month. I was wearing a mask. Mask off now. I'm Penny Catcher. First single is a free download. It's called "Feel Like Dyin." It sounds like it's someone who wants to die, but it's really about sex. *La petite mort,* the little death, that's Victorian slang for orgasm. Fun fact, hey? So the song is about wanting to have sex whenever the singer sees the person they love. Cool, n'est-ce pas? Anyway, I did my first show tonight. Maybe you saw that crazy stunt I pulled onstage? What was that, right? I'm going to tell you the truth about how we did that. Ready? You aren't going to believe it, but here it is.

That was magic. Not like some stage illusion, but actual fucking magic. I do real magic, and you can, too!

You probably heard about the Abyss Protest, right? I didn't start it, but when I heard about it, I started putting everything I had into it. My time and energy. And believe it or not, my magic. Lots of people have been working on it, spreading the word everywhere. There is no way you haven't seen the hashtag or watched a post about it. Some of the idea has to do with *Gyre,* and we did some organizing from inside that game and a bunch more outside it. Can you say *self-organizing global mass-protest movement*? It's pronounced like this:

Fuck the establishment!

Tonight at the Abyss Protest in Downtown Los Angeles, we are going to make something happen. Me and about eight hundred thousand people, that's how many are there right now, we are going to cast a massive magic spell! That spell is going to piss off a lot of very powerful assholes because it is going to turn the world literally inside out.

If you like the sound of that, you can help. If you're in L.A., come on down. If not, get together with your people. Online or in person, it doesn't matter. Follow me and you will be there. Do what we're doing with us, and you'll be part of the spell. I know that some cities are doing their own Abyss Protest, so go join it. The more of us we have, the better and stronger the magic we can make.

After tonight, the world is going to be totally different. Literally, totally different. So take a look around at what the world is like right now. Is that your vibe? I thought not. So let's change it. I wish I could do it all myself, be all of you and have all your magic so you wouldn't have to take this on tonight. But it's too big for one person, we have to work together.

Now, someone is going to get the blame, and that will probably be me. So let's get one thing out of the way. If people are going to say I'm the villain, I am sure as fuck going to tell my own story my own fucking way. And also, I won't be using the word *mojo*. You may have heard people talk about mojo. Yeah, guys? Life's dirty little secret? Well, I don't do that shit, I do magic. It's not some groove you get on if you're among the hot elites. Magic is power you can use to change shit, and anyone can use it. It is power to the people, and all it takes is knowledge and will and a little imagination.

About villains, guys. We supposed villains are always the hero in our own story, and I am a hero. Fuck everybody who says different because I know who the real bad guys are, and you probably do, too. All the people you think suck? A lot of them literally suck. Like they suck up all the magic so they can keep it for themselves, and that fucks things up for everyone else.

Think of something terrible in the world, guys. Especially think about when terrible things happen on top of each other and it all seems too crazy. Like, *Oh, fuck, how can it possibly be happening like that?* It doesn't make sense, yeah? Like, it really can't be happening. Guess what? A lot of the time, it shouldn't be happening. A lot of the time it's happening because some assholes are forcing magic to flow to them and that screws up everything else.

How did it get this way?

I'm glad you asked.

Start with magic being everywhere and in everything and anyone can use it and it is infinite and can do whatever you want and there are no rules. But like everything in history, it has to be found, figured out, whatever. So probably by accident someone wished for something and did some things that they didn't know they were doing and it tapped them into magic and they got what they wanted. Fucking shit, they tried it again. So how it works is, the more someone does magic in one way and to get one thing, the better it works for that one thing, and the easier it is. The problem? It starts creating a current that makes more magic flow that same way.

The first starving, muddy asshole who ever wished for a bison to kill and had that wish granted in some improbable way, they sure as hell took note of what they'd done. They tried it again and maybe told some friends about it. Whatever. The point is, once someone figured out a reliable way to increase their luck or crops or make them win in battle or get the guy they were after or whatever, they tried it again and again. They put down the first *courses,* and the more they did it the same way, the better it worked. And they were invested in keeping it that way. When people tried to do something else, make magic work some other way, the assholes with the power messed with them so nothing would change. Same fucking story all the time.

Here's a resource, it's infinite and all around us and anyone can use it. But a few assholes use it to make themselves richer and more powerful, and then they use their riches and power to make sure they keep magic locked up and working the way they want it to work. And the more assholes who come along and do the same thing, the harder it is to change how the magic works. Until only assholes have magic.

Which is opposite of how magic should be.

It's everywhere and in everything and we can all use it. Doesn't that suggest a purpose? I mean a natural purpose. Like the universe or whatever you call it has been set up with this resource that is meant to be evenly distributed and used by everyone. Why? I don't fucking know. You'd think it serves something or is the natural outcome of something. Really, I give a fuck. The point I'm making is that the so-called chaos the assholes are afraid of is maybe the actual point of magic. It's not supposed to run in massive courses that draw it in limited directions and to just a few ends. It's meant to be used discreetly, in small amounts by everyone, so that everyone can make their lives a little better. If you keep it small and intimate, your magic won't step on anyone else's. When you get greedy with the shit, it fucks it up for everyone else. Is that so hard to understand? I guess it is hard to understand if you're a titanic asshole. Am I trying to blow up magic and ruin it for everyone who has it? I sure as shit am. I am ruining magic for all the assholes who have been hoarding it instead of trying to use it to make the world better.

Okay, guys, so that's it. Magic is real and a few assholes have it trapped so they can use it the way they want, and that's a lot of the reason why the world is a hot mess, and tonight we break that shit open and see what the fuck happens. And I know a bunch of you think this is a crazy stunt I'm pulling to be hugely famous and rule all socials and brand myself as the crazy witch girl and next week, when I have a million followers, I'll be posting about my favorite face cream and putting all my ad revenue into crypto.

I get that, but so fucking what? Do you want to miss whatever crazy shit I'm doing? You do not. It is going to be insane in Downtown L.A. tonight, guys! You have to watch, you know you do. Fuck, you watched this hella long video so you know you have to watch live tonight and see what happens when yours truly tries to fuck up the entire world!

Is it going to be a huge fucking mess when I succeed? I don't know. Maybe. Probably yes. But it's a huge fucking mess now. The current mess is totally predictable. Spoiler alert! The world is fucked and the rich get richer and everyone else eats shit. So what's the cost of trying something else? What's the impact of purposefully doing something massive and unpredictable instead of waiting for the next predictable global disaster? What will happen if we stop fucking around and use the magic at our fingertips to try to make it all better?

I do not fucking know. Nor do I fucking care. I did not fuck this shit up. I am not going to live with the consequences of someone else's fucking mess. Me and my friends, if we have to deal with a mess, it will be the one we make. Not yours, you assholes. And you know exactly who the fuck you are.

They want people to think there are rules for how magic works. But they make those rules.

Fuck the rules.

I may be the villain in your story, but I am totally my own hero. Later.

THIRTY-SEVEN

"POST THAT SHIT, Clay," Circe said as she wrapped.

There was silence for a moment, nothing but the sound of Clay's tapping fingers on his phone as he posted Circe's insane video. Iva and I were sitting in kitchen chairs, audience of two.

Iva was the first to speak.

"What the fuck?" she said.

"Mom," Circe said, "I'm gonna go out. I'm gonna course a shitstorm of magic through my room. It's a conduit that goes right to me. I'm going to pull it downtown to the Abyss Protest. When all those people join the ritual I've created, it's going to rip open the banks of the major courses of magic all over the world. Then shit will happen. I know you want magic to not be real, but it is. You don't want me to have anything to do with it, but I'm all about magic. Mom, this world."

She came to her mom and knelt next to her chair.

"This world is broken, Mom. Help me change it."

Iva shook her head. Nodded. Shook her head again.

"I don't know. I don't know how."

"It's easy, Mom. You just have to let me go."

Iva put her arms around her daughter, pulled her in, buried her face in her little girl's hair, and inhaled.

"I love the way you smell," she said, and let her daughter go.

Circe stood, looked at me.

"My album. The conduit needs to be complete or it won't

handle what's going to pour through it. Shit will break loose and I don't know what will happen."

I stood up and freaked out.

"You don't know what will happen anyway! You want to change something? Okay, start to build a course. You're amazing. You're like the most talented and gifted person I have ever met. I can see that you can auspice and vehemance. You know how to pull and course mojo. But you have to build inside the thing the way it works. You don't blow up the house and then try to live in it. What happens when you break everything while Carpenter's suicide mojo is still all over the place? No way. Your heart is in the right place, but no way. I mean, even if I wanted to help, and I don't, I haven't got the album. It's over. This is all over right now."

"Sid," Clay said, "you can help. You know you want to help."

"Leave me alone," I said, looking at the floor. "Just leave me alone."

Circe stepped close.

"What the fuck are you afraid of?"

I looked at her.

"I'm afraid of being wrong! I found out tonight that I have been wrong my whole life. Saying the wrong things, doing the wrong things, thinking the wrong things. I'm one of the assholes you were talking about, and I don't know how to change that if I'm always wrong. I can't help anyway. Munroe has the album. She has it locked up. No one can get it now. I took it and I traded it away and she ended up with it. That's me, screwing everything up. So, no, I can't help. I can't make anything better. I just make things worse."

Clay stuck his hand out to Iva.

"Give me that gun. I'll go get the record."

Circe looked at her phone.

"You have to take me downtown first. I need to get to the protest and start the ritual."

Clay was straightening his tie, preparing for action.

"I can drop you at the stage through the mirror I set down there, then go straight to Munroe's. I know where she keeps her curiosities. I'll bring the album back here to your room and put it in place. Don't wait for me to start the ritual. I'll have it ready."

Iva was handing Clay the little automatic. Circe was already walking toward the hallway to her room and the mirror they'd have to go through. Everything was moving forward no matter how much I wished it would stop. It was too much, too big, too out of control. I needed time to figure out what it all meant. What was going to happen.

I needed time to figure out what I was feeling.

What was that feeling? It felt bad. I felt sick in my stomach, like I'd done something terrible that I couldn't take back. At the same time I felt like something amazing was under that feeling and that if it could grow, it would push through the terrible feelings of guilt and regret. It couldn't replace the bad feeling, but it could soothe it. It could make it easier to live with the terrible feeling. They were all moving, Iva and Clay and Circe. They were moving toward something that they didn't understand and weren't sure they could reach. They were together and wanted to make something good happen together. They were acting as if their actions could make something better. And I was sitting in my chair doing nothing.

It's a girl, Sid, we're having a girl, Abigail had said to me. And then she'd whispered the baby's name.

Hope.

Our daughter's name was Hope.

Life is like that sometimes. Stupidly sentimental. And everything is connected sometimes. And the most improbable things happen when you least expect them. And people change and do the things they didn't know they could do.

That's why it's called magic.

I thought of the name of our daughter, and it was also the name of the feeling that I couldn't bear.

Why does it take so long and why is it so hard to do the simplest things?

Like hoping.

Like helping.

Once you give in to hope, you are at its mercy.

I stood up.

"I want to help," I said.

They turned, looking at me.

Iva spoke first.

"When did the security lights come on outside?"

Glass shattered. The window over the kitchen sink exploded inward.

"Where's Circe! Where's my daughter!" one of the Crispins was screaming as it shoved its head through the window.

More glass breaking, windows falling in shards, someone hammering on the door.

"Where's Circe!" all the Crispins were screaming. "Where's my daughter!"

Something flew in through a broken window, a bottle with a tail of burning rag stuck in its neck crashed against the corkboard wall. Gasoline splashed on the memories and they began to burn.

I'd waited too long to help. Too long to hope.

It was all too late.

THIRTY-EIGHT

THE HOUSE WAS ON FIRE.

We'd been rapt in our own world. No one had been facing a window. Iva had left her phone somewhere. All that security, and it did no good when Carpenter drove a Sprinter van full of Crispins to her house, because we were distracted by Circe making a YouTube video.

Fire and smoke. A Crispin crawling through the window over the sink.

"Where's Circe? Where's my daughter?"

Those words being repeated everywhere outside the house, coming into the house.

I saw Iva pulling the ring of keys from the lanyard around her neck, fingering the gun cabinet key from the jumble, running for the front hall. Circe. I'd not seen her look scared. Now she looked scared. I was ripping my jacket open. Clay raised his gun, pulled the trigger. But Iva, a woman who lived with guns, had put the safety on.

The Crispin was halfway in, eyes locked on Circe.

"My daughter! My daughter!"

I held Minerva's giant phone as tightly as I could and swung as hard as I could and plastic and glass shards hit me in the face as the phone and most of the Crispin's head exploded against each other. It fell over the counter onto the floor. Its face was intact from the upper lip down, mouth still moving.

"Where? Where? My daughter!"

I kicked it, smashing what was left of its face.

More windows breaking in the house.

Shots fired. One after another. The distinct sound of thick glass, dense, being blown to tiny bits. Shotgun blasts hitting the trunks of manikin bodies. Boom! Boom! Boom! One after another.

Iva, screaming over the gunfire.

"I hate you! I hate you! I hate you!"

And the house was still on fire.

I was yelling at Circe.

"Go!" I was yelling. "Go!"

She had Clay by the hand, pulling him.

"Sid?" he said.

I was opening drawers, pulling them out too far, contents spilling on the floor. I yanked open a drawer full of tape and picture hooks and half tubes of glue. I dumped it over and a tack hammer fell out. I picked it up.

"Sid!" Clay shouted.

I waved the hammer, urging them away.

"Take her downtown. Start your ritual. I'll do the rest."

Clay grabbed me.

"If she starts to course the ritual and you don't have it ready here . . . !"

"It'll be ready. Go!"

It was the last I saw of them in the burning house, running down the hall to Circe's room.

If she started the ritual, if she started to course all that mojo without her room ready to flow it to her, she'd be overwhelmed. She'd explode.

Shotgun blasts from another room.

"I hate you!" Iva's voice on the heel of each gunshot.

"Iva!" I was screaming, searching for her.

Something grabbed me. I swung the tack hammer and it bit into the meat of a shoulder.

Carpenter.

"They're all dead," he said.

For a moment I thought he meant Circe and Clay and Iva, but that wasn't it.

"All my people, all my players, they're killing their characters. Harrow won through and they're all jumping into the Chasm. All those people are spilling blood in my land, grieving and celebrating, and all of it is going to her! She is stealing my mojo. Where's my map?"

I swung the hammer again, but Carpenter was a guy who knew how to fight and I was a guy who knew how to swing a hammer. He took it from me and knocked me down and stood over me, ready to bash my head in.

"Carpenter!"

He looked away from me. He wanted Circe, his sister. He got Circe's mom instead.

"Get out of my house, Carpenter."

He raised the hammer, took a step toward her.

"Where is Circe? Where is my sister?"

She shot him in the stomach.

Oh, man. Oh, man. I hope I never see anything like that ever again. Carpenter was a mess. On his back, rolling side to side, smearing himself around on the carpet. Making noises that I could hear over the fire. I got to my feet.

Iva was reloading her shotgun.

"Where's Circe?" she said.

I jerked a thumb at the hallway.

"They got out. I have to help."

"The house is burning."

"Don't let it reach her room," I said.

I ran away from her, down the hallway to the magic bedroom, where it all had started.

The house was on fire. The fire would reach the bedroom soon. Circe was starting her ritual, but she needed the altar of her room to be complete for it to work. There wasn't time for everything. Clay could take her to the protest, the heart of the ritual, but he didn't have time to also go to Munroe's. The fire had to be slowed. But I couldn't help with that. I had to get the album and bring it here and repair the altar. Fix what I'd broken. I didn't know what would happen if Circe completed her ritual, but at least I knew she wanted to make something better. If she failed, all the force behind it would go off the rails. It would become a flood rushing into the major courses. All that was wrong about the world would become worse.

And Circe would die.

I walked into her room. I climbed on her bed and leaned into the mirror. I heard Iva fire her shotgun. The sound of Carpenter's life ending. I blocked it all out. I remembered again that the world was not real.

Still, it was on fire.

Still, we had to try to put it out.

THIRTY-NINE

I KNEW where Munroe kept her best curiosities. She had them behind a green door in her bedroom. She made no secret of it, just like she made no secret about the huge mirror hung above her bed. The dare to all the slys who'd ever done a job for her. A mirror in her most private room. An unlocked door behind which she kept her treasures.

What did she care?

No one would dare steal from Munroe. Where would you run? Where hide? Knowing that she'd be sending Perilous Sue after you.

I knew the way. It was an easy sly from Circe's bedroom to Munroe's. I'd scouted a path there many times, and always come up short of diving through. Those desperate years I'd been scrabbling around, I'd thought plenty about ripping off Munroe. But I'd never had the confidence. It wasn't Perilous Sue who held me back. I was frozen by Munroe's mirror. Given how wicked Munroe was, I knew that mirror had seen things. Plunging through it would have a cost. Whatever it had seen would still be in it. You don't pass through without picking something up. So I turned back every time. There was no more turning back now, no other path, no going home and crawling into bed and hiding. There was no time for anything but jumping and hoping. I should have known what I'd see in that mirror, what I'd feel.

I saw myself. An idiot spread-eagled on the bed below. I

saw Sue and her knife. I felt it slide into me, I felt her pry my ribs apart, I felt the wish that I'd die, and then I felt the certain knowledge that I would live. I felt despair. No. Not that. I didn't want to feel that. I'd lived so long without hope. No more of that. I pushed through the hopelessness of who I'd been. All I could hope for was something soft to land on.

I landed on Perilous Sue's legs.

I rolled onto the floor and started crawling away from the bed, staying low to make it harder for her to throw her knife in my back. I heard a groan. Nothing else. It was very quiet. I looked back. Sue was on the bed. She was in bad shape. She'd lost a hand and half her forearm. It had been thrust through the disco ball mirror when Francois let go of me. Snip. I'd forgotten about that.

I stood up.

"Clay?" she said, eyes barely opening before they closed again.

I went to the side of the bed.

"It's me, Sue."

Her eyes opened and shut.

"Fucking Catchpenny."

She was bone-white. Her mangled arm was wrapped in bed-sheets, blood seeping through.

"You need a doctor, Sue."

She bared her teeth.

"Where's Clay?"

Sue, she killed people. She did unforgivable things. She saw a world of monsters and made herself a more terrible monster. I'd been her lover. But not her true love.

"Is he okay?" she asked.

"Yes, he is. He's helping the girl," I said.

She grunted.

"Him and that girl. Most broke-backed idea I ever hatched, sending him to save that tadpole. Set him on a wrong path.

What a tender heart he has. The fights we brewed over that girl.
I didn't know what they were up to, but I didn't like it. He can't
help himself from helping others. He's not like me and Munroe
and you, Catchpenny. He doesn't have the gift for hurting that
we three pirates have. But he hurts me all the same."

I put a hand on her forehead. Dry and cold.

"I'd like to help, Sue, but I don't have time. I'm with them
now, Clay and Circe."

"You're a fool, lover."

"I know. Where's Munroe?"

"Use your eyes and leave me alone. I'm trying to lay a course
to save my life and it's not easy. It's all a-fuck out there tonight.
Not even my own mojo will go where I tell it."

"Sorry, Sue."

"Fuck off," she said, "and tell Clay to call me."

I used my eyes, like she said. The door to Munroe's treasure
chamber was open, light spilling out into the otherwise-dark
bedroom. I glanced out a window at the terraces and patios
below the house. A few partiers and manikins were wandering
around lost. I heard a wild scraping fiddle. The ghost of Charlie
Daniels calling up the devil. The party was over. Dead. Munroe
had moved it to the Echoplex to use its mojo to launch Circe
and her app, and now it had dispersed, following the suicide girl
to her ritual downtown.

Munroe was in the treasure room, notorious dragon lady of
the music industry brooding on her hoard. She was in a chair
that had once been in the Oval Office, a chair that had seated
six presidents of the United States. War had once been declared
from that chair. Peace proclaimed. A moon landing announced.
It was a nice piece. Her feet were on a kneeling stool from the
Vatican. Popes had prayed there. It was a room as dense in curiosities and clutter as Circe's was. The least of these was more
valuable than any one thing Circe had, except maybe Carpenter's map. But the room didn't vibrate like Circe's. It was all

treasure, and none of it treasured. Munroe had never taken the time or had the imagination to arrange it so that it related to itself, added up to more than its parts. She only knew the major courses, the way power had flowed when she first heard about the racket. She'd joined the game and played it as it was being played by people she hated. Munroe was one of Circe's assholes.

She looked up from her phone. A video was playing. I heard Circe's voice.

"Have you seen this?" She shook her head. "What is this child thinking, Sidney? I had her cut out for great things. She was going to be the new sensation. Here she is, throwing it away to make a joke out of herself. She doesn't know a thing. So sad. Pathetic. It is to laugh and weep at the same time. Sigh."

She threw her phone at the wall and it smashed into a poster for the first ever Grateful Dead show at Fillmore West.

"Fucking phones. Awful things, Sidney. Truly awful. They are ruining the world. What was I thinking, getting involved with that shit?"

I stepped into the room, my eyes searching. I needed to find that album and get out.

Munroe waved a hand.

"Are you, by some chance, looking for this, Sidney?"

She reached behind her chair and pulled out the album, still in its jacket, and held it carefully by the edges at top and bottom, like a good collector of vintage vinyl.

"It's very important that you let me have that, Munroe."

"So I have surmised, honey baby."

She inspected the album with the eye of an expert.

"It is not, I'll tell you, in pristine condition. The jacket is very rough. Wear on all edges, foxed corners. The original paper sleeve is browned on one side. The LP itself is only fair. No big scratches, but considerable hiss and popping. It's a first pressing, so I wouldn't put it in the bargain bin, but it won't add luster to any serious collection. Of course, like all vintage items with a well-known provenance, the real value is the story it tells. This tells one of the saddest stories I've ever known. With all that in mind, what am I bid?"

"It's too late to change what Circe is doing," I said. "She can't be stopped now. You're going to have to start over, but you don't have to ruin everything for everyone else at the same time."

"Going once," she said, flexing the album between her strong hands. "Nothing to offer, Sidney? Very well. Going twice." She bent it further. "Going thrice."

"Please, Munroe, I don't have anything left. But I know what I'm doing. Please help me."

Her hair was awry, her outfit wrinkled and stained, her makeup smeared. The lines in her face cut deep, pulled down. Her hunger was clawing at her, and she didn't know how to feed it anything but more.

I couldn't make her give the record to me. I wasn't strong enough to take it from her. I didn't have a ritual to make that happen. I had nothing except the sad history I was dragging around. Things I'd said and done, more things that I'd failed to say or do. There was, if nothing else, a chance to say something before it all blew to pieces. In that moment, it seemed very important that I try to make something better. Use what was left of my voice to say something kind. Something heartfelt.

"Munroe," I said. "When I told you Abigail was having a baby, you were great. Everything you said was the right thing. You made me feel so much better. You made being a dad feel like something I could actually do. That's the closest I got, you know? When you told me it was going to be okay. That was the only time I really felt like I might be able to be a dad. That's a special memory for me. Thank you for that."

The record was flexed to the breaking point between her hands. A tremor would snap it in two. I waited to hear it go. Instead, Munroe was the one who broke.

"Catchpenny!" she screamed, and flung the album across the room.

It Frisbeed toward the wall. I dove, arms out. I could see the paper sleeve slipping from the jacket, the black disc slipping from the sleeve. There was no magic for this. Only luck. And I was not a lucky man.

Except maybe this one time.

Fingertips closed. Cardboard, paper, vinyl all sliding through my grasp. And then. Got it! A tenuous grip. But I'm still falling. Please don't hit anything too hard. Don't let go.

I hit the ground.

Luck found me and gave me this little thing. I had the album in my hands.

I got off the floor, sliding the album back in the jacket, but not before I saw the black-ink scribble on the paper sleeve: PROPERTY OF ABIGAIL CATCHPENNY—HANDS OFF!

"Nice catch."

I looked at her.

"Thank you, Munroe."

She stood up.

"Go away, Sidney." She headed for the door. "Sue needs my help."

If there was more, I didn't hear it. She had mirrors in her treasure chamber. The mirrors of the famous dead, waiting to be limned for the entertainment of her guests.

I picked a mirror.

I jumped into it.

Abigail's treasure under my arm.

FORTY

WHAT DO YOU SAVE when your house is on fire?

I looked out Circe's bedroom door. Heat seared me. I opened my mouth to yell Iva's name. Smoke choked me. I coughed so much I almost lost the album. I backed up. Was that a shadow on the other side of the flames? Please, Iva, please be somewhere else.

I backed up into the room and closed the door. Was there anything I could do to keep the fire out a little longer? No, no, no. Move. I slipped the album from its sleeve and put it on the turntable. I hit play, closed the clamshell lid, and set the jacket in place. There was still electricity in the house. The tone arm lifted and glided and dropped. I looked at the room. Was everything as it should be? I felt the rush of magic deep in the center of the room as it began to flow again. The pull heavier than before. So much, too much. I stepped out of it. How could Circe course all that? No one could.

Smoke seeped in at the edges of the door.

Sirens? Did I hear sirens?

Sinéad began singing.

I'll remember it
In Dublin in a rainstorm
And sitting in the long grass in summer
Keeping warm

It rushed through me then, a realization.

I didn't have to do anything else.

I could stay right there.

I could stay and listen to Abigail's favorite album, her actual favorite album, and let the house burn down around me. I'd done what I could do to help. It was up to Circe now. Whatever happened after, it wasn't my business. I didn't have to be there to see it or to do more. I'd done something to make it all a little better, and now I could be finished. Smoke thickened in the room. As much as I wanted to be on my back on the floor, I should stay on my feet where the smoke was thickest.

Wait till it knocked me down.

I'll remember it
Every restless night
We were so young then
We thought that everything we could possibly do was right
Then we moved stolen from our very eyes
And I wondered where you went to
Tell me when did the light die

FORTY-ONE

WHAT DOES A SELF-ORGANIZED global mass-protest movement fueled by the magic of a teenage cult survivor inspired by a video game look like?

It's beautiful.

It is faces in the night as far as you can see. City streets in Downtown Los Angeles packed so tight you can only move when other people move with you. Nothing gets done unless everyone moves the same way. Hundreds of thousands of phones in the darkness, beaming up and out. Filming and sharing and lighting up the faces. You've never seen such a thing. Or maybe you have. Maybe you were there. If not, there are no end to the posts.

I'm glad I decided to live long enough to see it.

What does it look like when hundreds of thousands of people join together to create a magic ritual to change everything in the world? It's beautiful, but it also looks like everyone everywhere messing around on their phones, waiting for something to happen.

And then it happens.

The mirror Clay had mentioned was on a platform on Skid Row. That's where the nominal organizers had created the center of the Abyss Protest, at ground zero for homelessness in Los Angeles. There were *Gyre* banners, screaming Abyss Protest mouths, and placards for and against anything you care to name.

Circe said she'd drafted off something that was already in the air. There would have been an Abyss Protest without her, but I was certain that it would never have reached this fever pitch and scale if she hadn't been channeling that course of mojo through her room, feeding it from her own great store along with everything she had been eking from her theater troupe. People had felt the pull to be there whether they knew it or not. How deft was Circe's guiding hand? Certainly it couldn't be a coincidence that Carpenter had preordained this very date for the final battle in *Gyre,* and that Munroe had set it for the premiere of the Penny Catcher concert. Circe couldn't have begun to dream of success without access to the massive twin courses those two had set in motion. If she truly intended to break the levees of the major courses and set all that magic loose, she needed an overwhelming countercurrent to rip them from their banks. It couldn't have just come together like this; she must have been planning and manipulating for years.

All of it connected.

There the hundreds of thousands were, and the courses of great powers were flowing into Circe's. The course of her childhood and her father's cult, the course she'd plucked away from Bruce at the Old Barn, Carpenter's course, and Munroe's, and now all the mojo behind these people, their anger and fear and hope. She had the desire and the means. Perhaps she had the talent and the skill to shape it all. People were waiting for her. Some were eager followers, longtime online fans or newbies who had never heard of her before her performance that night, but most were there for the protest, most had no idea what or who they were waiting for.

A song, some of them had been told, and word had gone around.

There will be a song, and that will be how we start.

Start what?

This brat, thinking that in her sixteen years she had come up with a formula to make the world better. It would never work. Destruction and chaos would be the outcome. I'd had to make a choice, and I hadn't been willing to stand still any longer. I'd crawled out of my bed and gotten on my feet and gone out the door, and just as I'd feared, there had been consequences. I'd chosen, and now I would see the cost of that choice.

It would never work.

But, oh, how I hoped it would.

I left Circe's bedroom and came out of the mirror on that platform into a tangle of bodies.

"Circe!" I was yelling. "Where's Circe?"

No one heard. But I could see her, and Clay next to her. There were too many people between us for me to reach them. I wanted to tell her to hurry before it was too late, the house was on fire, but she hadn't waited for me. I'd told her I could do it, and she'd trusted me.

I was at the back of the platform. Just another guy who didn't know exactly what was going to happen. She was up at the front of the platform, her voice was being picked up and echoed around in tiny fragments from thousands and thousands and thousands of phones. She was telling them what to do, but I couldn't translate the sound of her voice as it broke over the crowd. When the moment came, I didn't know what to expect. A bunch of people on the platform were pointing phones at her, projecting her into the world.

Circe started a countdown.

"Seven, six, five, four."

What would happen next?

"Three," she counted, "two, one!"

I thought it would be a song. She'd said she had a song to

play and wanted everyone to join her. And I guess it was a song. Fierce and angry and throat-shredding and loud.

She screamed.

And everyone sang the scream with her.

I joined the scream.

They called it the Abyss Protest.

We were screaming into the abyss that was the world. The chasm that had opened beneath our feet. All our frustration and anger and fear and sadness and regret, all our guilt and desire and desperation. We had to breathe, we had to gasp and sip water to soothe our throats and then scream some more. Screaming hope.

It went on and on. And over it and above it and never stopping came Circe's scream. Endlessly reeling out of her, piercing the world to its core, calling, summoning, bidding. Coursing. A scream in my voice, carried on all the magic she'd gathered and set loose. A shredding violence that ripped into the major courses and took with it all the voices that were shattering the night around us.

The scream from inside a house on fire.

I have only one gift for magic, opening doors into a place where everything stops existing. I do not create or forge good fortune. But I screamed a single wish, willing whatever meager magic I had in my life to join hers, urging her to succeed, refusing to stop even when each inhalation burned my throat and I could feel droplets of blood on my lips. Even when I knew I had stopped making a sound other than the rasp of air forced up my throat. My one wish over and over again.

Circe, I wished, *don't blow up.*

And I got my wish.

The sun rose, she was there. As all the thousands trailed off into exhausted silence, she was there.

Screaming.

Using my voice to do something I never could have done. Using it to do something more than to praise itself.

Was this where my life had been coursing all along? The path I thought I'd been on, the life I lived—was it ever mine? I could imagine that the invisible limner's hand that drew what I needed to see inside the Vestibule had been drawing the world around me since I had been born. It drew the circumstances that led my parents to abandon me. It drew me into the corner of the group home, alone and unwanted. It drew my voice from my throat, drew my songs from my hand. It drew me across the country, drew me to Abigail. The ocean we lived next to, my dreams of glory and being loved, Abigail's despair, our daughter. All of it a design I was meant to live so that I would pointlessly sacrifice my voice. Pointless for me, but not for Circe. Did she need my voice for this? Would it have been possible any other way?

I let myself imagine that it mattered, my voice. Vanity again. But also this. Imagine this. I let myself dream that my voice had a place in this that nothing else could have filled. Dreaming it made my distant heart hurt a tiny bit less. If my personal sacrifice to my personal demons helped Circe to break the world open, it would bleed just that much grace into me. Abigail slipping below the cooling water in the bathtub, never rising again. She and our daughter lost. That was a part of this, too.

Circe screamed with my voice.

And Abigail was there.

Whatever she'd intended, Abigail, the accident of our lives colliding also led here, to this. I heard her voice, and I knew that the world could not have been changed without her.

The girl, Sid. Remember the girl.

EPILOGUE

I WAS RIGHT IN THE END.

Circe did screw up everything.

Everything she wanted to screw up.

Which means everything that keeps the world in kilter. It's a mess. What kind of a mess it is and whether it's a better mess than it was before is open for debate, and it is being hotly debated. Hotly and violently. I could have stayed in my chair in Iva's kitchen and done nothing and none of this would be happening. So blame me.

What can I tell you?

Here are good things I can tell you.

Those were sirens I heard at Iva's house. The fire department stopped the fire before it got to Circe's room, so she did not explode and Iva did not die. The shotgunned body found in her home has presented some trouble, but even in California you are on good ground when you shoot a home invader. And also, now that the major courses are broken, the legal system does not grind so relentlessly. American jurisprudence is ill prepared for the impact of small acts of magic.

Yes, the major courses have been broken. Thus the big mess. The magic currents that have tilted the balance of luck and power for centuries are all out of whack now. Guys (almost all of them are guys) who are used to getting every break are now finding the breaks not going their way. Some strange recent election outcomes, odd happenings in the financial markets. It's all utterly unpredictable, and the results are not all good.

Also, you can announce that magic is real and everyone can use it, but that doesn't make a believer out of everyone. Most people do not buy it. Magic is all the rage, but it is mostly talked about as a metaphor for something else. You can lead people to the witch well, but you cannot make them brew a potion. Belief is slow in coming. Who knows if it will ever break through.

That said, there are plenty of people giving it a try and figuring out how it works. People are doing it because it is so much easier to tap into magic now. Look online and you see it everywhere. People want to use magic for the same old stuff, mostly. To make their lives better. They want to tilt the wheel of fortune in their own favor. That's where the new major course Circe cut helps out.

She kept that part a secret. She wasn't just setting all the magic loose, she was laying a new major course. She calls it a sacrifice course. That's where a lot of the suicide energy that was floating around was coming from. Circe was laying a course for personal sacrifice, and that got churned with Carpenter's *Gyre* course, and the ideas of sacrifice and suicide got mixed together. Circe's sacrifice course runs strong and pure now. It is the only major course left, and it pulls magic toward its path, making it all but impossible for anyone to use magic unless it runs a complementary course. What that means is that your ritual needs to have an element of self-sacrifice. You have to give something up, sacrifice something to get something. Not blood and not animals. Her course requires that your ritual include something good for someone besides yourself. Even the most selfish desire must benefit someone else and be done at no one's cost but your own.

Nice.

Naturally, it takes constant upkeep to keep her course running true, because most people can't stop themselves from getting greedy when they have access to power. Circe has to pour all her own magic into that sacrifice course to keep it strong. But it is sort of working. The more people use small magic in small ways to help themselves and the people close to them, the stronger Circe's course becomes, and the easier it is to keep magic circulating freely. On the other hand, there are a lot of powerful creeps out there who lost a lot of magic when the old major courses came down. They are not interested in the new world order. Grass roots does not suit their aims.

Circe says it was never going to happen overnight. She says the idea was to let people know that they had the power and to show them how to use it. After that, they have to take over for themselves.

She is showing them how to use that power.

Circe's magic-using videos are in the top ten for views across every platform. She has friends all over the world helping her out, doing little rituals online. Showing how to improve local crop yields, how to stabilize a hostile work environment, purify a polluted stream, help ensure unrigged elections, remove small amounts of carbon from the atmosphere. It's amazing what magic will do if it's coursed carefully. They also demo rainbow making and levitation meditations and tantric sex charms and magic hangover cures and stuff like that. The world is still the world.

Also, Circe is in fact hustling face cream. She needs a revenue stream to launch her own social media platform so she doesn't have to rely on the *Silicon Valley warlocks,* as she calls them. The major courses broke open, but whatever protections those guys in the tech racket have around their internet magic, it was too strong for the Abyss Ritual to break it.

Circe says that's where the real trouble will come from when it comes. Big-tech mojo.

What else is there to know?

Gyre crashed after everyone killed their characters. Demon did not rise, online or otherwise. Iva has been struggling with having killed Carpenter. He attacked her and burned her house down and tried to kill her daughter, but she still remembers him as a kid on the compound. Part of her family. She saved my life. I tell her that. She saved my life and I was able to help Circe. Whether that helps her, I don't know. She says she has to do something. She wants to try to find Carpenter's mom. All she knows is that his mom once lived in Nevada, and Crispin refused to talk about her except to mention her name exactly once. Lilith. I hear that and I remember Munroe's story about Adam's rib and the original mother-wife and I think, *Yep, everything is connected.*

Penny Catcher is working on a studio album. Circe is too busy to tour. I hear that her producer is losing patience with her other interests. Magic, saving the world, oil painting.

Munroe vacated the Laurel Canyon house. Word is she's in New York. She lost the party, but she's still sitting on the most potent collection of curiosities in the world. That gives me pause. Munroe has enough juice to blow a hole in the side of Circe's sacrifice course if she can get the right ritual lined up. The more time that passes without hearing anything about her, the more I don't like it. I wonder about her giving me the album. Sort of giving it to me, anyway. Did I really touch her heart? I don't know. Maybe she just saw the tide turning. The old ways didn't work for her anymore so maybe she wanted to see what would happen if the game changed. Giving me Abigail's album might have been a gamble she was willing to take to see how it would play out. Anyway, Munroe is not one to stay out of the limelight. Not unless she's preparing a big new show.

Clay. That guy. Man, I don't like that guy. It's a mutual feeling. He's with Sue. They worked out their stuff, I guess. Sounds like a bit of a reversal. He spends all his time helping Circe the way Sue used to always be helping Munroe. Meanwhile, Sue's back at the house watching a lot of TV the way he did when he first came out of the mirror. Her amputated hand won't be growing back, but she's still scary. Restless woman. Is she lying around or is she lying in wait? Unnerving.

Lloyd still has my heart and has me under indenture. He can kill me whenever he wants. Two things keep him at bay. The first is he likes to have me at his mercy. But it's the second consideration that really stops him from sticking pins in my heart. Because my heart is not just my heart. I share it with Clay. He still needs my mojo to be able to sly. Messing with Clay would mean Sue would take an interest. Lloyd is a creep. But not a stupid creep.

I feel bitter about it sometimes—the invisible connection between me and Clay that nourishes his impossible talent. Sometimes I'd like to march into Lloyd's office and smash my heart with my own hands just to spite Clay. Other times I feel proud. Like I'd be willing to sacrifice any magic I have left in me if I knew it could help him to be who he wants to be. I don't know what all of that is about.

No, that's a lie. I know what it's about.

Clay is my responsibility. He didn't ask to be here. I might have helped spawn him by accident, but I can't pretend that he didn't come from me. And from Abigail. He is what we made together. So if he needs a share of my heart, I have to give it to him. I owe him at least that much.

My debts and what I owe are still very much a matter for my concern.

After everything, I didn't get a massive payday out of the deal. I got the same thing as everyone else in the world. Access to minor magic to do small, unselfish things. Not the windfall I'd hoped for. Nothing that can get my heart out of hock or pay off my creditors. Although I did get Klarnacht those tapes I promised him. He might have sold me out to Minerva, but I'm not in a position to judge. He quit the D&D campaign, bought a car with a tape deck, and drove cross-country. Said he had to get some fresh air after forty years in Bob's mom's basement. He's now living with his sister, helping his niece and her friends learn how to use magic to fix broken stuff.

Wendell and Horace can afford to be patient about what I owe them because their business is booming. Their kind of small magic fits in perfectly with the new situation. Shingles has teamed up with them to create a line of necromantic touch-stones. People have realized that they can preserve the emotional lives of their dead loved ones, and that is driving a terrific walk-in trade at their shop.

And how am I?

I'm okay. I'm terrible. I'm okay.

The initial rush I got when Circe's course pulled me out of my depression faded after a couple of weeks. I'm no longer buzzing and hyper and getting on everyone's nerves. Well, I get on everyone's nerves, but not like that.

There have been bad days. Very bad days, when I feel myself closing in on myself and I wonder if it's back. It still feels like a viscous, alien monster, my depression, a hostile being that's lurking in darkness at my feet, waiting for me to misstep so it can suck me under. I am more afraid of that than I am of anything else. I could have a small course put down, something similar to what Shingles does for herself. A stream of magic to keep depression away. But if I let magic do all the hard things for me, I'll never grow up. I would like to grow up. As much as I can. Besides, I need all the magic I have for a project I'm working on.

I need to get away from here for a little while.

When you've been shattered, you don't just put yourself back together again. I haven't begun to come to terms with what I learned that day and that night. Abigail and me and what I thought we were and what I still don't want to admit we really were. The baby. Our baby. What I wanted and didn't want. I still try to convince myself that the truth about all that is not the truth. It hurts too much. Then I hear Abigail again. *Her name is Hope.* And I remember that hurting comes with life.

No magic will change that.

I'm in pieces, and it will take some time to put them together. If I can put them together. I need to be somewhere quiet, without distractions. I also need something to do when I'm there. Something more than navel-gazing. I'm afraid that if I stare too deeply into the pieces that used to be me, I'll start feeling sorry for myself. Sorrier, I mean. So I need to have a job while I try to fit myself together. A quest, call it. Which you'd think I'd have had enough of, except that this time it isn't a phantom I want to find. It's my best friend.

Francois is lost in the nothing. I'm going into the mirrors to find him. That's going to take a load of magic, so I'm coursing everything I can into my trusty Sinéad O'Connor T-shirt. Circe gave it back to me. I would have stolen it from her anyway, but it was a nice gesture.

The problem with my quest is that you can't find someone once they're lost in the mirrors. Not ever. It's one of the impossible things. There are rules, after all.

But Circe said it best.

Fuck the rules.

I have to try to save my friend. I have to try to do the impossible. Whether or not you have magic, you always have hope. How do you know if your ritual has been successful, your spell cast?

You scream until you feel it.

Can you feel it yet?

Scream louder.